Chasing
Tanzanite

Shirley Gould

Scrivenings
PRESS
Quench your thirst for story.
www.ScriveningsPress.com

I dedicate this book to one of my dearest friends, Carol Adams. For over fifty years, she has shown up during my darkest hours. I'm forever grateful to call her my friend.

Prologue

L eaving Kenya behind schedule put Tanner arriving late in London. Scanning the departure board, he realized his flight to Dallas was already boarding. He couldn't miss this flight. He'd promised to see Angie receive her master's degree, and he wouldn't let her down. Again. The miles between them had put distance in their relationship that needed to be remedied right away. That was his plan.

"Paging Tanner Zarello. Paging Tanner Zarello for flight BA 572 to Dallas, Texas, now boarding at gate C33. The doors are closing in five minutes."

Hearing his name over the loudspeaker, Tanner panicked and sprinted the last hundred feet to the gate. He had to see Angie, the love of his life, and if he could make the flight, he'd be with her in fifteen hours. "I'm here. Don't shut the doors yet!" With a wrinkled pass in his hand, he rushed through the door and boarded the plane.

Yes! I made it! While trying to catch his breath, Tanner found his row in first class, stored his carry-on, and almost fell into his assigned seat.

"Close connection?" The guy in the next seat asked.

"Too close. My plane was late, and I have to get to Dallas for a graduation celebration of a dear friend, so I ran. Jumping over two carry-ons surprised their owners but helped me make it. I can't wait to see her again. The next flight from London to Dallas isn't for five hours, and I promised her I'd be there."

"That's a huge deal." Jake put his hand out. "I'm Jake Stevens. Glad you made the flight."

"Me too. Tanner Zarello." He shook Jake's hand. "Her name's Angie. We've been friends since childhood, but I want to take our relationship to the next level. We need some FaceTime. Working in Kenya for the last few years has cost us."

"And you are about to remedy that situation." Jake fastened his seatbelt.

"That's the plan. My job in Kenya has been successful. I've proven myself to the execs, but it's ending soon, and I'm ready to take some definite steps toward our future. That's my goal for this trip. So, where are you coming from, Jake?"

"I've been doing children's ministry in Kenya. I'm on my way home."

"It must pay well for you to be in first class." Tanner fastened his seatbelt.

"My seat in coach was double-booked, so they bumped me up." The flight attendant served sodas in stemware. "I hope you make it in time."

"Thanks." Tanner settled in as they took off from London Heathrow.

After a long nap, Tanner smiled as the British Airways flight landed in Texas. "It's good to be home." He gave Jake his business card. "Let me know when you're in Kenya again, preferably in the Mombasa area. If I'm in the country, we can grab a meal together."

"I will. Thanks." Jake pocketed the business card and left the plane.

Tanner was right behind him. He had a schedule to keep and couldn't wait to see Angie.

Traffic hindered his trek to the university, but rushing inside, he arrived as they started calling the graduates. He got himself in a perfect position to video the moment, and it didn't disappoint.

"Angelica Joy Ward, Master in International Business."

Applause filled the auditorium. Tanner stopped the video on his phone and joined in the celebration before slipping out the door to drive to the Windsor Mansion for the celebratory dinner in Angie's honor. Being there to greet her upon her arrival would be perfect. But parking his SUV in front of the building hadn't been his smartest move. He had to wait for the main lot to empty, where the graduates parked, before he could join the traffic flow.

He arrived at the mansion right after the reception had started. An attendant took his arrangement of red roses with daisies to put it on Angie's gift table. "Mr. Ward is presenting his granddaughter. Slip inside this side door so you can join the celebration."

"Thank you." He did as suggested and stood behind Harry Connick Jr., the evening's musical guest, and listened to Alexander Ward.

Tanner's mom, Olivia, joined him. She'd worked for the Ward's family for twenty years and was like family to Angie. "Hi, Mom."

"I'm glad you made it," she whispered. "You're just in time."

Tanner put his arm around his mom, focused on Angie,

who was ravishing, and listened to Alexander Ward talk about his granddaughter.

"Angelica, you're an amazing young woman, but first and foremost, you're my granddaughter. Watching you mature has resembled the blossoming of a rare rose. It is my honor to present you to our guests."

Well-deserved applause filled the large marble-tiled foyer, and the chandelier glistened over the momentous occasion. The place was regal, and Angie was stunning in her tanzanite blue gown, highlighting her blue eyes. Her grace was not unlike royalty. "I've missed her."

"I know you have." His mom put her hand on his elbow.

His eyes caught movement in the crowd as Mason Malone, the pompous brown-nosing VP at Ward Enterprises, plunged through the guests to reach Angie. She nodded and accepted the roses he presented before he knelt on one knee.

"No! Tanner, he's proposing to Angie." Olivia stared at him.

Tanner held his breath. His ringing ears made it hard to hear. He wanted to yell, to plow through the crowd and slug Mason.

"Mom, he's just a suit."

"I know. I thought things were good between you and Angie. What happened?"

"He's not worthy of her."

"I don't understand."

"This is a nightmare." Heart pounding, wound crushing, he couldn't stay another moment. "Mom, I can't stay—forgive me."

"Go, dear. I'm so sorry."

Easing out of the crowd, he escaped using the door through which he'd entered. Rushing toward a bush, he lost his stomach's contents. Using the small scarf from his front pocket, he wiped his mouth. Sliding into the seat of his black

Hummer, he turned the air-conditioning on high and leaned his head on the headrest. *Lord, help me. I can't think straight. I've lost her.*

The intro to Angie's favorite song played on the radio, and Tanner slammed the on/off button, cracking the knob. He scrubbed his hand down his face and cranked the SUV. It was time for a quiet exit. It was time to return to Kenya.

Chapter One

A ngie slipped into her Vera Wang gown and stood so Sarah, her assistant, could zip the deep blue creation.

"Your shoes, Miss Ward." Sarah retrieved a pair of stilettos and placed them in Angie's hand.

"Thank you. Would you get my jewelry?" Angie slipped on the shoes and turned in front of a full-length mirror.

"This is your prettiest gown yet. You look like a million bucks." She held out a diamond tennis bracelet and secured it on Angie's wrist.

"Some see me as a spoiled debutante, Sarah. But I want people to look past the wrappings and see my heart." Angie lifted her hair so Sara could fasten her tanzanite necklace.

"Don't feel bad for receiving a blessing, even one that's financial, from when your parents passed suddenly. After tonight's gala, you can show the real Angelica Ward. Enjoy being honored. You're at the Windsor Mansion, and Alexander Ward spent major bucks to present you to the business world. Try to relax and have a good time." She gathered the dress bag, the shoe box, and the jewelry pouch.

"Thanks, Sarah, I'll try—I wish Tanner were going to be

here. It would make it worth walking down the winding staircase in these stilettos."

"Are you sure he won't be here?" She opened the door of the suite for Angie.

"He didn't RSVP. I don't think he will come." Angie sighed. She'd waited for his calls, checked for his emails. It slowly broke her heart. Like trying to grab smoke, he slowly faded from her life.

"Sorry, Zarello is quite the looker—but there's always Mason Malone hovering near." Sarah straightened Angie's hair over her shoulder.

"He is handsome, isn't he?" Angie faced her friend. Sometimes a man entered a woman's life and captured her heart forever. Tanner had done that to her before he left for Africa. Sadly, the promises of a long-distance relationship fizzled as time and distance competed with his increasing work demands.

"If you doubt it, just ask him." Sarah laughed at her joke.

"You make me smile." Angie stepped through the door.

"They're playing your song. That's your cue. Knock 'em dead, Miss Angie."

When the vocalist began, Angie whispered a quick prayer. "Lord, please keep me steady on this new path, especially these steep stairs in front of me."

She exhaled and walked to the top of the polished mahogany staircase. Her eyes scanned the crowd for a certain profile—black hair, dark chocolate eyes, and tan skin on a toned body. Disappointment weakened her resolve. She sighed, stepped forward, and pasted on a smile. The sturdy banister, steadfast and strong, sent a surge of strength through her even as she shivered in the chill of the air-conditioning.

When she looked toward the musicians, Harry Connick Jr. pointed in her direction and winked as he sang "The Way You

Look Tonight" in her honor. She smiled her approval and continued her gradual descent with the grandeur of royalty, posture perfect, not showing a hint of the nerves clinching her stomach. *Left foot, right foot, smile, and don't forget to breathe.* Step by step, she drew closer to her audience. Pausing three steps from the floor, she scoped the gathering.

He didn't come. Her heart wilted a little, but her smile remained. Hiding her pain had become routine.

Grand-Papa stood straight and tall on the platform at the base of the stairs—definitely the most handsome man in the room. His black hair with a touch of gray at the temples framed his chiseled features, which spoke of the authority he carried, while his smile portrayed the softness of his heart. He kissed Angie's hand when she arrived to stand beside him, placing it in the crook of his elbow and facing their guests.

"Good evening, ladies and gentlemen, friends and business associates. We're elated you've chosen to spend this evening with us. It's my distinct honor to present Miss Angelica Ward, an accomplished young woman who has earned a master's degree in business with an international focus."

Her eyes blinked as two photographers lit up the room.

"Angelica will lead us into the future with excellence." He paused.

His eyes moistened as he faced her.

"Angelica, you're an amazing young woman, but first and foremost, you're my granddaughter. Watching you mature has resembled the blossoming of a rare rose. It's my honor to present you to our guests formally."

Applause electrified the atmosphere as photographers captured the moment. Angie smiled at the crowd as she graciously accepted the accolades.

Making his way through the throng, Mason Malone stepped forward with a gorgeous bouquet of long-stemmed red roses. Angie traveled two additional steps to accept the bouquet. Mason turned to be photographed as he presented the blooms, the applause decrescendoing.

"Angelica, congratulations on your accomplishments. These distinguished guests have gathered to honor you, to celebrate you. I want to add another dimension to your happiness."

Before she could thank him, he knelt on one knee and opened a black velvet ring box.

Silence electrified the moment. Angie stood frozen. *No! Not tonight. This can't be happening—how manipulative to propose in front of this crowd.*

"Angelica Ward, you know I love you. You're beautiful, sensitive, and intelligent—truly one of a kind. We're a great team. You're the woman I want to spend my life with. Will you marry me?" He waited, statuesque, for her response.

She wanted to run. Mason was a nice guy, but he didn't own her heart. She'd given it away a long time ago. The anticipation among their guests was palpable. The room hushed—one heartbeat passed, two passed, three—

Perspiration dotted her forehead as a knot tightened in her chest. She wanted a proposal, but from Tanner. She looked at her grandfather. He smiled, nodding his approval. She wanted him to be happy, but—scanning the crowd—she sought Tanner's face.

He wasn't there.

She forced her gaze to Mason, who awaited her answer.

He whispered. "He left you, but I'm here. I won't desert you, Angelica. Please say you'll marry me."

Her mind raced through the facts. He was handsome, a bit overprotective, kind in a professional way, and quite successful. They came from the same world, Ward Enterprises. Grand-Papa would be pleased, and making him happy was important. *But I don't love Mason. His one strong point is that he shows up—he doesn't leave me. Everyone I love leaves.* Would Tanner ever make her a priority and stick around like Mason did? Should she take a chance and hope it worked? In time, she could learn to love him. Couldn't she?

Lord, help me! What do you want me to do? She squeezed the bouquet. Thorns pricked her palm.

There was no voice from Heaven.

Sensing the pressure of the moment, she forced a tight smile.

Mason's brow furrowed. He tilted his head. "Angelica, is that a yes?"

She gathered her breath. Embarrassing him in front of this audience would be tragic, but she couldn't say 'yes.' "Mason—"

"Yes," Mason said as their audience erupted in cheers and applause. He stood and embraced her as his expensive cologne, which needed to be replaced, seeped into the pores of her skin. With practiced pageantry, he put a Harry Winston diamond on her finger. Harry Connick Jr. started singing "It Had to Be You" as her diamond's sparkle competed with the photographer's blinding flashes. A perfect beginning to a perfect evening, or it would have been—if she were ten thousand miles away with the man who held her heart.

Grand-Papa waited for the cheers to fade. "Please join us for dinner in the grand ballroom as we celebrate with Angelica on this momentous occasion. The future before her is bright indeed."

"You look radiant tonight, Angelica." Mason offered his elbow.

With light brown hair, hazel eyes, and a perfect build, he filled out a tux in grand fashion. She allowed him to escort her as the crowd parted.

"It's a pleasure to have you on my arm, Angelica. Thank you for saying 'yes.' You won't regret it." He put his hand on hers, resting in the crook of his arm, and strutted with the confidence of an executive.

She leaned toward him and whispered, "But I didn't say yes."

"That's a minor detail. You know we make sense." Mason reached for her roses so she could greet their guests.

Leslie, one of Angie's best friends, rushed to her side and whispered in Angie's ear, "Tanner was here. He just left through the side door."

Angie eyed Leslie. "Are you sure?"

"Yes. He could still be in the parking lot."

Angie looked around, assessing the scene.

"What is it, Angelica?" Mason leaned close.

"Mason, allow everyone to be seated. I need a breath of air. I'll be in soon. Just give me a minute."

"Sure, I've overwhelmed you. Sorry." Mason turned and began talking to their distinguished guests.

Angie greeted some of their friends and business acquaintances as she hurried to the front door. Stepping out into the late afternoon heat took her breath. Scanning the parking lot, she spied Tanner's SUV coming down the aisle toward the exit. Stepping in front of his truck, she stood her ground until he stopped his forward movement.

Once his window lowered, she walked to his side of the vehicle. "Hello, Tanner."

"Angie. Congratulations on your master's degree."

"You were there?"

"I promised I'd be there. Didn't I?"

"Yes, but things have grown distant as of late. I thought maybe it had slipped your mind."

"Nothing about you slips my mind, Ang—"

She stared at his handsome face, completely speechless.

"You look stunning. You always wear tanzanite blue so well, maybe because it matches your eyes perfectly."

"Thank you. You're leaving again? Why so soon?"

"After Mason's proposal, I felt sick to my stomach. I need to leave, Angie."

"You weren't going to say 'hello.' Just going to ride into the sunset without a word."

"Angie, I thought *we* were going to have a future together. Watching you get engaged was a kick in the gut. I've worked hard to prove myself worthy of you. But it seems you have other plans. So, tell me, how do I let go of a dream I've held on to for so long?" His eyes were teary.

"I didn't say yes to his proposal, Tanner."

"Then why is that rock on your finger? Look, Ang—you've got a crowd waiting on you. Go and enjoy your party. Be the belle of the ball. I wish you the best." Tanner smiled, put up his window, and left her standing in the parking lot.

Sarah and Leslie were waiting for Angie when she returned to the gala.

"Angie, we have your makeup case. Let's stop at the ladies' room so you can freshen up a bit." Sarah opened the ladies' room door.

"Thanks, Sarah. I need that." Angie wiped tears from her cheeks. "Leslie, thanks for the heads-up. I spoke with Tanner." She worked on her makeup.

"And?" Leslie waited for her response.

Angie wiped a tear from her eye. "Could we talk about it later?"

Leslie squeezed Angie's hand. "Absolutely. You dry those tears. People are waiting to celebrate you. This is your night. So, shake it off. Reapply more lipstick, and let's get this show on the road." Leslie grinned and clapped her hands.

"Good try, Les." Angie smiled. "Okay, I'll pull myself together. Go sit with Elise and Missy, and I'll be out in a minute."

"That's what I wanted to hear. I'll see you out there." She blew Angie a kiss and left the ladies' room.

Entering the ballroom, Angie came face-to-face with the Chairman of the Board of Ward Enterprises. "Good evening, Mr. Everest. Thank you so much for coming tonight. I hope you enjoy your dinner."

"Congratulations, Miss Ward."

Mason shook hands with Mr. Everest. He slipped his hand to Angie's lower back and directed her to the head table.

As Angie took her seat, Mason pushed her chair forward.

"Thank you, I—"

"The elite of the business world are among our guests. It's good for them to know us—I mean you, as Ward's beautiful granddaughter, and me as his vice president in charge of the American holdings." He waved at someone of importance as he pulled out his chair. "I told Ward this was a good idea."

Is this about me, Mason, or about you? Scanning the magnificent venue, she eyed the gorgeous ice-sculptured centerpieces glistening as the melting process began, almost without notice. Beautiful today, but gone tomorrow—nothing but puddles on the floor, similar to Tanner's presence in her life.

A parade of seven courses of culinary delicacies was presented to the guests, who were serenaded by a string quintet. Caviar led the procession.

"Angelica, try this." Mason put caviar in her mouth when she faced him. "It's plump and savory. Probably the best I've ever tasted."

Angie grabbed her napkin to rid her mouth of the horrid fish eggs. "Mason, you know I don't eat caviar."

"Sorry, but you must learn to tolerate it for appearance's sake." His stiff demeanor betrayed his fake smile.

She reached for a piece of imported cheese from the charcuterie board to remove the strong, salty taste lingering on her tongue. Tanner would never have done that. *He knows I hate caviar. He would slip me a petit four before they're all gone, or slip my favorite candy bar into my purse, or buy my favorite sodas from Kenya and surprise me.*

Sarah stepped forward to exchange Angie's napkin for a fresh one and handed her a glass of ice water. As she stepped away, the waiter presented Angie with a shrimp cocktail in crystal stemware, Angie's favorite.

Mason, being overly demonstrative in a conversation with the mayor, hit Angie's cocktail with his butter knife, breaking the glass. The waiter caught the cocktail sauce before it touched her gown, but not before a shrimp went airborne and landed on Mason's tux. Angie used her napkin to hide a grin.

"Incompetent waiter. Get me some soda water to get the stain out." Mason scrubbed the stain on his coat to keep the sauce from staining the fabric. "Can't get good help these days." He motioned for the waiter to bring him another linen napkin.

"That was a good catch." Angie made light of the incident and took the focus off Mason's bad behavior.

"Sorry. I'll get you another cocktail right away." The waiter hurried to retrieve her appetizer.

The cocktails were followed by lobster bisque. Tender filet mignon with roasted asparagus was served under silver domes, removed with flair. Sorbet to cleanse the palate prepared the taste buds for the petit fours, very apropos for this elegant evening.

Angie walked the ballroom perimeter, greeting guests until she reached her best friends. "I'm so glad you're here!" She hugged Missy, Elise, and Leslie. "Thanks, friends," Angie whispered.

"Anytime."

"Angie, you look amazing. And this place is gorgeous." Elise Kensington grabbed her hand to admire the ring. "It's beautiful."

"This place is amazing." Missy Anderson, a feisty redhead, expressed her exuberance. The chandelier highlighted the orange tint of her bouncy locks. Her bronze lipstick matched the sprinkle of freckles dotting her nose.

Angie smiled. "Glad you like it." Angie touched Missy's shoulder. "I'm glad you three made it."

"We wouldn't have missed it. A master's degree in business with an international flair is pretty impressive." Missy imitated an announcer's voice as she spat out Angie's credentials.

"Yes, it is, and we promised to have each other's backs, so here we are." Leslie Morgan ducked behind her camera and clicked a candid shot. She checked the photo on her digital screen, then smiled. "You look amazing. The mermaid-style gown is elegant with a touch of sexy?"

Leslie leaned close. "Your ring is magnificent. Are you okay with this engagement?"

"Not exactly. I haven't had time to process it yet. Can we talk later?"

"Sure, anytime." Leslie squeezed her hand.

After coffee was served, speeches of congratulations preceded the presentation of exquisite gifts. Her Grand-Papa unveiled a leather-embossed desk set for her corporate desk and added a check for a quarter of a million dollars. Angie hugged him, pulled back, and wiped her eyes.

"I appreciate everything you've done for me. I'm so blessed you took me in when I was orphaned. I don't take it for granted. You're the best." She kissed his cheek and then turned to their audience. "Isn't he amazing?" Applause built once again.

"While I have the microphone, I want to share something that's on my heart with you, my dearest friends and colleagues. During my travels to Kenya, I've seen thousands of orphans roaming the streets, eating garbage, and begging for handouts. Being orphaned myself, I have a soft spot for the two hundred and fifty thousand children who are cold, hungry, and afraid right now. It's not their fault that their parents died of AIDS, typhoid, cholera, or malaria and left them to fend for themselves. I can't adopt them all, but I want to build an orphanage in Kenya. It's a big project requiring ongoing financial support. I'm going to need donors, so I will be hitting you up for some big donations." She paused for their laughter. "I want to be your hand extended to these precious children. Together, we can make a difference."

The guests applauded.

"You've won their hearts, Angie. They will support you all the way." Grand-Papa squeezed her shoulder.

The thrill over the support for her orphans was short-lived. Her heart hurt from her moments with Tanner, and her growing irritation at Mason's public proposal was gaining traction, but as a professional, she had to shelve her emotions and finish the task at hand. Ignoring her pain, she enjoyed the time with her friends almost as much as Mason enjoyed the limelight as master of ceremonies. It put him in a position of power where he seemed to thrive.

"Are your guests enjoying their evening?" Grand-Papa leaned close.

"Yes, they are. This is quite lavish for their tastes, but they're having fun."

"I'm glad. Mason outdid himself by putting this gala together for you." Grand-Papa whispered. "And he's doing a great job tonight."

"Yes, Mason's leadership abilities are shining." She sipped her latte, enjoying the touch of cinnamon, savoring the warmth of the cup. Her mind wandered to the leadership roles Tanner had excelled at in college and how he had exceeded Grand-Papa's expectations. His integrity was impeccable.

"Mason loves you. He will keep you safe. That's vitally important."

"Don't worry about me. I'm a Ward, and I have your inner strength." She hugged her grandfather, lightening the mood. Quickly pulling back, she searched his face. "Grand-Papa, you're burning hot, and it's freezing in here. Are you okay? You have a fever."

"The leg's been bothering me again. Maybe it's a change in the weather. Doc Ellis ran some tests, so don't worry, sweetheart. Enjoy your party. I'll be fine." He patted her hand. "Why don't you go thank your guests and let's bring this evening to a close?"

"Sure, you need to get home." Angie stood, placed her napkin on the table, and stepped to the podium. "Dear friends, I'm honored you've spent this evening with us. I appreciate your well-wishes and gifts. As I step into the business world, I'm blessed to have you as friends and—"

Alexander Ward grabbed his chest, closed his eyes, and gasped for air.

"Grand-Papa! No!" She dropped the microphone and rushed to his side. "Someone call nine-one-one!" Joseph, Ward's personal assistant, rushed to his side. "Joseph, Grand-Papa needs you." Angie knelt beside his chair. Their guests stood.

Mason made the 911 call and stepped to the podium. "Is there a doctor in the house?" He looked for a response but found none. "We appreciate your concern, but let's not crowd too close. Give him room." He motioned for some waiters to move the head table back, instructing them to keep the path clear, then strode to the entrance to bring in the EMTs.

Joseph removed Ward's tuxedo jacket and loosened his tie as he moaned and grabbed his right arm. Joseph helped him lie down on the floor.

Angie stood frozen. "Grand-Papa, try to relax. Help will be here soon. I can hear sirens. We're near the medical center."

Leslie stepped close to Angie and put her arm around her shoulders.

"Clear a path. The ambulance is here." Mason took control. "Tell your guys to bring a gurney and come this way." He led them to his boss and stood near Angie. "How's he doing, Angelica?"

"Not good, he's in severe pain and very pale."

The medical team wasted no time assessing Ward. Joseph rattled off Ward's medical information as a tech started an IV, preparing to transport him to the hospital.

"Leslie, I can't believe this is happening. He's all I have. Everyone I love leaves." Angie leaned toward her friend.

Leslie spoke softly, comforting Angie.

"Now, Angelica, he's not all you have. What about me?" Mason grabbed her hand. "They're taking good care of your grandfather. Try not to worry." He led her a step away from the workers. "Why don't you ride in the ambulance since the hospital is so close? I'll stay and close things up here, then meet you there."

"Right. Thanks, Mason. I have a change of clothes in the limousine." Angie turned to Leslie. "Will you, Elise, and Missy take the gifts and roses to my residence at the estate? I'll be there later."

"Sure."

"Angie, I've summoned your limo. It will pull up when the ambulance leaves."

"Thanks." She followed Grand-Papa's gurney as EMTs rolled it out of the ballroom. At the door, she pivoted and faced their guests. "You've honored me with your presence. Thank you for coming tonight. Please say a prayer for my grandfather as you depart. Blessings to each of you." She waved and disappeared through the entrance.

With the heat of the day gone, the night air cooled her, sending a chill down her spine. She stood under the Windsor Mansion's canopy as her limo stopped. After sliding onto the leather seat, she released the sobs she'd been holding since Tanner left her standing in the parking lot. Grand-Papa wouldn't leave her alone, too, would he? Panic gripped her at the thought.

Exhausted from his return trip and the emotional roller-coaster he had been on, Tanner let Paul, their Kenyan worker, carry his suitcase to his upstairs suite/office. The palm trees swaying over the ocean at high tide usually gave him comfort, but not today. His world had imploded. Everything he had worked for was now out of reach. How had he messed everything up with Angie? Didn't absence make the heart grow fonder? *Can't prove it by him.*

When Paul passed him on the stairs, he requested hot tea and warm soup. He showered while it was being prepared, hoping the hot water would ease the pain in his chest that wouldn't let up.

"*Bwana* Tanner, I have your tray. I added some cake." Paul stood inside the door holding a wooden tray.

Tanner exited the restroom, rubbing his hair with a towel. "Thank you, Paul. You can put it on my desk." Tanner hung the towel around his neck and added sugar to the tea. "Is everything okay here at Paradise Inn?"

"Yes, *bwana.* Dylan and the team left yesterday for the mine. They will return on Thursday afternoon. Your mother called earlier today and left a message." He turned to leave but pivoted. "Are you okay, *bwana*? You do not look well."

"I haven't slept for several days. I'm exhausted. But I appreciate your concern. It was a rough trip." He sipped his brew. "I don't know how long I'll sleep, so don't make breakfast."

"*Ni sawa, bwana. Lala salama.* Okay, sir. Sleep well." With that, he was gone.

Tanner thumbed through a few pieces of mail accumulated in his brief absence. He enjoyed his oxtail soup and tea and stretched out on the bed. Rain pelted the tin roof above, providing a personal sound machine. Overwhelmed by his loss, he cried out for help. *Lord, I've been kicked in the gut. Please help me catch my breath.* After quoting scripture from *The Message* Bible, he wiped his eyes and drifted off to sleep.

~

"Hey, Boss, you're back. Paul said you arrived at the beginning of the week. How did it go?" Dylan turned his ball cap backward and sat in the lounge chair beside Tanner.

Lifting his sunglasses, Tanner eyed his friend. "I don't want to talk about it. It was a disaster."

"Sorry, man. And you went all that way. I hate that. I'll be around if you want to talk." Dylan stood. "Put your sunglasses back on."

Dylan walked toward the lobby, where the team brought in their things. "Tanner's resting by the pool. Jet lag has taken its toll. We'll see him at dinner, so either swim or take a shower because you guys smell."

The group shared a laugh and went their separate ways, leaving Tanner to deal with his devastating heartbreak alone.

~

Swaying palms protected Tanner from the intense rays of Africa's morning sun as his future lay at the bottom of a seventy-foot black hole.

He shoved his sunglasses to the top of his head and edged closer to the mine's entrance, where the scent of the Indian Ocean's salt water mingled with the smell of moist dirt. His worn leather boots crunched loose gravel unearthed by three years of hard work. His heart quickened as debris plummeted into the darkness, bouncing off the walls. Just like his thoughts, bouncing all over the place concerning the prima donna who wreaked havoc with his life.

But he had a job to do and couldn't stop now. Too much was at stake. As the maid's son, he'd received his education and landed this opportunity as head of this mining project for

Ward Enterprises, a perfect chance to prove himself worthy of Angie. He had to see this through. And his team depended on him and needed their payout. If they surpassed the boss's expectations, Tanner Zarello would return to Texas a success, more than a peon among the prestigious upper class.

The rainforest underbrush camouflaged their hidden location. Squawking drew Tanner's eyes heavenward to marabou storks circling overhead like vultures in search of a meal.

Waves splashing against boulders along the shore brought him back to reality. With a dangerous job to do, he had to keep his team safe until they completed this assignment. Tanner breathed a prayer, scanned the area, checked the position of their guards, and waved as his employees arrived. "All right, team, listen up." Tanner stepped on the weathered ten-foot by twelve-foot mining platform and eyed his motley crew, three Americans and four Kenyans, who stood patiently waiting his instructions.

"Great job, guys. We've pulled a lot of rock out of that hole. You've worked hard. The boss will be pleased. But we're not done, and we're burning daylight. Remember our safety protocols. You know your assignments, so get to it."

Dylan Calloway, Tanner's project manager and best friend, pulled out a pocket knife and fought the tight packaging of C batteries. "Don't worry, Boss. We'll get the work done, and you won't have to get your get-up dirty."

Tanner smirked at his jab. He put his clipboard under his arm, leaned on the banister attached to the decking, and listened to the melee among his team.

"If you're willing, you can make a shilling." Daniel Mwangi, one of the Kenyan miners, gathered his tools. His grin had a hole where a tooth used to be.

"If that's Kenyan humor, it's not working." Dylan brought

his lighted helmet and a stack of buckets to the mining platform as Vickie, their gemologist, invaded their space. "Hey, Ponytail, do all divas chew gum?"

"Only the really cool ones. What's it to you?" She brushed a palm branch off her covered workstation at the end of the right side of the platform.

"Well, if you'd work your hands as fast as you chomp that gum, we'd get this job done in no time." Dylan jerked his thumb over his shoulder to the males working on the team.

"Listen, you focus on your tan, big man, and you'll be eating my dust within the hour." Within minutes, using generator-powered tools, her sander sent fine particles into the air as she honed tanzanite, precious orbs of deep blue color valued in the diamond category. Vickie was obviously focused on her task. Her ponytail swayed, probably in sync with the music flowing through her earbuds.

Drew, the team's professional miner, fired up the generator and started the process of getting cords to their equipment.

Tanner enjoyed his team. One of his favorite scriptures was, 'A cheerful heart is good like a medicine,' and their sparring was a healing balm to his soul. He needed that.

The waves on the Indian Ocean coast slapped the shore, drumming a rhythm into the day—a day where Tanner should be ten thousand miles away, meeting with Angie and attempting to salvage their relationship.

I'm nothing to her. He tossed his empty soft drink bottle.

"Hey, are you okay?" Dylan removed the batteries from his helmet lamp and pitched them.

"Yeah, I'm good." Tanner removed his hat and wiped the sweat from his forehead with his sleeve.

"We haven't discussed your quick trip to the States."

"There's nothing to talk about. It's over." Tanner put his wide-brimmed fedora on his head. "I was kidding myself thinking I could make a long-distance relationship work." His hopes of a future with Angie diminished on the breeze.

"Since you haven't clued me in about your quick trip, I cannot give you my widely sought-after, expert advice." Dylan checked the new batteries.

"Now is not the time, but she is wearing another man's ring."

"Sorry, I've been down that road, and it hurts." Dylan laid their tools out, preparing to get the day started.

From a makeshift desk connected to the mining platform, Tanner maintained his connection to the action while an ocean breeze made the heat bearable. He liked getting his hands dirty, but today, paperwork demanded his attention. He scanned the report, needing lists of expenses, and he would fax it to Ward Enterprises when he returned to Paradise Inn. The sound of work boots interrupted his focus.

"*Bwana*, it is your turn to go into the mine." Daniel adjusted a lighted helmet on his balding head.

Tanner glanced up from his work, then returned to filling out the Ward Enterprises paperwork, while Daniel spoke.

"You are busy. I will go down first today. *Ni sawa?* Is it okay? It is cooler in the mine." Daniel sported work pants too short for his stature, held up with a rope double-knotted for security. He'd slipped on an old flannel shirt over a worn T-shirt Dylan had given him some time ago. The mine offered a reprieve from the extreme heat of the East African coast.

"Okay, Daniel, work in the quadrant Dylan was chipping yesterday. The stones he sent
up showed a deep blue-violet mix."

"You got it, *bwana*." He headed toward the hole in the ground.

"Dylan, anchor Daniel's lines and send his equipment

down the shaft." Tanner picked up another receipt and posted it in its proper slot.

"Sure, Boss. I'll watch the ropes." Dylan grabbed a bucket handle, tied a strong knot, and attached it to a hanging array of tools, clanging a haunting tune.

"Going down!" Daniel mounted the ladder attached to the opening of the mine. After he secured his ropes, Daniel gave Dylan a thumbs-up and grinned. "See you later, alligator."

Dylan smiled and echoed through habit, "After a while, crocodile." He handed him the rope holding his tools. "I need to teach you some new clichés. That one's getting old."

Tanner flipped through the week's receipts, then focused on his monthly report. He had to make it shine to prove himself to Alexander Ward. He'd just posted an entry on the spreadsheet when a screech pierced the air. The pulley holding his worker spun out of control.

"No!" Daniel's voice pierced the air. "Help!" Daniel's cry, loud at first, diminished as he plummeted into the depths of the mine. His bucket and tools resounded, echoing in the darkness.

"Tanner, Daniel's in trouble!" Dylan jerked on his rope, bracing his feet for Daniel's weight. But the rope went slack in his hands.

"Grab the main line. Pull him up!" Tanner hurried to the entrance.

Daniel moaned when he reached the base of the mine and hit the water.

Dylan dropped to the platform, lay prostrate on the wood, splayed his fingers, and extended his arms, but grasped thin air.

"He's seventy feet down." Jerking his boots off, Tanner barked orders. "Dylan, hurry. Get the winch cables on the Land Cruiser." He pulled on Dylan's gloves. "Vickie, call an ambulance." He turned and mounted the ladder. "I'm going down."

"Kick, Daniel, kick!" Dylan yelled as he raced to the truck.

"Daniel, can you hear me?" Tanner listened for a response as he waited for Dylan. Only palm trees rustled in the wind, and Tanner's chest tightened. Daniel was more than a diligent miner. He'd become a friend. "I'm coming, Daniel. Hang on."

"Take my helmet." Dylan tossed it to Tanner before linking the winch cable around his chest, directly under his arms. He gave him another cable and a body sling. Tanner put his phone on the mining platform and started down the ladder.

Tanner locked eyes with Dylan. "Pray, man. Pray."

Lord, we need a miracle ...

Chapter Two

The dank earth swallowed Tanner as the winch lowered him into the murky depths. The whoosh of cold air enveloped his body as inky darkness stole his ability to see.

"Daniel, I'm coming. Kick your feet. Keep your head up." Still, no answer. He turned on the helmet lamp and pointed it into the darkness, but he was too far away. *Dear God, don't let him die.* Tanner gripped the hard cable with one hand as he guarded his body from the jagged walls with the other. The cable dug into his torso while the cold invaded his bones. Gooseflesh rose on his arms like pea gravel.

"Daniel, keep kicking. I'm almost there." Scanning the water, he located Daniel's body, unmoving, floating face down. "Don't give up on me." The cable lowered Tanner closer. He nudged Daniel with one foot, trying to get movement as he dropped into the cold water. No success. Easing closer, Tanner turned him over. He wasn't breathing. Blood gushed from a cut over his left eyebrow.

Tanner was glad when his foot felt the base of the mine. "Daniel, breathe—this is not the day to die." Tanner pressed his fingers to Daniel's neck and located a faint pulse. He attempted chest compressions but hit his elbows on the jagged walls in the tight quarters. Not having Daniel on a solid surface made this attempt futile. Sweat slicked Tanner's forehead despite the cold temps.

He strapped Daniel in the body sling, allowing it to hold his weight, and compressed him around the middle to rid his lungs of water.

Daniel let out a quiet moan.

Tanner squeezed him again.

Daniel coughed, sputtered, and expelled more water.

"Come on, Daniel. Breathe, man, breathe."

Tanner pressed into his lung area again with force. Water gushed from Daniel's mouth again. Daniel coughed, then gasped. Grabbing Tanner's shirt, he opened his eyes and whispered, "Take. Care. My family." His eyes rolled back as his body went limp, his breathing shallow.

Sirens blared in the distance, screaming Tanner's failure. Stray dogs howled, echoing the sound. Tanner jerked on Daniel's cable. "Pull, Dylan, hurry."

The hasty assent of the limp body left Tanner dangling in the heart of the mine. Defeat, like an ominous sign, flashed across his mind as Daniel's body eclipsed the sunlight. His Kenyan friend had taken Tanner's turn in the mine. *It should have been me.* The jagged walls pricked at his skin as bile rose in his throat. In his quest to prove himself capable, focusing on the paperwork instead of the mine, he'd lost a good man.

With a jerk, the winch began its ascension out of the depths. When the cable returned Tanner to sea level, he squinted against the bright rays of sunlight and mounted the ladder at the mine's entrance.

"Is he breathing?" Tanner asked Dylan.

Daniel's still body lay on the mining platform.

Emergency technicians administered CPR, and another pressed a bag, forcing oxygen into his lungs. A nurse held an IV bag above his body, allowing fluids to flow through a needle in his arm, while Dylan pulled the mining rope from Daniel's body.

"I think he's got too much water in his lungs," Dylan spoke in whispered tones, squatted beside the ladder, his knuckles white as he held onto the pulley.

"Don't say that. He has to make it." Tanner freed himself from the cable and moved closer to the emergency technicians. "I did CPR in the mine. He expelled a lot of water and talked to me before I sent him up."

Dylan handed Tanner his cell and a towel to wipe his hands.

Tanner stepped toward Daniel's body. The nurse changed a blood-soaked rag for a new one on his head wound. "Please back up and give us room."

Frozen and helpless, Tanner stood while the EMTs and the nurse worked to save Daniel. Bloody water dripped from Tanner's clothes, seeping into the weathered wood.

Sirens announced the arrival of the local police as they careened into the area, coating the scene in dust. Two officers joined the medical team on the mining platform.

The palms swayed overhead, signaling a storm approaching as time crept by. The nurse reported Daniel's vital signs every fifteen seconds, which declined with every report. After fifteen minutes of CPR, they hit Daniel's body with electric paddles. When he didn't respond, they hit him again. After the third attempt, the technician leaned back on his haunches, looked at his watch, and pronounced Daniel dead as the other tech covered his body with a clean cloth.

"Eight fifty-two." He noted the time on a chart, then stood and faced Tanner. "I'm sorry, sir, we did everything we could."

SHIRLEY GOULD

The tech confirmed the time of death with the police investigator at the scene, having him sign the report.

For a long moment, all were silent except for storks calling overhead. Tanner couldn't believe this turn of events. *The buck stops here. I should have checked those ropes. It was my turn, so it should have been me in the mine.* Now, their mining permit would be under review and possibly revoked because of the death of a Kenyan. The cards were falling, but not in his favor.

"Who's in charge here?" The emergency tech pivoted, wiping perspiration from his brow with his sleeve.

Tanner stepped forward, still wet from his trek into the mine. He extended his hand. "I'm Tanner Zarello. This mine belongs to Ward Enterprises, a mining company based in Dallas, Texas. Daniel Mwangi has been our employee for three years. I have his work permit."

"We're taking his body to the city morgue. The police will make a complete report of the incident. I have a form for you to sign, and we need to see his papers."

"Sure." Tanner strode to the Land Cruiser, jerked the door open, and slid into the driver's seat. He shouldn't have put paperwork above getting his hands dirty. He could have been down there. Maybe with his experience, the situation would have turned out differently. Tanner's heart broke for Daniel's family, and he said a silent prayer for their comfort and for what was going to come next for the mine and the rest of his team. He took several deep breaths, trying to regain his composure.

Opening the glove compartment, he grabbed a stack of work permits and thumbed through them until he located Daniel's. Fanning himself with the laminated card only stirred the stagnant air. The buzzing of his cell snapped him out of it. He scrubbed his hand down his face and pressed Accept to a call from the States.

"Hello, it's Tanner." Could this day get any worse?

"Tanner, Alexander Ward here. How's it going?"

Speared by the question, Tanner shook his head. "Not a good day. There's been an accident at the mine, and I'm currently sorting out the details. Can I get back to you?"

A beat passed.

"Shoot me the bottom line."

"Please trust me, sir. Give me a little more time." Tanner hoped his voice sounded positive.

"Yes, call me." He drew in a deep, raspy breath. "I'll be waiting."

"Sir, are you okay? You sound out of breath. Aren't you supposed to be resting?"

"The doc has it under control."

"Get some rest. I'll call you in the morning with more details then." Tanner waited.

"Okay, son." With that, the phone went silent.

Tanner lay his head on the headrest and stared at the ceiling. *Lord, what do I do now?*

With the weight of responsibility on his shoulders, he climbed out of the truck and took Daniel's permit to the EMT, who shared the information with the investigating officer.

"Could I speak to my team before you start your interrogation?" Not waiting for an answer, Tanner turned and surveyed his employees. Vickie wept openly, tears dripping off her chin. Paul, a quiet Kenyan on the team, hung his head and covered his eyes. Drew, their mining expert, stood silent next to Dylan, watching Daniel's body being taken to the ambulance.

The scraping of metal upon metal grated on Tanner when the gurney hit the base of the ambulance as the techs loaded their deceased passenger. The final slamming of the doors rang out, marking the end of a life, the loss of a friend.

Tanner exhaled. "Hey, guys, come out of the sun." They gathered in the shade of a jacaranda tree. "Paul, get everyone a bottle of water. I need you to hydrate and stay close. We've been through a trauma, and the police will want to question each of us. This could be a long day." Tanner failed to sound reassuring, even to his ears.

He stepped toward the ambulance and signed the body over to the EMTs before they drove away, dust billowing behind them.

The police didn't waste any time. Their litany of inquiries added to the barrage of soul-searching questions Tanner had churning in his heart.

The officer in charge handed Daniel's work permit to Tanner. "I'm Karani. I will be the investigating officer on this case. Walk me through the morning, starting with Mwangi going into the mine."

The officer took the steps of the mining platform two at a time. Tanner and Dylan followed, explaining moment by moment how the accident happened.

"Who put this rope on the pulley?" He bent to inspect it.

"I did. I loaded a new sixty-foot rope on the spool yesterday before we left for the evening." Dylan squatted next to the officer and pulled a portion of rope still dangling in the mine. "I secured it through the loop attached to the ladder, checked the pulley, and threaded it perfectly. We change the ropes regularly to keep the team safe in the mine."

The officer wrote the detail in his spiral notebook.

"Dylan, pull it up. I want to see the end of the rope." Tanner's brow furrowed as Dylan complied, laying it in a coiled pile that reminded Tanner of the circling of a drain. After about twenty-five feet of rope, the end appeared. Tanner grabbed it. "It's been cut. Look, it's severed at a slant."

The officer checked the cut and called his partner. "Kimiri, did the medical team leave the rope they extracted from the victim's body?"

"Give me a minute." Kimiri searched the area, moved some bloody clothes, and unearthed a thick piece of sisal twine.

Tanner put the ends together. "A perfect match." His stomach knotted.

The officer sighed and surveyed the property as he walked the platform. "Kimiri, cordon this entire area, then go toward the beach and search the perimeter for footprints."

Officer Karani pivoted. "And, Zarello, keep your team at a distance—away from the scene."

"Why?" Tanner rubbed his chin.

The officer's eyes locked with Tanner's gaze. "Your employee was murdered."

"Did you say murdered?" The word scorched Tanner's tongue.

"Murdered! Who'd want to hurt Daniel?" Dylan leaned forward.

"I don't know, Dylan, but we'll find out." Heat surged up Tanner's neck as pressure built in his chest. He wiped perspiration off his brow.

Officer Karani recorded something on his tablet, then faced Tanner. "Do you have night guards employed?"

"Yes, they left before we arrived this morning."

"I'll need their names and addresses. Did they leave before your day guards arrived? Was the mine left unattended at any point?"

"Henry would have those answers." Tanner pointed to their day guard.

Karani turned, dismounting the platform to question the current guard manning the gate.

Tanner retrieved the work permits from the glove compartment of the Land Cruiser and returned to the crime scene. With the laminated cards in hand, Tanner paced the graying boards of the mining platform. News of a murder would put them under review and possibly cost them their work permit. Kenya was strict on such matters. Keeping the location of the mine under wraps was next to impossible, but incredibly essential due to the extreme value of tanzanite. Apparently, someone wanting to hurt him had found the mine's location and killed the wrong guy. Would more attacks come? Should he be watching his back? He sighed, not realizing he'd been holding his breath. It was a lot to take in.

The police officers walked the perimeter and stopped at the footsteps on the sand.

"Drink some H_2O." Dylan handed him a bottle. "One minute we're horsing around, the next he's gone."

"It should have been me." Tanner removed his hat and ran his fingers through his hair.

"Don't say that!" Dylan jerked his head in Tanner's direction.

"I mean—it was my turn to go down first today." He plopped his hat on his head and eyed the officers.

"Do you think someone was trying to kill you?" Dylan kept his voice subdued. "Why?"

"Don't know, but I hope these Keystone Cops know what they're doing. Can you investigate a murder using only pens and carbon paper?" Tanner downed the water in gulps.

"I know the law and have followed evidence many times, but their methods are antiquated. Look, he's pouring plaster of paris into a footprint in the sand." Dylan watched the officer work the beach.

The platform moved as the investigator mounted the steps. "Did any of your team see the night guards today?" The chief investigator flipped to a new page in his steno pad.

"You'll have to ask them. They will answer you truthfully."

Tanner gave the work permits to the officer. "One guard is currently in Tanzania. His name is Juma Wanjiri. The other guard is Wycliff Matua."

"Wycliff's absence makes me think he knows something. The gate guard said Wycliff left as soon as he arrived."

Tanner spoke loudly to his employees. "Did anybody see Wycliff this morning?" They shook their heads.

"He was here yesterday, when I put the new rope on the pulley and learned our work schedule. Tanner, you may be on to something." Dylan faced the officer. "Tanner was supposed to be in the mine today. He may have been the target."

Karani scribbled something on a new page and then looked up from his notebook. "We're calling in the DCI on this case since Americans are involved." He paused. "They're the FBI of Kenya."

"Can we keep this out of the news?" Tanner chucked his water bottle. "We don't need reporters swarming the mine." The mid-morning sun added extra heat to a fiery situation.

"Yes, I'll make sure the investigation is kept mum, or under wraps, as you say in the States. Let's let them think they got their man. We will follow the evidence while the trail is warm." He joined his partner on the beach looking for clues.

"Dylan, tell Vickie and Paul to package yesterday's tanzanite for shipping." Tanner looked at his clipboard. "Have Drew turn off the generator and load the equipment. As soon as the officers have finished questioning the team, we're calling it a day. Everyone's too upset to work. Losing Daniel ... And we've got to buy another rope." Tanner gave instructions to his team.

"Sure, what are you going to do?" Dylan asked.

"Gather some clues of my own. Then, I'm going hunting. Whoever's responsible is going down." Tanner grabbed his cell phone to take pictures and a pen to make notes. No one would take the life of their friend and get away with it.

~

After a long night in the waiting room, Angie stood at the end of her grandfather's hospital bed, taking in the seriousness of the situation. Reading him like a book, Angie knew he hated it when he couldn't purchase what he wanted. Good health couldn't be bought. Sensing his frustration, Angie moved closer. "Grand-Papa, relax and let them do their jobs. We need to know what's going on."

"You sound like your mother." He reached for her hand.

"I'll take that as a compliment." She rubbed his weathered skin.

Doc Ellis opened the door. "Good morning. How is our patient?"

"Hi, Doc. When I arrived, he was on his cell phone." Angie frowned at Grand-Papa.

"His work ethic is his biggest enemy." He pulled a stethoscope out of his jacket pocket. After listening to Ward's heart, he read his medical chart.

"Angie, would you ask Joseph to join us?"

"Sure. He's in the hall with Mason."

"I want to speak to you both." He checked Ward's pulse and watched the heart monitor.

Angie returned with Joseph, leaving a miffed Mason hovering in the hall where she'd asked him to remain.

"You wanted to see me, Doc?" Joseph motioned for Angie to take the seat beside her grandfather's bed.

"Yes, I'm glad you both are here." He turned to face their patient. "Alexander, I spoke with your cardiologist. You have pericarditis, an infection of the lining of your heart.

Though your heart is strong, stress and overexertion for an extended period have made it susceptible to this infection. Rest and relaxation are mandatory, as well as strong antibiotics."

"So, he's going to be okay?" Angie was hopeful.

"Well, we have another health issue we need to address." He faced the patient. "I've been your physician for more than thirty years, that is—when you allowed me to be. You haven't taken your health seriously. Ignoring your symptoms has led us to today."

"This sounds serious, Doc, give it to me straight."

"We've run a battery of tests, at your request, regarding the aches and pains in your right lower leg. They've brought us to the diagnosis—it's cancer, and it's metastasized."

Ward froze. Didn't blink an eye.

"Cancer!" Angie was on her feet. "Are you sure?"

"Yes. The aching in his bones, which he's called arthritis, is bone cancer."

He showed no emotion. *Grand-Papa must be in shock.*

"How bad is it?" Alexander put a shaky voice to the question that hung in the air.

The doctor sighed, paused, and let his gaze land on Joseph, then Angie, and finally Grand-Papa head-on. "Alexander, I'm sorry, but it's terminal."

"Can't you operate, do chemo, or radiation? He can't die!" Tears pooled in Angie's eyes.

"Terminal." Joseph stood, talking at the same time as Angie.

"I know you both have questions. This is a shock for all of you. The cancer started in his bones, spread to his lymph nodes, and is now in his blood." Doc Ellis hung his head.

Grand-Papa's shoulders slumped as he sighed. "How long do I have?"

The physician met his gaze. "Probably six to eight months. I'd advise you to get your affairs in order."

Tears streamed unabated down Angie's cheeks. She sat beside her grandfather's hospital bed and slipped her hand into his.

"Does he need surgery or treatment? What do we do next?" Joseph searched for answers.

"The cancer is of an aggressive nature. It started in his right leg. If it had been diagnosed immediately, we could have amputated to keep it contained. Chemotherapy and radiation might give him another three months, but the formula he would need will make him very sick."

Joseph turned to his friend. "Alexander, do you want to try chemo?" Joseph spoke with a strained voice.

Alexander didn't hesitate. "No, I want to be as well as possible for whatever time I have. I need to keep a clear head as I transfer my assets and train the ones who will lead Ward Enterprises after I'm gone." He was adamant. Left no room for discussion. He turned to Doc Ellis. "Thanks, Doc, for not mincing words."

Angie stood, leaned closer, and hugged him. A sob escaped as she pressed her cheek to her grandfather's.

"Everything is going to be fine, my dear. Trust me." He cupped her cheek and dried her tears with his thumb. "The Lord and I have spoken frequently about your future." When she pulled back, he managed a small smile. "We may question His timing, but He can be trusted with the details of our lives."

She wiped her face. "I do trust Him, Grand-Papa, but I don't want to lose you. I love you so much. Everyone I love dies."

"I taught you to believe in miracles. We're people of faith, so let's pray for a miracle. Healing me is His choice. However or whenever my life ends, the Lord won't leave you, my dear.

Always remember that." He released her hand and looked at Joseph.

"Joseph, will you discuss this further with the doc? Get the details concerning the disease's trajectory. I don't want to hear anymore."

"Absolutely." Joseph followed the doctor as he left the room.

Angie's grandfather's heart monitor levels rose. "You okay, Grand-Papa?"

"Tough news. A hard pill to swallow."

"I know."

The head nurse hurried in with a cup of water and a tablet. "You need to rest now, Mr. Ward. Your heart rate is elevated. Try to sleep. You've had a rough night. You'll be released sometime tomorrow with new meds." She wrote something on his chart and dimmed the lights.

"You think you can sleep for a while?" Angie kissed his cheek and gathered her things.

"I will try."

Mason hated it when the door closed, leaving him on the outside. But it didn't latch. He could hear the doctor talking. As Angelica's fiancé and Ward's VP, he should have been invited in. *I'm practically family.*

Thumbing the screen of his cell, he acted as if waiting in the hall was his choice, but he gleaned bits and pieces of the conversation coming from Ward's bedside as he leaned against the door frame.

He noted Ward's impatience. Hearing the heart doctor's diagnosis—Cancer! He didn't see that one coming.

Mason walked the length of the hall. This put a new spin

on things. He needed to be made head of the company sooner rather than later. His marriage to Angelica needed to happen quickly so Ward could walk her down the aisle. They must set a wedding date. It was a lot to think about.

Returning to the door, he caught Ward's silence, Joseph's groping for treatment answers, and Angie's crying. That was to be expected.

Now, he could be a hero and help her through the grief process.

But when she said, everyone she loves leaves—what about him? He was still here. Or did she mean Zarello?

This was a wonderful turn of events.

He grabbed his phone, scrolled through the directory, dialed an overseas number, stepped outside the ICU unit for privacy, and waited for it to ring through.

"Wycliff—yes, I'm fine." Mason held his phone away from his ear, impatient with the litany of greetings the Kenyan used to start conversations. "How did it go?" Mason waited.

"The plan worked as we discussed. I paid the other night guard. He was helpful and is now hiding in Tanzania."

Mason paced the halls. "So, Wycliff, you did a good job for me? That's great news."

A stunning blonde strode in his direction. The nurse noticed him, and he winked.

"When I went back to see what was happening, there was a covered body, an ambulance, and the police investigators."

"Did you make sure it was Zarello?" Mason stopped short.

"I couldn't get close. They would see me and take me to jail. They hang people who kill in my country."

"I have to be certain it was him. Go find out and call me as soon as you know. This is critical. More benefits are coming your way if you don't fail me, Wycliff."

Mason pressed the Off button on his cell with force, then

strode back to the intensive care unit, frustrated by the incompetence of others, of things out of his control. But traveling to Kenya would be too risky. He had to trust the man he'd hired.

Clean hands spelled innocence.

Angie strutted into Ward Enterprises sporting a designer suit as if she owned the place. She arrived early, determined to relieve her grandfather's workload. Greeting secretaries along the way, she proceeded to the fifteenth floor and met Joseph in the hall.

"You're taking him home soon, I hope."

"Yes, after our budget meeting. I've convinced him to take a couple of days off." Joseph opened the office door for Angie.

"Thank you, Joseph."

Grand-Papa's private office suite exuded the power he carried. He smiled when she entered and held up one finger, then pointed to his computer, letting her know he was on a video conference call. She moved quietly on the plush carpet to join him.

"It's good to hear from you, Tanner. How are things?" Alexander Ward smiled at the computer screen.

Angie hesitated. *Tanner.* Hearing his voice sent her emotions reeling. Wouldn't Tanner be better at helping them through this? Which was unfair because Mason was doing his best. It wasn't his fault he excelled in business, but he was still learning the ropes of a serious romance. Would the news about Grand-Papa bring Tanner home for a visit? Probably not. She just had to get it through her thick skull, Tanner's plans didn't include her anymore. Even still, it hurt to believe it. She had to suck it up. The tables had turned, and Grand-Papa needed her now.

Inching closer to her grandfather, she stayed away from the camera. Since their conversation in the parking lot, she didn't want him to read the pain in her eyes.

"Not so good, sir. That's why I'm calling. As I mentioned yesterday, there's been an accident at the mine. We have lost a good man, Daniel Mwangi, and our equipment was sabotaged during the night. After looking at the evidence, the police determined it was murder. What's worse is they killed the wrong man, because I was scheduled and their intended target."

Angie covered her mouth to smother a gasp, placed her hand on Grand-Papa's shoulder, and entered Tanner's field of vision.

"Why do you think you're their target?" The force of Ward's words betrayed his grave concern.

"I was next in line to work below the surface. Daniel took my place." Regret tinged his words.

"Who would be targeting you? Were they after the tanzanite? Are the police investigating this?" Questions tumbled out of Angie faster than Tanner could answer.

"Hello, Angie." He paused. "Don't know anyone who would want to hurt me. If they were after the jewels, they would have attacked during the day, when we were bringing them out of the mine. The police are conducting an investigation, and I've started a search of my own. They've hurt one of ours. Now, it's personal."

"Is it safe to work at the mine after today?" Ward leaned forward.

"I've hired extra guards. We'll resume mining tomorrow. But the Kenyan government is investigating the incident, threatening to revoke our work permit. I know you have friends in high places, sir. Do you know someone in power we can appeal to?"

Angie read desperation in Tanner's deep mocha eyes, shadowed by furrowed brows.

"I have some acquaintances still in office from my last visit to Parliament. Let me make some contacts." Ward made a note on his iPad. "Since this has transpired, I want to hear from you more frequently."

"Yes, sir. It's my mess. I'll clean it up." Tanner sounded convincing.

"Be careful, son. And watch your back." Ward cautioned.

"Tanner, accidents happen in mines. This isn't your fault. Don't beat yourself up and don't try to be a hero, Tanner. Just finish the job—"

"Are you the boss now since you have a master's degree? Watch out, Mr. Ward, she will take over if you let her." Tanner teased.

"You're so funny. Don't quit your day job." She drew near the screen. "I was going to say, 'finish the job and come home safely.'" Without a goodbye, she stepped away and moved to the huge window overlooking Dallas, not seeing past the glass.

He'd let their relationship dwindle, allowing her to slip out of his life without explanation. After their brief encounter at her gala, she didn't know what to say or do when it came to Tanner Zarello.

Alexander Ward completed the call and faced Angie. "You okay, my dear?"

"I will be in a minute. Seeing Tanner again took me by surprise." She fanned herself with a piece of linen stationery. "I miss him, Grand-Papa."

"You two were pretty close at one time."

"*Were*, is the operative word. I don't know what happened. But trust me, it won't be a problem concerning me working at

Ward Enterprises." She closed the conversation, tucking the turmoil deep within.

"He's doing a stellar job running the mine for this company. It's a great position for him at this point in his career. He's a man of integrity, Angelica. I'm proud of him." Ward pressed the intercom. "Carol, bring me my international phone list."

"How long are you working today, Grand-Papa?"

"Only a couple of hours. Joseph is bringing lunch in, and we have a budget meeting. Then I'm going home."

"Please don't overdo it. You've only been out of the hospital for a couple of hours."

"I'm pacing myself." He took his phone list from Carol, his assistant.

Angie paced the office, thinking of the most effective strategy for the Kenyan situation. She understood their relationship was over, but her heart still wanted Tanner to be in this world ... he made it better by being her partner in mischief when they were young, by being her dance partner when she had to take lessons, by doctoring her skinned knees, and by rescuing her when she fell in the lake unconscious. "Are you going to call the vice president's office? I'm sure Saitoti will help us."

"It would be best to see him personally, but I'm not up for the trip."

"I can go. He'll remember me, and you can glean some benefit from the college bills you paid. I studied international business, so let me negotiate to keep the mine open until all the tanzanite has been harvested. They are close to the end of the project. I can do this, and you can save your strength, Grand-Papa. I want you around for a long time."

A challenge of this magnitude would help her shake off the wounds Tanner's loss inflicted. A trip was just the ticket. She could put distance between herself and Mason and spend some time alone searching her heart.

"I don't know. Africa is a dangerous place."

Reading worry on his countenance, she cut off his pondering before he could say no. "I can handle myself in foreign countries. Give me two weeks, and I'll get the job done and return safe and sound." She leaned over and brushed a kiss on his cheek.

Her cell vibrated in her pocket. "My phone is buzzing, and I need to take this. Let's talk later." Before he could stop her, she hurried out the door with her phone to her ear.

Tanner may think he's Tarzan. But Jane was the one with the brains.

Seeing Angie stunned Tanner. He'd dreaded making the call but didn't expect Angie to be present. She looked amazing, perfect, except for the disappointment he read in her eyes when he saw her face. No matter how far away he was, she remained embedded in the recesses of his heart.

"You okay, man?" Dylan slid into the Land Cruiser as he ended the call.

"Yeah. Ward has some friends in power here in Kenya. He's going to appeal for our permit to stay in effect until we complete the job." Tanner ran his fingers through his hair.

"Was he upset?"

"No, just matter-of-fact like usual. Angie was there. I guess she's working at the company now." Tanner started the truck.

"By the look on your face, I assume it didn't go well."

"Nope, seeing her feels like dancing with a porcupine. But it hurts to lose her." He gunned it and wove them into the traffic flow. Chaotic Mombasa traffic would get his mind off the lovely Miss Ward.

~

"Sarah, will you get my luggage for me? It's the three-piece set I use when I travel overseas."

"Yes, Miss Angie."

Angie retrieved her passport, checked the expiration date, and put it in her cross-body purse along with her money, hiding each in different compartments. As she entered her walk-in closet, her cell vibrated.

"Hello, Betty." Angie listened as she selected some sandals. "That will be perfect. Thank you for getting this done so quickly. I have urgent business in Kenya for Ward Enterprises. Please send the itinerary to my email address and charge these tickets to the company account."

"I'm glad there was a vacant seat for you in first class. Am I understanding right, you want the return open-ended?" The travel agent double-checked her facts.

"Yes, I'm hoping to get this done within two weeks, but it could take a couple more days. I'll book my return after securing the mining permit for Ward Enterprises." Angie surveyed her closet while talking to the travel agent.

"Your itinerary will be in your inbox momentarily. Have a safe trip and call me again when I can be of service."

Angie ended the call and packed her suitcases. Two business suits, some casual outfits, three sundresses, jeans, tennis shoes, and a bathing suit, in case she could relax around a hotel pool for an afternoon. With sunscreen added to her toiletry collection, a set of international plugs and adapters, and a 220-volt hair dryer, she closed the first bag. Her excitement built as she put in the last pair of shoes and some reading material for the long flights.

Her phone dinged, signaling a text.

> Hello, my fiancé ... thinking of you ... going
> into a meeting ... will call you tonight. Mason

But Angie would be flying across the ocean tonight. She'd inform him of this overseas trip by text once she got past security. Mason was a lot of things, but especially protective—there was no way he would approve.

She texted back a smiley face. He would think she was driving or really busy and couldn't talk.

And she was busy preparing for an African adventure.

Chapter Three

T he budget meeting for the expenses on the mine in West Texas droned on, but Mason had perfected the role, showing interest in each boring agenda item, especially when they discussed finances. Knowing his future would glean from the successes of Ward Enterprises' holding, it was important to know these details and the players making it happen. After two hours of tedious details, Ward adjourned the meeting in his usual fashion.

Mason finished his soft drink and put his notes in his portfolio as he listened to a conversation between his boss and Joseph.

"I saw Angie here this morning. Did she approve of the office you had designed for her?" Joseph, Ward's personal assistant, gathered Ward's folders and briefcase.

"Yes, she loved the décor." Ward reached for his cane and stood beside Joseph with its assistance. "The black oval desk and shelves look great on her white carpet."

"I hoped she would like it. Is she still here?"

"No. She's at the estate packing her suitcases. I'm sending her to Kenya to meet with the vice president. There's a problem concerning the work permit at the mine. She knows Vice President Saitoti and can take care of it and be back in a couple of weeks or so."

Ward and Joseph left the conference room, conversing like two old friends.

Mason hid his anger as he greeted the chairman of the board and asked for an invoice from the caterer. He was incensed. Angelica had been in the office earlier and hadn't looked him up, and now she was traveling abroad without telling him. What part of being engaged didn't she understand? Why hadn't she called him?

He stomped back to his office, shut the door, and paced, devising a plan. He reached for his wallet and got comfortable in his leather chair. With the company credit card in hand, he made a call and then requested the company limousine be brought to the front of the building. Once his plan was in place, he strode from his office, punched the elevator button several times, and checked his watch.

If traffic wasn't too bad, he'd get there in time to thwart her plans.

Angie slapped her palm on the British Airways counter. "What do you mean you can't find my reservation? Please look again. It's a first-class ticket in the name of Angelica Ward. I need to catch today's flight."

The agent's manicured nails tapped the keyboard as Angie fanned herself with a computer-generated itinerary, propelling a cool breeze across her perspiring face. Each click of the keyboard grated on her nerves. Frustrated at this glitch in her plan, she bit her bottom lip, probably removing the last of her lipstick. She reached into her cross-body purse and retrieved a lipstick case.

As she reapplied a burgundy hue to her pursed lips, she used the case's mirror to survey the mass of travelers behind her. She wanted to get past security before Mason had time to show up. He would pressure her to change her plans to travel with bodyguards, or want to go with her, which would not be fun. His overprotective tendencies got annoying.

Angie took a deep breath and relaxed as moments ticked by. "Any luck?"

"Yes, Miss Ward."

"Did you find my reservation?"

"There's a reservation for you from Dallas Fort Worth to London Heathrow, but the computer shows the reservation to Nairobi was canceled about an hour ago."

"There must be a mistake. I have the itinerary right here." Angie presented the flight schedule.

"I'm so sorry this happened. All I can tell you is someone with access to this credit card canceled the Kenyan portion of your trip." She clicked the keys. "There is one available seat in first class. May I book it for you?"

It was Mason. He didn't want her to be anywhere near Tanner, so going to Kenya would be out of the question. His insecurities fueled his actions too often. He would blame it on his love for her and his valid concern over her safety. But she would not be micro-managed and would need to discuss boundaries when she returned. *I'm going to rethink this engagement while I'm away.* "Yes, please. Here's my personal credit card."

"Don't worry. This will only take a few minutes. You have plenty of time to make it to your gate before they begin the boarding process."

Angie scanned the growing crowd. No Mason. Her pulse

quickened when a black limo slowed along the sidewalk. Drawing a deep breath, she prayed for a parting of the Red Sea to get her boarding pass printed and past security.

"Miss Ward, here's your credit card, passport, and travel documents. Please enter your signature on the machine." The agent put tags on her matching luggage.

"You'll be flying out of gate D24, Miss Ward." She placed her baggage claim stubs on the counter. "I hope you have a wonderful trip."

Angie grimaced as her luggage disappeared through the chute with duffel bags and Samsonite pieces. "Oh, I hope it doesn't get lost this time." Knowing she had to trust the airlines, she smiled at the agent. "I appreciate your help. You've been very kind."

She straightened her designer jacket, clutched the handle of her carry-on, and hurried toward the security line, coming face to face with her fiancé.

"Mason, what are you doing here?" A pasted smile hid her agitation as he greeted her with a kiss on the cheek.

"Angelica, could we talk? I learned of your trip to Africa at the end of today's business meeting because your grandfather and Joseph were discussing it. Why didn't I know about this sooner from you? I have grave concerns we must address." He grasped her elbow and turned toward a coffee shop, leading her to an empty table. "You should have discussed it with me before making this decision. As your fiancé, I need to have input in all important issues. You should be busy planning a wedding, not flying to the other side of the world to fix Zarello's mess." He unbuttoned his jacket and took a seat.

"Why, Mason? This is a business matter requiring personal attention, and my grandfather isn't well enough to make the trip. I've been there many times and have a good relationship with the vice president." She met his stare with an unbending determination. "Did you cancel my flight from London to Nairobi?"

"Yes. I needed time to discuss this with you."

"This upsets me, Mason. And it was quite embarrassing. Why did you do that?"

"Because Africa is dangerous for a woman alone. Couldn't this business be accomplished through a series of phone calls?" He leaned forward, putting his hands on his knees, his brows furrowed. "And as your fiancé, I'm nervous for you to travel without security. I could cancel my upcoming appointments and go with you, but it will take a few days to make that happen."

"I appreciate your offer, but no. Your expertise is in American investments. I'm familiar with foreign protocols, and this needs to be done right away. Vice President Saitoti will help me. Try not to be overly concerned. I'll take all precautions, get the job done, and be back before you have time to miss me." Perhaps her smile would persuade him.

He reached for her hand. "Angelica, where's your ring?"

"In the safe at the estate. Wearing it in Kenya would make me a target. I can't take a chance." She hoped it proved her cautionary mindset.

He squeezed her hand. "You're right. I'm just surprised to see you without it." He paused. "Are you going to see Tanner? I'm concerned. He hurt you once, and I don't want it to happen again."

"No need to worry about that." She patted his arm. "I don't plan to see him. I'm going to Nairobi. He's in Mombasa. I'll go straight to the vice president's office, take care of business, and get back to Dallas." Why did her stomach lurch at the thought of Tanner? "Don't worry, Mason. I'll be careful. I have my pepper spray and won't hesitate to use it."

"That doesn't make me feel better." Mason took in a deep

breath and blew it out. "I'm not going to be able to dissuade you, am I?" He took keys from his pocket and flipped them, probably to veil his irritation.

"No. Kenya's rules are strict. We're being investigated and can't lose the work permit on the mine when we're so close to the end of the project. We need this extension. It's business. So, hug me and let me go." She stood and gripped the handle of her bag. "I need to get through security and to my gate. They'll be calling first class soon."

"I'm not happy about this, Angelica. We must discuss some limitations on your leadership role when you return. Your security is vital to me. It's because I care. You do understand, don't you?" He stood and hugged her, kissing the top of her hair, as expected, not being comfortable with public displays of affection.

"Mason, you're being controlling and limiting of me and my work at Ward Enterprises. I don't like it, and neither would Grand-Papa. We will discuss this when I return. I'll e-mail you when I arrive." She turned and moved toward security. *Maybe I should've said 'no' to him in front of the crowd at the gala. He needs to be brought down a peg or two.* With a final wave, she lost sight of him in the crowd. Inching through the security checkpoint, she donned her peep-toed heels from the bin, her mood lighter. Not being sad to see him go should have told her something. Throwing caution to the wind, she raised the handle of her carry-on and proceeded to her gate, ready to take on the world.

Mason raked his hand through his hair and flipped his keys, his jaw tightening. He stepped out of the throng of travelers to a window and searched for the company limo. Didn't she know it wasn't advantageous to make Mason Malone angry? If Tanner Zarello was still alive, and she connected with him, it could ruin everything. That woman was entirely too headstrong. *Go ahead. Enjoy your independence, because as soon as you become Mrs. Mason Malone, I'll temper that trait.*

He spun on the heel of his expensive Italian loafers and marched toward the entrance of the British Airways terminal. Once on the sidewalk, he punched a number on his cell. "Pick me up, and hurry." The Texas heat merged with exhaust fumes, choking him as perspiration dampened his suit. Patience wasn't a virtue he possessed, especially when he didn't get what he wanted.

When the limo pulled up, he opened the door. "James, take me back to the downtown office." Mason slid into the luxurious sedan, retrieved a Perrier from the fridge, and rubbed its damp coolness on the back of his neck. Opening the green bottle, he guzzled its contents. With time to kill, he allowed his thoughts to churn, plotting forward moves. Dallas traffic gave him time to dream. He envisioned the power soon to be his and smirked. Just a few minor details stood between him and his future.

Upon arrival, he left the confines of the limo, Mason straightened his tie and smiled at the receptionist as he strutted into Ward Enterprises. *Angelica needs to count her blessings.*

Angie's anticipation intensified as the inertia of the lift-off pinned her to the seat. Her thoughts ran the gamut, from her doubts about Mason to the task ahead, from their resort, Paradise Inn, to her grandfather's failing health, from Kenya to Tanner Zarello, and there they stalled. Why does he constantly invade my thoughts? Tall, dark, and oh-so-handsome stabbed the heart every time.

Flying first class was the only way to travel the long overseas flight. In the comfort of expensive recliners, Angie relaxed, enjoyed great food, and arrived refreshed at her destination, unlike the exhausted passengers who'd been packed in coach like sardines. Angie's heart went out to young mothers exiting the plane with cranky toddlers in tow.

Jomo Kenyatta International Airport sported faded paint and cracking linoleum, but the people seemed friendly. Signs of new construction showed things were changing soon. In the customs line, strong body odors of perspiring travelers standing uncomfortably close assaulted Angie's senses. The ceiling fan stirred the heat among the crowd of Africans. Aging linoleum crackled as they stepped forward.

"It's hot in Nairobi, isn't it?" Angie made small talk with another tourist dressed in pink attire.

"And very humid." She fanned herself with her visa.

"I know." Angie pulled her shirt away from her body. "Oh, it's my turn." Angie hurried forward and put her fingers on the screen to be scanned.

"Lots of travelers tonight." She made small talk with the officer manning the desk. He had to be hot in his uniform since the breeze from the ceiling fans wasn't reaching his desk.

"Many visitors want to see our fine country." He stamped her passport before handing it to her.

She left the crowd behind, like a bird out of its cage, and headed to baggage claim.

After exchanging money at the forex—foreign exchange—she got a cart and positioned it by the luggage belt. A Kenyan man stacked her bags like a pyramid and followed closely as she parted the crowd, vying for a spot in the customs line.

Angie's hands were clammy, a mixture of nerves and

perspiration, when the customs officer took her passport. He perused the visa, compared her photo to her face, then waved her on. She boarded a gray London cab with backward doors, her chariot to the Nairobi Hilton, a welcome sight after twenty-six hours of travel.

As the noonday sun glared, baking the parched terrain, Tanner followed the hearse bearing Daniel Mwangi's body on the potholed tarmac. This part of the job tore at his heart. The title 'Boss' meant failure today since part of his job was to take care of his team. With the loss of Daniel, he had failed this family.

Mwangi's humble dwelling, their destination, was in Karen, a Kikuyu area on the outskirts of Nairobi, made famous by Karen Blixen, known for her *Out of Africa* fame.

The hearse came to a halt, sending a dash of sand bathing the waiting mourners. Tanner stepped out of his truck to a wave of sobs piercing the air, ramming his heart. It was his fault—all of it. No one would be gathered here today if it weren't for him. He shut the door and bowed his head. The dust settled on the worn leather of his boots—ashes to ashes and dust to dust. The casket was removed and carried inside the house. Tanner scanned the area and followed the wooden box as a bead of sweat coursed down his back.

Surveying the property, Tanner discovered a meager garden of corn stalks and stems of greens, called *sikumu wiki*. An outhouse at the back corner of the yard meant running water hadn't been installed. A few scrawny chickens roamed the yard, scratching in the dirt. The home was a humble dwelling, with walls of wood and floors of painted cement covered with a tin roof. Old calendars decorated the main room among a few family photos. His mind went to Daniel speaking of his home as a wonderful dwelling with an ample garden.

After giving Daniel's wife time to weep across the rough-hewn casket, he stepped forward, presenting her with a bouquet of roses. "Mrs. Mwangi, I'm Tanner Zarello, your husband's boss. I'm sorry for your loss. Daniel was a wonderful man, a great worker, and my dear friend."

Tears filled his eyes as his words were interpreted into Kikuyu. "His last words to me were, 'Take care of my family.' His care for you filled his last moments." He paused for her son to relate his words. "I have brought his belongings and shillings, including this month's salary."

She nodded and said, "*Asante,* thank you." Mrs. Mwangi grasped his hand and held it before taking the money.

As he met her eyes, his mind raced to his hard-working mother, who labored to raise him as a single mom, saving money for his education. One day soon, he would have enough to relieve her of all financial burdens, a goal met.

Tanner reached into his jacket pocket and retrieved an envelope. "This is from Ward Enterprises. You will receive this amount every year on the date of Daniel's death as long as you live."

She took the envelope, listened to his words in her tribal tongue, opened it, and wept again. After regaining her composure, she spoke in Kikuyu.

Her son, a younger version of Daniel, relayed the lengthy message. "She wants you to know how grateful she is. Your company has been very generous. Many times, she asked my father how they would make it when the job was finished. He always said, 'The Lord will provide.' And he has. Thank you." He paused. "And, from our family, I express our gratitude."

Tanner shook the son's hand, solidifying his pledge.

"Here's my contact information. If your mother needs additional help, please don't hesitate to call."

Breaking eye contact, Tanner stepped to the wooden casket, placed his hand on the lid, and paused, remembering the tooth missing in Daniel's easy smile. *After a while, crocodile.* He left, not looking back. It hurt leaving one he cared for behind. He'd felt this pain before when he left Angie, the love of his life, standing alone in a parking lot.

Mason looked at his watch as he finished his morning coffee, a perfect brew, in his corner office. He grabbed his portfolio and headed to Ward's office. When his phone buzzed, he checked the number, stopped walking, and pushed a button. "Malone here."

"Greetings from Kenya. This is Wycliff."

"This can't take long. I have an early meeting. What news do you have for me?" He stood and tossed his cup in the trash.

"*Bwana*, I have been watching the mine as you said."

"Are you there now?" He put his portfolio under his arm.

"Yes."

"Is he there?" Mason paced his office.

"No, the man with yellow hair is leading the team. There are extra guards in place."

"That's good news." He smiled. "But are you sure Zarello is completely out of the picture?" Losing patience with his hired man, he checked his watch. "We haven't been notified of his death. Check further to be sure. You boasted of your connections in Kenya. I'm depending on you to complete this job. So, call me back with definite proof." He disconnected the call and blew out a long breath before joining the meeting in the conference room. He hated being late.

"Sorry, I was caught on the phone. Ordering a surprise for Angelica got complicated." He hoped his excuse would touch a tender spot in his boss's heart.

He laid his phone beside his portfolio and tensed when the boss reached for his cell.

"Mason, is this the same phone I have, or is it a newer model?" Ward pressed a few buttons.

"Mine is one model newer than yours. Do you want an upgrade, sir?" Mason sounded accommodating, sweat dotting his brow. Was the air-conditioning working today? He searched the old man's eyes as he examined the screen, his reaction unreadable. Mason lifted his hand to retrieve his phone.

"No. I don't have time to learn a new phone. I've never been one to keep up with technology. But, get Angelica one when she returns." He handed back the cell. "Now, let's look at the profit margins on the Shafter mine here in Texas."

Had Ward seen the overseas number in his phone? If he did, would he recognize the country code?

He didn't seem to, but not knowing made Mason nervous.

Dressed in a sharp business suit, Angie stepped into the Nairobi sunshine.

"Taxi!" She raised her arm to get the driver's attention.

"I need to go to the office of the vice president of Kenya, please."

Nairobi traffic had increased since her last visit. The normal ten-minute drive took half an hour in stop-and-go, bumper-to-bumper chaos. She fanned herself to keep exhaust fumes from making her car sick.

"*Bwana*, please wait for me and keep the meter running."

"*Ndio, dada.* I will be here."

Angie moved toward the security gates connected to seven-foot stone walls with electrified barbed wire perched on top, protecting the grounds. Guards had watchdogs on leashes as they patrolled the compound.

"Passport, please." A uniformed guard scanned her documents and checked her fingerprints before allowing her to pass the gate.

With her passport in hand, she strode with confidence into the presidential office building and endured further security screening. Approaching the receptionist's desk, she smiled. "Could you direct me to the vice president's office?"

"He is out of the country. He had a death in the family that took him away for the week. Would you like to make an appointment?" The lady was nice enough, but her bun was too tight, making her smile taut.

"Yes, please. When will he return?" Grand-Papa's secretary had confirmed the vice president would be available to meet with her. She didn't expect this.

The government employee searched through a calendar. "One week and two days from today, he has an opening. Want me to put your name on his register?"

"Yes, please." She placed her business card on the receptionist's desk.

Sliding a piece of carbon paper under the appointment book page, she wrote Angie's name. The receptionist smiled and made eye contact. "Fifth of June at ten in the morning. *Ni sawa?* Okay?" She gave her a reminder card.

"Yes, thank you." Hating such a long delay, Angie turned to leave. This would keep her in Kenya for more than two weeks. Mason would be miffed. But losing the work permit would be a great financial loss for Ward Enterprises. She had to see this through.

"*Bwana*, I need to return to my hotel, please." Bouncing along on the streets of Nairobi, the driver dodged potholes and circled roundabouts with a steering wheel on the wrong side of the car while driving on the wrong side of the road. A *piki piki*, a motorcycle loaded with goods, cut in front of them. The driver dodged the bike and honked at a donkey trotting on the edge of the tarmac. Acrid smoke from burning refuse floated in her direction as they passed a garbage dump.

Ignoring the mayhem, Angie decided to go to Mombasa. With time on her hands, she could visit Paradise Inn, their resort on the coast of the Indian Ocean.

"*Bwana*, when we reach my hotel, can you wait for me again? I want to collect my bags and then travel to Wilson Airport."

"I will accommodate you, *dada*."

Her mind raced to the swaying palms and white beaches at the inn. Some relaxation would be wonderful. After making flight plans to Mombasa and retrieving her luggage, she used her cell to make a reservation at Paradise Inn. She punched in the number but ended the call before it went through.

"You need me to make a reservation for you in Mombasa, Miss Ward?" The concierge offered as he loaded her luggage into the taxi.

"No, but thank you. My grandfather owns the resort. So, I don't think I need a reservation. In fact, I think a surprise visit is a great idea."

Chapter Four

"Welcome aboard flight AK421 bound for Mombasa, Kenya, on the majestic coast of the Indian Ocean. We're proud you have chosen to fly Air Kenya. We appreciate your business. Please relax and enjoy your forty-minute flight. Make sure your seatbelts are fastened."

The flight attendant replaced the microphone and walked the short aisle of the thirty-seater plane, checking if seatbelts were fastened. Her bright red uniform with Kenyan fabric on the collar and pockets matched the airplane seats. Kenyans loved bright colors, even on airplanes.

With the click of her seatbelt, Angie tuned the flight attendant out. She was relieved the seat next to her was vacant since her emotions, like a roller coaster, lifted in excitement as the plane left the runway. This wasn't a flight where she wanted to make small talk with a stranger, though Kenyans were friendly people. Today, she'd decided to go where she wanted, and no one knew where she was headed. *I could get used to this freedom—make it on my own. Who needs a man placing demands on my comings and goings?* Huh, she'd thought about Mason but didn't miss him at all. Even though Grand-Papa was so high on Mason, he only saw the business side of him, not who he really was as a person. Wanting to please Grand-Papa should not mean spending her life with someone with domineering tendencies ... someone she didn't love. He wouldn't want that if he knew the whole story.

Kibera, the largest slum in Kenya, could be seen out of Angie's window as the plane took off. She'd heard about the country's slums, but seeing them gave her pause. Rows of shanties were built using rusty tin and cardboard, and sewers ran between the meager dwellings of the destitute amid rampant crime and disease.

Angie diverted her eyes to the skyline of downtown Nairobi in the distance. The scene contrasted the flow of well-dressed entrepreneurs walking with purpose among the high-rises, their windows reflecting the noonday sun. Villages dotted the landscape as they left the city. Square plots of gardens checkerboarded the hillsides.

Flipping through the *Inflight* magazine, her eyes caught a highlighted line—*Kenya offers a mixture of culture and cuisine with adventure lurking around every corner.* Sudden turbulence brought her thoughts to the dangers prevalent in the air over Kenya. Closing her eyes, she willed her stomach to settle. Her knuckles whitened as she gripped the armrests, thankful it was a short flight. Air sickness wasn't apropos for a classy businesswoman on assignment. Watching out the window passed the time and warded off nausea.

When palm trees and the Indian Ocean came into view, Angie smiled. Their descent went smoothly except for a baby screaming in the back of the plane—the air pressure must have caused his ears to hurt. From the air, the Mombasa International Airport seemed minuscule compared to Jomo Kenyatta International in Nairobi. The building appeared modern except for the lack of jetways to get on and off the planes. The bumpy landing jarred Angie, causing her to bite her tongue. *Did the pilot hit a pothole?*

"Please mind your head as you disembark. Transport will be waiting for you." The flight attendant's voice was loud on the microphone.

A spiky-headed boy about eight years old spoke up. "Hey Mom, what did she say?"

"She said, 'Don't bump your head as you get off the plane. A bus is waitin' for you.'" His mother grinned and popped her gum.

Angie smiled. The instructions sounded better with a southern drawl in the mix. She joined the passengers mounting the wobbly staircase they'd rolled to the side of the plane. The heat stole her breath as she walked across the tarmac under the African sun. The ocean's trade winds offered relief as they cooled her moist clothing. Her luggage was circling the baggage claim area, waiting for retrieval. Having cleared customs in Nairobi, entering Mombasa was a breeze.

"Angeleeka Ward, Angeleeka Ward." An African man roughly five feet tall, wearing flip-flops too big for his feet and sporting a watch with a cracked face, heralded her name as she trudged out of the terminal behind a cart stacked with luggage.

Angie touched a hand to her chest. "Are you speaking to me, sir?"

"Are you the one called Angeleeka Ward?" She shoved the cart in his direction.

"I'm Angelica Ward. Are you my driver?" She smiled

He returned her smile and opened her door. Wearing an old, but clean T-shirt that hung on his small frame, baggy pants, and a New York Yankees ball cap, the gentleman's hole in his grin where two teeth had been made her wish for her camera.

"Yes, *dada*, I received a call from my cousin in Nairobi, and I take you to the inn." He pulled an old phone from his pocket. *Does his antique cell really work?* Even without cutting-edge technology, he still seemed like a happy man, working his job.

A taller Kenyan man dressed in a wrinkled suit stared as she waited for her luggage to be loaded.

Her hair stood on the back of her neck. She memorized his face as she eased into the safety of the cab, all while he held her gaze until she slipped on her sunglasses.

"Miss Angeleeka Ward, you ready to travel?"

"Yes, I am ready." With her luggage jammed into the trunk, the driver launched the cab into the chaos of Mombasa traffic.

Angie clung to the armrest as her body slammed against the back seat. They wove in and out of the lanes as if challenging other drivers to a race, while Kenyan music blared from kiosks, beckoning those with shillings to come and spend. Several goats chewed fruit piled by an open market, donkeys brayed in the distance, and scrawny dogs dug through fermented garbage in search of food. The smell of roasted corn permeated the humidity.

It was smoother to stay on the shoulder of the road since the tarmac was riddled with potholes, resembling a war zone. Each vehicle created dust clouds, bathing pedestrians along the way. Angie imagined herself smiling with dirt in her teeth and opted to be tight-lipped for the duration of their trip. Horns trumpeted, overloaded vans cut in the cue, and people darted around vehicles. Concerned for the dirty children begging in the street, Angie strained to watch them.

"Where are their parents? Why are they out here alone? They could get hurt."

"They are orphans. Their parents have died." He honked at a bus cutting in front of them.

When traffic stalled, a motorcycle with three paying passengers breezed past, getting his riders to their destinations, dusty but with haste. Two bicycles loaded with trays of eggs zig-zagged a path between cars, trucks, and exhaust-emitting buses. Though choking on fumes, Angie absorbed the movement, the animals, the people, and the challenge.

They passed shop after shop with stacks of shoes, a clothesline of underwear, various vegetables stacked with precision, and fly-covered meat displayed in butcher shop windows. Gorgeous flowers were offered next to a casket shop with various sizes on display for grieving families. The whole experience reminded her of stories from fifty years ago.

Mombasa, a hot, humid place, left her skin gritty, ready for a shower after being in the city for thirty minutes.

The driver stopped at a rusty gate and waited for a herd of cattle to meander along. The mooing milk makers blocked the entrance of the inn while they grazed on the tall grass surrounding the property. When the dust settled, Angie saw Paradise Inn for the first time.

"No! No! No! We've taken a wrong turn somewhere. Check the address again. This can't be the place. There must be some mistake." She rustled through her bag and dug out a wrinkled pamphlet, leaned forward, and tapped her manicured nails on his shoulder. "Here's the brochure. It says, 'Paradise Inn, a beautiful resort on the Indian Ocean.' Does this look beautiful to you?"

"*Pole sana*, so sorry, this is the place. You have arrived." He honked his horn to signal for someone to let them in. "One thousand shillings, please."

"No, you don't understand. I can't stay in a place like this. You can't leave me here."

The squeaky gate opened. Angie's stomach tightened as they neared the main building. Grand-Papa would be horrified at this atrocity. A weathered sign hung from one hinge. Where there had been flowers, weeds stretched waist-high. Burnt garbage reeked in the steamy air. She exhaled and stared, listing the travesties—the paint curling on the buildings, a filthy open-air lobby, trash everywhere, and sand coating the floor.

"Welcome to Paradise Inn. The staff will take care of you. Not to worry."

Angie eased her door open and stepped out of the taxi. Dodging trash near the steps, she stood statuesque on gritty concrete, lifting the hair that had escaped her clip and was now plastered to her neck by the humidity.

The driver unloaded her luggage. He cleared his throat, stepped forward with his hand extended, and smiled.

She placed wrinkled shillings into his sweaty palm and cringed when he skidded her luggage onto the grimy tile. Everywhere she turned, sand, gravel, and debris crunched under her peep-toed pumps. *And he said, 'Not to worry.'*

He smiled, waved at Angie, and sped out of sight, his taillights fading amid a tsunami of dust, leaving her standing alone, deserted in the lobby of Paradise Inn amid a cloud of exhaust fumes. Being the strong woman her grandfather raised her to be, she usually knew what to do. In this situation, she stood staring, speechless.

"Hello, hello. Is anybody here? I need help." Silence. She spotted the 'Welcome to Paradise' sign on the counter. *Now, that's an oxymoron.*

She eased through the lobby, past a couple of tables,

toward a swimming pool. Chlorine scented the breeze as a sifting of sand blew at her feet, settling on her shoes.

"Anyone here? Hello." Angie weighed her decision to keep her arrival a secret.

A young Kenyan man wearing khaki pants and a T-shirt hurried toward her. "Yes, I am here. I closed the gate when your taxi departed." He stopped and stared. His face lit up with a grin. "Miss Angeleeka, you are here. I am the one called Julius."

How does he know my name?

"I'm glad to meet you. Where is Tanner?" *I'd like to interrogate Mr. Zarello right now.*

"*Bwana* is not here. He and his team are working at the mine. Do you need a place to stay, Miss Angeleeka?"

His kind mannerisms helped her relax a bit. "I hoped to stay here but didn't expect the resort to be so run-down, so dirty. It was much nicer when I stayed here three years ago with Tanner and Grand-Papa when they bought the property where the mine is located."

"Bungalows are nice. I have one ready. Do you need dinner?" He reached for one of her suitcases.

"Yes, is that possible?"

He put her carry-on under one arm. "*Ndio, dada.* Yes, miss. Samson, our cook, is in the kitchen. Come, I will show you where to stay. Then, we will cook for you." He smiled and grabbed a key attached to a small African hut keychain. Angie followed him from the lobby through an area that had once been a restaurant. Only two tables were clean, but the kitchen was pristine and amazingly modern.

Olive-green lizards, like the ones in those insurance commercials, scampered across the sidewalk. *I hope Grand-Papa took fifteen minutes and insured this place.* Angie shivered, hoping they weren't regular guests. *I may torch it.*

Just beyond the restaurant, a beautiful in-ground pool gleamed. The seascape beyond the pool was amazing. The waves of the Indian Ocean rhythmically licked the white sand, while tall palms cast long, moving shadows on the beach, mimicking the sway of hula dancers. Seagulls soared through a cloudless sky, sending their cries competing with the pounding surf. A sailboat washed across the horizon, framed by slow-moving vegetation. Pure, postcard perfection. What a contrast to the entrance.

The bungalow Julius opened was a quaint cottage decorated with a tropical island theme. It had a sitting area with a small television, a modern restroom, and a tiny bedroom where a window unit labored against the humidity to cool the cottage.

"I will return with your other bag." He slipped out. By the slap of his flip-flops, he was running to the lobby.

Dropping onto the soft bed, she pushed a mosquito net aside, slipped her shoes off, and searched for the television's remote control. This cottage might not be the Ritz-Carlton, but it would rival any African touristy spot she'd seen online. And it was spotless. Nothing like the inn itself.

What was Tanner thinking, letting the inn decline like he had? Well, there would be words with Big *Bwana* Tanner, and he was not going to like it.

A soft knock signaled Julius's return. He delivered her luggage and wiped the dirt off her expensive pieces.

"Thank you, Julius. Where is the remote for the television? These are new since I was here."

He paused. "I do not know this thing *remote*."

"You use it to turn the television on."

"*Ndio,* yes, I understand." He went to the TV. "We use these knobs. This one turns it on, and this one changes the programs."

Angie smiled. "Thank you, Julius. You've been so helpful." A phone rang. "That's my phone. Where did I put it?" She dug in her bag.

"Here it is." Julius found it on the table by the television. He touched the screen as he brought it to her, accepting the call unintentionally.

It was Mason. "Hello, Mason." Angie stood and paced the room.

"Would Miss Angeleeka want a soda?" Julius waited.

"Yes, do you have a Coke?"

"We do. I will get one for you." Again, he ran to serve her.

"Angelica, who are you talking to? And where are you?"

"Sorry, Mason. I just got in my bungalow, and a young man who works here asked if I wanted a soda." Angie said. "How are you?"

"A bit perturbed. I called your hotel, and the concierge told me you had checked out. You left Nairobi."

He was miffed—again. "I've made an appointment to see the vice president and have a few days to relax. So, I'm at the hotel Grand-Papa owns. I am a grown woman. I can decide to change my plans."

"Tell me you're not in Mombasa! Angelica—"

"Mason, I'm in Mombasa." She cut him off. "Tanner and his team are at the mine. So, I'm the only guest."

"But we decided you weren't going there."

"Listen, I'm safe here and could use some time in the sun." Angie sat on the bed again.

"It scared me when I couldn't locate you. I have to know you're in a safe place with adequate security. I'll make you another reservation at a more appropriate locale. How does a five-star hotel in Mombasa sound? I'll hire a man to come for you and take you there. You won't have to lift a finger."

"I'm not leaving here. So, don't even think about making those plans." *The nerve of this guy. He doesn't own me.*

"Angelica, don't get upset. I'm concerned for your safety. You're very important to me."

"You say that, but you manipulated me into allowing everyone to think I said yes to your proposal, and then you canceled my ticket to Kenya then showed up at the airport. Now you're seeking me out again. I'm not happy. Micromanaging me, controlling me, isn't love. We will discuss this later."

"I plan to have a future with you. I can make you happy. Getting some rest is a good idea. Bye for now."

Angie ended the call, stood up, threw her cell onto the bed, and paced the bungalow. Mason had pushed the limits. "I'd rather be single than deal with this pressure." *Unfortunately, Grand-Papa is happy about this engagement, and I want him to be happy with me, especially since he is so ill, but somehow, he doesn't see the kind of jerk Mason is.*

Julius returned carrying a tray with a Coke, a glass of ice cubes, two bottles of water, one cold and one room temperature, a plate of cookies, and a vase of fuchsia bougainvillea.

"Miss Angeleeka, are you still on the phone?"

"No. What do you have, Julius?"

"This water is for brushing your teeth, and the cold water is for drinking. Do not use water from the faucet in Kenya. Use the plug box to charge your computer or use the hair dryer. It will make American things work in Africa."

Angie jumped when a gecko hurried up the wall.

"Do not fear. They are our friends. We have many mosquitoes, and they eat them." He stuck his hand in his pocket and pulled out a bottle opener.

The familiar movement, the pop and clink of the bottle top, transported her to childhood memories of her and Tanner savoring soft drinks in returnable bottles. Tanner.

Julius edged out of her bungalow. "Your food will be ready in one hour. Lock your door when you leave. Monkeys get curious and take things to the trees." The sound of quick footsteps faded as he rushed back to the kitchen.

With her things unpacked, Angie took a quick shower, brushed dust out of her hair, and put it in a messy bun. She grabbed her camera and headed to the restaurant.

"Would you like some tea, Miss Angeleeka?" Julius pulled a chair out for her.

"That would be nice." Through her lens, the view was amazing with brilliant hues of the ocean reflecting the vibrant purples and oranges of the sky. The blazing shimmer of the sun sparkled off the crashing waves. A massive yacht glided across the horizon, boasting its wealth and luxury, a vast contrast to a dug-out canoe filled with a few Kenyans as they fought the waves, hand-fishing as they went.

Amid the beauty of the scene, using her high-powered lens, she focused on some pale hermit crabs scampering across the sand. They disappeared into holes and reappeared at will. When waves threatened to overtake them or seagulls got too close, they ducked into another hole, unreachable—hiding much like Tanner's perpetrator, causing havoc at the mine.

He may hide—but Grand-Papa will make sure he'll be caught.

With time on her hands, she wanted to be part of the action, to know the murderer was being pursued. Maybe a trip to the mine would glean some info. Grand-Papa would want an update, and since she was here representing Ward Enterprises, she'd go looking for answers. But not until she enjoyed her meal of steaming beef stew and warm rolls Julius just delivered. While she ate, she pondered what to wear for her surprise appearance.

"Miss Angeleeka, a man is here to see you." Julius' brow was furrowed.

"I'm not expecting anyone. What does he want?" She moved her chair back and stood.

"He said he is here to take you to a different hotel. Do you not want to stay here?" Julius wrung his hands.

"I'm not going anywhere. Walk with me, Julius." Angie glided toward the lobby with Julius behind her. A man waited beside the open door of a London cab.

"There has been a misunderstanding. I do not wish to change hotels. Sorry for your trouble. You can leave." She smiled demurely.

The man stepped forward and reached for her arm.

Angie jerked back at his touch. "Wait, I saw you at the airport. Who are you? Has Mason Malone sent you to watch me?"

"I'll be sure to report back about how uncooperative you are. I will take my leave now." He got in the cab, closed the door, and cranked the vehicle.

"Open the gates for him, Julius. He seems to be in a hurry."

The man left, leaving red flags flying in his dust.

With a cell to his ear, Tanner watched his team work as he listened to the police chief, Karani, drone on with an update regarding Daniel's murder. Tanner added a couple of notes on his tablet where he'd created a list of evidence. "Where do you think the perpetrator is hiding? Here in Mombasa?" He wrote more info in his spiral notebook, thanked the officer, and ended the call.

He pocketed the tablet and his cell, then took the stairs to the platform. The dank darkness of the mine shaft took him back to the trauma that cost Daniel his life. What kind of leader would send his friend into danger before he checked it out? *Though Dylan put the rope on the equipment, I should have done more. I should have checked the rope as his boss. He took my place.* Tanner had to bring the murderer to justice no matter the cost. He must complete this assignment as safely as possible—as soon as possible before someone else got hurt. He inhaled the salty sea air and massaged the tension tightening the nape of his neck.

"Still gathering clues, Sherlock?" A smirk tugged at the corner of Dylan's mouth.

"Yes, Watson. I am. The police chief thinks the perpetrator may be hiding on Lamu Island based on a ticket purchase. I— Do you see that?" Tanner shaded his eyes, trying to see who was in the approaching taxi. The London cab approached faster than it should. Its tires ground against gravel, drowning out the sound of squawking seagulls taking flight.

"We don't have visitors at the mine. You expecting someone, Boss?" Dylan fanned dust away from his eyes.

Tanner started toward the taxi but stopped mid-step on the wooden platform as the car skidded to a halt in the dirt driveway. Dust billowed behind them, coating the mine and Tanner's team.

"No, I'm not expecting anyone." He headed for the cab but stopped when the back door opened, and stilettos touched the dirt. The perfect curve of tanned legs moved beyond the back door. A tight skirt hugged a too-familiar body. His heart pounded in rhythm with the banging sounds from the mine. *Angie.*

Deep blue eyes peered over the rim of her overpriced— what did she call them? Oh yeah, Bvlgari shades. And to top it off, the breeze tossed her ebony hair, lifting it from the curve of her neck. *Angie. She can still hold me captive.*

He strode with purpose toward her.

"Hello, Tanner." She brushed a strand of silky hair off her face. Her smile faded when he got close. "I thought I'd come to see the scene of the—"

"Did you take a wrong turn at Albuquerque?" He smiled. "This is Mombasa, Ang—"

She pushed her shades to the top of her head. "That's what my boarding pass said."

Tanner braced himself. Flirty eyelashes framing those blue eyes couldn't be his undoing, but she was gorgeous. Time had been good to her. "Have you come to take a turn in the mine?"

"That's not really what I expected. Not 'Wow, you look great' or 'How have you been?' You want me to do your work for you."

"I don't know how we ever managed without you?" Tanner cocked his brow. "Angie, you could've let me know you were coming."

"I came to help—"

"Help! What can you do? Stomp a murderer with your spiked heels or hit him with your purse? Africa isn't ready for you." *You're beautiful, but there's no place for you here in Kenya.* He had to finish this conversation before his wounded heart went into cardiac arrest.

"If you would let me finish! I know the vice president personally and have an appointment with him next week. I'm going to appeal for an extension on your work permit. Grand-Papa couldn't make the trip right now—"

"I know, busy conquering the world. So, he sent you?" Tanner hung his head and gripped the back of his neck. What a low blow. Ward didn't think Tanner could take care of it, so he sent his fancy girl to do the job. That was great, just great.

"I hate being interrupted—"

"Oh, please continue. By all means." Tanner made a show of checking his watch before he folded his arms and braced himself. "I'll give you about three minutes before I get back to work. My team is shorthanded. So, say what you came to say. Then you can get your mani/pedi, book a massage, or enjoy your photography hobby and take some pictures."

"Very funny, Tanner, you're still full of yourself. Aren't you?" Angie dotted her forehead with the back of her hand. "Tanner, I need you to bring me up to speed. But first, could we move into the shade, out of this blazing sun?"

Angie struck off for the shade ahead of him, unaware of the havoc she was causing within him. As they made their way across the sand, he inhaled the familiar scent of her perfume mixed with a flowery shampoo, which brought back a deluge of memories, of summer fun and adventures with love growing between them. Her beauty drew him like a jeweler to diamonds.

Angie's ridiculous heels sank into the dirt with each step. "I assume you're working closely with the local police? Have you got any leads on the murderer? Why would someone want to do this? Do you think he will try again?"

Focus, Tanner. Don't let your feelings show. She wants information, not a relationship. Weary, Tanner faced her when they reached the shade of a jacaranda tree.

"Yes, we're working together, and yes, we've been gathering information."

"Well, has there been a recent update?" She raised her voice, competing with the work at the mine.

"The authorities believe the perpetrator is hiding on Lamu Island at the moment. I'll keep you informed."

She squinted her eyes like she was planning an attack. He

could read her. Her intense stare and rigid stance told him she'd stand her ground like a dog with a bone.

He changed his approach. "Listen, Angie." He stepped closer and lowered his voice. "Kenya is dangerous for a woman alone. You're the only family Ward has left. He wouldn't want you in harm's way. Go home where you're safe. I don't want anything to happen to you, Ang—" Feelings he'd buried threatened to surface. Her presence meant trouble in many ways, especially for his heart. "I don't want to spar with you. Please do this one thing, Angie. Go home. Stay safe."

"Fine, I'll head back to Paradise Inn for a few days until my meeting with the VP."

He glanced back at his team. "Angie, this is a dangerous job. My team needs me. Let me walk you back to your cab."

Her heel caught on the root of a tree, pitching her forward. Tanner caught her around the waist and held her until she got her footing.

"Oh, my goodness. I'm sorry, Tanner. My shoe got caught on something. I didn't mean to—"

"I know." Of course, she didn't mean to fall into his arms. She was wearing another man's ring.

He opened the taxi door and caught her wrist, turning her toward him. "I can handle things here. Go home. Be with your Grand-Papa." His eyes lingered on her lips, causing his heart to speed up. It was a mistake to get this close. He was glad it was her turn to speak.

She held his gaze. "Tanner, I didn't want to travel this far and not see you. I want you to be safe. If he was targeting you, you could be in danger … I'll let you know what the vice president says." She put her sunglasses back on as she slipped into the taxi and rolled down the window. "Tanner—"

"Yes, Ang—" He stood at attention, waiting for her departure.

"I've missed you." The window lifted—a barrier between them.

Just go home, Angie.

He blew out a long breath and hurried to the platform to escape the haboob, the dust storm her taxi created.

"So, that's Angelica Ward?" Dylan handed him a bottle of water.

"Yes, the one and only." He guzzled the water, glad for a moment to recover.

"I take it you didn't know she was in Kenya." Dylan pitched his empty bottle into a burn barrel.

Tanner put the water bottle on his neck, allowing the condensation to dampen his sun-scorched skin, but nothing could cool him today.

"You okay, man?"

Tanner wiped his face with his shirt sleeve to keep salty perspiration out of his eyes. "Yeah, I'm okay. Just caught off guard, that's all."

"Well, what ya' going to do now?" Dylan leaned against the railing of the mining platform.

"Let's work till the end of the week. I'll finish the report for Ward Enterprises. If you can handle things here, I'm going to Lamu Island for a couple of days. Karani said the man we're looking for has booked passage, and if he's there, I'd like to find him. The sooner he's captured, the safer we'll be." *The safer Angie will be.*

"I like her."

"What? Man, you don't know her."

"Maybe not, but any chick who can put you in your place is all right in my book."

"You don't even have a book."

"Just saying. I know my stuff."

"Right." *I know her too well. I've memorized every curve of her face. She's kind to house workers and maids, thoughtful in so many little ways. Her laughter is contagious, and her sense of humor entertains with ease. She is smart, creative, adventurous, and brave.* Her soft skin felt like velvet when he held her last. Making her happy was his greatest joy ... until now.

Chapter Five

"Julius, I need to send a message to the US. How does *bwana* send an e-mail?" She stood at the table in the restaurant with her laptop in hand.

"Miss Angeleeka, he sits here at the table and puts this cord into his computer. Then he waits a long time."

Angie smiled at his description and plugged in her laptop. "Thanks."

She sent an email to her grandfather, asking for an update on his doctor's appointments, asking about how he was feeling, and threatening to call Joseph if he didn't speak openly with her about his health issues. She updated him about her upcoming appointment with the vice president before she contacted her three best friends, Missy, Leslie, and Elise.

After pressing Send, the computer made a squawking sound, then a phone dialed the overseas number, like an antique rotary, followed by an unusual noise, then silence. *So, this is dial-up.* She waited a few minutes and pressed Send again. Same sounds, and the same sequence. She waited and tried again. Julius's description of the process became her reality. After thirty-two minutes, the message went through.

Then she focused on receiving incoming emails, which further lengthened the process.

Julius brought a tray to her table, "Tea, Miss Angeleeka?"

"Thanks, Julius." She stirred sugar into the steamy brew as her computer connected.

Three emails came in from Mason. *He must be getting antsy.* Angie read his apology. His second email broached their upcoming nuptials, asking about specific dates for the wedding before he gave his suggestions for the venue. The third email had manipulative innuendos.

You've got to be kidding!

The last message, which fueled her mounting anger, forced her to take a couple of deep breaths before she started typing her reply—

Mason, I appreciate your apology, but if you'd canceled your plan, I would feel you're truly sincere. Your man came to take me to another hotel, and it wasn't a pleasant experience.

About the wedding, it's the bride's job to plan the wedding—it's something I've dreamed about since I was a girl. And NO, I do not want you to hire a wedding planner and get things rolling. Please hear me on this—don't do anything! We need to talk when I get home. Angie

She pressed Send before she could second-guess herself.

An engagement isn't supposed to be like this. Where's the desire to be with him, the excitement about the wedding, and thoughts of a future together? It's non-existent. While Angie sipped her tea, a sailboat moved across the horizon. *Lord, I need help here.*

Putting Mason from her mind, she opened the emails from her friends. Missy made her laugh. Elise told her a touching story about one of the children she taught, and Leslie asked questions about her adventures. They were good for her. She typed her replies.

Angie hadn't noticed the weather changing. Without

warning, the skies opened with a deluge of rain. She enjoyed the sound of water as it pelted the tin roof over the restaurant, mirroring calypso drums as she answered her messages. Steam rose from the concrete when the shower had moved on, creating a sauna effect. Sparrows bathed in the puddles pooling on the sidewalks. Waiting for the internet dial-up again, she breathed deeply. Though humid, the air smelled amazingly clean.

"Julius, this is the cleanest scent I've inhaled since I arrived in Kenya."

"The rains have washed the air. This happens many times during the rainy season." He placed a fresh pot of tea on the table.

"When is the rainy season?"

"March through April, then late September until the first part of November. It rains every day, making the ground muddy, and there are many mosquitoes, but the crops grow tall. It is a blessing from God."

"I haven't thought about it that way. To survive, you need the rain, but it makes life difficult for your people. This is a hard place to live."

"*Ndio*, yes, *dada*. But it is a good place. They say, 'Once you drink the water of Kenya, you will always be thirsty to return.'" He smiled and walked toward the kitchen.

Angie lowered her voice. "That is, if you don't get an amoeba."

The old dhow rocked to and fro, tossed by the waves of the Indian Ocean. The antique pirate ship was slow, but sure, as it creaked, taking the journey in stride. Using this inconspicuous means of transportation, Tanner approached Lamu Island posing as a tourist. Arriving late evening, he made his way to the Dar El Eden hotel under the cover of dusk's lengthening shadows. This location put him smack dab in the middle of the historic part of Lamu Town. Perfect. From the rooftop restaurant, he could observe the movement of the islanders undetected.

A variety of ships and sailboats docked in the Lamu Channel overnight and rode the waves of high tide, adding to the nocturnal noises of the island. The footfall of donkeys clomped by, making their last haul as the sun dropped into the horizon, putting an end to a long day.

As is the custom in Lamu, dinner was a late evening event. Tanner took a seat at a table in the rooftop restaurant of his hotel. The beef curry was offered along with nans and a variety of toppings that cooled the spicy heat of the dish. Kenyan chai tea was served. Its warmth made him thankful for the evening's island breeze cooling the atmosphere. He planned to stroll the small island after a night of rest to see if he could find the man who took Daniel's life. After a long day, sleep would come easily for this weary traveler.

The next morning, the rooster's crow competed with the Adhan, the Islamic call to prayer, sending eerie cries across the island as dawn bathed the landscape. After a quick breakfast, Tanner left his room key at the front desk.

"Have a good day in Lamu, sir." The receptionist took the key.

"Thank you. It looks like another sunny day in Africa." Donning his brimmed fedora and sunglasses, Tanner set out on his quest to familiarize himself with the lay of the land, the alleys, and possible hideouts. Alert to anything suspicious, he tracked every inch of the small island, looking for Wycliff. As he turned a corner toward the canal, he purposefully bumped into a Kenyan man the size of Wycliff, but when he saw his face, it wasn't him. "So sorry. *Pole sana.*"

He kept moving—took photos, bought curios, and ate samosas—a fried pastry with beef, onion, chili powder, garlic, and Chinese parsley, a delicacy of the locals.

After touring the business district, he returned to the hotel's rooftop restaurant. Tanner ordered a cold drink and a pastry. He sketched a map of the island utilizing the digital pictures he'd taken, studying the streets and alleys of Lamu. If he were to find Wycliff, being familiar with the lay of the land would help him to apprehend him.

The waitress brought his order. "You've made a map."

"Yes, it is a good place to visit." He tasted his fried delicacy. "*Asante, dada*, it was *safi sana.*" Tanner told her it was good.

"*Karibu, bwana.*"

As he ate, he studied the layout, preparing himself to apprehend his man if he surfaced. Wearing a knife in a sheath at his ankle and carrying a rope in his pocket, he felt prepared if he found him. His strength training as a quarterback in high school and college helped him stay fit and fast on his feet. He watched the island activity from his perch on the roof. The head wraps and robes of the men made his task next to impossible since everyone looked the same.

With his map in hand, Tanner walked the island all afternoon to commit the terrain to memory. Being familiar gave him an advantage. He decided to watch and wait like a lion lurking in the shadows until his prey edged into a clearing —even if it took days for the culprit to appear.

After enjoying grilled tilapia and chips for lunch, Angie asked to see Julius and Samson, the cook, at her table. She was wearing casual clothes and flip-flops.

"I want to talk to you about something." She motioned for them to sit.

Julius caught Samson's eye, paused, and pulled out a chair. The legs of Samson's chair scraped with a gritty sound across the sandy floor.

"I want to clean the inn, paint the walls, repair the sign, and plant new flowers. These cushions are worn, and the chairs are wobbly. They need to be repaired. Will you help me?" She looked from one man to the other. Before they could answer, she kept talking. "We need the help of a carpenter, a painter, an electrician, and a seamstress. Do you know some good workers I can hire?"

Julius looked at Samson, then spoke. "Miss Angeleeka, I will serve you, as you ask, but—"

Samson broke in. "I do not know if *bwana* wants us to change Paradise Inn."

"Wait, I know *bwana* means mister. Are you talking about *Bwana* Tanner or *Bwana* Ward, my grandfather?" Angie sipped her Coke.

"I'm speaking of *Bwana* Tanner. He asked us to leave things as they are. He is happy with the inn this way. But—" Samson hesitated. "But you are the granddaughter of *Bwana* Ward, so we will do what you ask us to do."

"We will help you. You will tell *bwana*, yes?" Julius asked.

"Don't be nervous, guys. I'll tell him. My grandfather wouldn't be happy with it being in disarray." She could see they didn't understand. "He would want it clean and painted."

They smiled.

"Julius, I need to hire a man to oversee the work. Do you know someone I can trust?"

"*Ndio,* yes, his name is Timothy. *Bwana* Tanner hired him to make the bungalows nice."

Angie checked her list. "Is there a nursery nearby?"

"For a baby?" Samson was confused.

"No, no, for plants and flowers. I'll need a driver. I want to purchase some colorful plants for the gardens. There were some along the road as I traveled to the inn."

"Julius knows where to go and what to buy. You can ride with him and show him the flowers you like. Then, let him return alone to make the purchases. If you go, the price will be big. If you send Julius, the price will be small." Samson held his fingers close together.

"That makes sense. Together, we can make this place nice again."

On their afternoon excursion, they bought plants, some clay pots, a pair of chaise lounge chairs, and a park bench. The talents of these hard-working people presented so much potential for decorating the grounds that her head was spinning. It reminded her of the days she would help her Nana Joy in the rose garden at the estate. They loved seeing the place transformed by their hard work.

Wearing capri pants, tennis shoes, and a baseball cap with her ponytail sticking out of the back, she picked up trash near the front entrance. Samson ignited a fire in a barrel to burn the debris she had collected. He provided a pair of gloves to protect her delicate hands. She picked up old newspapers, plastic grocery bags, several smelly milk cartons, and a molded rag with a slug on it. Plastic bottles with a slimy growth inside reeked with the pungent odor of glue. It gave her a sense of satisfaction to do physical labor and to watch the transformation of the inn. *Grand-Papa would be proud. I'm perspiring.*

While collecting paper that had blown in through the gate,

goosebumps ran up her arm. Senses on high alert, anxiety left her feeling watched.

She would not be easily deterred. As she retrieved some flattened juice boxes, she grew certain eyes were on her. Her adrenaline soared. *Did Mason send some bodyguards to watch me?*

Again, she discreetly surveyed her surroundings. There weren't any men in black suits hiding behind dark glasses. *Is the murderer lurking in the shadows?*

I'm a Ward. Could I be his next target?

Swallowing back concern, she edged to the fire, emptied her hands, and reached for a limb at the base of a jacaranda tree.

Freezing, she waited for movement.

A voice caught her attention, and she jerked around to find a couple of street boys peering over the perimeter fence. Surprised to see dirty faces, she breathed a sigh of relief, dropped the limb, and stepped closer. "Hello."

"*Jambo,* Mama." The taller boy spoke, then looked away. His courage must have waned.

"What is your name?" She perused the waif of a boy.

The older boy took a deep breath. "I am Nicolas. He is Robert."

Nicolas was probably thirteen years old, despite his tattered clothes and matted hair, he wore an easy smile. Robert looked ten or eleven by his undernourished size. The whites of their eyes appeared yellow, a sign of poor health.

"Why are you boys watching me?" Angie edged closer to her visitors.

"Because we never see *mzungu* work." Nicolas hung his head.

Angie was intrigued. "What is *mzungu?*"

"A white person. We never see white people working. Why you work?" Nicolas's courage grew.

"This place needs cleaning. It is hard work for very strong people. Are you strong?" Angie watched them. Waited. "Do you want to help me?"

"We are hungry. Can we have food?" Nicolas sounded hopeful.

"If you work, you will get food."

"We get food?" Robert's eyes grew wide.

"Yes. Come inside the gate." Angie opened the latch and let them pass. After removing her glove, she extended her hand. "Nicolas and Robert, I'm Miss Angelica, but Kenyans say Miss Angeleeka." Their dirty hands left grime on Angie's palm. She wiped her hands on her capri pants. The boys were quick to begin gathering trash. *They must be starving.* Her heart wrenched at their plight as they worked.

"Samson, would you prepare some food for my friends?" Angie called out when she neared the lobby.

"Friends, Miss Angeleeka?" He came out of the kitchen, wiping his hands on a towel. When he saw the street kids, he hesitated before approaching the boys.

"Yes, we'll work for two hours, then, my friends will need food before they leave. Please pack something for them."

"I will do it for you." He pointed his finger at the boys and spoke sternly in Swahili. They nodded and went back to work.

Angie eased closer to the boys when Samson was out of sight. "Nicolas, what did he say to you?"

"He warned us to be good and do what you say. In Kenya, women are not in charge. He said you are different. You are *Mtu Mkubwa,* the big boss, the one in charge. So now, we work for you." He smiled and headed for the burn barrel with trash in his hands. His eyes lit up when the blaze leaped heavenward as he fed the fire.

They worked side by side and cleared the front lawn. With her arms full of trash, Angie startled at the voice of someone in pain blaring through a loudspeaker from downtown Mombasa. It continued for several minutes, prickling her with foreboding.

"Nicolas, what is that? What is he saying?"

"That is Adhan. He is telling the Muslims it is time to pray. We hear it five times a day. They stop their work and kneel to pray to Allah. It is the way of Islam."

The appeal to worship a false god left her with a creepy awareness. To witness Islam firsthand made it real. Taking it in stride, she decided to counter their 'call to prayer' with petitions of her own, starting with prayers for her two smelly friends.

Working near the lobby in the shade of some banana plants, Robert helped Angie pick up broken soft drink bottles. When he moved some tall grass, a small, glossy green snake slithered in his direction. Quickly, instinctively, Angie put her foot on top of the reptile as it wiggled and stretched, its split tongue licking at the air.

Robert stepped away from Angie. "Nicolas, *nyoka!*"

Nicolas dropped the debris in his hands and ran.

"I've only seen snakes in the zoo. Now, one's under my shoe!" Panic hurried her words as they increased in volume. "Help!"

Nicolas put his foot on top of Angie's and yelled. *"Nyoka! Nyoka!"* He added pressure to her foot, careful to keep away from the head of the serpent, whose tail slapped Angie's foot.

Angie was glued to the spot. She stared at his grimy foot. Her shoes had been clean when she started this project.

Julius ran toward them with a *panga*, a large knife, in his hand. With a swift blow, he killed the reptile and held it up by its scaly tail. Its long, rectangular head hung by a thread severed by the deadly blow.

"I've never liked snakes. Thanks for killing it. It's a grass snake, isn't it?"

"No, Mama, this is a green mamba. It lives in trees and is very deadly. If it bites you, you die soon." Julius tossed the snake into the burn barrel.

Angie gasped. "It's poisonous?"

"No, this one is deadly, Miss Angeleeka. There are two kinds of snakes in Kenya: poisonous and deadly. The deadly one kills you by attacking your system of nerves. The venom makes your heart and lungs stop working." He wiped his panga on his pants leg, seeming unaffected by the incident.

"Oh, Julius, I had no idea. We must be more careful." Her adrenaline vanished, legs wobbly. The phrase 'weak in the knees' came to mind as she took a seat on the steps. That was so very close. She replayed the feel of the mamba under her shoe. A shudder gripped her body.

"Miss Angeleeka, you saved me today. *Asante,* thanks. I will not forget." Robert's grin revealed dirty teeth.

"You're welcome, Robert." She placed her hand on his arm and shot her gaze at Nicolas. "Thanks for keeping me safe. I didn't know. You were very brave."

"It is the way of the street. We look out for each other." He held his hand out to steady her as she stood. "Are you okay? You look whiter now."

"Sure. Let's finish cleaning the area."

Accustomed to street life and its difficulties, the boys resumed their work as if nothing had happened. Apparently, danger defined their everyday lives.

Angie studied the boys for a few minutes, amazed at their resilience, their strength—orphans without a ray of hope for the future without the Lord. Their smiles tugged at her heart and challenged her to make a difference in her life, starting with these boys.

~

Mason reached for the financial report his assistant had prepared that highlighted his success. It looked good. Real good. Closing pending deals, firing unneeded employees, and collecting outstanding debts made a substantial difference in the bottom line. Ten days of strong-arming delinquent clients had paid off. He'd been relentless. Once in power, he planned to mend the fences he'd destroyed with these gutsy moves later, but looking stellar in Alexander Ward's eyes was critical at this juncture.

He eyed a framed print adorning his wall with a man climbing a mountain. It expressed the passion driving him. The view out of his corner office was a perk at this pinnacle, but it would only get better from here, and he loved it at the top, figuratively and personally.

He'd known his share of sorrow. His father chose his career over being a father to him or a husband to his sick mother. "Mason, you're just like your mother's side of the family. You've got their good looks, but you'll never be good enough to carry the Malone name."

Proving his father wrong had become his life's mission, the force driving him. And now, he could see the peak from this distance. *Look who's on top now, old man. I will buy your measly company once I'm in Alexander Ward's chair.*

"Leslie, please print another copy of today's financial report. Ward wants a copy. I'll take it to him." Mason released the intercom button and sighed. After removing a piece of lint from his slacks, he sent a text to Angelica. He needed to appear as a devoted fiancé, ensuring the future he deserved.

Answering phone calls took most of his morning. One last look at his email before leaving for lunch brought a smile to his face.

Angelica.

He opened her message, read it, and slammed his laptop shut. While blowing out a hot breath, he ran his hands through his hair. *She's out of control.*

He stood and faced the window. Knowing his next move was critical, he reined in his temper so he could think straight.

Some major groveling will be in order. I have to fix this. I can't risk losing her—she's the queen that will take down the king in this chess game.

After a short flight to Nairobi, Angie retrieved her carry-on suitcase, hefted her camera bag strap onto her shoulder, and hailed a taxi to take her to the government offices. The bumpy taxi ride mixed with clouds of exhaust fumes churned her stomach. She waited in the hot cab behind locked gates for permission to enter the government complex. Recent attacks in the country warranted these strenuous security procedures. She fanned herself as the moments ticked by, thankful less dust billowed through the windows since paved roads surrounded the governmental properties. Just to be sure she was presentable, she pulled out her compact and reapplied her lipstick.

"*Bwana*, please wait for me," Angie said to her driver.

He agreed.

Moving in slow motion, the uniformed security guard scanned her passport, made a phone call, and checked her fingerprints. The gates opened, and she was allowed to enter, being escorted by an armed guard. Angie carried herself like an executive even though perspiration had glued her power suit to her slender body.

Being the finest buildings in the country, she expected air-conditioners to be cooling the offices. But no. Body odor assaulted her. She understood why ladies carried perfumed handkerchiefs before air-conditioning was invented. After checking in with the receptionist, the Ward constitution fueled her steps as she neared Saitoti's door.

"Vice president, it is so good to see you again. My grandfather sends his greetings. He speaks of you as a dear friend. His health is failing, and he was unable to make the trip but wanted you to know he missed having this time with you." Angie shook his hand and remained standing until being asked to sit.

"It is good to see you again. Has it been three years since our last meeting?"

"Yes, but we hosted you and your family in America on your last trip to the States."

"And it was a wonderful event. Thank you again. Please send my heartfelt greetings to Alexander upon your return. It saddens me to hear he is not well. Is his condition grave?"

"I'm sad to report that it is, sir. It's cancer."

"Please be seated. This brings me great sadness. Tell him my heart is heavy for him at this time."

His sincerity was moving. "I will. Thank you."

His secretary entered with a tray of tea and shortbread.

"Please join me for tea." He leaned forward to the table between them and prepared his drink. Angie followed protocol and fixed her brew.

"*Dada* Ward, what brings you to Kenya? Are you on holiday?" Saitoti sipped his tea.

"No, sir. This is not a vacation, though I always enjoy visiting your beautiful country. There is a problem at my grandfather's tanzanite mine along the coast." She stirred additional sugar into her steaming beverage.

"What sort of trouble?" He set his tea on the table and studied her.

"One of his workers has been murdered at the mine. An investigation is underway as we speak, but our work permit is being revoked because the man who was killed is a Kenyan citizen. They're nearing completion of the job. I've come today to appeal for your assistance. The incident is being investigated by your police force. My question to you today is, is there a way to keep the permit in force, allowing them to complete the mining effort?"

The vice president stood, went to his desk, and thumbed through a Rolodex. He retrieved a card and returned to his chair across from Angie. "Work permits are not under my jurisdiction, but I can call the man who heads that department. I'll remind him of the vast income Ward Enterprises has brought to our country and request a three-month extension. Would that suffice?"

"Oh, yes. It will give adequate time to complete the work. I appreciate your help in this matter."

Mission accomplished.

"I'll inform Tanner Zarello, the man in charge representing Ward Enterprises, of your kindness. Thank you for seeing me today and for the extension on our permit. My grandfather will be pleased. *Bwana*, I know your time is in great demand, so I will take my leave now." Angie rose and placed her empty teacup on the tray.

"Before you leave the premises, there's an office in the adjacent building where all criminal activity occurring in Kenya is reported daily by our police investigators. Give them my card and request information on this unfortunate incident. Tell them you are representing Ward Enterprises at this time." He reached into his inner suit coat pocket and offered her a business card. "If there is anything I can do to assist my friend, Alexander, please let me know."

"Thank you, sir. I know Grand-Papa would like an update on their investigation."

"Please convey greetings to my friend, Alexander Ward." He waved his fingers as a gesture of greeting, then shook her hand.

Angie walked the long hall, greeting guards posted at various positions throughout the building. She paused to thank the receptionist before leaving the building.

Stepping into the police headquarters, a barrage of activity caught Angie's attention. As she stood in a room full of offices without dividing walls, a fax machine spat out pages, secretaries answered calls, officers yelled orders in Swahili on short-wave radios, and people shuffled reports from one desk to another. Her presence went unnoticed for several minutes.

An officer finally spotted her and hurried to help. "Hello, may I be of assistance? I am Officer Kamau." He extended his hand.

She shook his hand and showed the vice president's business card. "I'm Angelica Ward. I would like an update on the murder of Daniel Mwangi in Mombasa. My grandfather, Alexander Ward, owns the business where the murder occurred, and with our continued operations, we're very concerned about the ongoing safety of our workers." Angie was careful not to mention the mine by name.

"Miss Ward, please take a seat. I am working with Karani on the case. I will retrieve the latest update."

Angie studied him as he pivoted, went to a desk, and opened a file. He wrote something and then stopped at another desk, ran his finger down a clipboard, and noted something in his spiral notebook. A secretary pointed toward the fax machine. Angie assumed he was asking about the case. He checked the machine, retrieved two pages, and stopped at a copy machine. Her request had taken him around the station before he headed back in her direction.

"I'm assuming you have news for me." She stood as Officer Kamau approached.

"Yes, in this envelope is a photo of the man we're currently pursuing. This is the case number, a list of the charges against him, and his address on file. This man has been a suspect in some robberies in Mombasa and one in Nairobi, but those charges haven't been proven yet. He has been on the run since the murder, and our last intel reports he's hiding on Lamu Island. We think he traveled by bus under another name, but only one surveillance camera was working. Please inform Alexander Ward we're striving to bring this man to justice."

"Thank you, officer. I appreciate your attention to this matter. You've been most helpful. Just one more question. Is there a plane that flies to Lamu from Nairobi?" She waited.

"One each afternoon, at three, from Wilson Airport."

"Well, I've taken too much of your time. Have a great afternoon."

Angie took the stairs with a spring in her step, slipped her shades on, and went through security to the waiting taxi.

It's a sunny day indeed, Tanner Zarello. He'd allowed their relationship to fizzle. Accepting this career move, she understood, but he didn't have to leave her in the dust. That road was riddled with potholes.

With updated information on the case and a photo of the suspect in hand, she slid into the taxi, her mind devising a plan. She checked her watch.

"Wilson Airport, please. I have a plane to catch." Angie punched a number into her cell phone and called the concierge at the Nairobi Hilton.

"Hello, *bwana*. This is Angelica Ward. Could you book a

seat for me on the three o'clock flight from Nairobi to Lamu, leaving this afternoon? I'll stay for two nights."

"Absolutely. Do you need hotel accommodations?"

"Yes. Could you arrange that for me and text the information to my phone?"

"I will get it arranged."

"*Asante.* Thank you, *bwana.*" She pocketed her phone and smiled.

On an excursion to Lamu Island, with my camera in hand, I'll do some investigating on my own, just like those pretty police investigators on TV. After all, I'm smart, brave, and have great hair like they do. I can pull this off.

Stop-and-go traffic delayed their arrival at the airport. While waiting again for traffic to move, she opened the envelope the officer had given her. When she flipped over the file, it was topped with the perp's photograph, his name scrawled messily at the top, a Wycliff Matua, the cab driver who got her to change hotels—the man who watched her at the Mombasa Airport.

Her breath caught. What had Mason done?

The murderer had found her, followed her.

She checked her surroundings and remained calm, to breathe normally. *Am I a target now? Or was he looking for Tanner? I have to be more careful.*

She retrieved her carry-on, paid her cab driver, and went through security at Wilson Airport. After paying for her ticket, she enjoyed some tea until her boarding class was called. She scanned the passengers heading for the terminal exit—not seeing Wycliff—and mounted the shaky steps into the eight-seater plane. With no in-flight service, the pilot/steward of this flight offered her a small bottle of water and a mint.

Chilled by an overactive air conditioner, Angie watched the

steamy tropical scenery along the coast of the Indian Ocean out her small window.

The roar of the engine hampered any conversation, which was good.

Angie was lost in thought. If Wycliff knew who she was and her net worth, was she his next target? Or was he looking for Tanner to try to take his life again?

The looming danger was vividly real. Staying in Lamu could be dangerous to her health. Maybe she should shorten her stay and keep herself in crowded areas. Playing the tourist card could draw attention, keeping her safe.

When she mixed memories of Tanner coming to her rescue, such as when he saved her from almost drowning, with the present danger and included questions about her future, like whether Tanner still loved her and if she could win him back, her heart was caught in the crosshairs.

Chapter Six

The short flight to Lamu put her on a dirt airstrip. Angie grabbed her camera case and squeezed past the seats of the small plane. Making her descent down the rickety ladder attached to the exit door, her feet found purchase in a mixture of sand and dirt.

"*Bwana,* is there a taxi?" She took her carry-on bag from the Kenyan pilot who was emptying the cargo hold.

"There are no cars on Lamu Island. You have two choices: walk or ride a donkey." He didn't crack a smile.

"You're serious—"

"Are you from Kansas?" He raised his sunshades and made eye contact.

"No, I'm from Texas. Why?"

"One visitor from Kansas said, 'This ain't Kansas, Toto.'" He smirked and moved to load the bags of his departing passengers.

Angie wasn't amused. She retrieved her carry-on, unzipped her bag, and changed her shoes. After stopping in the small shack, not enough to be considered a terminal, she used the internet to get the text from the concierge at the Nairobi Hilton and collected the rest of her luggage he'd sent. Finally, she began the trek to her hotel, Dar El Eden, dragging her bags behind her. The twenty-minute stroll left her with a sheen of perspiration on her upper lip, her clothes sticking to her body, and beads of sweat rolling down her back. A slight breeze swept in from the ocean, offering a bit of reprieve.

In Lamu, the ground floor was the main floor, with the second floor designated as the first floor. Angie's room was on the first floor, and meals were served on the rooftop terrace. The building's stucco reminded her of homes in New Mexico. After depositing her luggage, she took the stairs to the rooftop for an early dinner.

Angie captured the setting in her camera while she waited. Lamu intrigued her. A pirate ship called a dhow was docked in the channel with an array of fishing boats riding high tide. Swaying palm trees added a bit of green to the landscape. The earth-toned buildings with intricate designs on the walls and colorful canopies provided respite for tourists from the evening heat. Stacks of baskets, loaded donkeys, and an array of pottery made her think of the story "Ali Baba and the Forty Thieves," and its Arabian culture with men in flowing robes and turbans. The smell of curry pierced the air. Indian dishes were popular in this setting. It would perfectly end this long day.

A rooster's crow served as Angie's alarm. She dressed and had toast, fried ham, and runny eggs on the terrace before joining those exploring Lamu. Under the guise of a tourist, she moved freely, seeking a certain face among the Kenyan men on the island.

Strolling among the Arab-style architecture, she put her camera to work. Being discreet with her camera, she shot images of signs, buildings, curios, and people, looking for the man who murdered their employee. With the men wearing turbans and flowing robes, Wycliff could be hiding in plain sight. Pausing to buy a bracelet made of old coins gave her a chance to take some random shots of her surroundings.

A pastry from one shop reminded Angie of the baklava Tanner's mother made for them at the estate. The shop owner gave her a Coke in a glass bottle, sparking a barrage of childhood memories of her and Tanner toasting their adventurous futures. He would try to catch the bottle top as it flew through the air and grin with each successful catch. Beating him at billiards was so much fun since he taught her how to play. He always won when they raced the jet skis on the lake, until she tampered with the engine of his machine and won! The look on his face was priceless. More memories threatened, but she quickly moved on, shaking the dust out of her sandals.

The dock area was alive with fishermen unloading their catch, tourists boarding the dhow for a cruise, and vendors stacking goods onto carts. The air carried a mixture of sea salt and raw fish. Palm trees swayed as if trying to rid the area of the scent. The sun's rays scorching her white skin sent Angie down a shaded alley with a row of colorful shops. Canopies flapped in the breeze, their colors stark against the brown stucco walls. Women showed her their beautiful scarves.

"These are nice. *Bei Gani? 'How much?'*"

"One thousand shillings." The mama smiled.

She bought a couple that matched her coats. Perfect for winter.

"Thank you. *Asante.*"

Angie framed a perfect shot of a baby riding on his mother's back, tied securely with a stretch of cloth. When the mother turned, Angie moved closer, stepped wrong—her foot falling into a hole, and toppled a huge display of woven baskets in the process of trying to catch herself. Colorful baskets went airborne, then rolled into the alley, and some fell backward, covering the woman who was selling her handiwork. Angie caught three of them to keep them from the dusty path.

"I'm so sorry. *Pole sana.*" She apologized in English and Swahili as she grabbed the baskets in the walkway, dusted them off, and helped reconstruct the display, working with the shop owner. The woman patted Angie's arm to express that things were okay. Angie nodded, understanding the gesture, as the woman's sandpaper skin rubbed against her sensitive skin.

Angie pivoted and came face-to-face with an African, a replica of the man in the picture the police officer had given her. His breath was hot on her face—his strong body odor assaulted her senses. She gasped.

"Stop!" She reached for her camera. She had to prove it was him and report an accurate location to the police.

His eyes widened. Dust rose between them as he ran away. Angie couldn't get the shot. She planted her feet and snapped a picture when he turned back to check if she'd followed. Was it the murderer? With the camera close to her eye, she was tense. Focused.

Without warning, a strong arm slid around her waist, and a large hand covered her mouth and pulled her behind the tower of baskets. Angie went into attack mode. She'd taken a self-defense course after a paparazzo stalked her a few years back. Her adrenaline was in overdrive. She kicked his calves and bit his hand.

He's lucky this isn't a frontal assault. She struggled against his strength.

He released her, pivoted, slammed her body against a wall, and pressed himself close. She ignored the rough stucco hurting her back. Now, face to face, with eyes wide, she took in her captor.

"Tanner, move your hand."

He removed it and pierced her with a stern look. "Quiet." Then looked for Wycliff, who had fled the scene.

Angie stared at him.

"Keep your voice down. What are you doing here?" He rubbed his hand.

He's still so handsome, even with a sheen of perspiration coating his forehead. She could stare into his deep chocolate eyes all day. "What kind of question is that? I'm a tourist taking in the sights. I should ask you the same question. I thought you were running the mine for Ward Enterprises. Do you take unscheduled vacations often?" She spoke in hushed tones.

"I was following Wycliff when you got in the way. You could get yourself killed. You know that?" He stared at her with concern.

"How would that happen? By an alluring man pressing so hard against me, I can't breathe?" She smiled as he eased back a few inches.

"Sorry, you scared me."

"Then we're even." Angie straightened her clothes.

He blew out an exasperated breath. "We can't talk here. Where are you staying?" He scoped their surroundings.

"I'm at the Dar Eden by the channel. Why do you ask? Was that the murderer? The turbans and robes make all the men look alike to me." She let him study the area while she enjoyed the scenery, loving his closeness.

"It's called the Dar El Eden. Let's go there." He took her arm and marched toward the hotel, dragging her along. His stride betrayed his agitation.

"Easy, now." She whispered. "Shouldn't we try to look like friends, so we won't attract attention?" She put her arm inside his elbow, slowed their pace, and put on the tourist act, keeping up their much-needed facade. "Have you noticed the different doors on these houses?"

Tanner huffed out a breath and schooled his voice. "Yes, the doors represent the dignity of the owner or head of the household. It's measured by the size of the door, the weight of the padlock, the size of the iron studs that nail the door together, and the weight of the timber used to construct it." Tanner pointed to the massive doors they passed.

"These spikes are huge. Wouldn't smaller nails work?" She enjoyed goading Mr. Know-It-All.

He led her down another alley toward the hotel. "The spikes were added during the medieval period to protect them against war elephants. These spikes, and the amount of carvings on the doors, are there as a display of the family's importance."

"So, I assume your door would be very ornate, Mr. Zarello." She loved watching him squirm.

"Never as fancy as yours, Miss Ward."

They stepped into the lobby of Dar El Eden. He drew her close and whispered. "Angie, go to the rooftop restaurant. I'll be there in a few minutes. I've got a call to make."

"Sure." Angie sensed his absence as soon as he stepped away.

"I want some tea. Order it black, with two sugars."

"Yes, sir." She saluted him, mocking his direct order like she did when they were teens. The return of a bit of bantering between them felt nostalgic. Taking her back to when she fell for this man.

He hurried up the stairs. His shirt, damp from perspiration, outlined his muscular physique, ruggedly handsome. His black hair and olive complexion betrayed his Italian roots. *He's easy on the eyes but bad for the heart. It's too bad he goes AWOL regularly.*

A salty ocean breeze gave her a reprieve from the scorching heat of the day. She needed this opportunity to cool off. Being close to Tanner, with his masculine scent of leather and spice, had her hot and bothered, confused, and vulnerable.

She chose a table at the rooftop's edge, placed her order of tea and pastries, and stood to photograph the island from her elevated vantage point. These prints would deserve framing, a souvenir that would transport her to this exotic place, remembering the unique moment when God tossed her back in Tanner's arms, even if ever so briefly. Why would he do that? Tanner was her first love —her last heartbreak. Could there be a future for them?

Tanner dialed his cell and waited. "Lieutenant, Tanner Zarello here. I've spotted our man in Lamu. Thanks to a camera-toting tourist, he saw me. So, Wycliff knows I'm alive, and he's probably headed your way again."

"His sister has a place in the Mombasa slums." The call was wrought with static.

"You think he'll go to her house to hide?" Tanner grabbed the pad and pencil off the nightstand and was poised to write.

"My men are watching it now. I don't think she's involved, but he will see her before he attempts to leave the country," Lieutenant Karani said.

"Do you have the address?" Tanner waited.

"I can retrieve it for you. It's in a file on my desk. I'll be at the station in a few minutes."

"Can you call me back with the address?" He thanked him and ended the call.

After locking his room, Tanner took the stairs two at a time to the terrace restaurant. He paused before joining Angie to collect himself before invading her space. Hiding his feelings for her had been difficult. To touch her again did crazy things to his heart. She could rattle him with a look, with the bat of an eye. He sighed, took the chair across from Angie, and surveyed the chaos of Lamuans moving in the alley below. It kept him from staring at her. He tasted his tea and finally brought his gaze to his close surroundings within the restaurant to see who sat within earshot.

"So, Angie, why are you in Lamu? Do you enjoy tempting danger? Most of these people don't want their picture taken. Did you know that?"

"Really? I was discreet." She took a sip of her tea.

"Well, they believe you stole their soul, and it's captive in your Nikon. Some get angry and could try to take your camera." He spoke in a forceful, hushed tone. He scrubbed his hand down his face. "Ang—there is something you don't understand." He took her hand and softened his voice. "You've been raised in a bubble with bodyguards watching your every move. But they aren't here now. You have a false sense of security that doesn't work in third-world countries. This danger is real. With one plunge of a knife, you could have been left bleeding in that alley." He ran his thumb across the back of her hand. "I just want you to be careful, Ang—" Tanner held her gaze.

"I hear your concerns, and I'll be more careful. I promise."

"It's dangerous for you to travel alone. Why don't you finish your business with the vice president and go home?" *She's a Ward. The killer could target her next.*

"I met with Vice President Saitoti yesterday morning. He has requested a three-month extension on your work permit, which he can make happen with his influence." She picked up her cup of tea.

He stared, speechless.

"You didn't think I could do it, did you?" She didn't hide her smile. "You're welcome." She raised her tea as if toasting.

"Thanks, Angie. That'll help us finish the job. And you're right. I didn't think you could pull it off. But you did. I'm proud of you." He picked up his cup and saluted her.

"Are you sticking around for the next few days?" Angie poured herself another cup of tea and stirred sugar into the brew.

"No, heading back to Mombasa early in the morning. What are your plans?" He released her hand and leaned back in his chair, admiring the view. Black hair blowing in the breeze made her incredibly appealing with a striking seascape as a backdrop. *Yes, putting kilometers between us is a good idea.*

"I think I'm going to soak up some sun tomorrow. I'd go back to Paradise Inn, but the place is a mess—"

Tanner's phone buzzed. He answered it as he pulled a pad and pencil from his pocket. After a greeting, he wrote something on the paper, tore the top sheet off, and folded it. "Thanks. I'll let you know what I find." He ended the call.

The waitress offered another pot of tea. Tanner held his hand up, indicating he didn't want any more. "Angie, thanks for getting us an extension on the work permit. I'll tell the team we're still in business."

"You're welcome. I'm glad I could help. Is there anything else I can do?"

"Not for the mining project. But I do wish you'd go home so you'll be safe at least until this is over."

"It sounds like you might want me to come back."

"You're welcome anytime. I wish you had come sooner."

"I do too."

"Enjoy your stay in Lamu and be careful. I think Wycliff is long gone by now. The police think he will go visit his sister in Mombasa before he leaves the country." He took her hand. Squeezed it. "Goodbye, Ang." He turned to leave.

"Tanner ..."

He stopped, pivoted, and met her eyes. "Yes, Angie." She looked like she wanted him to stay but couldn't say it.

"Watch your back." She bit her bottom lip.

"I will. Thanks." He turned and walked away—again.

Angie's heart skipped a beat as she watched him go. There was only one Tanner Zarello. She finished her tea while attempting to guard her heart. There was no comparison. Hot and husky Tanner won out over controlling and demanding Mason hands down. There was no contest.

She stared at the chair Tanner vacated and noticed his pad and pencil remained. She pulled it closer, took the last bite of her pastry, and turned the pencil at an angle. When she gently rubbed the lead over the imprint of his writing, an address appeared. Another clue. Thanks to years of watching old *CSI* reruns, she knew what to do. Returning to Mombasa was her next order of business. She could swing by this address with a police officer in tow on her way back to Paradise Inn. If she found Wycliff, she could send the officer to catch him, keeping herself safe.

She retrieved a skeleton key from her camera case and hurried to her room. Safe behind the locked door with her Nikon in hand, she searched for the pictures she had taken of the African. Finding the frame where the man looked back, she cropped the picture to enlarge his face. When she compared it to the photo the police chief had given her, it was a match. She'd found him.

She studied the perp's face more closely. Wycliff wasn't looking at her. His eyes were focused on the left side of her body. On Tanner. *He is the murderer's target.*

Mason put the stellar report in a presentation folder and strolled toward Alexander Ward's office. Being a wealthy, well-dressed executive, he enjoyed attention from lovely members of the secretarial staff. After a flirtatious advance from a bleached blonde and a business card slipped into his pocket by a redhead in a skirt two sizes too small, he eased into Ward's office and closed the door. He walked the length of the luxurious study, then sat in Ward's massive leather chair and eyed priceless paintings, expensive curios from around the world, and a killer view of Dallas, Texas. Ward had the best of everything. Rubbing his hand along the wood grain of the desk, Mason spoke aloud, "This will all be mine one day soon."

He placed the updated report on the desk so Ward would see it as soon as he arrived first thing tomorrow morning. He noticed a handwritten note.

Daniel Mwangi was killed at the mine in Kenya.

Mason took in a deep breath at this news. His man had failed him. Zarello was alive. He swallowed a curse and slammed his fist on the desk.

In his haste to return to his office to place an overseas call, he almost missed a folder marked '*medical.*' After checking to make sure he was still alone, he opened the folder. In Ward's handwriting along the side in the margin, he wrote ... *Terminal —six to eight months to live.* Mason had heard the doctor say the word 'cancer' and knew his prognosis was grave, but this confirmed it would happen sooner than he expected.

He rushed back to his office. Reaching under his calendar, he retrieved a business card and punched an overseas number. International calls stretched his patience. He paced as the overseas operator took her sweet time to do her job. On the third attempt, the call rang through. Finally.

"Wycliff, Mason Malone here."

"Yes, *bwana*." Wycliff sounded as if he'd been asleep.

"Tanner Zarello still lives. You killed the wrong man. I'm paying you well for this job, and I expect my instructions to be carried out as directed."

"I know, *bwana*. I saw him today in Lamu. I checked the schedule, and Zarello was to be first in the mine. I do not know what happened." He sounded awake now.

"I need you to finish the job. I'll compensate you generously. This time, make sure you take out Zarello. Shoot him in the heart, then steal some of the stones they've mined. Make it look like a robbery. Understand?" He changed his phone to his other ear. "Stake out the mine. He'll return to check on his employees. Be ready and move swiftly. Then, get out of Kenya."

"I will finish the assignment as we have discussed. Do not worry." Static crackled on the line.

"You gave me the impression you were the man for the job. Just get it done. Are we clear?" Mason demanded success.

"Yes, *bwana*. I will not fail you."

He punched the Off button, slammed the phone on his desk, and blew out a hot breath.

~

Paradise Inn was looking great. Grand-Papa would be proud. After one week, the entrance was inviting with fuchsia bougainvillea planted around the fence, a manicured lawn, and colorful flowers around a bird bath in the center of the circular drive.

"Julius, it looks much better, doesn't it?" Angie put two chaise lounge chairs in the shade of a jacaranda tree with lavender blooms and a park bench in front of some banana plants. "I think *Bwana* Tanner will be amazed at our work. Don't you?"

"*Ndio, dada.* It is very clean. I am going to spread the gravel in the drive now."

"Get the street kids to help you. It's a big driveway, lots of work."

"I will, Miss Angeleeka. Our number has grown. We are feeding nine children now, eight boys and one girl."

"That's good. I don't want to turn a hungry child away." A sense of satisfaction swept over her. She loved it when a plan came together.

The chocolate brown ceramic tiles of the lobby floors gleamed in the afternoon sun. The painter used a brush instead of a roller to paint the walls, not dropping a drop. It took a while, but it looked great when he finished.

Angie placed a huge vase of bird-of-paradise flowers on the polished check-in counter and hung a seascape on the wall behind the desk. Julius had planted small palm trees in the two clay pots she'd purchased. They added a tropical feel to the area as a salty breeze invaded the space.

The fax machine on the check-in counter came to life with the sounds of an incoming message. Angie retrieved it. "Samson, could I have a Coke, please?" She got comfortable in a lounge chair by the pool. The first page of the fax was a report from Ward Enterprises for Tanner. The second page was from Mason.

> *Angelica,*
>
> *I'm sorry our season of engagement has experienced such a rocky start. I had envisioned quiet, intimate dinners, exciting afternoons of planning the wedding, and our engagement appearing in the Dallas Morning News. Let's start over when you return.*
>
> *We must move quickly to get married before your grandfather's health deteriorates further. I know his medical issues are serious by the oxygen tanks he's using, the limp in his gait, and Joseph's hovering with meds given at strategic intervals. It has to be difficult for you to be so far from him. We will walk through this together. So, to help relieve some of the stress, I'm listing my condo with a realtor so we can move closer to him. What do you think?*
>
> *Please be careful and take care of yourself.*
>
> *I miss your smile—Mason*

Angie sat in the lounge chair and closed her eyes. *Lord, I've made a mess of things. Saying no to his proposal would have put a damper on the gala and disappointed Grand-Papa. But I don't love him. Help me untangle this web.*

To shake off Mason's fax, she took a deep breath and refocused on the renovations of the inn. Hearing the gate open, she walked to the lobby as a lorry was pulling through the gate. The driver delivered a large cage housing a talking African gray parrot. Angie bought him to add life to the resort.

"His name is *Mzee,* meaning old man in Swahili. You like him, Julius?"

"Yes, *dada.* He is a good bird. I will take care of him, Miss Angeleeka."

Mzee had a fluent vocabulary, which proved entertaining. Angie knew he'd been owned by Americans. His repertoire included whistling *The Andy Griffith Show* theme, saying "Polly wants a cracker," and "Help, get me out of here. They're going to eat me!" Angie loved it when he would make the ringing sound of a phone, carry on a complete conversation, laugh, and say goodbye. He was a perfect addition to the lobby, making it inviting for future guests.

"Miss Angeleeka, do you like our restaurant?" Samson was putting new tablecloths on the tables. "Our seamstress did a fine job on the cushions. Sit and you will see." He pulled out a chair.

"It looks amazing." She sat. "And they're comfortable."

"Rest, *dada,* I will get you the soda you requested and some banana bread fresh from the oven." Samson hurried to serve her.

"Thank you, Samson. It smells delicious. I love cinnamon."

The new slow-moving fans with woven paddles stirred a welcome breeze. She'd seen fans like these in an African movie and knew they'd add a perfect touch. Soon, this would be a slice of paradise for weary travelers seeking peace.

Mzee wolf whistled and yelled, "Hey, good looking!"

Well, I take back the peace part.

Perched on the rail of the mining platform, Tanner watched his team harvest a fortune in tanzanite. Losing Daniel had stolen their spunk, but they labored harder to take up the slack caused by his absence and make it to the finish line now that they had the extension they needed, thanks to Angie.

"Great job, team. You've filled in the gap Daniel left. I appreciate your extra effort. You've processed a lot of stones today. Let's wrap it up and get some rest." He moved to the ladder attached to the side of the mine and grabbed the rope, jerking it three times, signaling for Dylan to return to sea level. As he manned the ropes for his friend, Tanner's mind replayed the events of the day they lost Daniel, questioning if he had missed any detail, any evidence.

Dylan mounted the ladder and climbed out of the mine. He guzzled a bottle of water and retrieved his tools hanging at the end of the extra rope. "You're quiet. What's up?"

"Just wondering about some things. You said Wycliff was here when you threaded the new rope. Did he watch you?"

"Let me think." Dylan stared toward the beach area. "Yes, he relieved the day guard ahead of schedule that day and the day before."

"Two days in a row?" Tanner rubbed the back of his neck.

"Yeah, he swapped days with David, who needed to visit family in Tanzania. He squatted across from me and made small talk while I threaded the rope on the pulley. I didn't think anything about it at the time. Sorry, man." Dylan picked up the stones he'd mined and moved toward Paul and Vickie in the processing area.

"It's not your fault. You were doing your job. I just want to make sure we're after the right person. He seemed like a good man. Why would he do it? There has to be more to this story." Tanner began threading the ropes on the pulley.

"I agree. Wycliff lived in a very modest house in the valley. He was a friendly guy. He took a couple of weeks off recently for some family business and seemed stressed when he returned. Dylan turned off the light on his helmet.

"We'll catch Wycliff, but it's the man behind the scenes I have to find."

With their equipment loaded, Tanner sent his team to the Coastal Hotel close to the mine, where they stayed while working, and made his way to the low-income part of Mombasa to locate the apartment of Wycliff's sister. Bringing Wycliff in for questioning would end this fiasco and let things go back to normal.

He drove to the area and parked the Land Cruiser with a view of her home. He checked the address with his binoculars and phoned Karani to tell him he was doing surveillance. Karani said the police had been circling the area but didn't have the manpower for a continuous stakeout. Twisting the cap off his Coke, Tanner took a long drink and settled in for the evening.

Wycliff didn't seem like a murderer, but Daniel was gone, and his family deserved answers—Tanner needed answers. What would cause Wycliffe to murder Daniel? If Tanner waited for the understaffed police force to solve this case, Wycliff could get away.

Watching a continuous stream of pedestrians proved tedious. So many fit his description, but kept walking. After forty-five minutes, a young woman entered the apartment carrying two bags. She was alone.

With his interest piqued, Tanner searched the path, compared the height and weight of the men, and watched for anything out of the ordinary. Stray dogs, street kids, women with babies on their backs, a beggar hobbling by as bicycles darted in and out of traffic. It was Mombasa's afternoon traffic. Among a group of men, one wore a hoodie in Mombasa's heat. It had to be Wycliff!

Tanner pressed the last number dialed on his cell. "He's here. Send a car."

He slipped his cell into his pocket, slid out of the SUV, and locked it manually so it wouldn't beep. Edging across the street, he hurried to catch up. He rushed past a guy roasting ears of corn, around a woman with a load of sticks tied on her back, and past a bicycle piled high with eggs, and ran into Angie. A police officer was right behind her.

"Ouch!" She stumbled and reached for something to steady her.

Tanner grabbed her arm. "Angie, what are you thinking? It isn't safe here. You could disappear in this crowd and never be found again." Using a forced whisper, he willed himself to remain calm, to not blow it. The last thing he needed was for her to get offended.

She stared at him. "But I knew you'd be here." She paused. "Would you search for me, Tanner?"

Tanner scanned the surrounding crowd. "Yes, I would search for you to the ends of the earth, Angie. It's a habit of mine to come to your rescue on a regular basis." Lots of curious faces, but one was missing. Wycliff.

"He's gone. Again." Tanner stared at Angie.

She pointed to the police officer standing beside her. "He was about to catch the murderer and would have, if you hadn't gotten in the way."

"If *I* hadn't gotten in the way? You're kidding, right?"

Tanner turned to the officer. "Thank you for keeping her safe."

"You're welcome. I'll continue to search the area for our suspect. Karani and his men are on their way to assist."

Pivoting, Tanner came face-to-face with Angie.

Chapter Seven

"Angie, let's get out of here. The Cruiser is across the street." He led her through the flow of bicycles, donkey carts, and street kids and punched the fob, opened her door, and hurried to the other side. He pressed the last number dialed on his cell and told the Lieutenant he didn't catch Wycliff and was leaving the scene.

"Ang—I was following the murderer." Tanner stared at her stunning profile. He'd loved her looks since he saw her in shorts and a tank top, with her long, black hair in braids.

"So was I." She met his gaze.

"What were you going to do, hit him with your stilettos? Screaming for help doesn't work here, princess. How did you know to come here, anyway?" He blew out a breath, upset, but relieved she was safe.

"I got the address off the pad you left on the table. I told you, I'm a good detective, and I wouldn't try to take him in myself. I had a police officer with me. I planned to stay out of the way and let the police do their job." She rubbed where he had grabbed her arm.

"Listen, I think we need to work together if we're going to

get this guy." *So I can keep you alive.* Worrying about her safety was keeping him on edge. He would give his life for her ... if he got there in time.

"Work together? Are you sure? I thought you wanted distance between us."

"But you keep getting—" Tanner ran his hand through his hair.

"In the way? I've kept up with you at every turn."

"This isn't a contest. We're dealing with a murderer who could take your life. There's safety in numbers, and to catch this guy, we'll have to combine our efforts." He had to sound convincing because keeping her near was the only way to keep her safe. And despite the ring on her finger, she owned his heart.

"Look, Tanner. I'm not strong enough to fight with you." She thought about his suggestion for a second. "Okay, can I go now? I'm not feeling so good." She gave him a weak smile.

What, no objections? That's out of character. "Yes. Go straight back to the resort and stay there until we can make a plan."

"All right." She slipped out of the truck.

He sat stunned, watching her walk away. She didn't put up much of a fight, very uncharacteristic for the Angie he knew. Maybe he'd helped her understand, finally.

Among pedestrians struggling under loads of goods, garbage-eating goats, and scrawny dogs, she turned back to him, mouthed his name, then fell in the dirt-covered street.

"Angie!" Tanner bolted out of the truck, slammed the door, and rushed to her, dropping to his knees. He checked her head for cuts where she'd hit the rocks and felt warm moisture. She was bleeding. He brushed hair off her forehead, which was pasty and pale. She was burning up. "Angie, Angie. Wake up!" He scooped her into his arms, parting the gathering crowd, and rushed back to the truck.

A street boy opened the back door.

"Thanks, kid."

Tanner maneuvered into the back seat with Angie cradled in his arms. He grabbed his duffel bag off the floor, slid it under her head, and saw blood on his hand from her wound. He scooted out from under her limp body, gently laying her on the seat. After putting some shillings in the street boy's hand, he hurried around the Land Cruiser and slid into the driver's seat.

"Lord, I need your help here."

With the truck in first gear, he dug out his cell to notify the police he'd left the scene. When the traffic came to a halt, he scanned his phone list for Dr. Ruiru's number and requested a house call. It would cost extra, but he'd rather have her at Paradise Inn. Moments mattered.

Horns blared around him when he cut in front of a *matatu*, an overloaded van. Reaching back to steady Angie's body, he took an off-road route around a traffic jam of honking, brake-slamming drivers all trying to get home. Maneuvering the demolition derby, after thirty-five minutes, Tanner neared the inn as dusk bathed the sky.

He lay on his horn as they approached the gate so Julius would get it open. The gate opened without its annoying squeak. Once in the resort compound, he eased forward.

What happened to this place? It looked clean, painted, inviting—completely transformed.

Adrenaline fueled Tanner. He jammed the Cruiser into gear and hurried to Angie's side. Dirt fell from her clothes and hair as he checked her arms, legs, and torso for any injuries he might have missed. She was smart, capable, funny, entertaining, endearing, and challenging all in one beautiful package. He eased her into his arms.

She moaned at the movement.

"I've got you, Ang—" Tanner cradled her like a treasure.

"Julius, get the key to Angie's bungalow. She spiked a fever." He strode through the lobby and halted in the restaurant. "What happened here?"

"*Bwana*, Miss Angeleeka had the repairs done while you were working the mine, staying in the Coastal Hotel. She said she would tell you—"

"Don't worry, Julius. I understand. I really do."

Julius ran ahead, unlocked her quarters, and held the door as Tanner stepped inside with Angie cradled in his arms.

"The doctor should arrive soon. Bring him here. I'll need some broth and tea for Miss Angie. Bring some bags of ice and the fever reducer out of the medicine cabinet. Tell Samson I'll need something to eat."

"*Ndio, bwana*. I will be right back." The slapping of his flip-flops confirmed his haste. Tanner stood in the bungalow with Angie in his embrace. He should have put her in bed, but didn't want to let her go. The feel of her against his body stirred a love he'd denied, had buried. Her ivory skin and ebony hair glowed in the first hint of moonlight slanting through the windows. He placed a soft kiss on her forehead. "I love you, Angie. There's never been anyone but you. You're the best friend I've ever had. I've loved you since you were twelve, and I helped you with your dance lessons on a rainy day. Marry me." Too bad she was asleep.

Angie stirred, opening her eyes.

"Tanner?" She spoke in a whisper. "I'm hurting and so cold."

"You're sick, Angie."

"Why are you holding me?"

"You fainted in the street."

"I remember calling for you. Then, everything went black."

"A doctor is on his way. We need to get you into bed. Can you stand?"

"I don't know." She rested her head on his shoulder and attempted a smile. "Can't I just stay right here? You feel good."

"Well, I wouldn't mind that. You'll be out again soon, though, so we should get you into bed. Let's try to stand, okay?" He eased her into a standing position. She swayed. He held her shoulders as she clutched his shirt to steady herself.

"I need some pajamas. They're in the top drawer."

He got her something to sleep in and walked her toward the restroom.

"Why am I so dizzy?"

"It's a symptom of several contagious things here in Mombasa. The doctor will help us figure out what exactly." He helped her into the small room. "Wait, Angie. Let me check your hair."

Tanner flipped on the light and lifted the hair behind her ear on the right side of her head. "You've got a cut on your scalp from where you hit the gravel. There's blood in your hair."

"Blood in my hair."

"You had fallen in the middle of the street when I got to you."

"Is it a big cut?"

"I can't tell yet. I'll get a flashlight and clean this up for you. Can you change by yourself?"

"Yeah, if I hang on to the walls." She shut the door. "I got some mosquito bites right after I arrived in Mombasa. I hope it's not malaria." She talked through the door. "We have a killer to catch."

Tanner waited. She got quiet. "You okay in there?"

"Yeah, I'm moving slowly. If the room would quit spinning,

it would help." When she opened the door, her eyes were glassy against pale skin.

He helped her to a chair. "I need to pour water on this area to clean the wound and get the blood out of your hair." He put a thick towel under the area to catch the water. "This may burn."

"Do what you need to do."

Tanner separated the dry hair from the bloody area and poured bottled water on the cut. "You may need a couple of stitches, Angie."

"I have a headache right there too."

"The doc will be here soon, and he'll fix you right up." Tanner brushed the dry part of her hair.

As he ran the brush through her silky hair, particles of dirt and tiny rocks hit the floor. The intimacy of the moment was hitting him where it hurt, in his heart. She leaned against him and closed her eyes as he brushed.

"That should do it. Let's get you in bed."

"I'm for that." She stood and grabbed onto his arm. "Can you make the room stop moving?"

He put his arm around her and led her toward the bed.

"I'm going to put a clean towel under your head."

"Thanks for doing this, for taking care of me."

"You're welcome. That's what friends do."

"You're still my friend?" She grabbed his hand, turned, and met his gaze.

"You're fading fast. Let's get you in bed." He pulled the cover back and tucked her in.

She grabbed his hand when he moved away. "Thanks, Tanner."

"You're welcome." He winked, breaking the connection. "You want some water?"

"No, but I need more blankets. Why am I so cold when

Mombasa is hot?" She shivered. "My bones hurt like they're breaking inside my body."

Tanner searched the bungalow. "I'll be back with more blankets. You stay in bed."

"I'm not going anywhere. It hurts too much to move."

Tanner met Dr. Ruiru in the lobby as he came from his upstairs suite with an armload of blankets. After the traditional greetings, Tanner showed him the way to Angie's bungalow, stepping aside to allow him to enter. He eased a chair to the side of the bed, giving the doctor access to his patient.

"She got sick suddenly after saying she didn't feel well. Then she passed out in the street." Tanner said.

"Several tropical diseases come on quickly. Let me determine what illness she has acquired." He pulled a pen from his pocket and started a chart for Angie.

Tanner eased to the other side and sat on the bed. He smoothed her hair from her face.

"Angie, wake up. Dr. Ruiru from Mombasa Hospital is here to help you." Tanner added blankets over her trembling body.

"Okay." Angie's voice was weak. She didn't move.

"Doctor, there's a cut behind her right ear. I washed the area. It looked like it might need some stitches."

"I will look at that after I assess her condition." The doctor reached for Angie's wrist and checked her pulse.

"I've never seen her so sick." Tanner rubbed the nape of his neck and paced the room as the doctor opened his bag and displayed his instruments.

"Miss Ward, I'm going to check your vital signs and take some blood." Moving with precision, the doctor checked her using old-fashioned instruments. He looked into her eyes with a small flashlight and wrote down his findings. He pinched her skin, checking for signs of dehydration, and drew blood from her arm.

"*Bwana*, her fever is one hundred and three. You must work to bring it down. Her blood pressure is fine, but you must pay attention as the chills, high fevers, and body aches from malaria are almost unbearable, ten times worse than the flu. Did she complain about body aches?" He noted information on her chart.

"Yes. She said it felt like her bones were breaking." Tanner paced.

"Nausea?"

"No, sir. She was dizzy and very cold."

"She will be weak and dizzy. Miss Ward has contracted malaria. I'll know the severity of this strain once I get this to the lab. If this fever isn't down within twenty-four hours, we must hospitalize her. I'll give her medicine now. She must have these tablets every four hours." He opened the vial, put two tablets in his palm, and handed Tanner the bottle. "It will not cure the disease, but it'll keep it from going to her brain, endangering her life. Drinking fluids is crucial to keep her hydrated. She cannot be left unattended. Do you have someone to stay with her?"

"I'll stay until her fever breaks and she's on the mend." Tanner was quick to answer.

"Do not hesitate to call if her condition worsens. Any questions?" He leaned over Angie and elevated her head so she could take the tablets with the water. "I cannot stress this any stronger. She's very ill. Bring her to the hospital if her fever does not come down." He took a close look at the laceration on Angie's head. After shaving a small area around the cut, he bathed the area with an antiseptic before putting three stitches to close the wound. "You need to clean this every day."

"You think it's a deep cut, doctor?"

"Not too deep. I'm more concerned about a mild concussion. When you give her medicine or wake her for food and drink, be sure she is completely awake. If she has a severe headache, excessive dizziness, or any seizure activity, get her to the emergency room."

"I'll take good care of her. I appreciate you making a house call." Tanner walked him to the door.

Julius and Samson hovered near, worry marking their faces.

"Samson, please walk out with the doctor and pay him for this visit. Julius, do you have the ice?"

"*Ndio, bwana.*" He entered carrying a tray with steamy broth, a pot of hot tea, a fever reducer, and bags of ice.

Tanner gave her the fever reducer, spoon-fed some broth and tea, and held ice bags on her forehead to fight the high temperature, just like Dr. Ruiru suggested to keep down the chance of cerebral malaria. A constant prayer stayed on his lips. The vigil was tiring, but every moment mattered. She was critical.

He called Dylan in between tending to Angie's needs, letting him know to run the job for the next several days.

Samson and Julius stayed close. Much to his relief, Angie's fever subsided around midnight. Knowing her temperature would rise again, Tanner left his loyal workers with Angie and went to his upstairs suite for a shower and a shave. Panic quickened his steps. Malaria had killed so many in Africa. Ang—couldn't be one of them.

The shower gave Tanner his second wind. This vigil would take several days. Pausing briefly, he sent a quick note to Alexander Ward, letting him know Angie had contracted malaria and was receiving around-the-clock care, promising to give him updates on her condition daily. Typing the words to her grandfather made it all the more real, adding to Tanner's angst.

He returned with his laptop, Bible, journal, and a change of clothes, ready to see this through. Julius had just placed a cool cloth on Angie's forehead when he came into her bungalow.

"*Bwana*, she was beginning to moan. I fear the fever is coming again."

"I will check it. Thanks for staying." Tanner reached for the thermometer.

"Samson is preparing a tray for you. He will bring it soon. Call if you need either one of us during the night."

"Thanks, Julius."

As Julius left, Samson brought in a tray with soup, bread, and tea in a Thermos bowl and containers to ensure warmth for hours. They left him quietly with his patient.

Her fever was 102 again. He cooled the rag and placed it on her forehead and onto the top of her head and prayed. *Lord, we need a miracle right now. Angie is very ill. Please do what you are famous for and bring healing to her body. We know you care about the details of our lives. She is so very important to me. I ask this in your holy name. Amen.*

The early morning call from Dr. Ruiru confirmed his fear. Angie had contracted a serious strain of the disease. Tanner didn't leave her side for three days and nights except for brief showers and a change of clothes. He administered meds at the correct times, bathed her face, and spoon-fed her liquids. When her fever spiked, she would cry out.

"Tanner, where are you? Tanner?"

"I'm here, Ang—" He bathed her face with a cool cloth.

"Leslie, are Missy and Elise okay?"

"I'm sure your friends are fine. Don't worry about them."

"Tanner, come closer. You're so far away. I'm sorry."

"Just get well, and everything will be okay."

"Don't be mad. Why did you leave me?" Tears dampened her cheeks.

"I'm so sorry I left you. Please forgive me." He wiped her tears away.

He'd talk softly to her till her temperature subsided. It reminded him of the times he'd watched over her, when he was her hero. He thought his heart would stop the day a drone hit her head, and she plunged unconscious into the lake. He sprinted from the lawn to the end of the pier and jumped in frantically trying to find her body. When he brought her to the surface, she wasn't breathing. Doing CPR, he saved her life. If only he could save her from this ...

Angie's bones ached, and her spiking fevers caused her to go from freezing to inflamed in record time. She couldn't stay awake. *Am I dreaming, Lord?*

She opened her eyes. Tanner slept in a chair beside her bed with her hand in his. *Yep, it's a dream.* Sleep overtook her again like a heavy blanket—hours slipped by.

Unsure of how long had passed and with the sun streaming in, Angie woke and surveyed her surroundings. A pile of blankets on the floor blocked her way to the restroom. *Those will have to be moved soon.* A bag of melting ice cubes was dripping on the rug. *Where is Julius when you need him?* And a very attractive man was lying across the foot of her bed.

She smiled. "Tanner?"

He opened his eyes, smiled as he massaged his neck. "Welcome back to the land of the living."

"I'm sure I look like the living dead right now. How long have I been sick?" She finger-combed her hair, forcing it into some resemblance of order.

"Four days and nights." He got up, stretched, and started folding blankets. "Feeling better?"

"I feel weak. But I'm hungry."

"That's a good sign. Your fever broke around three this morning. I think you'll live." He smiled.

"Did you doubt?"

He stopped stacking the blankets and met her gaze. "Angie, you've been really sick. You scared me."

"I seem to be doing that a lot lately." Angie got out of bed but had to sit back down. "Whoa." She grabbed her head.

"Here, let me help you." Tanner slipped his arm around her waist and walked her to the restroom. "You want to get a bath?"

"You going to help with that too?" She smiled and turned, their faces somehow inches apart. Her smile faded as Tanner's demeanor shifted. *Do I see love in his eyes?*

"I think not, but I'll get you some fresh pajamas and a towel." He tenderly touched her cheek, sliding her hair behind her ear, then met her eyes. "You'll feel better after a warm bath. You can wash your hair if you want. I wouldn't put shampoo on the stitched area, but getting the blood out would be good. Then, it will be time for your medicine."

Angie paused, wanting to cherish the feeling of being in Tanner's arms. His closeness brought back a rush of memories and buried feelings. "Thank you, Tanner. For everything."

"You're welcome, Ang—" He opened the door to the restroom, turned the water on, and released her to enter. "Enjoy your bath. I'll have Julius change your sheets."

Tanner gave her some time to get cleaned up before he came in with a tray sporting a vase of fresh flowers, a black currant soda, a glass of ice, and a pot of tea.

"It's time for your medicine. You up for some company?"

"Sure." She patted the bedside for him to join her.

He put the tray on her bed and opened the malaria meds. "Here you go." He poured her drink.

She took the tablets. "Julius said you stayed day and night. I appreciate it especially since I've been a nuisance lately."

"But you've always been a challenge, Ang—That's one thing I love about you. You have grit, tenacity. You're creative and fun. You're my best friend, and you were so sick. I couldn't leave." He smiled.

"There aren't many men who would do that." Her hand shook as she held her glass.

"Angie, we've been friends for a long time." He stared into her bloodshot eyes.

"Friends?" She speared him with a look.

He paused. "Well, more than friends." He poured two acetaminophen into his palm while he searched for the right words. "Why are you here, Angie?" He gave her the tablets.

"We needed to appeal to the VP for an extension on the work permit. It's my first assignment, and I wanted to prove myself. Besides, I heard you and Grand-Papa talking about the murderer. You're not the only one who can worry, you know. Then I got caught up in trying to help you from afar when they gave me a photo of the murderer at the police station." She took a deep breath.

"Any other reason?"

"I wanted to be close to you, Tanner. I've missed you."

He held her gaze. "And, I've missed you."

Uncertain what to say, he changed the subject. "Why didn't your grandfather make the trip? Was he too busy?" Tanner took her glass and put it on the tray.

She paused. "He's dying, Tanner." Her eyes pooled with tears. "It's cancer. He has six to eight months to live."

He grabbed her hand and moved closer. "Oh, Angie, I'm so sorry. I didn't know."

"He's preparing to turn Ward Enterprises over to someone else in the next few months." She hesitated. "It's hard to believe."

"What are you going to do?"

"That's the question of the hour. I've given it some thought. Many people assume I'd take the top position, but I haven't aspired to replace my grandfather in leading the company. I'm not sure where I fit into the Ward Enterprises paradigm. It will depend on who takes the lead." She paused. What would Angie do if Mason were next in line? Would she want to work with him? "It will be according to what positions are available once they restructure. I'd like to do more with my life. I just haven't discovered what that is yet."

"Your name carries weight. I think you'll have your choice of positions. I hate that he'll leave you so soon."

He didn't want to destroy the little bubble her illness created between them, but the pain was still there, hiding in her eyes, dividing them.

"I looked for you as I descended the stairs." Tears filled her eyes.

"There was engine trouble on my plane, and I was four hours late reaching Dallas, but I watched as you received your Master's degree. I rushed to my mom's place to change into my tux and slipped into your gala as your grandfather presented you to the prestigious guests on the platform at the base of the staircase. No one could miss Mason plowing through the crowd, giving you roses, and proposing. I didn't wait for your answer. I left to the sound of applause."

"Where were you standing?"

"Behind Harry Connick Jr., beside the platform he performed on."

"The huge bouquet of roses surrounded by daisies. You brought them, didn't you?"

"Guilty."

She hesitated. "I don't know what to say. I'm sorry I didn't see you. It means so much to me that you were there. Did you stay with your mom?"

"No, I flew back to Kenya that night."

"The same day you arrived? That's horrible."

"I couldn't stay. You're engaged."

"Please let me explain. Everyone was waiting. The crowd was silent. I looked for you, but you weren't there. I weighed my options and saw encouragement on Grand Papa's face. I need to please Grand-Papa to make him happy. I smiled at Mason, and he took that as a 'yes.'"

"So, you didn't say yes?"

"No. He took it for granted. You and I haven't had a chance to talk until now. I'm sorry."

"Sorry you didn't tell me, or sorry you're engaged? I didn't hear you calling out for him when you were delirious with a fever. So, do you love him?" He had to know.

She hesitated. "He's been kind to me, protective. Maybe too protective. I've seen another side to him since I arrived in Kenya. Grand-Papa is proud of how Mason has worked his way to the top of the corporate ladder at Ward Enterprises and—"

"And what?"

"He has one outstanding quality—he doesn't leave me. Everyone I love leaves, Tanner."

He paced the room while running his fingers through his hair. "So, do you think Mason is being groomed to take your grandfather's place at Ward Enterprises?" Tanner pulled a chair beside her bed, turned it backward, and straddled it.

"No. He may assume he'll be chosen to lead the company, but my grandfather is looking at other candidates."

"Are you in love with Mason Malone?" Tanner's voice came out quiet, husky.

She stared into his eyes. He furrowed his brow. "No," she whispered.

"What do you plan to do next, Angie?"

She looked weary. Getting comfortable in her bed, she said, "I don't have the answers. I don't know what to do. I'm too tired to think. For now, can I sleep? This is good. Can we do it again later?" Her eyes were heavy. "I'm so weak and shaky. Why am I so tired?"

He didn't answer—just sat there and watched her drift off to sleep, memorizing the spray of long lashes on her cheeks.

The malaria had run its course. Each day, Angie grew stronger. The doctor said she must extend her stay for at least two weeks until her blood tests proved she was recovering. Tiring of her bungalow, she eased outside for some fresh air. Listening to waves lapping the shore was music to her ears. The palm trees offered filtered shade as the wind swayed their branches. Resting by the pool, Julius waited for her. He served oxtail soup, fresh bread, and a Coke over ice for lunch. As she took her last bite, he returned to remove her tray.

"Julius, when will Tanner return from the mine?" She shaded her eyes to see his face in the sunlight.

"They are scheduled to be here in nine days. Do you need something else?" He stood, awaiting her answer. "No, the lunch tasted great." She finished her soda and put her glass on the tray.

"Are the street children okay?"

"They are *sawa sawa*. They are okay. We fed them as you instructed. They rake the grounds every day. They prayed for you. While you were sick, they cleaned the grassy area outside the fence. It is *safi sana,* very clean. They have missed the *mzungu* working with them."

"I've missed them. After tea time, you can let them play soccer inside the fence. When I first met the street children in Matharie Valley, they were playing soccer in a cleared section of the dump. I questioned where they got their soccer ball. The missionary who was with me had the children bring me their ball. It was homemade. They made it using plastic grocery bags, tying their creation with rubber bands or twine, whatever they could find. Adding more and more bags, they kept working until it was the size of a real soccer ball. The oldest boy applied string last, making indentations like a regulation ball. That has stuck with me."

"So, I bought a new ball in town before I got sick. It's in my bungalow. Do you know the rules? They need to learn how to play the game properly."

"*Ndio, dada.* I will teach the rules before I let them use the new ball." He hurried to retrieve the object. His grin said he was as happy about the soccer ball as the children would be.

Tanner descended into the mine. Utter darkness cocooned him like the challenges he faced. With a murderer on the loose, a job to finish, his boss dying, and Angie engaged, his mind jumped from one problem to another. Pounding rocks relieved his stress, and the manual labor helped him focus and process his next move. Without answers, he banged the wall of the shaft, followed the final strain they were working, and retrieved a gorgeous chunk of stone. It sparkled with promise when he held it in front of his headlamp. At least something was going his way.

He filled one bucket, sent it up, and waited for another to reach him. Dylan lowered an empty bucket with a note attached.

Stay in the mine. We're being watched. They're looking for you. I called the police. I'll let you know when things change.

Frustration fueled him. He chiseled the thread of tanzanite and prayed for the safety of his team. He kept working so things would seem normal to someone watching and listening to the scene. Time crept by. Moments stretched at a torturous pace. He labored to pass the time, to work out the stress of this cat-and-mouse game the culprit was playing.

When sirens chased the murderer away, Dylan jerked on the rope tied to his bucket and signaled Tanner's safe ascent to sea level. The squeak of the pulley grated on his nerves as it returned him to the sunshine. He squinted, mounted the ladder, and removed his helmet.

The lieutenant and his men were combing the area for additional clues. His team was tense and concerned. The danger was real. Close.

Officer Karani wrote in his notebook, gave orders to his assistant, and faced Tanner. "I think he came back looking for you, Mr. Zarello."

"He's a bold one. I'll give him that." Tanner ran his hand through his hair.

"He is not giving up. But neither are we. He left some shoe prints and a Coke can with possible fingerprints. I have work to do. I will be in touch." The officer descended the steps.

"Lieutenant, did he ever show up again at his sister's house?"

"I have cars patrolling the area. But no one has seen him there since. He will visit her before he flees the country. It's what Kenyans do." He got in the patrol car and left with sirens blaring.

"Hey guys, let's close up for today." Without comment, the team spun into action. The generator now off, the silence among the team seemed amplified. They needed to distance themselves from the mine—from the scene of the crime. Their murderer was now a thief. He was stealing the life out of his employees.

After five more days of lying around, Angie was stir-crazy. She couldn't just lie around waiting for a murderer to find her, but she needed to continue resting. So, she decided to go on a safari, booked a flight to Masai Mara for three nights at a five-star tent camp, and packed her carry-on bag. She needed time away from the city to think and pray. What better place to do that than among God's handiwork? After an hour's flight, she would be safe from any threat while in the Mara, and the deluxe accommodations would be a great place to rest. With her camera bag hitched on her shoulder, she rolled her luggage toward the lobby. Julius hurried to carry her bag. Samson had wrung his hands when her taxi arrived.

"Miss Angeleeka, please take care of yourself and get rest. You were very sick." Samson opened the taxi door for her.

Julius loaded her suitcase. "It is soon, *dada*. You must be careful."

Angie sensed their angst. "I will, the beds are so comfortable in the tents. The doctor said it would be okay if I rest every afternoon and do not take extra trips into the Mara. I promise not to overdo it. I'll see you in a few days. Teach *Mzee* some Swahili while I'm gone."

"*Ndio,* Miss Angeleeka." Julius smiled and closed her door.

The taxi driver hit every pothole on the way to the airport. Or maybe her body wasn't ready for Kenya's roads just yet. Fortunately, the short plane flight was smooth sailing to Masai Mara where God's creation roamed free. The pilot had to buzz the runway to get a herd of impalas to clear the path. Angie loved watching the animals scatter. The sun shone brightly in a cerulean sky when they landed on the dirt airstrip and took the rickety steps off the plane. Safari vehicles were lined up. Their drivers were ready to carry new arrivals into the wilds of Africa.

Angie climbed into the middle seat of a three-level, canvas-covered safari truck, pulled her camera out, and changed to a stronger lens. A cute couple about sixty years of age took the front seat and settled in for the safari. Angie loved how the lady doted over the gentleman, making sure he was okay.

A Kenyan in uniform greeted them. "Welcome to Masai Mara. I am Peter, and I'll be your driver. We will now begin to search for animals as we make our way to the tent camp for you to take lunch. Get your cameras ready and hang on. Africa can be bumpy."

Angie leaned forward. "Hello, I'm Angelica Ward from Dallas, Texas. You can call me Angie."

"We're Buford and Betty James from Albuquerque, New Mexico. Glad to meet you. Are you alone on safari?"

"Yes, but I don't mind. Look, there are warthogs in the weeds. Their tails look like radio antennas when they run." Angie grabbed her camera, but they were too quick for her.

"Do not worry. Warthogs live within the confines of your camp. They have been raised around humans. You will see many and get close-up photos. But do not corner them because they can grow aggressive, but otherwise, they run from danger." Peter assured his passengers.

"Angie, are you a professional photographer? You have an

amazing camera, and those lenses must have cost you a pretty penny," Betty said.

"No, I'm not a professional. It's just an expensive hobby I enjoy."

They rounded a curve and stopped to watch several species of gazelles grazing together.

"The largest is called the Grant gazelle, the smaller one, with a black stripe and a white stripe on their side, is the Thompson gazelle." Peter pointed them out.

"I like how their tails move back and forth like windshield wipers." Angie took several pictures. "Peter, what's that small one called?"

"That is the *dik dik*. He is full-grown. Notice his coat is darker, and his horns are shorter. They are *wasi wasi*, very nervous."

Peter eased the truck through the grazing animals to a rutted dirt road. Rounding a corner, he slowed to a stop. A giraffe stood in their way, dining on a thorn tree, not bothered by the invasion of his privacy or the thorns scratching his long, long throat. His eighteen-inch, black, slimy tongue worked the limbs for a few minutes before he sauntered to the next tree for dessert. "Thank you, Peter. That was awesome. I got some great pictures."

"His family is feasting in the forest. Watch for their heads as we pass. Where there is one giraffe, the journey is close by."

"A group of giraffes is called a journey, Peter?" Betty asked.

"*Ndio,* yes, Mama. Some call them a tower of giraffes."

"I hadn't heard that, thanks." She noted it in her travel journal.

Pausing at a guard post, their driver reported in. Once cleared to enter the camp, he drove a winding road through a rainforest of tropical birds, beautiful flowers, and monkeys swinging from limb to limb. When they reached the lodge, Peter parked.

"Welcome to the lodge, Kichwa Tembo, which means 'head of the elephant.' Please disembark and take your lunch. Meet me here at four o'clock for our afternoon game drive. The animals will be waiting. We expect to see many lions today."

Friendly smiles greeted them with words of welcome and a refreshing glass of cold pineapple juice. Angie checked in, paid her game park fees, and identified her luggage. A porter balanced her luggage on top of his head and led her to a five-star tent directly across from a pristine swimming pool. Her tent was constructed of green canvas with mesh windows welcoming a breeze. Flaps hung from each window awaiting closure for evening privacy. The floors were polished stone, the bed was soft, and the bathroom was modern. *Now, this is my idea of camping.*

A thirty-minute nap in her tent had given her a second wind. She zipped her tent to keep monkeys from taking her undergarments to the trees and went on a warthog search.

Just past some bamboo, Angie approached the neighboring tent and found Betty and Buford lounging on their porch. They waved her over.

"Isn't this an amazing place? Is your tent like ours?"

"Yes, isn't it great? I love it. Hey, give me your camera.

Angie put her camera strap around her neck while she used Betty's. "Take a seat by Buford, and smile." Angie took three shots from different distances using the telescopic lens and then returned the camera. "Look at those and see if you like them."

"I hadn't thought of getting a picture. We'll frame it. Our daughter, Susan, would love to see that shot. She gave us this trip. Thanks, Angie."

"You're welcome. I think lunch is ready, and it smells good. I hope it's not a warthog."

Chapter Eight

Tanner took his team to Paradise Inn for a few days of rest. They weren't as jovial as normal. Watching for the murderer had them on edge. It was time for a reprieve.

Drew, their mining expert, eyed the grounds as they drove in. "Wow, what happened here? Where's the place we called home?" His smile betrayed his complaints.

"You said she renovated the place, but I didn't expect it to be transformed. It doesn't look like the inn I knew, but I could get used to it." Dylan stood staring at the improvements.

"She who?" Vickie pulled her luggage to the lobby. "Hey, there's a bird in here."

"Angie remodeled, but keep your comments to a minimum."

"Why?" Vickie dropped her bag at her feet.

"Ward suggested we leave it in shambles to keep away unwanted guests since we're bringing in valuable tanzanite. It was merely a safety measure on his part." Tanner grabbed his duffel bag and closed the truck.

"Don't worry about us, Boss. Mum's the word." Drew made the action of zipping his lip.

"I have to admit, it does look wonderful. Alexander Ward planned to update the facility for resale soon. She's done him a favor." Tanner couldn't wait to see Angie.

Samson greeted him as he entered the lobby, sporting a new apron and drying a shiny pot while humming a Kenyan tune.

"Welcome back, *Bwana* Tanner."

He returned the greeting. "Where is Miss Angie?"

"*Bwana*, she is gone." Samson studied Tanner.

Adrenaline slammed through him. *Did I leave her too soon?* "I thought she was getting better. Her fever broke before I left."

"No, *pole sana,* so sorry, *bwana*. She is better. She went on safari." He slung the kitchen towel to rest on his shoulder as he picked up Tanner's luggage.

Tanner held his breath. "A safari to America?"

"No, she went to Masai Mara. She will return to the inn soon. *Unataka Chai?* Do you want some tea?" As if giving constant Swahili lessons, Samson would say something in his language, then interpret it in English.

Malaria had sapped Angie's strength, leaving her pale and fragile. Would she be up for a safari already? Still, Tanner breathed a bit easier knowing she'd not left for America, or worse. Relaxation among God's creation could be a tranquil place to heal, but her sudden trip was odd. "Yes. Thank you, Samson. I'll take tea on the veranda after a quick shower." He took the stairs to his upstairs suite two at a time. A reprieve was a good idea. If Angie had the same thought. She could be grabbing rest, but out of the way, so the murderer couldn't find her. He fought a bone-weary exhaustion as he reached the door to his suite.

Samson served Tanner a steamy pot of tea. "*Bwana*, a fax arrived while you were away. It is still on the machine."

"Would you bring it to me?" He stirred sugar into his tea.

"I will return with it in hand."

Tanner added warm milk to his cup. Perhaps Wycliff was doing the same somewhere in Kenya. Was he close by?

Shuffling his feet in his oversized flip-flops, Samson returned with the fax.

Tanner expected it to be something from Alexander Ward, but after reading the first few lines, he knew this missive spelled heartache for Dylan. Tanner folded the slick paper and would wait until his team finished lunch to deliver this news privately.

Angie dined alone, enjoying the solitude in her plush surroundings, wishing Tanner were with her. He would love the relaxed setting and the animals. Maybe one day ...

Beyond a three-foot rock wall, monkeys played in the trees next to the open-air dining hall. Butterflies flashed a rainbow of color as they stole nectar from flowering bushes in the meticulous landscape. Birds of different species flew in and perched on the backs of the canvas director's chairs in search of food. The waiters were on high alert to keep the wildlife away from the guests and their food. Angie enjoyed the live entertainment.

Grilled chicken, roasted pork, and sautéed ostrich were her choices. Angie chose the ostrich. She shied away from the salads but enjoyed the grilled vegetables. Dessert was their signature, macadamia nut pie. Simply delicious.

Her porter was also her waiter. "*Bwana*, can you help me?"

"Do you need more food?" He seemed anxious to serve.

"No, it was wonderful. I need to rest, but I do not want to miss my safari. Is there a wake-up system here at the camp?"

"Yes, I will wake you. What time do you want me to come? I will stand on your porch and call until you answer." He stood, awaiting instructions with her dessert dish in his hand.

"It's one-thirty now. We leave for our safari at four o'clock. Could you wake me at three-thirty?"

"Would you like a cold bottle of water to take on your safari?"

"Yes, that would be great."

"Glad to serve you." He removed her dishes.

She thanked the chef and returned to her tent. Safaris had been her favorite vacation since her first visit to Kenya when she was ten. On her visit three years prior, there wasn't time for an extended trip to the Mara.

Watching two monkeys scampering from limb to limb, curious about the *mzungu* that had invaded their domain, she caught their faces in her camera. Resting was a good idea. She needed her strength built up again if she was going to pair up with Tanner when he returned from the mine. She prayed he was safe as he moved about Mombasa.

Once she stepped into her tent, she secured the zippered opening to deter mischievous guests during her nap. Snuggled into her feather mattress, she listened to hyenas laughing in the distance. The grunt of a warthog let her know they were resting nearby. It was siesta time. Life was good. She dozed off, replaying her last conversation with Tanner in her mind. Things were looking up ...

Samson served lunch to Tanner and his team at Paradise Inn. The scent of spicy seasoning filled the air.

"Man, I'm starving. You're working us too hard." Drew plopped himself in a chair. "I think you'll survive. You ate a big breakfast and haven't broken a sweat today." Tanner took a seat at the table.

"All the equipment has been cleaned and loaded to go back to the mine. That's a big job for one morning." Drew grabbed some chips and stuffed them in his mouth. "It took me a whole hour on my day off to do the work. Does anybody feel sorry for me?"

"Not in this crowd. And who's eating again before we've prayed?" Dylan chided.

"He thinks he's bordering on malnutrition." Tanner poured his Coke over purified ice cubes. "Is Vickie back from town?"

The striking blonde joined them at the table. "I'm here. I got back an hour ago. There wasn't a line at the shipping office. What's for lunch?"

"Tacos and guacamole." Tanner smiled.

Drew talked with his mouth full. "You're kidding, right?"

"Nope, Angie taught Samson how to make it and told him Americans liked tacos."

"Thank. You. Angie!" Drew was all smiles as Samson served tortillas, guacamole, and refried beans. Steam rose from the seasoned hamburger meat, filling the air with south-of-the-border flavor.

The group devoured the welcome touch of Tex-Mex while conversations jockeyed from subject to subject. Tanner loved seeing a few smiles among his team. But he couldn't quite bring himself to feel it himself. The threat was still out there. Waiting for any of them to make one wrong move.

"Dylan, I need to see you for a minute after we eat." Tanner kept it light.

The team was finally returning to a more natural feel after two weeks of grieving.

"Tanner, can I use your extra laptop? Vickie said she would help update my resume. I need to get a line on my next job since we're wrapping up in a few weeks now that the water level is rising." Drew asked between bites.

"Sure. It's on my desk. Help yourself. But, don't forget to tell them what a bum you are."

"Oh, don't worry. I'll tell them the truth—how you lazy no-counts would've failed miserably without my expertise and skill." Drew headed to the office.

Vickie trailed Drew. "Let's work in the office. The air-conditioner works better in there."

Dylan finished the last of the guacamole while condensation formed on their soft drinks. The revolving fans overhead sent a breeze into the dining area.

Tanner took the fax out of his pocket. "This came through while we were still working at the mine. After reading the first two lines, I realized it wasn't for me. I thought you might want to read this in private." He handed Dylan the fax.

"Man, you're scaring me. Is something wrong at home?" Dylan sat up and gripped the table.

"No." He paused. "It's from Amy."

Dylan rolled the paper up. "You didn't read it?"

"Nope, it's not my business. But I'm around this afternoon if you want to talk." Tanner opened his laptop. He had some emails waiting for his reply.

"Thanks, man." Dylan stood and pushed his chair in. "I'll find you later."

Tanner watched him trudge past the pool, toward the beach area. He climbed the outcropping of rocks where the shore met the ocean at the left end of the property. He fought the ocean breeze as it blew against the paper. Low tide would give him a dry place to sit to read the fax.

Tanner wished he could shield those he loved from the

pain of broken relationships. He knew heartache ran deep. Time away from the States had given Dylan a chance to heal after being jilted at the altar. The strength he'd gained was being tested—thanks to Amy's fax.

In Tanner's conversation with Angie, she'd said, "... *he doesn't leave. Everyone I love leaves.*" His heart wrenched. Tanner was one of her deserters, and he wanted to find a way to try again.

Waiting for an email to go through, Tanner propped his feet onto a chair and watched as Dylan walked the shoreline. The saltwater washed over his feet several times before he turned and marched to the veranda, stopping to rinse off the sand.

"You all right?" Tanner read his expression.

"What's the scripture in *The Message* Bible you told me about that you stand on when difficult things happen?" Dylan stood, waiting.

"It's Psalms 34:13. 'When you're kicked in the gut, He'll help you catch your breath.'"

"Yeah, that's the verse. I like the 'kicked in the gut' part. Here, read this." He held the wrinkled scroll toward Tanner.

Tanner took the fax. "You sure?"

"Yeah, read it." Dylan headed to the kitchen, and Tanner read. He skipped the part where Amy asked him to give the letter to Dylan.

> *Dylan,*
> *You probably thought you'd never hear from me again and didn't want to since I left you at the altar. I'm sorry for that. I know I embarrassed you and your family. I feel bad. You didn't deserve that.*
> *You need to know the truth. I was struggling the week of our wedding. You called it wedding jitters, but that wasn't the*

problem. To be your wife would have been a dream come true. You're an amazing man of the highest character—and so good-looking. You saved yourself for me and stood there pure and righteous. But I wasn't pure. I hadn't been faithful to you.

When I returned to my hometown for my class reunion two months before our wedding, I spent time with my old boyfriend. I let it get out of hand, and things happened. I found out I was pregnant the week of our wedding. When I saw you at the end of the aisle, I couldn't dishonor you like that, so I ran.

He's married and wants no part of me and my little girl. I'm a single mom, working to build a life for me and my daughter. But every day, I think of you. I miss you and who I was when I was with you. I thought it would help if you knew the truth. You did nothing wrong. The mistakes are mine. All mine.

You always said, 'The truth will set you free.' I need to be free. I hope you can forgive me. Please accept my apology. I'm very sorry.

Hoping time has healed at least some of the wounds I inflicted. If you still have any feelings for me, would you be willing to try again? It's asking a lot. I know. But I can't seem to forget you and move on. You're on my heart every day.

Still loving you,

Amy

(505) 442-7302

Tanner folded the fax and handed it to Dylan, who guzzled the last of another Coke as he took a seat at the table. "Dude, that stinks. She stabbed you in the back, and now she's turning the knife."

"I thought I knew her. Count how many times she said 'I.' I didn't see her selfishness so clearly before. She's probably been rejected by her family, which leaves her penniless. She's lonely, desperate, and grasping at straws. But I'm not going to be one of them. I've been down that road."

"What are you going to do?" It wasn't his place to tell Dylan what to do, but Tanner couldn't help but see his relationship with Angie in this. Was Tanner being selfish too?

Dylan shook his head. "It hurts, but I can't trust her. I won't go there again."

Tanner sat forward and looked Dylan in the eye. "She hurt you, but, as a Christian, you have to accept her apology." Would Angie forgive Tanner for his selfishness? Could he forgive her for seeing Mason? "It's scary to risk your heart again. You've healed, and you're ready to go home and start your law practice. You've been working on your faith, and now that this job is coming to an end, it's time to follow God's path for you. In a way, she's done you a favor."

"A favor—how's that?"

"Now you know what happened. She'd been unfaithful, and this fax gives you closure. You're free to make a new start."

"You're right." He clinked the ice in his empty glass, watching it melt under the midday sun. "Is this what you're doing with Angie, forgiving her and making a new start?" He held his hand up. "Don't answer that. It's none of my business." He stood and headed to the lobby. "See you later. I've got a call to make."

Tanner's thoughts went to his mistakes with Angie. He assumed she'd wait for him for almost three years to prove himself successful without keeping constant communication between them. He should have made more trips to Dallas to keep their feelings intact.

At three-thirty, Angie's waiter stood on her porch.

"*Dada, dada*, miss, miss. It is time for your safari. Are you awake? A bottle of cold water is here on your outside table."

"Yes, I am. Thanks." She sat up to keep from dozing off again. The bed felt so good, but adventure waited. She donned a khaki vest and pants, matching sun visor, and designer sunglasses.

At the gift shop, she bought some potato chips and a candy bar imported from Europe, then hurried to the truck and climbed on board.

"Peter, can we see some zebras this afternoon? They're my favorite."

"Yes. A herd is to our east. We will go that way." He started the truck.

"Good afternoon." Buford greeted Angie as they climbed into their row of seats. "Let the fun begin."

Squeals rose from the surrounding forest. "It sounds like the monkeys are upset, Peter." Betty got her camera out of her bag.

"The vervet monkeys have one screech they use as a warning to take to the trees when a leopard is near, and another cry when eagles are approaching, which signals for them to drop to the ground. They work together." Peter cranked the truck and eased them into the rainforest.

One of the vervet monkeys should have been there the day the murderer ran into Angie in Lamu. The moment was seared into her mind. If she'd had any warning, she might have done more than frozen to the spot.

The ride was bumpy as they entered the savanna, but Angie loved letting the wind blow through her hair. It felt freeing.

"I love these flat-topped trees." Angie zoomed in on one with a vulture perched on an extended limb. She snapped a photo, thinking again of the man trying to steal from Grand-Papa's mines and murder Tanner.

"Those are the giraffe's favorite, acacia trees. A neat fact, they do not fight over the leaves. The male eats the higher leaves, and the female eats the lower leaves. The Africans believe demons dance on these trees at night, causing them to be flat on top. But I have never seen them." He spoke as if it were a common occurrence.

In the distance, a group of safari vehicles circled like a wagon train in the Old West. As they grew closer, a lion's roar shivered in the air.

"It is a pride of lions. I will get you closer." Peter eased their truck between a van with the roof raised for its passengers and a privately owned Jeep. There were four young males, two lionesses, and three cubs. Parking seven feet from a female and her nursing cubs, the clicking of cameras filled the air. It made her think of how Tanner nursed her back to health. Tender. Caring.

A distant roar of a large black mane lion woke the two females. One ignored him and finished her nap. The other lioness yawned, stood, and stretched before she roared back in his direction. "That's it, girl. Roar at him, but play hard to get. That's what I do to Tanner. And maybe I shouldn't anymore. Maybe …" She let the thought go. After looking around, the lioness lay down and closed her eyes, ignoring the gawking tourists.

"Angie, I heard you speak of Tanner. Is he your significant other?"

"He was until he broke my heart. He's an amazing man, and I still have strong feelings for him. I guess you could say I'm trying to get my footing again." *Maybe I have been playing too hard to get.*

"Well, don't rush into anything. Wait for complete peace.

The Lord will lead you into the future He has planned for you." Betty reached back and squeezed her hand.

Peace sounded nice. "Thanks, Betty. I needed to hear that today."

When the camera noises stopped, Peter moved them away from the pride. "They sleep during the day, hunt, and eat at night. The females do the hunting, but the males eat first. The lion is the only social cat we have in the Mara. They stay together, hunt together, and eat together."

"Betty, I don't think I've ever told you this."

"What's that, Buford?"

"Betty, there's an elephant behind you." He teased.

She turned. "It's a huge herd."

Angie laughed. A tiny part of her had imagined her and Tanner doing this one day.

Peter steered the Land Cruiser off-road across the plains. "Hang on. This area has pot-holes." He jostled his passengers as they hurried toward the pachyderms.

Angie counted fifteen elephants, including two small babies. The largest female, the matriarch of the herd, led the pack. Her baby struggled to keep up with her stride. The massive elephant's commanding presence and huge tusks confirmed her place at the front of the parade.

"Now, that would be me, a multi-tasker, leading the pack, getting the job done," Angie said. "A mover and a shaker in the business world." But why couldn't she seem to get it together when it came to her love life?

"I can sense that about you, but you would be kind and caring," Buford said.

"Thanks, Buford. Being domineering in the workplace makes everyone uncomfortable."

"I experienced a narcissistic boss at the end of my career.

It's why I retired." Buford watched the lions through binoculars.

"One of the females touches the young ones at least once every five minutes. We believe it is to make them feel secure. Elephants use their trunks to drink, pick up food, smell, and breathe. Sometimes they put their trunks in each other's mouths to say hello."

Peter fell silent, put the truck in reverse, and eased away. The matriarch had noticed their presence and flapped her ears, waving her trunk and showing her agitation. Peter eased them farther back. She trumpeted and charged toward the truck, stirring the dust.

Angie hung on to her camera with white-knuckles and photographed the encounter. Betty and Buford grabbed the seat in front of them, but Peter remained calm. "Do not be alarmed. She is warning us. We are not in danger yet."

The matriarch trumpeted again and charged, her tusks coming dangerously close.

Why was everything in Africa trying to kill Angie this visit?

When they were finally at a safe distance, they breathed a sigh of relief. Angie's heart was beating hard. "I was hanging on, scared. With the acacia trees in the background and the dust stirring at her feet, those shots will make awesome prints!"

"I thought we were in trouble for sure." Buford wiped his forehead with a handkerchief. "Great driving, Peter."

"If she had charged the third time, we would have been in danger. They trumpet when they are angry, scared, or excited."

Peter shifted the truck and took off for a forest area that shadowed a river several kilometers away. He eased the truck into a stand of trees. "A leopard lives in this wooded area. As I drive, look to the trees."

They searched tree after tree, limb from limb, reminding Angie of her search for the murderer. Funny how similar he was to this leopard—hiding, but in places people knew they could find him. Just as Peter predicted, they found a zebra carcass hanging across a branch ten feet off the ground with bee-eaters and starlings perched nearby. Peter stopped the truck, lifted his binoculars, and scanned the trees. They waited and watched.

"I can see marks on the trees where the leopard has climbed to higher elevations." Angie used her strongest lens to look for clues. That reminded her of Mason. *A leopard can't change its spots.* She shook off the thought.

Peter moved the truck slowly forward, scanning the area.

"There he is." Peter pointed to the sleeping leopard on a low branch of another tree.

"He's handsome." Betty focused her lens. "His spotted coat helps him blend into the scenery, to go completely unnoticed. No wonder he was hard to find. You could walk under the tree and never know danger was lurking."

It was strange how much Betty's words resonated with how Angie felt about Mason.

"When the leopard stalks its prey, it is quiet and cunning, approaching its kill with stealth and strength."

Like ambushing her at the Gala. Angie frowned.

"He steals up on the animal of his choice and pounces from close range. He killed the zebra this morning, ate his fill, and pulled his prey into the trees to keep other carnivores from stealing it. He will finish eating it tomorrow. Look, he is waking." Peter said.

"Will he stay there to guard his kill from other predators?" Angie stood for another shot, thinking about how Mason's possessiveness kept her from a lot of things.

"Yes, there is no need for him to leave. He will eat zebra for breakfast." Peter backed the truck out of the thick brush and headed toward the open plains again.

"Since he had a zebra, does this mean we're getting closer to them?" Angie perked up at the prospect. Imagine if she'd listened to Mason, she'd never have had this wonderful safari experience.

"*Ndio,* they are near."

Topping a hill, the sight was a zoo without cages. Zebra, topi, ostrich, and several species of gazelle grazed together. As their safari truck invaded their space, they turned away, giving the photographers a rear view. Peter slowed.

Angie took a photo of the back end of three zebras.

"Betty, I'm going to put that picture at the end of my photo album and write *The End* as the caption." Angie grinned.

"Great idea." Betty got a rear-view shot as well.

"Be ready with your cameras. They will turn and look at you." Which they did. As if posing for the camera, they put their heads on the back of another zebra. The stallion pranced, kicking up dust. The young ones remained close to their mothers for security. What would it be like to have such a large family? To have security. Angie again cut her thoughts off. It was too hard to think about Grand-Papa's future, or lack thereof.

"Peter, tell me about the zebra. Are they white with black stripes or black with white stripes?" Angie talked behind her camera as she focused on a close-up instead of the sorrow in her thoughts.

"They are black with white stripes. They have excellent eyesight, great hearing, and a strong sense of smell. Lions, leopards, cheetahs, and hyenas kill them for food. Most of these are a harem of females and one stallion. They sleep standing up. If a lion or leopard is near, they bray."

"You love them as much as I do."

SHIRLEY GOULD

Peter smiled.

"Are they called a herd of zebras?" Angie zoomed out to take a panoramic shot.

"No, they are called a dazzle of zebra."

"A dazzle. I like that."

Leaving the dazzle, they traveled a dusty road. The sun was descending in an apricot sky, the weary travelers heading back to camp, tired from the bumpy ride and chilled by the cooling temperatures of nightfall. At the gate, Peter told them when to meet for an early morning game drive. "We will take a boxed breakfast and eat while we watch the wildebeest and zebra cross crocodile-infested waters. It is a sight few get to witness because they only do this during the migration season. *La la salama*, rest well."

After bidding her safari companions goodnight, Angie went to the restaurant to request dinner be served in her tent. She'd pushed her body, and the remnants of malaria were taking their toll, so rest was crucial to prevent a relapse.

With a cup of tea in hand, her mind replayed the feel of being in Tanner's arms, of him sleeping on the end of her bed, and the look of desperation in his eyes when she talked about being engaged. She could sense his pain, but couldn't risk her own heart again.

Or could she?

Considering Betty and Buford's counsel today, she took their words to heart. Being away from Dallas was giving her a new perspective. Mason's controlling ways were not good for Ward Enterprises or her personally. She took her concerns to the Lord in prayer as she watched God paint the African sky across the Serengeti Plains. *Lord, I feel you have quieted me during this time away. I'm seeing things more clearly and sense you leading me in matters of the heart. Please continue to guide and direct me in the relationship issues I'm facing. Thank you for the many blessings you've given me. I'm so appreciative. Direct my path, Lord. I trust you ... Amen.*

∼

Tanner chose a chaise lounge by the pool and stretched out. His mind churned about the Angie situation. She wasn't the spoiled child shadowing his every move. She wasn't the debutante he thought she'd become either. She was a conundrum who loved dirty street kids, braved the unknown seeking justice, and with a wave of her hand, she'd transformed the inn into a paradise. She was a treasure to be cherished, but he'd messed up their relationship. He questioned his heart, weighing his options. Without answers, he sighed and hid his eyes behind some sunglasses.

"These are called lounge chairs for a reason."

Tanner lifted his shades and eyed Dylan, taking the chair beside him. "What?"

"You're supposed to lounge, relax, enjoy the view, and soak up some sun. Take in this gorgeous seascape. But, no, you're stiff as a board and blowing off steam like a hippo coming up for air. What's eating you?" Dylan flipped his shoes off.

"It's Angie. She's marrying a suit—a self-serving suit. I've known him for years. He struts his stuff when he enters the Ward Estate as if he is royalty, but he's got dollar signs in his eyes when he looks at Angie. He's a skunk. I can feel it in my bones. He's vying for power, prestige, and position, and she's a pawn in his game."

"Sounds like you've got it bad." Dylan poured a Coke over ice. "Are you going to go down without a fight, or are you planning your attack?"

"What can I do? Angie doesn't see his manipulation like I do. I can read him like a book. She said everyone leaves her, and Mason doesn't." Tanner put his sunglasses back on and attempted to relax.

"And you left her, so you're feeling bad while you know he's up to no good. Quite a dilemma." Dylan frowned, his gaze going long, probably thinking about Amy.

"I know." Tanner had no doubt.

"Want me to check him out?" He gulped the cold liquid.

"What do you mean?" Tanner leaned forward. "You can do that?"

"I'm a lawyer, from a family of lawyers with private investigators on retainer. Research is the name of the game. We can see where he went to preschool, when he had his teeth capped, and his favorite crush in junior high, in the snap of a finger. I can start an investigation today. Just give me the go-ahead."

Tanner thought for a minute. "He wouldn't find out?"

"Nope, totally confidential. We're good at what we do." Dylan got comfortable.

"Yeah, send a private eye after him. I want to know what he's up to." Maybe if Dylan found something, he could show it to Angie. Give her proof Mason was no good for her.

"I'll get it done. I'm glad to help. One email will get the wheels rolling." Dylan opened his iPad and turned it on. "No bars today. Can I get your laptop and use dial-up?"

"Sure. Do your thing, catch the slime ball, and I'll hang him out to dry."

Chapter Nine

Angie pulled herself out of bed. Not wanting to miss a minute, she climbed into the safari truck and wrapped herself in warm blankets to ward off the chill of darkness. They reached the Masai Mara's edge as the sun crested the Ngong Hills, where the movie *Out of Africa* had been filmed. As morning dawned, flocks of birds launched into the mist, ready to start their day. With the migration in full swing, safari vehicles were strategically parked for the best views. The crocodiles waited for breakfast to be served.

Hundreds of wildebeest, otherwise known as gnu, from the antelope family, and dazzles of zebra milled around, nervous about jumping into the fast-moving water. Their increased numbers forced them forward. The wildebeest hesitated, remembering danger lurking in the muddy drink, their young ones at risk. A female zebra plunged into the river, leading the way on their courageous trek for greener pastures. The dazzle followed her.

"You go, girl. That's what I'd do." Angie cheered her on. "Make a decision. Take on the task. Lead the way, leaving those indecisive gnu, wildebeest, behind in the muddy water."

After pacing back and forth at the water's edge, the wildebeest plunged in, catching the eye of a fifteen-foot crocodile, which slipped into the river and eased their direction. Cruel and calculating, the reptile wove his way toward the herd, watching for a wildebeest to make a false move.

He reminds me of Mason—though sometimes he outwardly seems kind, there's something insidious underneath that façade. Why haven't I seen this before? I'm getting out of my murky situation—onto greener pastures.

Angie attempted to eat her breakfast, taking photos between bites. Vultures circled overhead, waiting to feast on the croc's leftovers. The grunts of the gnu competed with the zebra brays as sleeping hippos lounged upriver, ignoring the chaos. When the croc took a young wildebeest, Angie couldn't watch. "Buford, did he make it?"

"No, he was on the breakfast menu."

"I know it's the circle of life, but it's still sad." Angie gave up on finishing her breakfast, not caring if it was her slow recovery from malaria or the gruesome sight before her that stalled her appetite.

"What a way to start a day," Betty said.

Angie couldn't agree more. A tough sight over breakfast, but the opportunity was a once-in-a-lifetime experience, and Angie was determined to appreciate it despite her seemingly failing health today. "It doesn't get better than this." She stored her video camera and picked up her digital camera for still shots.

"You've got that right. It's nature at its best." Angie took a couple more shots of the gnu mid-air as they launched themselves into the murky river.

Static on Peter's CB radio gave him a message only he could interpret. Without a word, he took off in another direction. They covered about three kilometers and joined a group of safari vehicles. Their passengers gawked at something to the left. Everyone huddled on one side, trying to catch a view.

Peter eased their truck between two others. A mother cheetah stood amid the onlookers, scanning the landscape for possible prey, as she protected her three cubs. Unable to see beyond the vehicles, she jumped on the hood of Peter's truck, rocking them inside with the impact of her weight, and everyone aboard didn't dare speak.

Angie took some amazing shots, then reached for Betty's camera and motioned for them to turn around. They smiled as she took a picture with the cheetah directly behind them.

When she rejoined her cubs, Peter drove them toward an area where vultures circled over a kill. Hyenas feasted on the carcass of a wildebeest.

"Peter, did the hyena kill the wildebeest?" Betty's gaze never left the bloody fight over the meat.

"There are lion prints in the mud, so I think lions killed the gnu. They ate some of the meat before the hyenas took their turn. Jackals are waiting in the high grasses to eat. The vultures will be last to clean the bones."

"An African pecking order," Angie added to his explanation.

Peter drove to their tent camp. "Be at the truck at four o'clock for your afternoon safari."

"Don't wait for me. I'm recovering from malaria and must rest this afternoon." Angie told the group. "I need to return to Mombasa on tomorrow morning's flight."

"We'll miss you, my dear." Betty patted her hand.

Buford gave her a fatherly smile.

After a much-needed nap, Angie toured the tent camp with camera in hand, pausing on the sidewalk for a warthog family to pass. The runt of the group stopped, looked at Angie, snorted, then hurried on, tail in the air like an antenna.

As dusk settled, Angie decided to turn in. She snuggled under her down comforter as darkness swallowed the day, bringing a chilly drop in temperature and memories of her warm whirlpool tub back home.

The next morning, when Peter got her to the airstrip, Angie hugged Betty and shook Buford's hand. "I've had a wonderful time. Betty and Buford, I've enjoyed the memories we've shared."

Angie climbed out of the truck and placed some shillings in Peter's palm. She knew it was wise to return to the inn because she was still so weak and shaky. If her fever rose again, she could relapse and didn't want to be alone if that happened. She'd ventured out too soon.

"We wish you the best." Betty hugged her again.

Buford waved. "Enjoy the rest of your time in Kenya."

With time to think, she made a decision to end things with Mason, to take Tanner up on his offer for them to team up in the search for the murderer, in hopes their time together could heal their wounded relationship.

On her return trip to the inn, Angie used her phone to click random shots. She didn't want to offend the people but wanted to capture the city at its best. An old man pushed a wheelbarrow loaded with pineapples, and a woman struggled under a load of wood tied on her back. Vendors sold fruits and vegetables, repaired bicycle tires, and built caskets. People with disabilities begged from everyone who passed by, pulling at Angie's heartstrings.

As they entered the gates of Paradise Inn, Angie breathed a sigh of relief. The safety and seclusion of the resort shone brightly in this dark place. She paid the driver and hurried through the lobby. Hearing Samson singing in the kitchen, she decided to slip to her bungalow for a nap. The cozy bed was calling her name.

With his team assembled in the remodeled Veranda Restaurant, Tanner instructed the group. "We'll return to the mine tomorrow morning. Security will be heightened. Watch for anything suspicious. Let's finish the vein we were working on. Working together, we should be able to close it up within a couple of days." He paused. He'd lost their attention. They were staring at something behind him. Curiosity made him turn—beauty made him stand.

"Angie—you're back."

"Yes. I returned this afternoon." The warm breeze off the ocean ruffled her gauzy white sundress, accenting her tan. Onyx hair framed her beautiful face and tanzanite blue eyes.

Seconds stretched. No one moved.

"Please don't let me interrupt your meeting." She stepped back to give them space.

Tanner moved to her side, placing his hand on the small of her back. "No, let me introduce you to my team." They edged close to the table.

"The blond is Dylan Calloway. He's a lawyer and is working as the foreman on this job. Next to him is Drew Winslow, the one with the mining expertise in the group. And this is Victoria Becker. She goes by Vickie. She's our gemologist. Team, this is Angelica Ward. You can call her Angie."

"I saw most of you working at the mine when I arrived. It's nice to meet you in person." Angie told the group.

"It's nice we finally met. I've heard a lot about you, Angie." Dylan came around the table to shake her hand.

Drew touched the bill of his ball cap. "Hi, Angie. I like what you've done to the place."

Vickie extended her hand toward Angie. "Well, I guess I missed the conversations about you. Tanner *must* fill me in." She put her hand on Tanner's arm like a lioness marking her territory. "Can't we finish our meeting tomorrow and ask Angie to join us for dinner? The food is almost ready."

Angie stiffened under Tanner's touch. "Finishing up tomorrow is a great idea, Vickie."

"You three enjoy your meal. I'm taking Angie out for dinner. We have a lot of catching up to do. Dylan, let Samson know of the change."

"Sure, you two have fun." Dylan tossed him the keys to the Land Cruiser and headed toward the kitchen.

Tanner led her to the Toyota and opened her door. Angie blushed. "Sorry, I interrupted your meeting."

"I'm not." He closed her door, slid into the driver's seat, and cranked the five-speed SUV. He didn't want Vickie to say anything about the run-down hotel being a front for the mining assignment. Vickie was a blabbermouth. It would be better if they separated from the group so he could see how Angie was recovering from malaria. Maybe an opportunity might present itself for him to explain why Ward left Paradise Inn in such a disarray. If not, he'd have to have a word with his team again, reminding them to keep the inn's backstory quiet.

As he drove through the gate, Angie put her window down. "Stop, I need to see the children."

Before Tanner could warn her about street kids robbing

people, she extended her hands, touching dirty faces and calling them by name.

"Thank you for cleaning the entrance area while I was sick."

Their smiles proved they shared a backstory he'd have to ask her about. They also showed Angie had won their hearts. Not unsimilar to how she'd won his.

Tanner shook his head as he pulled into the busy Mombasa traffic.

"What?"

"You never cease to amaze me. You're taking on those kids, aren't you?"

"Yes. They helped clean up Paradise Inn. I've been making sure Samson feeds them. I hope that's all right. They call me a nice, smart *mzungu*."

"*Mzungu*, you know what that means?"

"It means white person."

Tanner smiled. "Many years ago, it meant a crazy white man sailing around the world, namely Christopher Columbus. But today, it means a multi-tasking white woman talking fast and moving faster, going in circles. And, by the looks of Paradise Inn, that's what you've been doing."

"It did take some doing—"

"And calling you smart, they don't mean intelligent. They mean sharp-looking or pretty."

"That's good to know."

He shifted gears and eased through a roundabout right into a traffic jam. He ignored the horns honking around them and caught Angie watching him.

"You see my mom lately?"

"Yeah, right before I left. She's good, just busy, running the estate like a pro."

"That's Mom. I'm ready for her to retire and enjoy life. She deserves it."

"She may choose to retire after Grand-Papa is gone." Angie turned toward her window. "Everything will change when he passes."

Tanner thought he heard her sniff. "I'm sorry he's sick, Angie."

"Yeah, me too. Thanks."

She brushed moisture from her cheek as they pulled in front of the Tamarind Restaurant, famous around the world for its seafood.

"I love the food here, and the ambiance beats Paradise Inn with the rowdy inhabitants. And I wanted us to be able to talk without listening ears."

"I appreciate it, Tanner."

After being seated, Tanner ordered dinner, took a drink of bottled water, and broached a sore subject. "So, how is Mason Malone, your fiancé?"

"You want to talk about him?" She put her linen napkin on her lap.

"You don't?" He placed his glass in front of his plate and locked gazes with Angie. "There are so many things to discuss, so many things we should have already said, but we've danced around them for too long." He let his gaze drop to his hands steepled between him and his plate. He had to get this right. Had to reach her. If not for him, then for her.

"You've never liked him." Angie's eyes hardened on him.

He refused to devolve into their earlier antics and forced himself to remain focused on their purpose. "But you do."

"Tanner, he's worked his way to the top of the corporate ladder, he's respected in the business world, and is quite charming."

Tanner, needing something to do with his hands, shook his

napkin out of the decorative fold and dropped it across his legs. "That's a given, but have you considered it's the power and prestige he loves? He wears status on his sleeve like a badge, and with you as his wife, he'd be set for life." He could tell he'd hit a nerve when Angie pierced him with a look, but he kept going because this had to be said. "He rubs me the wrong way. I've never trusted the guy, and I don't want him adding *you* to his list of achievements."

Angie grew very still. She unfolded her napkin and took her time placing it in her lap. Then her gaze hit Tanner's with an almost physical force. "It's interesting your focus is all on Mason and not on the things you've done, or not done. You're being pretty hard on Mason when maybe you should be doing some soul searching yourself." She paused and sipped her soda. "Do you believe people can change?"

"A leopard can't change its spots." Tanner took a drink of water.

"Well, the jury is still out on that one." A familiar humor winked out from Angie's tight smile.

A fragrant aroma filled their space as the waiter placed a platter between them.

"What's this?"

"It's baked ostrich with prawns, or shrimp, as you call it in the States. Taste it. It's great."

She took a bite and chewed slowly as if savoring the flavor. "It's delicious. Good choice."

"Glad you like it." He cut his serving of ostrich.

"I'm tired of talking about Mason. Let's talk about you, Tanner. What happened? Did you lose interest in me? I waited for your calls, texts, and letters. They didn't—"

"Angie." He reached for her hand. "I'm so sorry. When I started this project, my singular focus was to rush it to completion so we could be together. But when I realized the danger of working below the ground, combined with the heightened possibility of being robbed as we took the stones out of the ground, I was overwhelmed with the vast responsibility as the leader. In retrospect, I should have communicated my situation to you. It was too dangerous for you to visit, and I had trouble leaving this responsibility to someone else. Since the project was coming to an end, I wanted to make future plans with you when I came to your gala."

"And we both know how that played out." She squeezed his calloused hand. "I wish you had shared this with me."

"I do too." He rubbed his thumb across the back of her hand.

"Let's finish our meal before it gets cold." She released his hand and tasted her entrée.

"Their desserts are amazing too." He offered her some bread from the basket on their table. They ate in amenable silence while listening to Kenny G's saxophone over the speakers.

"Penny for your thoughts." Tanner put his napkin by his plate.

"You're different. You're very secure in who you are as the leader of this assignment. I think Africa agrees with you."

He smiled. "Is that a good thing?"

"It is for Ward Enterprises."

Tanner scanned the restaurant and signaled for their waiter.

"Something wrong?"

"Not sure. I have a feeling we're being watched. You mind if we skip dessert?" He motioned for his bill when he caught the eye of the manager of the Tamarind.

"Sure. I'm stuffed. Great food."

"I'm glad you liked it." He counted out some shillings as he talked. "Samson should have something sweet at the inn if you change your mind." Placing ample shillings in the vinyl folder, he stood and helped Angie with her chair in one smooth move. His eyes roved the dining area as they made their exit, and he caught sight of Wycliff lingering outside on the patio, waiting for their exit. Tanner put his arm around Angie, protecting her, liking how she pressed into the safety of his presence.

On the sidewalk, he couldn't resist pulling her tighter and leaning into her like they once did years ago. "Play along, we're being watched. Wycliff has seen us."

She loved being in his arms, breathing his cologne, and relishing in his protection. Where would she be if he weren't there tonight? Dead. Tanner had instincts she had never noticed before. He was powerful and handsome.

He held her tight against his body, blocking her view of the murderer.

Tanner turned. "Angie, get behind me."

Wycliff lunged from the shadows.

"Tanner, watch out."

"Run for the truck." Tanner parried a blow from Wycliff and threw two that hit the murderer hard. He went down.

"Angie, go now." Tanner placed a guiding hand on her back and hurried her toward the truck. A crowd was forming outside the restaurant, and sirens blared in the distance. "I'm right behind you. Let's get out of here."

In the truck, Tanner's gaze analyzed their surroundings. "I don't see him anymore. Let's go."

"He's just going to try again. We have to find a way to make this stop. You can't live like this forever. And what if—"

"If he didn't recognize me in Lamu, he knows I'm alive

now. You're right. We need to find out where he's hiding."
Tanner maneuvered the traffic like a pro. "Hang on, Angie. This
could get bumpy."

"Don't worry about me. I'm just glad you're here to get us
out of there." She held the armrest as the truck hit a deep
pothole, and Tanner swerved. Things couldn't go on like this.
The danger left her weak. But another truth edged into the
recesses of her mind, pushing its way through the fear closing
in on her. Her heart ached for what had slipped through her
fingers.

"Excuse me, gentlemen." Mason stood to leave the late evening
meeting in the boardroom with his cell cupped in his hand. "I
must take this call."

"Mason Malone here."

"Hello from Kenya, *bwana*."

"I'm in a meeting. Do you have something for me?" He
paced the corridor.

"I have found the man, Zarello." Wycliff's voice came in
winded puffs.

"That's good news, very good news. You'll be compensated
for your trouble. Follow him closely." Mason checked if anyone
was in earshot.

"He has gone with a woman, lost to me for now. What
should be done with the woman when I find them again?"

"What woman?" Mason froze mid-stride, then hurried to
his office and shut the door.

"The American woman with ebony hair."

Angelica.

"She is there with Zarello?"

"Yes, *bwana*. He was holding her close to him outside the

restaurant by the coast. The woman complicated things. I was not sure of your wishes and didn't want to make another error."

In Tanner's arms ... Reconnecting with him thwarts my plan ... now she's gone too far.

"Hear me well. She isn't to be harmed. Do you understand?"

Unbelievable. She's with Zarello.

"Yes, *bwana*, I understand. She is not to be hurt. I will complete the job you have hired me to do."

"I'm starting to wonder if you are capable of such a task."

"Yes, *bwana*. I will take care of things as you've instructed."

"Exactly as I've instructed. Do not fail me."

Mason punched the Off button, reined in his anger, and took a couple of deep breaths before returning to the meeting in progress, taking his seat beside Alexander Ward.

Joseph stood between them, showing their employer a chart. Joseph moved his portfolio, knocking Mason's phone to the floor.

"Sorry, I'll get it for you." Joseph bent to retrieve the cell and put it by Mason's hand on the table as the last number displayed across the screen.

"Thanks, Joseph." Mason turned the cell face down.

"You with us, Malone? You seem distracted as of late." Ward's intense stare was unreadable. Had he glanced at the area code on his phone? No way he could suspect anything. Mason had been upstanding in every interaction with the sick man.

"Yes, sir. I'm concerned about Angelica traveling to Kenya alone." Mason's palms were sweaty. "But it hasn't affected my work. Did you see the report I left on your desk?" His gut churned.

"My granddaughter has a good head on her shoulders. I

wouldn't have sent her if I didn't know she could get the job done, which she did. She is safe at Paradise Inn. Let's focus on the matters at hand, shall we?" Ward returned to his agenda.

Mason attempted to interact, to look engaged, but under the façade, he was livid at Ward's dismissal.

Chapter Ten

After Tanner held Angie in his arms, smelled her perfume, and stared into those deep blue eyes, he knew he'd give his life for her. Once in the safety of Paradise Inn, he breathed a sigh of relief and relaxed his grip on the steering wheel.

"You okay?" Tanner stared across the Land Cruiser at Angie, reading worry in her eyes.

"No, I'm not okay. A killer just came after you with a knife, Zarello, and you don't seem shook up at all. This is serious, and you could have been hurt. Weren't you afraid? My stomach is in knots." She opened her door, stepped out of the truck, and turned in his direction. "You want something to drink? I need some tea to settle my insides."

"Tell Samson I want *chai*, tea, Kenyan style. I'll join you in a couple of minutes."

She saluted and strode toward the kitchen, the ocean breeze blowing her hair.

Taking the steps to his upstairs office suite, he hurried inside and placed first a phone call to secure additional guards for the inn and then an overseas video conference call on his

177

laptop. He tapped a pencil on his desk. The threat to his life had come too close and endangered Angie. This guy had to be stopped. The pencil broke in his hand as Alexander Ward's face appeared on his laptop's screen.

"Tanner. How are things with the investigation, and how's my granddaughter?"

"Hello, sir. Things are progressing. The police are doing the best they can. They're understaffed and using antiquated methods. We've got to catch him soon. The danger has become real tonight. I called to tell you the murderer knows he killed the wrong man."

"You sure?" Ward's brows furrowed.

"Yes, sir. Tonight, he spotted Angie and me at a restaurant in Mombasa and lunged at us with a knife."

"Was Angelica in danger?" Ward moved closer to the screen.

"No, sir, I put myself between her and any threat. I won't let anything happen to Angie. She's safe." Tanner sighed. "I've hired extra guards for the inn and the mine. This will come to a head soon."

"Be careful and watch your back. I'm praying for your safety. Keep an eye on Angelica. She's all I have left."

"I understand, sir. I do."

Ward ended the call.

The lights of a cruise ship eased across the horizon, slipping out of sight like Angie's relationship with Tanner had, without fanfare. Recurring waves slapped the shore with high tide's force, erasing all imprints left on the sand. She wished it could do that to her heart.

Samson served tea and cake while Tanner joined Angie at the table.

"Thanks, Samson. That will be all for tonight. Get some rest."

"*Asante, bwana.*" Samson bid them a good evening.

"Your grandfather asked about you." Tanner stirred sugar into his tea.

"You called him?"

"Yes, giving him an update about the murderer, knowing I'm alive. I think he'll make another move soon." He blew on his tea, cooling it.

"You think he'll try to take you out again? If that was his plan, wouldn't he have tried harder tonight? You were a sitting duck." Angie furrowed her brow.

"There were too many witnesses." Tanner sipped his *chai*.

She dipped her cake in chocolate sauce. "How did Grand-Papa look? I hate being gone this long."

"Tired. But he didn't complain. He was worried about you."

"And?" She waited.

"I told him you were safe and sound at Paradise Inn. Is the cake good? Sometimes their cakes are dry." He picked up a fork to taste.

"It's pretty good. Samson brought some chocolate sauce to put on it. You want some? The syrup mitigates the dryness." She reined in her emotions and was pleasant as he doused his dessert in a Hershey's imitation. "Dylan and I were talking about Wycliff. He's been covering a lot of kilometers to hide from you and the police, which is extremely expensive. What if someone is behind this with deep pockets and a vicious ulterior motive?" Angie took her notes out of her sundress pocket.

"What are you, a private eye?"

"I did take a forensics course at the university. I love the

179

challenge of putting the pieces together and solving a mystery."

"Well, officer." He teased. "No enemies. I've been welcomed and have met all the legal requirements to be here." He leaned over to read her notes. "What else have you come up with?"

"Seriously?"

"Yeah, let me hear it." He leaned forward, elbows on the table, his fingers steepled.

"I know you're concerned about your team because they could get hurt if they got in the way. But he's after you. You were supposed to be the first one in the mine. It's you he ran from in Lamu. Tonight, he was watching you, then following you."

She turned a page in her notes. "On a different subject—do you think the police could be in on it? There's always someone who can be bought." She finished her tea and pushed the cup away.

"You're probably right, but I feel good about the officers working this case. They seem honest and persistent." He licked the chocolate off his fork. "So, what's our next move?"

"This is serious, Tanner. I got the extension on the mining permit, and I understand you wanting to complete this project. But a murderer is after you. We need to get you home safe and shut down the mine. Grand-Papa won't care about a few tanzanite staying below ground if your life is in danger. Let's get out of Kenya. Let the police take it from here. He got too close to you tonight." She stared and took the fork out of his hand.

"So did you. But you didn't seem to mind." He held up his hand to keep her from speaking. "I need you to trust me, Angie. I know how serious this situation is, and I plan to check in with the investigator first thing in the morning and formulate a plan. I'll let you know what's decided."

She stood to leave, biting her bottom lip as she pushed her chair in. *He's going to get himself killed.* Shaking her head, she closed her notebook.

"Ang—you may be right about the funds coming from someone else. It's better to catch the guy here, so we can flush out whoever is behind this, or it will follow us home."

"Follow us? Are you coming home, Tanner?" She waited.

"Thanks to you, the work can continue at the mine. But the rising water is bringing this job to a close. I'll finish it for your grandfather and see what he plans for my future. So, yes. I'll move stateside soon."

"I'm glad." She held his gaze. "Thank you for dinner. I'm going to turn in now." She didn't move.

"You're welcome." He stared. "Angie?" He stood and touched her arm, keeping her from leaving.

She took a deep breath. Looked at his hand on her arm. Then met his eyes again. "First, I come face to face with you, I'm successful in acquiring the mining permit for you, but I get malaria and can't leave right away."

"I know." He leaned closer.

"We go to dinner, almost like a date, and we leave suddenly, and you protected me as if you cared."

"I do."

"You drove like a maniac because a murderer could be chasing us."

"Anyone would."

"My grandfather is dying, and I need to be home. His days are numbered. What I think about this case doesn't matter."

He eased closer, slipping his arm around her shoulders. "I'm sorry, Angie. This is more than you bargained for. Africa's a dangerous place."

"Tanner, I want off this emotional roller-coaster."

"Your grandfather looked good today, and we'll get you home as soon as the doctor releases you to travel. I'm proud of your educational accomplishments." He brushed a tear off her cheek. "I do care about you. We have history—but you're engaged. Things can't be like they were." He tightened his arms around her. If only the situation were different, and he still loved her like she loved him.

"I'm praying they get the guy."

"Me too. Get some rest. Hang around here tomorrow. I'll call you with the plan." He kissed her forehead.

She eased out of his embrace and started toward her bungalow. After she took three steps, she turned back. He was still watching her. "Goodnight, Tanner."

"Goodnight, Angie."

Mason Malone strutted through the halls of the high-rise, greeting the main players of Ward Enterprises as he went. *It's good for them to see my face from time to time, considering upcoming leadership changes.*

Once in the parking garage, he placed an overseas call as he pulled his Jaguar into the flow of Dallas traffic. He loved the feel of driving such a powerful machine, knowing he looked good behind the wheel. The click of static plagued the connection.

"Hello, *bwana*."

"Wycliff, how are things in Kenya?" Mason stopped at a red light.

"They are good. I am making preparations to do as you have requested, but there is a great deal to accomplish with little manpower. Is there something else you need from me?" The overseas line echoed, repeating everything Wycliff said.

"Yes, I understand. Hire an additional man to help carry out our plan. I'll reimburse you for his pay when you get to Texas." Mason merged into the left lane and took the ramp to the Interstate, racing toward home.

"*Asante, bwana.* That will help. There is a man I have worked with before. He's good at what he does and can be trusted. I will speak to you *hivi karabuni.*"

"What does that mean? Speak English."

"Soon, *bwana.* It means very soon." He ended the call.

Mason tossed his cell into the passenger seat and opened the sunroof on his Jag, allowing cooler temps to fill the car. He maneuvered through evening traffic across Dallas, taking the Broadway exit. He pulled into the Palms restaurant parking lot and allowed a valet to park for him. Meeting friends from the office, he took a seat between two lovely ladies who worked at Ward Enterprises' crowded table and ordered a drink for himself, taking in the large group of frequent partygoer employees. Having these relationships could be advantageous in the near future. Every king needs subjects, and this group would give him the respect he had earned. After enjoying their company and a wonderful meal, he'd see where the evening took him.

Tanner paced the police headquarters as he waited for his appointment, the linoleum gritty under his feet. A receptionist noted his presence on a pad of paper, duplicated by the carbon paper she'd inserted. Sweat chased tension down his back, predicting it was going to be a scorcher on the East African coast. Rotary phones rang, and officers shuffled from their desks to the interrogation rooms, then back again. Each focused on their respective tasks, unaffected by the chaos of their workplace.

"Mr. Zarello, please follow me." The receptionist led him down a hall and opened the third door on the right, leaving him in the doorway. The police investigator stood to greet him.

"Hello, Zarello. Please have a seat." Officer Karani flipped a couple of pages in his spiral notebook. "On the phone, you said the man we're after has found you." He leaned back in his squeaky desk chair.

"Yes, outside the Tamarind Restaurant last night. We had just finished dinner when I sensed someone watching us. I didn't see him until we were leaving the building."

"You said 'we.' Who was with you?" He held his pen ready to write.

"Angie, Angelica Ward. Her grandfather owns the mine where the incident took place."

Karani made a note. "Did he approach or threaten either of you in any way?"

"Yes. He came at me with a knife. Stared at my face, then fled the scene. I don't know if he followed us, but I made sure to lose him in traffic."

"Has your office made any headway on the case?"

"Yes, we've discovered he has a record."

"He's a repeat offender."

Karani nodded. "He and an accomplice robbed some missionaries last year, where he left a shoe print that matches the one we printed at the murder scene. Kenyans don't have a lot of shoes, which means they wear one pair until they are gone. That aids our investigation. We've been trying to track him, but he hasn't returned to his sister's apartment, so we're fairly certain he's been staying in hotels, changing his location often to keep us from finding him."

"Miss Ward thinks he's getting funds from someone in the States. Is that possible?"

"Whether the money is coming from overseas or not, I do not know. But he's being funded from somewhere. A Kenyan doesn't have the shillings to frequent these hotels." He checked his notes. "Our suspect has been in the States recently. I'll have that itinerary and see about locations he frequented this afternoon."

"Good. I'd like to know what cities he visited, and if you can track hotels he stopped at or restaurants he ate at, that would be helpful too."

"Do you have an idea who might have ordered an attempt on your life?" Karani leaned forward, his fingers hovering over his notepad.

Tanner shook his head. "Nothing concrete yet. Will you call me when you get that information?" Tanner stood to leave. With his hand on the doorknob, he pivoted and faced the officer. "Do you think he's after the tanzanite, or is it me he wants?"

"It looks like you're his target, especially after he tried to take you out at the restaurant. It was your turn to go first in the mine the day your employee died, and Wycliff didn't rob the mine the day he watched your team. Why don't you stay out of sight until we catch him? Spend some time at that resort Ward owns on the ocean." He eyed Tanner from across the room.

Tanner rubbed the back of his neck and considered his options. *Spend time with Angie? She doesn't love Mason. Does that mean she still has feelings for me?* "If I do that, I can't leave my team exposed. I would have to pull them off the job, and our permit is good for two and a half more months, but the mine is filling with water, which will bring the project to a halt very soon."

"Why don't you help me follow a couple of leads today and

do some surveillance this afternoon? We're short, and I could use an extra set of eyes. Then, tomorrow you can pull your team off?" He pocketed his pen.

"You have a point. Are these leads credible?"

"I think so. I'd like to catch him before he tries again." He grabbed his notebook and keys and led the way to their vehicles. "I will explain as we walk. There's a pattern in his activity. He lived in Lamu for three years. He may have owed some money or had a relative there he wanted to visit before leaving the country. Then he traveled to his home village and left some shillings with his father. It looks like he is tying up loose ends, getting ready to make a move. Which is why I'm certain he will visit his sister before he gets on a plane."

Angie's group of street kids had grown to eight, each child with a story of loss and hardship. There were seven boys and one sweet girl named Sophie, who would slip her hand into Angie's when they were walking, tugging on Angie's emotions since she'd been an orphan at this same age. *How many times did I want to hold my mother's hand after she was gone?*

"Sophie, what happened to your mama?" Angie squatted in front of the child and pinned her hair out of her face.

"My mama was sick." Sophie stared at Angie with wide eyes.

"Oh, no. What did she have?"

"Typhoid, then she got malaria and died."

Going through malaria was hard enough. Having it on the heels of another illness would be impossible. "That must have been so hard, Sophie. I'm sorry."

"It made me cry."

"Did you have to live in the streets after her death?" Angie stood and walked toward the beach, with Sophie's small hand in hers.

"*Ndio,* Robert is my brother. He finds food for me." She smiled, a tooth missing in her grin.

"Robert is a good boy for taking care of you like that. I'm glad you're here." Angie thought of her efforts with the gala. They weren't enough. She could do more. She had to.

"*Asante, dada.* Thanks, miss."

Julius kept an eye on the kids when they were at the inn. Today, the street boys swept the beach area till it was smooth and clean. Their brooms were made of a limb about two inches in diameter they'd cut and trimmed by hand. They tied several leafy twigs to one end. When it lost its leaves and would no longer sweep properly, they would replace the leafless twigs with new ones.

"Great job, guys. You're very hard workers." She touched Robert's shoulder, shook hands with Njiri, who bowed slightly as his tribe was known to do, and patted Taso's fuzzy head.

They soaked in her praise like dry sponges meeting water.

"Miss Angeleeka, you have guests." Julius pointed down the coastline.

Angie put her hand across her brows, shading her eyes so she could see the approaching entourage of men and camels. The men had a different look about them, sharper, chiseled features. Their skin was a different shade of brown, and their eyes were piercing and deep-set. Their flowing white robes and turbans bespoke of Arabian descent.

Julius greeted the men in Swahili. They instructed their three camels to sit on the sand. After disembarking, the men each shook Julius' hand. The leader of the group turned to Angie and smiled, a grin resembling a broken picket fence. She returned the gesture, flashing her perfectly maintained pearly whites.

He spoke to Julius, who interpreted for Angie. "He wants to know if the children want to ride the camels. Every day, he walks the beach, passing the hotels, offering camel rides. It is their way to make shillings."

"Where are they from?" Angie eyed the men. "Are they safe? The kids would love an adventure."

"Somalia, the country northeast of Kenya, and yes, they will not harm the children."

"Ask him how much he charges for each ride. Tell him they're orphans, and I require a fair price for the group." Angie placed her hands on her hips.

Julius conversed with the Somalian, then turned to Angie. "He wants five hundred shillings per camel."

"Tell him I'll pay four hundred shillings per camel, and ask how many children we can put on each camel." Her bargaining skills were shining. Hearing the kids giggle was worth ninety dollars any day.

Julius smiled and negotiated. "He said you can put as many children as you want on each camel."

She turned to the kids. "Do you want to ride the camels?"

Nicolas and Robert were the first to say 'yes.' The others took a little coaxing. "*Ndio*, Miss Angeleeka. We would like to ride the animals." Taso spoke for the shy group.

"Will you ride with us?" Sophie begged.

"Sure. I'll get some shillings and my camera. Would you stay with the kids for a moment, Julius?" Angie strode toward her room, gathered her things, and returned quickly.

With the kids loaded, the camels lunged forward as they raised their back feet, then threw their passengers backward as they stood on their front, which brought squeals from all aboard.

"Julius, take our picture as we ride and tell them to hang on."

"I will do it as I walk alongside the other camel." Julius hurried alongside the younger children as they rode.

"Is this sand hot on their feet?" Angie lifted her voice above the children's excited chattering.

Julius translated her question for the camel herders. "No, Miss Angeleeka. They have a layer of fat on the bottom of their feet that protects them from the heat of the sand."

"God made them that way so they could adapt. Amazing." She listened to her giggling young friends, enjoying their adventure.

Moving slowly, swaying from side to side, the dromedaries carried their passengers a kilometer down the coast, then turned for their return voyage. The experience, the children's laughter, the stares from tourists at neighboring resorts, the pictures Julius captured, would be a memory Angie would cherish when times grew sad, and times of sadness were approaching all too fast. It was not every day an American woman rode a camel led by Somali men on a beach in Africa with eight street children in ragged clothes.

Afterward, the experience left the smell of camels on the group. As the Somalis and their dromedaries grew smaller in the distance, Angie gathered the children under the shade of a palm tree.

"Julius, ask Samson for cold sodas for me and my guests." She led the way toward the resort, trailed by eight pairs of sandy feet.

"They like their sodas warm, *dada*." Julius paused.

"Warm soda, are you joking?"

Nicolas chuckled. "Yes, *dada*. We like warm soda. We are happy about the camels and the soda."

Angie touched his shoulder. "I'm glad to see you smile."

Nicolas remained close. "You don't shoo us away. We are safe with you."

Angie brought the children into a shady area and motioned for them to sit on the sand. "Julius, please give them the sodas, then interpret for me."

"Children, do you know any stories from the Bible?"

Julius interpreted.

"Only when we stand outside the churches and listen to their words," Robert answered.

"There is a story in the book of Luke about children wanting to come close to Jesus. Some of the men with Jesus wanted to send them away like people shoo you away. But Jesus said, 'No, let them come near. Do not stop them. They are part of the kingdom of God.' He told the crowd of adults *they* needed to be more like these little children."

Julius interpreted.

"This Jesus cares about street kids like me?" Taso asked.

"Yes, He does. And He hears you when you pray." God's truth struck the kids hard, a hand to Taso's chest, a silent 'O' on Sophie's lips, raised eyebrows on Robert's forehead.

"Is that why God sent you here, Miss Angeleeka, because I prayed? I asked Him to help me when I was hungry, then you gave me and Robert food. So, God sent you to help street children." Nicolas raised his voice above a rising murmur amongst the children.

All their eyes were on her. "I haven't thought about it that way. I want you to be cared for." Nicolas's assumption stunned Angie, giving her story a twist she hadn't expected. It was good to apply biblical stories to our lives, but this moment was life-altering. *Lord, is this what you've been speaking to me about? Is this what you want me to do with my life? I would be humbled to take on such a task. Make my way clear. You have my attention. I'm listening.* Her eyes filled as she scanned the children—her future.

Robert interrupted her thoughts. "You need us to work more today?"

"Yes, let's go to the pool area."

The pool had been kept clean, but the surrounding area needed attention. She and the children washed the tiled area around the edge. They were perspiring in the afternoon heat when they finished.

She asked Samson to join them. "Please interpret for me."

"Children, you've worked hard." They listened to Samson speak in Swahili. "But I need to tell you something."

The children looked serious.

She paused. "You stink!"

Samson laughed, then interpreted.

They giggled.

"So, I need you to jump in the water and play."

Before Samson finished speaking, they were in the pool, splashing and having a good time.

"Samson, I think we're going to need some towels and food for our friends."

She sat at the edge of the pool, watching them. Bursts of laughter filled the air, as sweet, orphaned children, down on their luck, were getting clean for the first time in a long time. They'd captivated her heart, changed her.

An orphan caring for orphans—who would have guessed?

In her Paradise Inn cottage, after showering and changing for the evening, Angie Skyped with Grand-Papa and got the update on his health, which sounded like a list of half-truths to hide his pain.

"I tell you, Angelica, I'm fine—more worried about you

than anything." He tilted his head in that all-knowing, all-seeing grandfatherly way.

Angie leaned closer to the screen. "But the dark circles under your eyes tell me another story, Grand-Papa. Please rest more."

"I will, Angelica. I promise. How are you, and what's the update on the investigation?" He leaned back in his leather desk chair.

"I'm much better. One more visit to the doctor and I'll be booking a flight home. The search for the murderer is ongoing. Tanner wanted me to tell you they're closing in on him. He'll get back to you soon." Angie smiled.

"That's great. Tell him I'm working on some things on this side of the ocean. We will need to talk soon." Grand-Papa said.

"I'll tell him. Would you let Mason know I'm feeling better?" Angie said as an afterthought. She ran her hand over the floral bedspread where Tanner was sleeping when she had malaria. It was a comfort to see him there. He was so close.

"I will. Please be careful, my dear. I'll be glad to have you home. Love you, Angelica."

"Love you too, Grand-Papa."

Then he was gone.

She stared at the blank screen. *Just that quickly—he'll be gone.* Her heart ached to feel his strong arms around her, his kiss on her temple. *How will I feel when those things are no longer a possibility? Will I be strong, or will I break?*

Punching the keyboard, Angie waited to connect with Leslie, whose face now filled the screen. "Les. How are you?"

"Great. Overworked right now. But let's not talk about me. How are you coming with your wedding plans? Michelle, the wedding planner you asked me to call the day you left, said she would love to work with you. She has a barrage of questions.

First of all, when is this wedding?" Leslie waggled her eyebrows.

"About that, Leslie."

Leslie shifted immediately into the professional she was.

"I see things differently since I've been away. I'm not in love with Mason. I'm giving his ring back when I see him, but he has no idea, so please don't say anything yet. I want to be the one to tell him."

"I'm not surprised." Leslie leaned forward, nearer to the screen. "Is it Tanner?"

"Oh, Leslie. I'll never love anyone the way I love Tanner, but he is different, guarded. I couldn't break through to his heart if I tried."

"Only you can know your feelings. In one afternoon, we can find the perfect dress, but choosing which man to spend the rest of your life with takes time. Pray, Angie. Ask the Lord to lead you, to show you His will for your life. He's faithful." Leslie glanced off toward the office.

"I'll do that. Pray with me."

"You got it. Hugs and kisses—gotta go. I'm late for an appointment."

The screen went blank.

Angie stared at the blinking cursor, replaying Leslie's words, soaking in the wisdom in her advice.

Chapter Eleven

"Miss Angeleeka, don't pay the price they ask. Offer much less. Bargain with them. They will think you have money since you are American. Make them give you a better price."

Angie touched Samson's arm. "I'll do that, Samson. Don't worry. I'll be fine." She slipped into the waiting taxi. "The driver will wait for me." She closed the door and waved. "McKinnon Market in City Centre, *bwana.*"

Samson spoke to the driver in Swahili, assuring Angie's safety and return trip to the inn.

Downtown Mombasa had its high-rise buildings, and Angie passed Carter House, Thuo House, and Barkley House before stopping in front of the city market. "*Bwana*, I want to shop here. Please wait for me."

"Yes, *dada.* I will be here." He opened his newspaper—a staple for cab drivers.

"*Asante, bwana.*" She slipped out of the cab, donned her cross-body purse, and entered the market inside a huge warehouse. Stairs led to rows of shops around the perimeter, every inch lined with colorful wares. Kenyans milled about, greeting friends, jawing with cohorts as they started the day.

All eyes focused on Angie. Just inside the building, an array of fresh flowers pleased her senses with a floral mixture. The mama watering the beautiful blooms pulled a rose from a cluster and presented it to Angie while greeting her in Swahili.

"*Asante,* Mama." Angie smelled the rose and smiled.

Moving from one shop to another, the owners begged her to shop, to open their business for the day, to help them feed their children. The shops offered paintings on canvas and mud cloth, soapstone carvings, placemats made of banana leaves, and Masai beadwork. One shop displayed antique items like spears, knives, and camel bells. Craftsmen made toys, earrings, and jewelry using Coke bottle tops. Leather shoes, purses, and belts were displayed next to etched glasses, vases, and plates.

She chose a set of three picture frames carved out of ebony for Olivia, Tanner's mother. The kitchen counter at the Ward Estate boasted an array of Angie's and Taner's escapades through the years. Olivia and the staff had hoped they would be a couple one day. *I hoped that as well. It's in the Lord's hands now.*

Angie stopped at a tiny shop. "*Bwana,* what is the price of the four monkeys, the carved apple, and the camera?" She picked up an ebony piece, rubbing her fingers across its rough texture, weighing it in her hand.

"*Dada,* I make a good price, just for you. Two thousand shillings for the monkeys, five hundred shillings for the apple, and fifteen hundred shillings for the camera. I can pack it for you." He reached for the carvings.

"Wait. Don't pack it yet. Your price is too big, *bwana.* I will pay one thousand for the monkeys, two hundred for the apple, and eight hundred for the camera." She stood her ground, unflinching.

"Give me fifteen hundred for the monkeys, three hundred for the apple, and one thousand for the camera. Okay, *dada*." He smiled and started wrapping the monkeys.

"No, I will give you two thousand two hundred for the monkeys, the apple, and the camera together. Deal?"

He thought for a moment. "How about two thousand five hundred?"

Angie smiled. "Deal."

"You are opening my business. Bring money." The Kenyan was happy.

At the next shop, an intricately carved walking cane caught her eye. A talented artist had created the meticulous detail of the cane. The weight told her it was made of ebony, but she wanted to be sure she was right.

"What type of wood is this, *bwana*?" She rubbed her fingers over the smooth surface.

"It is ebony, the second hardest wood in the world. Very strong. You want the cane, *dada*?"

"*Ndio*, yes, if we can agree on a good price." She didn't want to appear overeager.

He smiled and began wrapping the cane. "Three thousand shillings, yes?"

"No, two thousand shillings, yes?"

"Two thousand five hundred, yes?" He smiled as he taped the paper around the cane.

"Two thousand three hundred, and you have a deal." She refused to accept the wrapped cane he was handing her.

"*Leta shilingi*, bring money." He accepted her price and tried to sell her another cane.

"I only need one. But thank you." She paid him and left the market with her twenty-five-dollar carving, which would be worth over two hundred dollars in the States. Grand-Papa would love it.

After leaving her purchases in the cab, a feeling of being watched sent goose bumps rising on her arms. Scanning the crowd, she didn't see anything unusual and chided herself. *Would Wycliff be looking for me? I'm a Ward.* She again checked her surroundings and realized how silly she was being. *Everyone's looking at you—you're an mzungu.* She decided to shake it off and went to a kiosk for some chips and a warm Coke for her driver and a cold soda for herself.

"I got you a snack, *bwana*." She reached through the open window and gave him the chips and Coke before taking a long drink of her Fanta. The asphalt radiated heat from the midday sun. Without an ocean breeze, the humidity was stifling.

Re-capping her bottle, the fine hairs on Angie's neck rose at attention. Frustration mixed with fear had her pinned to the spot. *Would Wycliff try to kidnap me?* She forced herself to move, to search the area. Staying beside the taxi, she perused the crowd, looking for Daniel's killer. With hundreds milling around, her search proved futile. She slipped into the taxi's back seat, locked her door, and scanned the crowd, looking for a certain face.

"*Bwana*, please drive toward the south coast." She wanted to get out of town and didn't want anyone following her to the inn.

"*Ndio, dada.*" He maneuvered the car through the throng of people, motorcycles, bicycles, and donkey carts.

The chaos of the city passed her window, but she was lost to its intrigue. She watched for any vehicle following them. As they left the hubbub of Mombasa proper, she breathed a sigh of relief as kilometers passed.

"*Bwana, take* me to Paradise Inn. I'm ready to return." Angie relaxed in the back seat and allowed the wind to cool her damp skin.

He turned the taxi toward the inn, his meter chalking up a substantial fee, padding his pocket. "*Ndio, dada.* Yes, miss."

They retraced their path, taking a few turns she didn't recognize, probably adding kilometers to the meter. But it ensured they weren't followed. She chose not to complain.

As the cab left her breathing exhaust at Paradise Inn, the phone at the desk started ringing. Angie put her packages in the lobby and hurried to the desk. "Hello, Paradise Inn."

"Hey, Angie. It's Tanner. I'm doing surveillance with Officer Karani, and I'm hungry. Can you get Samson to put some food together for us, and I'll pick you and lunch up in twenty minutes, okay?"

"Why sure. I'll cancel my busy schedule and pencil you in. No problem." She was quick with a retort, maybe because her heart rate raced with excitement at spending time with Tanner.

He laughed. "Just be ready. Can't talk. I'm in traffic."

With that, the line went dead. Angie looked at the receiver, shook her head, returned it to the cradle, and headed for the kitchen, her packages in tow.

"The clock's ticking, Angie." Tanner loaded their food and opened her door. Dressed in khaki pants and a shirt, he looked like a safari guide.

"You can't rush perfection. Don't you know that?" She waved to Samson and boarded the Land Cruiser.

Tanner smiled and shook his head. "Glad you could break away for the afternoon, my African Queen." He started the truck.

"African Queen? Is that a term of royalty around here? It

took some doing, but I cleared my schedule just for you." She clicked her seat belt, metal meeting metal. "Let's get started."

He shifted gears and pulled to the exit. Glad for the distraction, Tanner listened to Angie's conversations with the street kids as they waited for a herd of cattle to pass the gate. When the last heifer moseyed by, he entered the traffic flow. The African Queen question was forgotten.

"Well, bring me up to date." Angie didn't waste any time.

"Officer Karani and I have been on a stakeout at Wycliff's sister's apartment. But he hasn't shown. Other crimes have taken Karani off the case for the afternoon, so we need to watch for the unsub, as you call him."

"Why did you think he would return to her place?" She pulled out her notebook.

"Karani thinks he'll visit her before he finishes his assignment and leaves the country. Says it's a part of Kenyan culture." He downshifted and dodged an overturned donkey cart.

"Tanner, where can you buy a bus ticket in Mombasa?" She flipped a few pages and found her notes.

"At the bus station or a ticket office downtown. Why do you ask?" He glanced at her.

"Is it near the McKinnon Market in the City Centre?" She pulled out her pen.

"Yeah, across the street. What's up, Ang—?"

"While shopping this morning, I got an eerie feeling I was being watched. Scanning the crowded area, nothing seemed out of the ordinary. So, I shopped at a few more stores. When I returned to my taxi, the feeling grew stronger. I searched the area for the unsub, but there were too many people. The feeling intensified, giving me goosebumps, so I left."

"Did you go straight back to Paradise Inn?" He sounded worried.

"No, I had the driver detour toward the South Coast until I was certain we weren't being followed. Then, he took me back to the resort along the scenic route." She stared at him. "You think the murderer was there, getting his bus ticket to make his escape?" Danger had come close again.

His stomach tightened. She'd been in danger. He took a deep breath and let it out in a huff. "You're correct, and I'm glad you didn't take any chances and got right out of there."

"I'm ready." She closed her notebook.

"Right now, I'm ready for some food. What did Samson send us?"

"Tacos, I think. You get this gas guzzler in a good parking space, and I'll get the food out."

He parked across the street, giving them a clear view of the block, and scanned the area. "Wycliff's sister lives in that first apartment on the ground level just inside the gate to the left."

"This is where I was when I got sick. Isn't it?" Angie pointed to the area.

"Yeah, you fainted in the street over there." Tanner pointed toward the center of the dirty walkway. "You collapsed between some scrawny dogs and a donkey."

"And you rescued me." She offered him some food.

"You remember that? You were pretty sick." Being her hero time and again had kept them close, built their friendship, their relationship. He accepted a paper plate from Angie, and they ate in silence while watching for their man to show up. The mixture of tribes living on the Mombasa coast made it difficult to distinguish one man from another.

Angie took out her photo of Wycliff to jog her memory.

"Where did you get that?" *Maybe those TV shows had taught her a thing or two.*

"From the police chief at headquarters. The vice president sent me to him after our meeting. You told me about Lamu but didn't give me any info, so I had to get the scoop my own way." She handed him a cold Coke.

It was good to spend time together. Maybe with time, he could rebuild what they once shared. Making opportunities for them to spend more time together would be in order. But for now, he had to protect her no matter how much it hurt if she walked away.

They ate in comfortable silence, though the sounds of Mombasa's streets surrounded them.

"So, tell me about those three friends of yours, the ones you called out for when you had malaria." He kept his eyes on the scene, analyzing each pedestrian. "I can watch and listen."

"We're a tight foursome that met in a photography class. I'd like you to meet them when you come home. Elise is an intern as a teacher of special needs children." She took a drink of her Coke. "Missy is a feisty redhead with bright green eyes and a personality to match. Her quick wit keeps us all entertained all the time. She has a BA in business, but we don't know what she'll be when she grows up. She's a hoot."

Tanner leaned forward, took a bite of his taco, and rested his arms on the steering wheel.

"Leslie is the reserved one of the group. She's a photojournalist who's quiet and unassuming unless she's behind her camera, capturing masterpieces. She has no family. Elise, Missy, and I are her family now." She paused. "What else did I say when I was sick?"

"Nothing of importance." He kept his gaze on the busy scene and took a swig of his Coke before stuffing the last of a taco into his mouth.

"I'm sure I was a picture of refinement in my sweaty pajamas, matted hair, and lack of make-up." She scrunched up her face.

"Funny, that's not how I remember it." He didn't want her to press him for more information. "Tell me more about your friends." "We've experienced a lot together, been there for each other through personal dramas. They're like sisters to me."

"Sounds like you've learned to love. They've been good for you." He glanced in her direction.

"What do you mean? I've learned to love?" She shifted in her seat to face him. "Maybe it's time you tell me why you let our long-distance relationship die."

"There's been a lot of water under that bridge. Are you sure you want to go there?" He took a drink of his Coke, not wanting to rehash the past. What good would it do?

"No, I need to know what happened. What got us to where we are today?"

He stuffed his trash into the sack, shifted in the driver's seat, and sighed. "Okay, I felt our love was solid, everlasting. I was so sure of our relationship and never doubted what we had. I know we talked more in the first year, and I loved every email, card, or phone call. You were the reason I kept going out here, your support, your sweet messages. Then your schedule got busy with your increased class load. I wanted to be understanding and supportive of your endeavors too. So, connecting less often became our new normal. I was okay with that, but I should have come home to see you. You needed me, and I was ten thousand miles away."

"Everyone I love leaves." Angie's eyes filled with tears.

"But everything I've been doing here has been with our future in mind. My feelings for you haven't changed, but I think I took you for granted. I've pushed myself and my team to finish this project. But in this last year, when the mine started filling with water, I knew our time was short, and we ramped up our schedule even more. Coming stateside was out of the question. I thought you understood. You saw this project from its inception. But I was wrong. When I watched Malone kneel in front of you, I knew I had been kidding myself. I had lost you."

"Don't cry, Ang—, that's why I didn't want to talk about this." He massaged the back of his neck.

"I thought your feelings for me had faded. When I met Vickie, I wondered if she had turned your head." She grabbed a napkin from the glove compartment and wiped her face.

"She made her play, but my heart was occupied. We're just friends. I'm not skilled in matters of the heart, but sometimes people do things that are out of character. I never meant to hurt you. Angie, I'm sorry." He took her hand.

"No, I'm the one who should be sorry. We should have talked about *us*. You were a constant in my life. You were my strength. I thought you knew how I felt about you and could read my mind. I never dreamed you'd gradually let me go. It shattered me. I felt so alone."

"Ang—, being away from you was the hardest thing I've ever done. You were my weakness and made me strive for strength. Your belief in me gave me confidence. I am who I am because of you. I'm forever grateful." He wiped a tear coursing down her cheek.

Sitting in silence for a while, Tanner watched for the murderer. *We had it great for a while, but I let it slip through my hands. I have to fix what I've broken.*

"I'm so sorry, Tanner?"

"I am too, Ang—"

The sounds of Mombasa filled the air between them.

She pointed to the apartment. "Is there a back door to

204

these apartments? He could be coming and going that way, and we'd never see him. And he knows this truck."

"You're right. Let's stay until six like I promised, then we'll call it a day." Tanner checked his watch.

"What happens now? Between us? We really botched things up, didn't we?"

"Yes, we did. When tested, we should have trusted our feelings for each other—"

Angie finished his thought. "But we didn't."

Mason greeted the secretaries as he strutted through the Ward building. He retrieved a stack of messages from Leslie, his personal assistant, and entered his plush private office with his gourmet coffee. He retrieved a number from his desk drawer, pressed the listing in his cell, and waited for an overseas call to go through.

After five attempts, it rang. "Wycliff, how are things in Kenya?" He paced his office.

"Hello, *bwana*. I am happy to report that everything is ready and finalized as you have requested. My friend is set to assist with the plan of attack." Wycliff sounded sure of himself.

"When is it going to happen?" Mason thumbed through his stack of messages.

"Tomorrow is the day."

"That's good news indeed. Have you planned your getaway?" Mason wadded one of his messages and tossed it into the trash.

"Yes, tickets have been purchased. Not to worry, *bwana*."

"Please notify me when the job is complete. I must know that the woman is safe." Mason demanded.

"I will call when we get to the mine. Then again, as soon as the job is finished, which should be when I get my shillings. Right, *bwana?*"

"Right. Do not get caught." Mason hung up and pocketed the phone.

He returned several calls, especially the ones that would strengthen his position at Ward Enterprises. He scheduled two meetings with the intent of squeezing additional funds out of companies with outstanding accounts. Making progress. It felt good.

He pulled out his top drawer where he kept business cards of female employees and associates, thumbed through them, and selected one. It belonged to a realtor, who happened to be drop-dead gorgeous. It only took a minute for her syrupy voice to fill the other end of the line.

"Hello, Daphne. This is Mason." He smiled.

"Mason, glad you called," Daphne said. "What's on your mind?"

"As we discussed two weeks ago, I'm in need of a realtor. Are you available?" He imagined her on the other end of the line.

"Why Mason? I'm always available to you. You have some land to sell?"

"No, I want to sell my condo, which will be ready to list in a week." He opened his calendar on his iPad.

"I know you're a busy man. You tell me when you're available, and I'll set a date for the property assessment." Her voice was smooth as honey.

"How about a dinner meeting tonight? I can have something catered. What would you like?" Mason smirked.

"Let's do shrimp again. Does that sound good to you?"

"Sounds great, how about eight o'clock? Bring your briefcase. I'm serious about listing my place." He smiled. "And don't be late."

Angie was glad the team was joining them for dinner, sparing her any possibility of private dialogue with Tanner. Their intimate conversations during the stakeout had left her shell-shocked. If he had shared the details and dynamics of the load he was working under, she would have understood and cut him some slack. It was the silence that was hard to read. But given the chance, she wanted a future with Tanner. But that was a big if.

After Dylan prayed over their meal, conversations bounced from one subject to another with some humor thrown in. Tanner was relaxed with this group. He laughed and bantered with ease. So different from their time together while on the stakeout.

"What are your plans after this job is done, guys?" Angie asked.

"I've got some resumes out with three mining sites. Haven't heard from them yet." Drew buttered his bread.

"I think I'm going to travel a bit before I start a new assignment." Vickie looked at Tanner and smiled. "I can always go back to the South African diamond mines. I left that contract open-ended."

"Well, I'll be in Kenya a while longer. I'm handling this case for Ward Enterprises, and I'm part of a pit crew for a race that's coming up in a couple of months. When all loose ends are tied in a bow, I'm going to return to the States and open a law firm for my father. What about you, Tanner?" Dylan handed his empty plate to Julius. "You going to keep working for Ward?"

"Yeah, that's the plan. I don't know where he'll send me for my next assignment." Tanner said. "But he pays good and treats me well."

"He pays me well too. So, I'm going to stay with Ward Enterprises." Angie smiled as they laughed.

"Listen to the silver spoon." Drew teased Angie.

"Don't bite the hand that feeds you, Angie," Dylan advised.

"From the mouth of a lawyer." Angie enjoyed being accepted into this tight circle. After dessert was served, she asked for a tray with a pot of tea to take to her bungalow.

"Turning in early?" Tanner asked as he finished his pie.

"Yes, I'm tired." She stood and bid everyone goodnight.

"Angie, if the water line has risen, we'll finish at the mine tomorrow. Why don't you go with us and photograph the day? Ward likes to document his holdings, and we haven't taken many pictures. Bring your camera and put it to good use. We're leaving around seven, okay? I don't want you out of my sight until this crime is solved. Wycliff won't have the opportunity to hurt you, because I've taken extra security measures. We should be safe."

"Sure, what time?"

"We're leaving around seven, okay?" He set his fork on the table and yawned.

"I'll be ready." With the team around, there wouldn't be any one-on-one conversations with Tanner that she wasn't ready for. Not yet. But finishing up at the mine was a great plan. Maybe he was taking her advice about getting out of Kenya before Wycliff showed up again. One could only hope.

Sleep wouldn't come. After twisting and turning for hours, Tanner gave up. He slipped downstairs and took a chair at a table in the restaurant. Nocturnal noises and the sounds of high tide went unnoticed as he thought about his stakeout conversation with Angie. Her sincere explanation, the tears coursing down her cheeks, showed him her heart.

"Hey, man. It's late. Can't you sleep?" Dylan came out of the kitchen with a bottle of water.

"Grab me one of those." Tanner was seated at the table, partially hidden by the shadows of evening.

Dylan handed him the water and turned a ladder-back chair around before straddling it. "Something on your mind?" He twisted the top off and upped the bottle, guzzling the water.

"Angie." Tanner stared at the half-moon's reflection on the ocean waves, enjoying the salty breeze coming off the water. "I know what I heard, but today, I got the rest of the story. Man, I blew it big time."

"But you did the best you could with the responsibility of this mine."

Tanner shook his head. "I dropped the ball. I should have kept communication open and taken your advice to visit her more frequently. She thinks everyone she loves leaves."

Dylan groaned.

"If I think about it, she's right. She lost her parents, then her Nana Joy passed, and I moved to Kenya." Tanner rubbed his hand over his overgrown five o'clock shadow and took a deep breath of salty sea air.

"And then when the mine started filling with water, you had to focus, to lead us, and she lost communication with you. Rough."

"I knew her heart, her character, and I let our relationship fade slowly by taking what we had for granted."

"So." Dylan put the lid on his empty bottle. "Has it changed your feelings for her?"

"Not in the least." He didn't hesitate.

"How did you leave it with her? She seemed fine during dinner."

"Once the truth was out in the open, it hung between us like a shroud. It pains me, knowing what we've lost." He paused. "How do I fix this?"

"You'll have to ask the Man Upstairs that question." Dylan pointed skyward. "You said, 'The truth will set you free.' Are you free?"

"I feel like I've been hit with a stun gun." Tanner stood and pushed in his chair.

"Is this that 'kicked-in-the-gut' feeling?"

"Yeah, but I was the one doing the kicking, and Angie is the one who was wounded and is now engaged to another man." Tanner reached for their empty water bottles. "But what do I do?"

"Why don't you give this to the Lord and get some sleep? There's a murderer out there gunning for you. And you've got a beautiful photographer focusing on you and the mine tomorrow. Getting some rest is a good idea." Dylan pushed his chair under the table. "And, the Lord hasn't failed you yet. He'll help you walk this out. I have no doubt."

"You're right. Trusting Him is my only recourse." Tanner prayed as he returned to his quarters. *Lord, please keep my team and Angie safe until this is over. And if it is your will, Lord, for Angie and me to have another chance at love, open our hearts and heal the hurt from the past. I'm trusting you, Lord.*

Chapter Twelve

S unglasses would hide the dark circles she attempted to camouflage with makeup after her inability to fall asleep. Angie grabbed her camera battery from the transformer as she left her bungalow. Mixed emotions weighed on her heart.

It wouldn't be right to tell Tanner she was breaking her engagement to Mason before she told him and returned his ring. And using that information to get Tanner back felt like manipulation. Nana Joy was big on doing things correctly and taught her to follow protocol in delicate situations. Their relationship was definitely tenuous. For today, she pasted on a smile as Tanner's team came into view.

"Coffee for me, Samson." She pulled out her chair, took a seat, and held her cup.

"You're usually a tea drinker, Angie," Tanner said.

"I need the extra caffeine today. It was a short night." She added sugar to her brew.

"Seems like insomnia is an epidemic around here." Dylan reached for a piece of toast with a knowing smile.

"There has been a lot to think about." Tanner finished his coffee.

Drew scooped the last of the eggs onto his plate. "Like finishing this job and getting out of Dodge before the murderer finishes what he's started. Right, Marshall Dillon?"

"Right, Drew."

Angie slid into the back seat of the Land Cruiser next to Drew, who was finishing a crispy piece of bacon. "Is that good?"

"Yep, good and salty." Tanner smiled in his mirror while the rest of the team loaded in for the forty-five-minute drive.

Friendly chit-chat among the group passed the time, but once there, Angie let the dust settle, then went to work with her digital camera. A new understanding dawned about Leslie's desire to hide behind a camera. It felt safe and blocked unwanted, or at least too soon, conversations.

Tanner mounted the steps to the mining platform and called his team together. "Well, friends, we've reached our last day of mining since the mine is filling with water. I want us to work half a day, retrieve as much tanzanite as possible, and help Vickie prepare it for shipment. This will give us the afternoon to lock the area down tight and load our equipment. Be careful. Take all precautions. I don't want to risk another life. Extra guards will be watching for danger, so stay focused on your work. Let's get this job done." He slapped his clipboard against his thigh and spoke to each employee as they went to their assigned tasks.

Angie took photos of Tanner from different angles. Through her lens, she caught his tightly toned muscles and a shadow of a beard, while an ocean breeze messed with his black hair. Seeing him in action gave her another layer of respect for the man he'd become. He led with confidence, was attentive to details, and was meticulous with the business side of mining.

The tropical setting, with swaying palm trees, birds overhead, and waves crashing on the shore, made a perfect backdrop for her photos of the mining activity. She climbed on top of the Land Cruiser for pictures from a higher vantage point, capturing the scene in one shot. Close-ups of the ropes passing through the pulleys and Vickie chipping away at the gems with dust filling the area would become frameable prints for the office. She kept quiet and stayed out of their way, using her lenses to get great shots Grand-Papa would love.

Drew started his descent into the mine. "Hey, Noah, it's time to build a boat. The water level's much higher."

"No, we're throwing Jonah overboard instead." Dylan teased Drew. "It's what happens to guys who don't go to church like they should."

"Hey, I said I would try it." Drew pleaded.

Tanner leaned over the entrance of the mine and interrupted their banter. "Drew, how much did it rise? Give me an estimate."

"Looks like about twelve more feet is underwater. It's up to the rock Daniel hit his head on when he fell."

"Work the vein you were working yesterday. It's the only one left showing promise. But stay above the water level. If anything changes, let me know." Tanner's brow was furrowed.

"You got it, Boss." Drew's voice echoed against the walls of the mine.

Angie was amazed at how hard the men worked and how well-oiled their operation was so that each of the stones made it to the light of day. Few were privileged to witness these jewels being harvested from where God placed them, and the immense effort it took to bring them to the glass cases in jewelry stores.

~

Mason punched his pillow. He hated to wake up before the alarm went off. This better be good. "Hello, Malone here."

"*Bwana*, it is Wycliff. We are near the entrance to the mine. Isaac, my hired man, is with me. It is time. We are ready."

"What's happening at the mine? What do you see?" His interest piqued, bringing him fully awake.

"The men bring stones to the surface every half hour or so. The boss, Zarello, or the one with yellow hair, retrieves the stones from the miners and takes them to the woman who chips rock and dirt off the gems. We are waiting for our chance to attack. Many shadows of big trees will give us an advantage."

Like a lion stalking its prey. "Are there many guards?" Mason sat in bed and turned on a lamp. His clock read 4:30 a.m., 12:30 p.m. in Kenya.

"I can see four guards. One is near the gate, two others are on the rise on the other side of the mine, and one is on the beach. We plan to use our clubs to knock them out as we begin. The noise of the generator will cover any sound they make. Then, we will attack and finish the job you have hired us to do. Kill Zarello."

"Is your hired man sure of his assignment?" Mason rubbed sleep from his eyes.

"Yes, he will hit the yellow-haired woman and the smaller man, then grab stones and make his escape. I will do as you have requested—shoot the boss and steal more stones.

"Is the other woman at the mine? The one with ebony hair." Mason hated trying to see through someone else's eyes.

"Yes, she has been taking photos with her big camera. She is walking to the beach now."

Angelica is at the mine. Unbelievable!

"Remember, she is not to be hurt. Have you made arrangements to assure her safety?" Mason paced his bedroom.

"Yes, *bwana*. I understand, and I have told Isaac not to hurt the one with ebony hair."

"Make sure he doesn't. Don't let this be like last time. Hit the target and let's be finished with this ordeal." Mason was wide awake now.

"*Bwana*, I will leave this phone on speaker. You will hear the shots ring out when the job is done."

Through the phone, car doors opened, squeaking their need to be greased, followed by footsteps, and then silence. Then, the whack of a bat hitting something.

The gate guard is down for the count.

Mason kept his cell phone on speaker as he went to turn on his coffee pot, watching and greedily listening as it dripped through the filter into the carafe. Retrieving his morning paper, he took a seat in the living room. He had just opened the *Daily News* to the business section when a shot rang out!

He pumped his fist—Yes!

Angie walked the perimeter of the property to take photos from different vantage points. She strolled to the other side of the mine, where the sandy beach bordered the Indian Ocean. With the sun directly overhead, she held her hand over her brow as a yacht glided across the waves. She removed her shoes and let the soft sand cushion her feet, shadows of swaying palms dancing in the salty breeze. A guard followed her, keeping watch for danger. When she reached the water, she turned back to the mine and got a picture from that angle. In her first shot, two guards were watching like sentries on point. She looked into her digital screen and took another shot to make sure the sun's glare wasn't too bright, but this time, both guards were missing.

Jerking her camera from her face, she searched the area. She couldn't see either of them.

"Tanner, the guards are gone! Tanner!" She slung her camera around to her back and ran with all her might. The sand seemed to suck in each of her footsteps, slowing her progress, forcing her legs to burn. She couldn't get there fast enough, and her voice wouldn't be heard over the ocean waves and roar of the generator.

She hurried, with a guard at her heels and her shoes in his grasp. Wycliff couldn't win this time.

As Tanner turned the generator off for the last time, he breathed a sigh of relief. Rolling up the extension cord while his team completed their tasks. He was closing a chapter in his life. Time to move on.

"Dylan, can you get the new locks out of the Land Cruiser and secure the entrance to the mine?" Tanner tied a long extension cord and reached for another.

"Sure, I'll get them." He hurried to the truck parked at the edge of the property.

Tanner surveyed the area one last time.

Quick, heavy footsteps made him turn. A whack, the sound of a sledgehammer on wood, pierced the air. Vickie screamed as Drew hit the ground. There were more footsteps and another loud crack as an unfamiliar Kenyan man hit Vickie's head with a club and grabbed the stones she had been holding. She cried out and dropped to the ground, blood staining the surrounding dirt.

"Vickie!" Tanner called, rushing up the steps of the mining platform.

No response.

He called her name again and grabbed a board to defend himself as Wycliff stepped out of the shadows.

"Wycliff!" Tanner swung the board at the murderer.

Wycliff blocked the flying timber, then kept coming straight for him.

"Why are you doing this?" Tanner stepped toward the murderer. "Dylan, we're under attack! Get my gun!" Not allowing his eyes to leave Wycliff, he reached down and picked up a large stone from Dylan's bucket and tossed it at the murderer's head.

He dodged the piece of tanzanite and drew his gun in one swift move. "Why—for money, for the tanzanite. Your life's over, Zarello." Wycliff spouted.

Tanner stopped in his tracks and stared down the barrel of Wycliff's weapon.

Angie climbed the steps, breathless from running. "Tanner, both guards are gone!"

Her guard was close on her heels. He dropped Angie's shoes and grabbed a board to fight off the guy who hit Vickie and was putting tanzanite into a cloth bag.

Tanner grabbed Angie's hand and put himself in front of her, protecting her body with his. "Angie, stay behind me. We're being robbed!"

"Robbed! No—he wants to kill you, Tanner!" Angie eyed Daniel's murderer over Tanner's shoulder.

He could feel Angie's body trembling behind him—feel her grasp his shirt as Wycliff moved closer. With his feet planted, Tanner looked him in the eye and braced himself for battle.

"Is someone paying you to do this? Wycliff, you can have

the tanzanite. I'll pay you double what he is offering you. You'll be a wealthy man. Take them and leave!"

Wycliff stepped closer to the mining platform and aimed at Tanner.

"Be reasonable, man—" A shot rang out.

Angie screamed.

Everything went black.

One second, Angie was breathless, holding on to Tanner for protection, then, in a heartbeat, he crumpled at her feet.

"Tanner!" She dropped to his side on the platform. "Speak to me. Tanner! Dylan, help! Tanner's been shot!" She put his head in her lap, checked the source of the blood staining his shirt, and pressed the wound, as Wycliff retreated.

Dylan drew Tanner's gun, aimed, and shot at Wycliff. When Wycliff took cover behind a jacaranda tree, he shifted the gun's trajectory and shot again.

The unfamiliar man fell and cried out, "Wycliff, help me. I'm hit."

Wycliff ran and yanked him up. After grabbing their stolen tanzanite, they disappeared into the shadows, leaving a trail of blood in the dust.

The man cried out in pain just before a car door slammed, and an engine revved as the vehicle took off.

Dylan hurried to the platform to check on Tanner.

Angie sobbed as she applied pressure to stop the bleeding. "He's been hit in the chest. Get the truck. We've got to get him to the hospital."

"Stay with him. I'll pull the truck closer to the platform so we can load him in the back seat." He ran to the Cruiser, leaving her cradling Tanner's body.

"Don't leave me, please. I need you to be okay." Her tears soaked his shirt, mixing with his blood. *I love you, Tanner. I always have.*

Dylan lifted Vickie's unconscious body and put her in the back of the truck, placing a rolled-up jacket under her head. Drew was coming to, holding his head. On wobbly legs, he got into the front seat with Paul, their worker holding him up.

Dylan moved the truck as close as he could to the mining platform and called for the newly hired guard who had been on the beach with Angie. Courage obviously wasn't his strong suit. He'd dove for cover when bullets were fired. Angie couldn't blame him, since he couldn't return fire, not having a gun.

"Come help me put him in the truck. Grab his legs." Dylan opened the door and put his arms directly under Tanner's. "Angie, keep the pressure steady. Let's get closer to the truck. You slide in with his upper body in your lap."

"Okay." She moved with caution as fresh blood warmed her fingers. She slid into the back seat, inching to the far side, as Dylan and the guard slid Tanner's body in. She pressed his wound, her hand cramped from the strain. But she wouldn't let up.

"Paul, check on all the guards, see to their injuries, and secure the equipment until I return," Dylan instructed their faithful worker as he cranked the truck and sped out of the lot as quickly as possible without injuring his patients. With a cell phone on speaker, he informed the police of the attack and the robbery, giving them the location of the mine and their estimated time of arrival at Mombasa Hospital. He asked the officer to contact the hospital and tell them one man had been shot.

An occasional moan let Angie know Tanner was still alive. She prayed for a miracle while Dylan dodged potholes and traffic. Drew threw up, sick from the wound on the head. Vickie didn't make a sound, and Angie wadded up a clean cloth left in the truck and pressed it to her head, strapping it there with the sleeve of one of Tanner's extra work shirts.

Sirens blared in the distance as the hospital came into view. Dylan swerved into the emergency room driveway.

A Kenyan police officer, Jackson Waruri, met them at the emergency room entrance.

Angie opened her door and motioned for them to bring a stretcher. She acknowledged the officer. "Let us get these three in for treatment, then we'll answer your questions. Please contact Officer Karani immediately. He's working another case that occurred at this same location."

Nurses in white uniforms, with stiff hats pinned to their heads, hurried out of the emergency room with a squeaky-wheeled gurney. Dylan and Drew helped get Tanner out of the truck and onto the rickety stretcher on wheels. Angie didn't let up on the pressure on his wound. She moved with his body as they rushed him inside the building into a curtained triage area.

An antiseptic smell stung her nose. Monitors beeped, highlighting the seconds ticking away. He was in trouble. Doctors and nurses scurried around his bed. They had to stop the hemorrhaging and get the bullet out. One doctor lifted Angie's hand so he could see the source of the blood.

She stepped back.

A nurse cut his shirt off, and another nurse began asking questions. His name, age, address, weight, height, and blood type. Knowing it was routine, Angie tried to help. They seemed short-staffed on this shift.

The young doctor kept his eyes on Tanner but wanted to know what had happened. He packed the wound to stop the bleeding, scheduled an X-ray and a CT scan to be done immediately, and then left the room.

Dylan spoke to the nurses about Drew having a possible concussion.

Blood seeped through the gauze, and a nurse applied pressure. Another nurse checked Tanner's temperature, pulse, and blood pressure. A tech from the lab took his blood and inserted an IV. Angie watched for sterile instruments.

An older physician entered the room. He checked Tanner's chart and stepped closer to inspect the wound. "I'm Dr. Gichui. The intern said he has a gunshot wound." He stepped closer.

The nurse lifted the pressure, and Angie could tell the bleeding had slowed considerably. Realizing her hands were covered in Tanner's blood, she stepped to the sink and scrubbed her hands and arms while a nurse assisted, and they taped the wound closed with butterfly strips to hinder additional blood loss temporarily.

Dr. Gichui noted his findings on Tanner's chart and faced Angie. "I have called in a surgeon, who is on his way. We're prepping the theatre for surgery, but we must get the bullet out as soon as possible."

"Who is the surgeon?" Concern etched her voice.

"Dr. Gittau. He was schooled in the States. He's the best in Kenya. They will take Mr. Zarello for an X-ray in a few minutes to determine exactly where the bullet is lodged."

"Thank you, doctor."

When the physician went to examine Vickie, Angie was glad for a few quiet moments. She wet some paper towels and wiped blood from Tanner's face and neck. Working her way down his side, she cleaned blood off his arm, the one he extended to put her behind him before he was shot. She owed him her life.

"Angie, what did the doctor say?" Dylan stepped into the room.

"They've called in a surgeon, a specialist educated in America. Tanner will undergo an X-ray soon, followed by a CT scan. How are Drew and Vickie?"

"Drew has a concussion and a black eye. He should be okay. He's asking about sick pay." He smiled. "Vickie's head wound and concussion are much more serious. The doc says the cut will take several stitches. They're doing a CAT scan now, checking for bleeding on the brain. She's still unconscious."

"I hope she comes around soon. I've heard the longer they're out, the more serious the wound is." Angie kept up her cleaning vigil, filling the trash can with bloody paper towels. It helped her to be busy.

"Are the police officers waiting to talk to us?"

"Yes, and they've called the investigator who was working on Daniel's murder case." Dylan leaned against the door jamb.

"I'm glad. This is unbelievable." Angie stepped aside when the lab technician and a nurse came to take Tanner for an X-ray.

"Angie, he's strong. He'll pull through." Dylan handed her a black T-shirt. "Here, it's Tanner's from the truck."

"You think I need to change?" Angie forced a smile.

"I know your outfit was expensive, but you need to throw it away. I don't think it'll come clean."

Angie examined her clothes. "I think you've got a point."

She slipped into the restroom to change. His T-shirt hung on her frame, so she tied one corner of the bottom to make it fit better. The moments stretched in slow motion as she waited for Tanner to return. Pacing the small area, Angie prayed for him and his team.

The squeaky wheel of Tanner's gurney announced his return. Angie stepped aside so they could bring Tanner into triage and reconnect his IV, moving to his side once they'd finished.

Why wasn't he waking up and saying something? Pale from too much blood loss, it seemed he stood on death's door. She washed his hands. Residue from gathering their equipment was evident on his skin. Careful not to get close to his wound, she cleaned as much as she could. As she scrubbed, Tanner moaned, moving his head back and forth.

"Tanner, I'm here. Are you trying to say something?" She threw away the dirty paper towels and straightened the sheet they had on him. He moaned again. She waited.

He mumbled something inaudible. Angie leaned closer, but he slept again, silent and still.

The surgeon arrived, introduced himself, placed an X-ray on a glass screen, and flipped on the light. "The bullet is lodged one-half inch above his heart in the chest cavity."

"Dr. Gittau, is he going to survive?"

"He has a very good chance. He's strong, in good shape, and I'm good at what I do." He smiled. "We will take him to the theatre in about fifteen minutes. This surgery could take several hours because of the location of the bullet." With that, he left the room with the X-ray in his hand.

Angie breathed a sigh of relief.

Tanner moved his head back and forth again, moaning. He mumbled something again.

"What is it, Tanner? What are you trying to say?" She held his hand to her cheek. "I'm here. I'm listening." She waited. Watched.

He took a deep breath, then groaned. Angie put her face close to Tanner's.

"Vickie, Vickie, I'm here. Dylan, they—" He moaned again. "Vickie, I'm coming. Oh, Vickie—"

Angie stood frozen on the spot. She couldn't breathe. She

gripped the bed rail with her free hand to keep from falling, as if her heart had stopped beating. *Tanner has feelings for Vickie. He is calling out for her. The Bible says, "Out of the abundance of the heart, the mouth speaks."* The truth hit like a wrecking ball. She couldn't move, couldn't think. She eased his hand onto the gurney beside his body, stepped back from his bed, and braced herself against a wall. His words stung like a slap to the face. *Lord, what do I do now?* "I think I've loved him all my life," Angie spoke to an empty room. "Lord, help me."

"Angie, you okay? You're as white as a ghost. He's going to make it." Dylan touched her shoulder. "I'm ready to catch you if you faint."

"I think it's all catching up with me. It's a lot to process. Lots of blood." She took a deep breath, locking her personal feelings deep inside.

"You kept him from bleeding to death. I'm glad you were there."

"Thanks."

He grabbed a chair out of the hall and put it next to Tanner's gurney. "Here, sit. We don't need another patient."

Angie pasted on a weak smile, determined to do the right thing. She held onto the bedrail, her knuckles white. The truth pierced her with a paralyzing reality. She had loved and lost him.

Angie listened to Dylan recount the attack. "This is the gun I used. It belongs to Tanner Zarello, the patient in surgery. It's a Colt .45 model 1911. This is the license and official paperwork we keep that proves our right to have a gun in Kenya."

Officer Karani noted the license number and collected the gun as evidence.

"Finished mining today. We were packing up for the last time when the thieves approached from the road through the trees, hidden by dark shadows. The noise of the generator covered the sound of the car and their attacks on our guards."

"When the boss turned the generator off, I heard Vickie, Victoria Becker, the wounded woman on our team, scream and Tanner's call for help. Then, a shot rang out. I grabbed the gun hidden in the truck. I shot one of the thieves in the arm. If you follow the evidence like you've done with every clue so far, you'll find Wycliff, his accomplice, and our tanzanite."

"Can you describe the killer's associate?"

Dylan gave an approximate height, build, and clothing description. This info would prove vital to the investigation, especially in a country where the average man didn't have many sets of clothes.

"It is essential we keep the thieves thinking their attempt on Zarello's life was successful. I'm going to ask you the same questions as before when Daniel Mwangi was killed, but do not share this information with anyone else. Please bear with me. Each case is handled separately until we prove they are connected." Officer Karani questioned Dylan, who responded appropriately.

Angie let Dylan fill in the details of the attack. Thinking through it caused a barrage of painful emotions, causing tears to threaten. *How many times am I going to let Tanner break my heart?*

The detective stood. "*Bwana*, I'll update the DCI of another attack upon this team. Their agents may want to question you again. Wounding one of the thieves will work to our advantage. He will need medical attention tonight. I will take my leave while the trail is still warm. I need information about the three who have been injured, namely, their work permits."

"Can you follow me to the parking lot so I can grab the

permits from the truck?" Dylan ran his hands over his scruffy beard.

"Sure." Officer Karani followed Dylan through the emergency room doors.

He returned within minutes and took a seat in a plastic chair next to Angie.

"You have to be tired, Dylan."

"I haven't really thought about it until now. I think we've both been running on pure adrenaline since the attack. It's been a long day."

"Yes, it has. I'm glad the police recognize the seriousness of the situation." Angie sat back.

"This one was a narrow escape—he got entirely too close." He leaned back and closed his eyes.

"So near to the heart this time," Angie wasn't just talking about the shooting either.

The day crept by in slow motion. Mason needed his phone to ring. During the last international call, a couple of shots rang out, then a car cranked, and someone yelled in pain. He hated not knowing what was happening. So much was riding on this. He stood at his window. Raindrops glided down the glass.

His secretary brought a report and laid it on his desk. He acknowledged her and sat to preview the file. It took effort to focus, especially with a lack of sleep dulling his concentration.

His phone rang. He grabbed it and swiped the screen.

"Mason Malone here."

"*Bwana*, I called to report our success." The overseas line crackled.

"It is done? I heard the gunshots." He sat straighter in his leather chair.

"We have just arrived at our hiding place. He was struck in the heart." Wycliff huffed, out of breath.

"The heart. Are you sure?" His adrenaline was pumping.

"Yes, he fell immediately."

"And you have something for me?" Mason waited.

"Yes, you will be very pleased. We have many stones for you."

"That is good to hear."

"Now, I must get my friend to a doctor, then I will make my escape as we have discussed," Wycliff said.

"Why? What happened?" Mason furrowed his brow.

"He was shot in the attack, but it is not serious. He will be fine. Not to worry, *Bwana.*" Wycliff sounded reassuring.

"I am happy about the heart," Mason smirked.

"We will talk again soon." Wycliff ended the call.

"Good."

"You on a call?" Alexander Ward surprised him. *How long had he been standing in the doorway? What had he heard?*

Mason scrambled mentally for a reply and tried to act nonchalant. "Yes, I was ordering a heart pendant for Angelica as a welcome home present." He met Ward's gaze.

"Good idea. Well, I'm calling it a day. See you tomorrow." With that, Alexander Ward was gone.

Mason breathed a sigh of relief and added buying a heart-shaped pendant to his to-do list. On second thought, a heart pendant was a good idea, a perfect gift in fact.

Ambulance sirens grated on Angie's frayed nerves. As the nurses hurried to help some Kenyans wounded in a car accident, the scene took her back to the events of the day.

"Coffee?" Dylan interrupted her thoughts.

"Yes." She took the cup and sugar packets. "Thanks."

"They're busy tonight." He sipped his brew.

"The people coming in were in a car wreck. Two of them are pretty banged up. Have you heard anything about Tanner?"

"The head nurse called into the theatre for an update. They said the patient is stable, and the doctor is still operating." He sat beside Angie. "He's strong. Try not to worry."

"He lost a lot of blood." She sipped her coffee.

"Sorry about all this, Angie. You got much more than you bargained for on this trip to Kenya. And it's not over yet. You'll probably be glad to get back to civilization."

"It's been a roller coaster ride for sure." If he only knew the truth in his words. "But I'm glad I could help Tanner."

"I'd call you a hero." Angie offered a smile. "Your eagle eye shooting stopped their attack, wounding one of them and forcing them to run before they finished Tanner off." Angie offered a smile.

"All in a day's work." Dylan tried to play it down.

"If you hadn't been quick on the draw, he might have shot him again. So don't quit your target practice."

He gave her a thumbs-up and a smile before they settled in for hours of waiting in a straight chair. A squeaky fan stirred the humidity, spreading the sweaty odor of locals suffering high heat and tragedy.

The clock ticked away the minutes. Angie finished her lukewarm coffee and threw away the cup. "Are we out of danger, Dylan? Is it really over?"

"I doubt he would try again. He saw Tanner fall after he shot him. They got some tanzanite. I'm sure they are leaving Kenya as soon as possible." Dylan said.

"How are Drew and Vickie?"

"Drew's fine. He's always had a hard head. He's resting until the doctor releases him. Vickie's concussion is more severe, but she's waking up. They'll keep her overnight for observation."

"I'm glad they're going to be okay. Paradise Inn will be a great place for them to recuperate. I can attest to that, though I'm almost totally healed now."

"Thanks to you, it's a much better place for healing, beautiful and peaceful, except when that bird starts singing off-key."

"Well—there's that." Angie smiled.

Chapter Thirteen

Angie stood, "I need to walk for a bit." Besides, making small talk with Dylan would be torture with so much on her mind. No matter how she replayed the events of the day, it still ended with Tanner wounded, bleeding, and calling for Vickie. Pacing the hospital hallways helped her rein in her chaotic emotions.

After an hour, she tried to get comfortable in a straight-backed chair once again and joined the waiting room crowd staring at a black and white television. A Kenyan reporter droned on in a monotone voice, delivering Mombasa's evening news. Dylan looked captivated.

"You interested in this?" Angie asked in hushed tones.

"I'm just making sure we're not on it. The location of the mine and news of Tanner's survival mustn't be made common knowledge." Dylan kept his focus on the screen.

"I didn't think about that. There weren't any reporters at the site."

"They could have obtained information from the police. Officer Karani said we need to keep the thieves thinking they took him out, but can everyone at the police station keep quiet? I doubt it." Dylan whispered.

Angie tried her cell but couldn't get reception. Staring at the walls, she replayed the scene of Tanner slipping from her embrace after taking a bullet. *Lord, please let him live.*

"Angie, are you okay?" Dylan interrupted her thoughts.

"Yeah, just thinking."

He handed her a tissue. "Your thoughts are running down your face."

"Oh, I didn't realize. It's been a long day." She wiped her cheeks. "Thanks."

"Did you get some good pictures today?" Dylan changed the subject, probably to help her manage.

"Yes, I really did. Some need to be enlarged and hung in the halls of the Ward building."

"Do you have pictures of Ward's other mines?" Dylan spoke softly, keeping watch on the news being reported.

"No, but that will change. It would help the staff to have a visual of the work being done in the field." Her wheels were turning, rethinking the events of the day.

Angie fanned herself with a rumpled magazine. Humidity hinted at a rain shower in the distance.

After five long hours, the surgeon came through the double doors and faced Dylan and her. Angie stood on shaky legs and hurried toward him.

"He is doing fairly well. The bullet was lodged one-half inch above his heart. Retrieving it was tedious. Excessive blood loss has left him weak, but barring any setbacks, he should make a full recovery."

"Thank you for all you've done." Angie smiled.

"I'm glad I could help. We must keep him sedated for the first forty-eight hours. Further blood loss could turn his situation critical. We'll allow him to wake gradually, and then he must have several days of complete rest for a while until he regains his strength."

"We'll make sure he does." Dylan smiled and shook the doctor's hand.

"The nurse will let you know when he's in a room. I will be checking on his progress over the next few days." He retreated through the double doors.

"Thank the Lord." Angie rubbed her tight shoulders.

Dylan ran his fingers through his unruly blond hair. "Yes. I'm going to check on our other two patients. You going to wait here?"

"Yeah, I'll make myself comfortable in these back-breaking chairs and watch for your picture on the TV." She pulled another chair closer to prop her feet up and tuned into the evening news, listening closely this time.

As the credits rolled across the screen, Angie eased to the nurse's desk to see if there was an update.

Placing her glasses on the end of her nose, the head nurse looked at a chart. Without speaking, she went to check on the patient, returning with a slow stride.

"You can see him now. He has been taken to a private room, number 118. It's down the hall on the left." She eyed Angie over her glasses.

"Thank you." Angie located his room and eased in quietly, with Dylan close behind. The hospital room was simple with pale mint green walls and aging tile on the floor. It appeared fairly clean—the smell of ammonia lingered. A mosquito net hung near the headboard for use in the evenings. The bed had to be lowered and raised manually, dating it to antique status. The IV apparatus and monitors were ancient but usable. Bars were on the windows to keep out intruders, both human and animal. A retro-looking rotary phone sat on a plain, weathered table.

"This is like browsing in an antique store. How old is this equipment?" Angie whispered.

"I'm glad this stuff still works." Dylan picked up the receiver on the phone and listened. "There's a dial tone."

Tanner was asleep, with wires attached to a breathing monitor, a heart monitor, and an IV. A nurse was checking his blood pressure. "He's still out. The doctor wants to keep him sedated. He doesn't want the hemorrhaging to begin again." She posted her findings on a chart and hung it on the end of his bed. After folding the blood pressure device, she silently left the room.

Dylan yawned and settled himself in another uncomfortable straight-backed chair. The monitor beeped the steady rhythm of Tanner's heart as Angie stepped to the end of the bed and studied Tanner's chart.

"It's in Swahili."

"This is Africa. What did you expect?"

"English." She hung it back on the bed.

The door eased open, and Officer Karani stepped inside and eyed Tanner's sleeping form. "Did the doctor give you a good report?"

Dylan stood. "Yes, he's strong. The bullet was lodged above his heart, but the doctor said he should survive."

"That is good to hear. Mr. Callaway, I have some new information. May I speak with you?"

"Yes, of course. You've met Miss Ward? Her grandfather is Alexander Ward, the man who owns the mine." Dylan included her as they took a seat.

"I know your identity. It is good to meet you." He opened his notebook. "Mr. Callaway, the one you wounded, is now in custody. We believe he is the accomplice."

"That's better news than I'd hope for so soon. How did you catch him?" Dylan ran a hand through his blond hair.

"He entered a local clinic and demanded immediate attention, claiming his wound was the result of a shooting accident. Usually, at our clinics, they demand drugs, but this one was suspicious. The physician pressed a silent alarm, signaling for help."

Angie leaned forward. "Thank you for working so hard on this and being quick to act."

"I don't think the other man will be hard to find. After we threatened to deny medical attention, the accomplice confessed to the robbery, saying their assignment was to hit your boss in the heart and the head."

Angie gasped.

"Did he say anything about who is behind the hit?" Dylan flexed his right hand.

"No, I don't think he knows who is behind these attacks. He was anxious to tell us all he knew, and that wasn't part of his knowledge. Mr. Calloway, the actions you took saved your friend's life." The officer closed his notebook.

"I'm glad you have one of the men. That's good news." Angie needed something positive to come from this difficult day.

The officer stood to leave. "Calloway, I have your number, and I'll be in touch. We're watching Wycliff's sister, the bus terminals, and outgoing flights. The person who hired these men is from America. A Western Union transaction from overseas is now part of the evidence stacking up against the shooter. Until we get this guy, I'll post an officer outside Tanner's door. I must take my leave now. There are new leads to follow."

Angie faced Dylan as the officer left. "Why would someone from the US want to hurt Tanner? Grand-Papa will be livid. I suspected funding was coming from the States. What do you think? Is he right?"

"They're probably after the tanzanite and think it belongs to Tanner. These stones are growing in popularity, and they're scarce. Once the mines are empty, there will be no more tanzanite."

"I didn't know."

"Yes, the tanzanite in circulation is all there is. That raises the value considerably. But Tanner is safe now, and the job's done."

"I need to call my grandfather. Will your cell get an overseas line?"

"No, but Tanner's will. Here, use it while you're here at the hospital." He took the cell out of his pocket.

After several tries, it rang through. She spoke in hushed tones as she relayed the news to her grandfather. He had a stream of questions and asked her to keep the news of this attack confidential. She told him the officer had already requested the same thing, but had also promised Grand-Papa.

"Are you sure you're safe, Angelica?" Worry tinged his voice.

"Yes, I'm with Dylan, Tanner's foreman. Please try to take care of yourself and not worry too much."

"He's a good man. Keep me updated."

"I promise. Mum's the word, as they say in Kenya."

"Love you, Angelica."

"Love you too. Bye." Angie held the cell to her chest. Treasuring the sound of his voice. Capturing memories was now more important than ever.

Dylan covered a yawn.

"You're exhausted. Why don't you get a shower and a few hours of sleep? I'm not leaving here until he is out of the danger zone." Angie took a seat.

"Are you sure?" He sat forward and turned to see her face.

"Yeah, I'm fine. There's no reason for both of us to stay."

"If you're sure. I need to get Tanner's work truck from the mine to the inn. I'll take Drew with me to drive the Cruiser. After a nap, I'll leave him at the inn and come back to check on Vickie and Tanner. Do you want me to bring you anything?" He stood and pulled some keys from his pocket.

"For now, I've got some bottled water and crackers, but later, I'd love some of Samson's cooking. Oh, and please tell Samson and Julius what happened. They need to be cautious in case anyone comes there looking for Tanner."

"Call if you need anything else. My number's in Tanner's cell." With that, he closed the door. She listened as his footsteps faded.

In the quietness of the hospital room, Angie prayed for Tanner's strength to return and for healing to begin. She thanked the Lord that the bullet didn't hit his heart.

The sun would be up in about five hours. Sleep was impossible since the guard with a hacking cough had started his nightly vigil. She covered herself with a blanket to protect her body from mosquitoes and planned to nap between the nurse's visits. The nightly routine fell into a rhythm: doze, be woken up, then doze again. She rested little in those five long hours.

After the third nurse visit, something had changed. The monitors beeped with regularity. Tanner still slept, but the guard wasn't coughing. She listened. The hacking had ceased.

Her internal radar peaked.

She slipped a hand into her bag, grabbed her pepper spray, twisted the safety, and inched toward the door. Hidden behind it, she poised for action.

Ten minutes passed.

Nurses chattered as they returned to the nurse's station,

their shoes squeaky on the tile floors. All was quiet except the ticking of a wall clock.

After fifteen nerve-racking minutes, the door eased open.

With a squeak, darkness dissipated.

Angie didn't dare breathe.

Light invaded the room. A gun pointed at Tanner eased ahead of a hand reaching forward.

Angie lunged, shooting pepper spray in the assailant's face and screaming for help.

The gun fell from his hands. With his forward momentum, he shoved Angie, knocking her against the end of the hospital bed.

Ignoring the pain in her wrist and ribs, Angie spun.

But the man reached for his eyes and charged out of the room blindly, slamming into the door frame.

Angie couldn't breathe. Pain pierced her side as pepper spray, lingering in the air, stung her eyes and nose.

Nurses notified the police and came running. Angie gripped the end of Tanner's bed and clutched her injured ribs.

Tanner was still alive.

Hospital guards barged into the room and searched for the intruder, but he'd disappeared into the night. Officer Karani had received the call, hurried to the hospital, and confiscated the weapon while other officers took fingerprints from the door. Police found the original guard in a storage closet. The guard reported he saw the suspect with another attacker from the mine who was seeking medical help. When the guard addressed the suspect, the man knocked him out.

"Angie, what happened?" Dylan stormed into the room. "I saw the investigator rushing into the hospital and followed him."

"He came back." She held her side.

"Who?" He offered her his hand.

"The murderer. He tried to shoot Tanner again." She rubbed her swelling wrist.

"Are you okay?" He helped her to a chair.

"It's just some bumps and bruises. Nothing's broken." She rubbed her side. "Can you get me something to wipe my eyes?"

"Sure, mine are burning too. What is that?" He stepped aside for a nurse carrying a fan into the room.

"Miss Ward used pepper spray to stop the attacker." Karani joined their conversation. "She saved Tanner's life. He must be an important person." He thumbed through his notebook and stepped closer to Dylan toward the oscillating fan that relieved their burning eyes. "Miss Ward, please walk me through the events of the last attack. Do you always carry that eye-burning spray with you?" He was thorough, asking a lot of questions.

She recounted the events for him. "And *yes,* I do carry pepper spray with me. Did anyone see him leave the hospital?" Angie wanted to make sure he wasn't hanging around to try again.

"He is gone, Miss Ward. Do not worry. A street boy told us he got into a blue truck. A woman was driving. I think his sister helped him. She probably doesn't know what he has done. I think he's going to leave Kenya. So, we must catch him soon." He tipped his hat. "I must take my leave."

Housekeeping came to mop the room. The smell of ammonia blended with the pepper spray, making Angie cough.

"Angie, let's get something to eat. Police are going to be here in full force for a while, and your new perfume is burning my eyes." Dylan gave her a half smile.

Angie laughed, grabbing at her bruised ribs. "I never thought about pepper spray having repercussions. Are you sure Tanner will be okay?"

"*Dada,* your friend will be in good care. Not to worry." The head nurse said. "I will not leave."

Something in the kind woman's eyes struck a chord of trust within Angie. "All right, but we'll be quick. I am hungry." She grabbed her purse and led the way to the parking lot.

Dylan commandeered the Cruiser. "I know it's early, but is Chinese food okay with you? There is a great place that's close. They start cooking at daybreak, and it will be fresh."

"Sounds good." Angie held on to her side as they hit a pothole. "Why are you in Africa, Dylan?"

"Tanner." He shifted gears and entered a parking lot. "I was left standing at the altar, and Tanner was my best man. He offered me a job, and I thought a change of scenery was a good idea at the time."

"Sorry, I asked. I remember Tanner telling me about it. That had to hurt." She slid out of the truck. "I've felt similar pain. It takes a while to recover. Some days you don't know if you'll ever get past it."

Dylan held the door for her. "You sound like you speak from experience. It has been rough, but I think I'm finally getting my bearings. It's time to go home and start my law practice."

"I'm glad." Angie picked up the menu. "Let's order quickly. I want to get back to the hospital."

"Sure, we can get it to go and head back." He stepped to the counter to place his order, then moved aside to allow Angie to make her selection. "This place usually has the food ready in no time."

Angie stepped back into room 118 and found it empty. "Where is he?"

She pivoted and marched to the nurse's station.

Dylan's stride got him there first. "Excuse me. The patient

in room 118 isn't there. Do you know where they've moved him?"

"Yes, please follow me." Without revealing the room number, she led them to the elevator. Once the doors closed, she faced Dylan. "He has been moved to a new private suite for tighter security. His location is being kept secret. He will be safe here."

"Thanks. Great idea."

Mint green sterile décor prevailed in the new, nicer accommodations. Its sitting area made her smile. A couch gave her the promise of much-needed rest.

"He looks unfazed by all the excitement." Dylan stood at Tanner's bedside.

"It's good he was sedated. He would have tried to get up, which could have caused him to bleed again." Angie studied his monitors, grateful for the indication he was alive.

"He loves you. You know that, right?" Dylan stared at Angie.

"We've always been close." She looked away.

"No, he's in love with you."

"He loves me like a sister or a friend. I don't think it goes any further than that. Did you sleep at all?" She needed to change the subject.

"For a couple hours. Samson sent you some food, and Julius sent you a flyswatter. He's worried about mosquitoes."

"I appreciate that." She smiled and pulled the flyswatter out of the bag.

Dylan's phone dinged, signaling a text. He read the message. "Let's enjoy our Chinese food, then, if you're okay, I'm going to take Vickie to the inn. She's better, and they're releasing her in about an hour. After I get her settled, I want to check with the investigator on their progress. I'll come back to relieve you." He moved toward the door.

"I'm good for today with the food Samson sent. But if you can stay here starting tomorrow until they release him, I'll get a bungalow ready for use while he recuperates. He doesn't need to climb stairs for a while."

"Sounds like a plan. Call if you need anything."

Angie found a blanket and pillow in a closet and made herself comfortable. Her ribs were aching, and her wrist was throbbing, but Tanner was still breathing.

On the third day after surgery, the doctor eased back on the sedation. Tanner woke up. His mouth dry, he spoke in a whisper. "Dylan, what happened?"

Dylan stuck a straw into a glass of water and put it in Tanner's mouth. "We were robbed, and Wycliff shot you. The bullet missed your heart by half an inch. After your surgery, they kept you sedated for a couple days to let your body heal."

"Where's Angie?"

He gave Tanner another drink. "She didn't leave your side for two days and nights. When the doctor said he was going to release you tomorrow, she left me here as your nursemaid and chauffeur. She's getting a bungalow ready because the stairs will be too strenuous for a few weeks."

"Are Drew and Vickie okay?"

"Both had concussions, some cuts and bruises, a couple of shiners, but they're fine. They're recuperating at the inn, probably poolside. They may hit you up for sick pay." Dylan smiled.

"I'm glad they're okay. That's a relief. Did we lose a lot of stones?" Tanner licked his chapped lips.

"We lost some. Don't know how much yet. I shot one of the

thieves, and Officer Karani followed the clues and caught the wounded man." He offered Tanner more water.

"But everyone is okay?"

"Yeah, Angie got a little banged up when the murderer arrived at the hospital to finish you off. She sprayed him with pepper spray, stopping him from shooting you—saving your life. She's doing okay, just a couple of bruises."

"So, he's still out there?" Tanner fought to process all the news.

"I'm afraid so."

"When can we get out of here?"

"Probably tomorrow. The doctor wants you up and walking first."

"That's no problem." Tanner sat. "Wow, the room's spinning." He grabbed the bed rail.

"Hey, slow down there, Speedy. You lost a lot of blood and have been down for days. You've gotta move slowly. We'll get you sitting up first, then try to stand." Dylan helped him by turning the crank at the end of the bed and raising the head manually.

"Now that the world isn't spinning, where are my clothes?"

"Sitting is all you're going to do today, but tomorrow, after they unhook all these wires and tubes, I'll get that big smelly nurse to help you dress." Dylan grinned.

Tanner smiled. "I thought you were my friend."

Angie chose the first bungalow for Tanner. Its proximity to the restaurant made it the logical choice. Open windows allowed the ocean breeze to drive out musty smells while Julius changed the linens. Angie checked out the television. "I'll have Samson exchange this TV with the one in my bungalow."

"If he is busy, I can do that for you, *dada*."

"Thanks. But you have a lot to do." She went to the storage room in search of a new mosquito net, picked up an extra blanket, and talked to Samson about moving the TVs.

"Hey, Angie. You need some help?" Drew rested by the pool near the bungalow.

Angie prepared for Tanner. "I think we've got it. Thanks for asking."

"You need to rest, Angie. You've been through a lot the last few weeks." Drew sat in his lounge chair and faced her. The sparkling pool beside him was forgotten while the injured on the team healed.

"I'll rest when I have everything ready for Tanner. We're almost done."

"I'll save you a chair." He lay back and closed his eyes. Both were swollen, and one was black.

"Julius, would you bring a couple of short-sleeved shirts with buttons and some pants with a stretchy waist from Tanner's closet? He'll need his toiletries and personal items as well."

"I will retrieve them, Miss Angeleeka." He hurried up the stairs.

Angie powered up her laptop, sent the email she'd written to Leslie sitting in her inbox, and typed an email to her friends about her delayed return. She promised to fill them in on the details when she got home. She initiated the email process and sighed when it went through.

Samson served lunch, humming as he worked. *Mzee* mocked him, singing in Swahili.

Drew laughed as he pulled out a chair. "Great duet, Samson. You're singing with a bird."

Their teasing helped Angie to relax until Vickie joined them.

"What's for lunch?" She pulled out a chair and sat by Drew. "It smells good."

"You feeling better?" Breaking the ice between them would be good.

"I still have a headache, but I'm going to survive." She put a napkin in her lap. "So, Angie, when's the boss getting out of the hospital?"

"Tomorrow morning." Angie wondered about just how tight Vickie and Tanner were. Had they professed feelings for one another? Was it one-sided? Maybe Vickie broke Tanner's heart? It had to be hard to be a woman out here, all alone, working with a group of men. Still, Angie could only feel one thing toward Vickie, and it wasn't completely kind.

Samson served beef stew and bread for lunch. Julius delivered cold sodas while Drew kept the conversation moving. Angie finished her meal and checked Tanner's room one last time before hibernating in her bungalow.

Having a late dinner, Angie ate alone. Swaying palms and ocean waves were great entertainment as they brought peace to the setting. Only a few more days left. Should Angie rethink this and bare her heart before she returned home? Let Tanner decide what to do with the fallout, or was it already too late because of Vickie? Either way, she was breaking it off with Mason. Then there was the stuff Dylan said about Tanner being in love, which didn't make sense, and made her feel like maybe she should tell him and let the chips fall where they may. She hated this uncertainty. Taking a deep breath, she turned back to her computer. *It's time to book my return flight.*

Traveling from the hospital mid-morning to Paradise Inn was

excruciating for Tanner, even though Dylan went as slow as he could without getting run over.

"Ouch," Tanner grabbed his bandage as he clung to the armrest. Every pothole Dylan hit sent earth-shattering pain ripping through Tanner's bones. They couldn't get to Paradise Inn fast enough.

"Sorry, man. I'm trying to dodge the potholes and stray animals. I think I hit a couple of pedestrians, though." Dylan smiled, but when he obviously caught Tanner's tight expression, he spun back to the wheel and spoke softly. "We're almost there."

"That's good." Tanner held on, bracing his body for another roundabout.

"Lean back and close your eyes."

"I'm ready to hit the sack. You're wearing me out."

"Lean back and close your eyes. They grated the road up ahead. You'll think you're riding a vibrating chair instead of a bucking bronco."

Tanner's arrival at Paradise Inn was a big event. Henry, the new guard, opened the gate while the street kids yelled greetings. "*Bwana* Tanner, *Bwana* Tanner. Welcome back." He waved to them, encouraged by their winning smiles. Angie really made some great changes around the place.

As they reached the lobby, Samson and Julius grinned. Vickie and Drew looked pretty beat up, but happy to see him. Angie's smile told him all was right with the world.

Exhausted from the ride across Mombasa, Tanner accepted Dylan's help into the bungalow. Samson's steamed fish and rice wafted on the ocean breeze as Tanner settled into the soft bed.

Dylan put his hands on his hips. "Take the pills the doc sent to help with the pain and rest until lunch. Angie's preparing a lunch tray for you."

Tanner closed his eyes as Dylan shut the door.

Sleep came easy.

~

Angie stood on the sidelines and let Dylan and Julius get Tanner settled in his bungalow. She discussed a meal plan with Samson for Tanner's first few days and busied herself with his lunch tray. His soup wasn't quite ready.

"He's pretty worn out, so he'll sleep until lunch." Dylan grabbed a water bottle out of the cooler.

"What were the doctor's final instructions about Tanner's medicine and follow-up doctor visits?" Angie stirred Tanner's soup on the stovetop, waiting for it to finish cooking.

"Absolute bed rest, keep him hydrated, watch for fever, continue the pain medicine for the first week, and the antibiotics for ten days. The doctor wants you to call his office about his follow-up visits." Dylan acted as though he was ticking off a list. "Here's the phone number."

"Good job." Angie took the paper. "I'll call his office while I wait for Tanner's soup." She headed for the lobby to use the landline. Now is not the right time to hash out matters of the heart. Tanner needed to focus on healing his body. Angie could wait.

Chapter Fourteen

"Julius, would you be sure the guards are diligent in their job? The murderer hasn't been caught yet. We can't let our guard down." Angie dusted the desk in the lobby.

"I will remind them, Miss Angeleeka." He walked toward the front gate.

Angie kept moving at Paradise Inn. Seeing Tanner in such a weakened state reminded her of how close they came to losing him. So, she delegated some of the day-to-day tasks to make sure he was cared for, but not available for lengthy conversations.

"Vickie, could you take this lunch tray to Tanner?"

"Sure." She hurried to assist, with Drew following close behind.

"Drew, it's time for his antibiotic and fever reducer. I just talked with his doctor. He has ordered an additional med. I'm going to the chemist to get the prescription filled."

"We'll keep an eye on the patient." Drew opened the bungalow door for Vickie.

"I'm sure he'll be entertained."

Drew gave her a thumbs-up.

With Julius tagging along, Angie downshifted the Land Cruiser and entered Mombasa traffic without incident. Still, she kept her eyes on the landscape, watching for Wycliff. She was glad it wasn't far to the chemist. Julius's firm grip on the dash let her know he was relieved as well.

"Julius, I might need your help with my Swahili."

"Sure, *dada*." He followed her into the pharmacy.

Angie spoke with the chemist, informing him of the antibiotic the doctor had prescribed, along with the exact dosage and prescription strength. He busied himself packaging the tablets. Angie paid for the meds and plowed into the roundabout chaos, laying on her horn like the other drivers did.

Julius remained quiet for the ride. *Maybe he's praying.*

She returned with the meds and tossed the keys to Dylan. "How's our patient?"

"Vickie said he didn't eat much of his lunch. He said he didn't feel good."

Concerned, she hurried to his room and knocked lightly. With no answer, she eased inside. Sweat dotted Tanner's brow, and he was shaking. Angie pressed the thermometer into his mouth—103 degrees. No wonder he had chills quaking his torso.

She rushed back to the kitchen. "Tanner has a high fever, which could mean an infection. Julius, get some blankets. Samson, grab a bag of ice and some cold water. Dylan, the extra-strength Tylenol is in the storeroom on the top shelf. Tanner has a high fever. This could mean he has an infection." She tore open the package of antibiotics. "Dylan, hurry. I need your help."

They worked in tandem. Angie gave the antibiotics, fever reducer, and pain meds. Dylan kept the ice bags coming for Tanner's forehead and body. The ice melted fast against his warm skin. Angie bathed his face and kept him drinking fluids every time he awoke.

She pressed the thermometer inside his mouth again. A wave of gratitude washed over her when she discovered the fever was going down.

"Angie," Dylan spoke in a hushed tone. "We might need to work this in shifts."

"I'm staying."

"Okay. I'll go to sleep for a while. Wake me if the fever returns. I'll help you get it down, then I'll stay with him and let you sleep."

"That's a good plan."

Tanner moaned occasionally.

Angie steeled herself to hear him call Vickie's name again, but he never called out for her or anyone. Angie was thankful. Caring for him, the intimacy of wiping his face, watching him sleep, and meeting his eyes when he woke tore at her heart. Torture enough.

"Thank you, Ang—" Tanner whispered.

"It's what friends do, Tanner. Rest now."

This routine kept them busy for thirty-six hours. The antibiotics helped, and Tanner's fever finally broke. With Tanner covered in perspiration, Dylan helped him to the shower and changed his bandages while Julius changed his bed linens. He slept peacefully for a couple of hours. He'd turned a corner—hopefully, the worst had passed.

Angie left Dylan in charge of Tanner's meds and went to rest for a minute in her bungalow. After a shower, she slept, exhausted after the round-the-clock vigil.

Since the shooting, she'd avoided intimate conversations with Tanner. Once he recovered enough, he would sense something was wrong. Unless he was surrounded by his team.

She would have to steer clear if she was going to give him time to heal and not delve into matters of the heart.

While Tanner slept in a lounge chair under an umbrella, his team sunbathed around the pool. Samson was singing, Julius wore a smile, and *Mzee* was whistling *The Andy Griffith Show* theme.

Angie took this opportunity to pack her suitcases. It was time to go home.

Wanting the coolest thing she had for this hot, tropical weather, Angie donned her white sundress. Grabbing her camera, she set out to take a few photos. Tanner was still sleeping by the pool. It was a great picture. As she took her third shot, she noticed him staring at her. She caught that pose, checked it on her digital screen, and smiled in his direction.

"Looks like you're feeling better." She walked closer to his chair. "You've got some color in your face."

"I am feeling better. It's good to be outside, even if it is under an umbrella. Those walls were closing in." He shaded his eyes with his right hand.

"Be careful out here. Your medication warns against direct sunlight. We could move you to another room if you want."

"No, it's fine. In a few days, I'll be able to go upstairs again." He paused. "Angie, where have you been?"

She sat on the lounge chair beside him. "What do you mean? I've been right here, taking care of you."

"You're here, but your heart isn't. There's something different in your eyes. I can see it."

"Tanner, I have had a lot on my mind, but maybe it's fear you're reading in my eyes. You could have died. The bullet barely missed your heart. You scared me, and I don't scare easily. I've nearly lost you twice. And Wycliff is still out there somewhere. So, the threat isn't over."

"I'm still here, Ang—and I'm not going anywhere." He reached over and took her hand.

Vickie and Drew chose that moment to take another swim, breaking up their conversation. Angie was thankful. Their laughing and splashing gave her a chance to retreat.

"It's time to feed the kids. I'm going to help Julius and take some pictures. See you later, Tanner." She squeezed his hand and left.

She served chai and bread to the kids and took pictures of them individually and in groups. They loved to pose, then see the shots of themselves on her digital screen. They'd won her heart. She cherished their smiles. "Julius, take a picture of me with our kids."

"Sure." He took the camera.

"Okay, guys, come in close and smile for me." Angie put her arms around the group—touching as many of them as she could—hating to let them go.

After depositing their tea cups in the kitchen, Angie strolled the beach alone, except for some hermit crabs scurrying across the sand. She left footprints behind as she listened to the waves. It created a perfect place to pray with only the seagulls to interrupt her thoughts as the coolness of the waves washed over her toes.

Lord, thank you for letting Tanner live. I've talked to you about him as often as these waves have washed this shore. My past and my future are colliding, creating warring emotions. I'm trusting you. I need your strength.

~

From the patio, Tanner studied Angie. He sat as if in a daze, memorizing her every move. She looked sultry with her white sundress blowing in the breeze while the wind whipped her hair. Framed by a backdrop of ocean waves and a setting sun, she was enchanting.

His tea cooled, ignored. When she reached the top step by the pool area, their eyes met. She paused, then slowly took the chair beside him.

"You've been watching me, haven't you?" She faced him, studying his expression.

"Some habits are hard to break." He took a deep breath. "Your work here has really made a difference. To me. To the team. To the children here. You belong here, Angie. You know that?"

"No, I'm an American girl, through and through. I can't make my home in Kenya." She was quiet for a moment. "When are you coming home?"

"I don't know. I have to get well first." He reached over and took her hand. "We haven't had time to talk. You're amazing, and I know you're going to be successful at whatever you do with your life. I'm proud of you for getting your master's degree, Angie. I'm sorry for leaving you alone for so long."

"Tanner, I—"

"Hey guys, dinner's almost ready. Samson said in twenty minutes." Drew yelled toward the pool area.

They ignored him.

"Angie, you look sad, disappointed. I sense you're struggling. What's wrong? You're searching. What are you looking for?"

She answered in a whisper. "To be loved. I want to be someone's priority, his soul mate, his happiest hello and hardest goodbye." She stood. "Tanner, not everyone gets a 'happily ever after.' It's time for me to grow up and face the future, whatever it holds. I need to go now." She leaned forward and kissed him on the cheek. "And you're forgiven." She turned and left.

"Ang—let's talk after dinner." She smiled, but it didn't reach her eyes. When she turned and left with a wave, refusing to turn around and answer, Tanner's stomach tightened. Something was very wrong. He watched her walk away, confused, but he'd find a time to get her alone and figure it out together. He wasn't going to make the same mistake again. This time around, he'd give her all the attention she needed, she deserved. He'd be the one with the happiest hello and hardest goodbye if she would have him.

As the sun set, Samson called the group to the table for dinner.

"Dylan, help me." Tanner gave him a piece of cloth.

"Sure." He tied Tanner's arm in a sling to minimize movement of the injured shoulder.

"Thanks, it helps with the pain. I'm still so sore."

For the first time since his surgery, Tanner sat at the table with the team, reserving a place for Angie.

"Hey, Boss, please don't let Dylan be in charge again. He's temperamental and a real slave driver." Drew smiled and plopped a piece of bread in his mouth.

Dylan laughed. "What do you mean, slave driver? You haven't done a lick of work since you started drawing sick pay. I think your concussion has made you delusional."

Vickie smiled at their teasing, but it didn't reach her eyes.

"You still have a headache?" She was quieter than usual.

"Yes, but it's getting better every day."

"Vickie, you rest tomorrow. Dylan put Drew back on

regular pay and find something for him to do." Tanner raised a glass of Coke to his team.

"Glad to have you back, Boss. But will you reconsider putting me to work? I still have a headache, and if I get tired, it could make my concussion worse." Drew held his head like a man in pain.

They shared a laugh. It felt good.

After serving their soup, Samson returned to the kitchen. Within minutes, he rushed back to the table. "*Bwana*, Tanner."

"Yes, Samson. What is it?" Tanner held his spoon mid-air.

"Miss Angeleeka—" Samson was wiping his hands on a dish towel.

"What about her?" Tanner scooted his chair back.

"She is leaving the inn." He pointed toward the lobby.

"Now?" Tanner got up, holding onto the table for support. He motioned for the team to stay put, and he walked to the lobby. Julius was putting her luggage into a London cab. Angie stood poised. Magazine material wrapped in skinny jeans with high-heeled boots to accentuate her height.

"Angie, you're leaving?" By her slight jump when he said her name, he knew he'd surprised her.

"I told you I had to go. You know goodbyes are hard for me." She bit her bottom lip, a trait he'd seen many times, designed to keep her from crying.

The driver waited at the curb as Julius placed her camera case in the backseat.

"Tanner, kiss me quick and let me go." Tears pooled in her eyes.

He stepped forward, wrapped his strong arm around her, and felt her sob against him. He didn't want to let go, but couldn't make her stay. She looked up with a tear-stained face. "I love you, Tanner."

"And I love you, Angie. I hope you find what you're looking for." He wiped her tears with his thumb.

Angie, staring, reached up, and touched his lips. She said, *"Nina penda wewe sana. Tutaonana."* With tears streaming down her cheeks, she waved goodbye to Julius and Samson, got into the taxi, and closed the door. When the driver reached the gate, she turned around for a final wave.

Tanner fought the new pain piercing his heart as Angie left the property—a pain that had nothing to do with his surgery.

Not ready to face his team, he retreated to his upstairs suite, climbing the stairs slowly, taking one deliberate step at a time.

"Julius, tell the others I'll see them tomorrow. Have Samson bring me a small plate."

"Yes, *Bwana.*"

"And Julius, what did she say in Swahili before she left?" Tanner waited.

He spoke sheepishly. "She said, 'I love you very much, and I will see you when you see me.'" He paused. "She asked me to teach her to say those words."

Angie didn't expect it to be so hard to leave Africa, the street kids, the staff, Paradise Inn, and especially Tanner. She wept all the way to the airport—through roundabouts, traffic jams, and a herd of cattle.

Pushing her pile of luggage, she started her trek through security. Her first-class status helped expedite the check-in process. Walking to her gate, she listened to the lilt of Swahili spoken along with broken British English and enjoyed seeing brightly colored mismatched prints on their attire. Some carried babies on their backs while others pushed modern strollers. Many men carried briefcases, and others had documents in plastic bags. Yet, all seemed comfortable in their status in life. The smells of coffee and tea for sale at curio shops reminded her of mornings at the inn. Like a dry sponge, she soaked up all of Kenya she could before they asked her to board the plane.

"Welcome, Miss Ward. Can I get you anything? You look upset." The flight attendant waited with a kind smile.

Angie wiped her tears with the back of her hand. "No, I just need to get home."

"If I can be of assistance, please press the button." She squeezed Angie's hand before moving on.

As the first-class recliner encased her, Angie covered herself with a blanket and let the 767 carry her to Nairobi, London, and then home to Dallas. *Lord, my heart is so heavy the plane may never lift off the ground.*

~

Comfortable in his executive corner office, Mason enjoyed the last of his morning brew as he read Alexander Ward's name on his cell.

"Yes, sir. How can I help you?" Mason poised his pen to make notes.

"Mason, I need you to set up a meeting. Give it high priority. You've always done an impeccable job for me in the past. I want it scheduled for ten days from tomorrow, on Friday morning at ten o'clock, here at Ward Enterprises. Let's use the small conference room that adjoins my office."

"Sir, would you like refreshments catered?" Mason recorded the date, time, and venue.

"Yes, have light refreshments, the usual fare. You know how I like things."

Mason made a note to call the caterer. "And who is invited to this meeting?"

"I will chair the meeting with you on my right and Joseph on my left. Please call my attorney. He is expecting your call. Ask him to bring my will and the documents we discussed. Angelica has returned. One seat will be for her."

"She's back?" He added her name to the list.

"Yes, she arrived yesterday and is struggling with jet lag. I'm sure the malaria has exacerbated her exhaustion. I'm going to have Doc Ellis check her blood to make sure she is still recovering as expected. I had Joseph see her home from the airport. He said she looked weary."

"Give her my love. I'll give her a few days to rest before I call her, but flowers are in order." *I'm her fiancé, and he sent Joseph to pick her up at the airport.* Mason reined in his temper, wadded a piece of paper, and threw it across his office.

"About the meeting, I'll seat Angelica on my right." Mason tried to sound authoritative.

"I have two more guests, so there'll be seven in total." Ward used that matter-of-fact tone Mason hated so much.

"And the names of your two guests?" Mason waited for the information.

"They shall remain nameless for now. That is all."

"Consider it done. Is there an agenda to be prepared?" Mason hated it when Ward didn't give him full disclosure. Despite his frustration, he remained professional.

"I haven't completed my notes yet. I'll have Judy prepare the documents for this meeting."

"I'll make these arrangements today."

"Thanks, Mason. I knew I could count on you." Ward ended the call.

Mason cursed under his breath. *He can't die soon enough for me.*

259

∽

A bubble bath never felt so good. Angie had thought about her large whirlpool tub while in Africa. But now, sitting among lit candles in these luxurious surroundings, she wished she were back in Kenya with the kids, the staff—and Tanner.

Having dinner scheduled with Grand-Papa, she fought a war of emotions, trying to get prepared to meet his piercing gaze. She blamed jet lag and unpacking for keeping to herself the first week after her return. Donning an amethyst necklace to match her lavender dress, she hoped he'd be pleased. He loved for her to look her best at dinner, even if it was being held at home.

Arriving promptly at seven, Angie rushed to greet him as he hobbled into the dining room. He kissed one of her cheeks, then the other.

"Welcome home, my dear. Did you have a pleasant journey?"

"Yes, Grand-Papa. But I'm glad to be home." She placed her arm in the crook of his elbow as they moved toward the table.

"I see Mason's flowers arrived." He motioned to her centerpiece adorning the table.

"Yes, this morning. It's the third bouquet this week."

"You look tired, Angelica. Are you well?" He moved to pull out her chair, always, the gentleman.

"My trip was eventful. The malaria drained me, but I'm recovering. My blood tests improved before I left the continent. Malaria lingers in the bloodstream, but the symptoms have subsided." She smiled, hoping he believed her ailment was physical, not emotional.

"Malaria is serious, my dear. I've taken the liberty of asking Doc Ellis to check your blood. He is seeing me tomorrow afternoon. I'll have him stop by."

"Sure, Grand-Papa. That will be fine."

The butler poured their water and served their soup.

"In Kenya, they have the best soups I've ever tasted. I don't know how they make them, but next time I'm there, I want to get the recipes." She tasted her broth.

Ward stared at his granddaughter. "You want to learn to cook?"

"Yes, I could give the staff a night off from time to time. They work round the clock. They would probably appreciate the rest."

"You care about our staff being overworked?" He sat back. "You've changed, Angelica." He shook his head. "You surprise me."

"They serve us faithfully."

"Again, you surprise me."

"I'd just like to show my appreciation to them." She patted his hand. "Eat. The soup's good."

They dined in comfortable silence, happy to be together.

"Well, did you have a good time in Kenya?" Ward pushed his empty soup bowl aside.

"A wonderful time." Caesar salads were served. "You would have been appalled at the run-down condition of Paradise Inn when I arrived. Uncut grass had grown three feet high, trash was scattered in all directions, and the sign squeaked as it hung on one hinge. The place needed painting and decorating. I got busy, hired workers and a seamstress, and recruited some street children. People were working everywhere. You would have loved it. In two weeks, we had the place restored to pristine condition." She missed eating salads while in Africa and savored the first bite.

"Did you get Tanner's okay first?" His brow creased in concern.

"No, he was off someplace with his team."

That brought a frown to Grand-Papa's face.

"Is it a problem, Grand-Papa?"

"Could be a minor one. We were using the run-down condition of the inn as a front for mining the tanzanite. It kept guests away while maintaining the security of the tanzanite. We didn't maintain the resort to five-star status by design to keep the team safe. They utilized the resort when taking R & R. During those times, they prepared the stones for shipment and shipped them from Mombasa. We didn't need extra eyes on our valuable stones."

"Oh, Grand-Papa, I didn't know." Her fork made a clanging noise when it hit the china. "I should have listened to Samson and Julius. They said Tanner didn't want it changed. But no. I took control and transformed the place." She sat back in her chair. "Did I put Tanner in more danger than before? Is that why he was shot?"

"Don't blame yourself, my dear. I think the attack may be connected with my overseas endeavors. It's a business matter that will soon be resolved."

"Why do you say that?" Angie's mind raced to process this news as her fear for Tanner collided with her concern for her grandfather and their business.

"Some things have been suspicious around the office lately."

"I'm sure you're taking steps to address the matter."

"Yes, I've hired an investigator and called for an audit. That will determine my next steps."

Angie frowned. "I wish you didn't have to deal with this right now. What can I do?"

"I need you to be in the conference room adjacent to my office next Friday morning at ten for a very important business meeting."

"Of course. My friends are visiting this week, but I'll be there. It's time for me to get to work."

"You've already done excellent work completing your assignment and getting the extension for the mine. And don't feel bad about your work at the inn. We were going to update the facility after the job was complete. You did us a favor." He squeezed her hand.

Angie sighed. "I hope so."

"I'm certain you transformed Paradise Inn into a showplace. And I'm glad you were there when Tanner needed you. I heard about the pepper spray incident." His eyes lit up. "You were quite the hero. I'm proud of you."

"I'm a Ward, and we play the cards dealt us." She waited for their waiter to place the entrees in front of them, her heart in her throat. "I'm thankful I was there. Even after the bullet missed his heart by half an inch and the attacker returned to finish the job, an infection created a bad fever. Dylan and I nursed him through the worst part. But he's strong. He'll survive." She tasted the steaming pasta, scorching her tongue. She grabbed her water glass.

"Tanner will recover, but will you? You're distracted, guarded. I can see you left part of your heart in Kenya—with Tanner."

Angie stared at her grandfather. "I thought you wanted me to marry Mason."

"But you don't love him."

"How do you know who holds my heart?"

"Angelica, you've been in love with Tanner for years. Mason clearly manipulated you with his proposal. But you have a good head on your shoulders, and I knew you would do the right thing."

Tears filled her eyes. "But he doesn't love me."

"I think the jury is still out on that one, my dear. Give it time and prayer. He's a good man. Valuable to Ward Enterprises and to you."

"Grand-Papa, why tanzanite?"

"Tanzanite is extremely valuable. The gems are a symbol of love, commitment, and permanence. The Africans who discovered the stones say its brilliance ignites passions impossible to measure as it embraces your soul for years to come." He tasted his lasagna.

"Well, they're beautiful."

They ate in silence, except for their forks tapping the china.

"Grand-Papa, if the mining job is finished, what are you going to do with Paradise Inn? It's a great property. Are you going to sell it?"

"Probably. We have no further use for it. I haven't given it much thought." He took a sip of water.

"Could we donate it?" She waited.

"Donate the inn? That would be a sizable donation, Angelica. For what purpose?"

"As a place for street children. An orphanage." She watched his expression.

"Street children?" He sat back in his chair.

"Yes. The streets of Kenya are overrun with three hundred thousand children whose parents have died of AIDS, typhoid, or malaria, leaving them to fend for themselves. They sleep on the streets and scavenge for food to survive. I've made some special friends who live around the inn and have worked with me to clean up the resort. We fed them at the gate every day. It's such a great need. Would you think about it?"

"That was quite a speech." He paused. "I'll consider it. Draw up a proposal, and we'll discuss it."

"Thanks, Grand-Papa." She squeezed his hand.

After they enjoyed red velvet cake and Kenyan AA coffee, Angie moved to her chaise lounge and stretched out.

Ward stood to leave, kissing her good night before limping out of her wing of the estate—pain in his steps foreshadowed the impending loss looming in her future. *If only he would let me do more for him. But at least I can be at that meeting.*

Tanner's cell buzzed in his pocket. He answered, swallowing a nervous thrill. "Hello?"

"Alexander Ward here."

"Yes, sir. How are you doing?" Tanner sat up with caution from his bed at Paradise Inn, guarding his injury.

"I think I should ask you that question. How are you recovering?"

"I'm healing and glad to be alive." He rubbed the stubble of his day-old beard. "Can I help you with something?"

"Yes, I need you to come home."

"Home? Is Angie okay? Is my mother well?" Tanner's adrenaline surged.

"Yes, they're fine. Don't be concerned. This is a business matter. We have many things to discuss, and I would like to do this in person. I've called a meeting for next Friday morning. Are you strong enough to travel?"

"The doctors won't be happy, but I can do it. I'll get a ticket for early next week. Can Joseph pick me up at the airport?" Tanner reached for his calendar.

"Yes, I would prefer to keep your arrival a secret."

"Absolutely. I'll send my flight schedule to Joseph. He can fill me in on additional details. I look forward to seeing you, sir. Our job is completed here. I think you'll be pleased."

"Tanner, you've far exceeded my expectations. Take care of yourself and come home safely." The line went quiet.

Tanner reached for his laptop. It took a few minutes for it

to power up. While he waited, his thoughts went to this important meeting. Would Ward reveal who was taking his place at Ward Enterprises? Or was this about assigning his next project in another part of the world? Maybe Joseph would give Tanner some insight. He typed his password, pressed Enter, and waited again for the internet to connect. It took twenty minutes for Wi-Fi to take him to the British Airways site. *I'm going home.*

Angie wiped salty perspiration from her brow as she dug through her moving boxes in the estate's garage. Two cartons fell off when she retrieved her box of books. After blowing dust off her find, she tucked the manual under her arm and went to work, using her dining room table as a desk.

Her presentation for the orphanage had to be formatted perfectly and professionally to make a stellar impression. Hours passed as she researched the plight of street children in Kenya. She sketched a diagram of a facility that would accommodate a hundred children and drafted a tentative budget. She prepared a fax for Julius and Samson, asking them to gather furnishing prices for her from within the country.

The cost of utilities for Paradise Inn would be included in Tanner's monthly reports on the project. This new facility would be comparable in square footage, giving an estimate of future expenses.

Putting this dream on paper to help precious orphans made her mental wheels turn, giving her a reprieve from the angst of her personal challenges.

Chapter Fifteen

"Okay, team, we need to finish things here, pack up, and start new assignments. You've been great teammates and gone above and beyond what was expected. I think we've all grown in our abilities while we worked side by side. I hope this stint will add to your resumes. If you need references, email me. I know you'll excel wherever you go. I'll be leaving in a week myself." Tanner looked from Vickie to Drew to Dylan.

"Are you sure you're up to it?" Dylan's brow furrowed.

"Alexander Ward needs me for a meeting, so I have to try. I'll be careful." Tanner put his hand on Dylan's. "Thanks for saving my life. I'm glad you're a good shot."

"You're welcome. I was worried we wouldn't get paid if something happened to you."

They laughed.

"Yeah, we have a local hero." Drew teased Dylan.

He punched Drew's shoulder.

Tanner smiled at their banter and flipped a page on his clipboard. "Let's make sure we finish earning that pay. Drew, inventory the equipment and organize it in the storage building. Get Julius to help you. Then, you and Dylan prepare the work truck for storage. Drain the oil out of the engine, remove the tires, and leave it on blocks until a decision is made about selling it." He paused, checking his list.

"Vickie, after you send the final shipment of stones to the States, you've completed your responsibilities. You and Drew can empty your bungalows. I have your bank information. I'll continue your insurance for three months from today and your pay until the end of the month. After the value of the tanzanite is assessed, a bonus will be sent to each of your accounts. There'll be a delay on the final amount until the courts release the stolen stones." He looked up from his notes. "I couldn't have asked for better employees."

"I think I speak for the team when I say thanks for the way you've led us." Dylan looked from Drew to Vickie, then Tanner.

"I appreciate that." Tanner closed his notebook.

"Well, if this is going to get sad, I'm out of here." Drew stood to leave the table.

"I don't like goodbyes either." Vickie put her napkin on the table and pushed her chair back. "I'll say it's been fun."

"You two can go. But let me know when you're leaving the inn."

"You got it, Boss." Drew saluted Tanner, keeping things light as he and Vickie left.

"Dylan, I need the court dates, so I'll know when to take the stand." Tanner pushed back from the table and stood.

"Sure. I'll be here long enough to see this thing through. I'll let you know when you're on the docket. Anything else you need help with?" Dylan pushed both their chairs under the table.

"Yes, I had a ring made for Angie. Would you pick it up for me?" Tanner handed him the receipt. "And, since they know you at the airport, can you help me get on the plane? I'll need a wheelchair and someone to help with the luggage."

"Consider it done." Dylan pocketed the receipt and headed to the work truck. "Don't forget to give me a big bonus. Good friends are hard to come by, and you need me."

Tanner laughed at Dylan's final jab as he picked up his Coke and made his way to the lounge chair by the pool. His body needed rest, but mixed emotions kept his mind churning. Saying farewell to his team tugged at him. They had become family as they worked side by side. His curiosity about Ward's meeting had him guessing. He knew his boss was pleased with his work in Kenya, but Alexander Ward kept his plans close to the vest, revealing them in his time.

Angie's heart-warming Swahili phrases replayed in his mind every time he slowed down. He determined to explore her meaning behind her words soon.

Fifteen minutes later, Samson approached Tanner, who was resting at the edge of the pool. "*Bwana* Tanner, you have a guest. He is with the police."

"Thank you, Samson. Bring him to a table in the restaurant." Tanner eased out of the lounge chair and headed to meet the officer.

"Officer Karani, please take a seat." Tanner pulled out a chair with his right hand.

"Thanks. How are you faring?" Karani took a seat.

"I'm weak, but the doctor says I'll make a full recovery." Tanner joined the officer.

"Excellent. Is Mr. Calloway still on the premises?" The investigator looked around for Dylan.

"Yes, he's working." He motioned for Samson. "Ask Dylan to join our meeting."

Dylan soon approached, wiping grease from his hands. "Hello, Officer Karani." He pulled out a chair.

"I came to ask if you wanted to go to the Waiyaki Way bus station. We're going to arrest Wycliff." Karani paused, a tiny grin threatening to break through his professional demeanor.

Tanner's pulse rose. "Right now?"

"Yes, my officers are following him as we speak."

"Hey, I'm up for it, but I don't know about you, Tanner." Dylan took the truck keys out of his pocket.

Tanner hesitated, his chest aching with every heartbeat. "Karani, can we park close so I can watch without getting out of the truck?"

"You can park on the upper road and survey from that post. The bus station is in a valley."

"Then let's go." Tanner eased forward and stood. "I don't want him to get away." He moved toward the lobby. "Dylan, you want me to drive?"

He laughed. "Not on your life."

They followed Karani's police car, maneuvering through the chaos of the evening traffic. Tanner held on as Dylan dodged pedestrians and stray dogs. He braced his arm to protect the incision.

On Waiyaki Way, they passed the officer's car and parked on the upper road for a bird's-eye view of the action at the bus station. Rows of brightly painted buses, crowds of people toting personal possessions, and crying babies created a cacophony. Workers yelled to passengers as they tied metal luggage, water jugs, and chickens to the roof of the buses while drivers called out bus numbers and destinations.

"This is a great place to disappear in a crowd," Tanner spoke loudly over the roar of conversations.

"I hope they know which bus he's supposed to be on. There are three going to Nairobi on this front row." After killing the engine, the air was heavy with exhaust and humidity. Dylan fanned himself.

"Isn't that Karani crouching down between those two buses?" Tanner pointed toward the officer. "Right there, next to the stack of metal luggage, the bus that's leaning toward the left."

"Yeah, that's him. I can see the headlines now: 'With the stealth of a lion, Officer Karani captured his prey.'" Dylan grinned.

"I think they'll keep this news under wraps for a while." Tanner kept his eyes glued to the scene.

"I'm going to join him. I'll give you the details when I get back." Dylan eased out of the truck.

"Hey, dial my cell and keep your phone on."

"Sure." Dylan hurried past a bus to join Officer Karani.

Tanner watched him slip beside the investigator.

"Calloway, you stay here at the back of the bus in case he tries to escape."

"Sure, I will be ready."

Karani crouched below the bus windows and slowly made his way to the open door of the Nairobi-bound bus. Karani showed his badge to the driver and motioned for him to step aside. With his gun drawn, he mounted the steps onto the bus and started down the aisle.

As Karani made his way toward the back of the bus, he sent passengers outside, quietly exiting the bus after he passed by. Wycliff might fight his way out when cornered. When Karani got close, Wycliff panicked like a wild animal. He looked around and tried to open the back door.

"It's the end of the road for you, Wycliff. Put your hands up. You're under arrest." Someone moved at the back of the bus.

Wycliff repeatedly banged against the back door. On his third try, it opened, and he fell to the tarmac. Dylan pounced on him instantly. Blow by blow, they fought. Dylan slugged him, breaking his nose as he knocked him to the ground. Wycliff slung his leg at Dylan's, taking his feet out from under him. Dylan rammed his body into Wycliff and landed on top of him. "Give it up, man. It's over."

The sound of guns cocking got Wycliff's attention. He looked up as police surrounded him, and Karani pointed his gun at Wycliff's head.

Karani yelled, "You're under arrest. Cuff him, men, take him to jail, and lock him up. No phone calls for him, and no one interrogates this one but me. Understand?"

His men answered in the affirmative and moved into action.

"Calloway, you want to confiscate his belongings?"

"Sure." Dylan wiped sweat from his brow as he entered the bus and grabbed the bag under the seat Wycliff vacated.

When he stepped off the bus, the passengers took their seats again. The officers directed Wycliff to a police vehicle, protecting the suspect's head as he got inside the car. Dylan gave Wycliff's bag to Officer Karani. As the police car pulled out, Karani shook Dylan's hand. "You okay?"

"Just a little scuffed up. I'll be fine.

"I appreciate your help today. I will call you after I interrogate him."

"Thank you, sir." Dylan dusted off his pants as he returned to the truck.

Dylan opened the driver's side door of the Land Cruiser. "Man, that was great, but it was over too quickly—not enough drama. I wanted a shoot-out at the OK Corral. But you should have seen his face when he realized it was over." Dylan slid in and cranked the truck.

"I'm glad he's in custody. Some of the sound was muffled. What did Karani say to his men about the prisoner?"

"He told them to book him, put him into a holding cell, and not allow him to make any phone calls. He made it clear no one was to question him. He wanted to do that himself." Dylan pulled into the traffic flow.

"Good, letting him make a phone call could have been a problem if he were hired from the States. We don't want his employer to know his plan failed."

"Karani said he'd call us once he'd been able to interrogate Wycliff and place him behind bars."

"I'm glad it's over." Tanner braced himself for the potholes ahead. "For now, let's get you back. You need rest."

"Now, you sound bossy." Tanner teased his friend.

"Well, the job's over, and you're not my boss anymore."

Tanner laughed.

Angie requested the company limo for her trip to the airport to pick up her best friends. She smiled when Leslie, Missy, and Elise descended on the escalator.

"Angie, I missed you." Leslie wrapped her in a hug.

"It's good to see you, Les."

Missy rushed to the luggage carousel, grabbing her lime-green bags. Breathless, she staggered back and hugged Angie. "I had the shortest flight, but thought I'd never get here. My plane sat on the runway in Houston for over an hour."

"I've missed your smile." Angie embraced her feisty friend. "I'm glad you came."

Elise rolled her suitcase toward Missy's neon pieces. "Angie, a tan looks great on you. Maybe I need to go to Africa." She put her arm around Angie's shoulders. "Glad you're back."

"Me too. Let's take your things to my place, then we'll do dinner in Dallas."

"Sounds like a plan." Leslie clasped the handle of her luggage and started toward the exit.

The driver opened the door for Missy. Once in the limousine, Angie offered them a cold Perrier as Les and Elise slid in on the other side.

"Where to, Miss Angelica?" The driver checked the traffic flow before leaving the curb.

"Back to the Ward Estate, James."

"Yes, miss. Is the temperature to your liking?" James asked.

"It's perfect. We're comfortable."

"We're in the lap of luxury." Missy ran her hand along the leather.

Angie smiled. "I thought we'd have lunch and visit for a while before going downtown."

Leslie squeezed Angie's hand. "Don't push yourself to do too much to entertain us. You've been through a lot, and we've come here to be with you."

"I'm fine. Besides, having fun with you three is medicine to me."

Her friends had lived in the condo with her in Waxahachie, Texas, while they were at Southwestern. But in showing them the grandeur of the Ward Estate, Angie trusted them with an intimate portion of her life, a cherished part of her history.

"I can't imagine living here." Elise grinned. "It's like a ritzy hotel. But you fit in these surroundings."

Angie put her arm around Missy's shoulder. "I love seeing things from your perspective."

"Tanner, I got an email from my dad. Mason Malone is already being investigated by some of the best in the business. Looks like someone beat us to it." Dylan cranked the Land Cruiser and loaded his bags to go to the airport. "If I get wind of any findings, I'll call you."

"Thanks for checking. I'll scope out the situation once I get home and email you an update." Tanner clicked his seatbelt and braced himself for the potholes. "He thinks he's untouchable on his pedestal behind all those titles. I'm anxious to see how this scenario plays out."

After the treacherous ride across Mombasa, Tanner was happy to see a wheelchair on the sidewalk. Dylan unloaded Tanner's bags while he eased out of the Land Cruiser. The chaotic crowd parted, giving them a clear path to the check-in counter, the security checkpoints, and the luggage scan.

Dylan gave Tanner's passport to the ticket agent. "He's the one who's flying today, but I have special permission to get him to the plane."

"We've been expecting you." She checked Tanner's passport against the image on the computer.

Dylan placed Tanner's luggage on the scale. The agent busied herself with boarding passes and luggage tags. Tanner sank into the wheelchair, thankful to be uninvolved.

With documents in hand, Dylan pushed his passenger toward the final checkpoint and the elevator. "You're quiet. What's up?"

"Just wondering what this meeting is about and Ward's next assignment for me." Tanner pushed the elevator button. "I'd feel better if I knew what was ahead."

"The mine has been a good fit for you. I'm sure Alexander Ward has another great plan. I hope you're in the States for a while so you can renew your relationship with Angie. But for the near future, you have two long flights with pretty flight attendants waiting on you hand and foot."

"You know that's not what I meant." Tanner moaned as they exited the elevator over uneven flooring. "Ward didn't give any hints about his plans."

"Must be earth-shattering since he's bringing you, barely recovered, ten thousand miles just to be in a meeting."

"Yeah, funny. It's time for a new assignment, but that wouldn't be important enough to bring me home early. He'd wait till I reported on this job, so something strange is up."

"Look at the bright side. You're going to come face-to-face with Angie soon."

"Yes, and I keep reminding myself she's engaged to a ladder-climbing suit." Tanner blew out an exasperated breath.

"Well, Romeo. Turn on the charm. Flash those pearly whites and win her back. She hasn't made a trip down the aisle yet." Dylan put the brake on the wheelchair in front of the gate.

"You think there's a chance?"

Dylan handed their documents to the gate attendant. "Yep, I watched her when you were shot. She cradled you like her long-lost love while she used all her strength to stop the bleeding. She risked her life to save you when the murderer returned to take you out. And didn't you say she cried when she left? You have a chance if you play your cards right."

"Thanks for the encouragement. Get me on this flight, and I'll strategize as I fly."

"Give it your best shot—pun intended." Dylan left him with a doting stewardess.

By the time he landed in Dallas—DFW Airport—arriving at passenger pickup, Tanner's strength was depleted. The air pressure change wearied the body on a good day, but it proved more than taxing after his surgery. He smiled. Joseph stood beside the limo when the automatic doors opened. Tanner relaxed inside the luxury sedan and allowed Joseph to tip the attendants who manned his wheelchair and took care of his luggage.

"To the hotel, James," Joseph instructed the chauffeur as they left the curb and merged into Dallas traffic. "It's good to see you, Tanner."

"You too, Joseph. I've missed you."

"How was your flight? Do you need anything?"

"It was fine, but I need to rest."

"You'll have time to relax and the best care. Alexander wants you to stay at the Wyndham Hotel downtown." Joseph offered him a cold Perrier out of the fridge.

Tanner took the bottle. "The new one next to the Ward building? That's a bit more luxury than I'm used to."

"Well, the Motel 6 was all booked up." Joseph laughed with Tanner.

"That was quick, Joseph. You eat your Wheaties this morning?"

"I had to, so I could stay ahead of you. I've arranged for your appointments to come to you at the hotel." Joseph reached for his portfolio.

"Appointments?"

Opening the leather folder, Joseph read. "Doc Ellis will see you after lunch today. Alexander will have dinner with you tomorrow evening in your suite." Joseph paused. "Are you in need of clothing?"

"Yes. I need something to wear to the meeting on Friday."

"No problem. I'll schedule someone to bring a selection for you to choose from."

"Also, your Hummer has been serviced and is parked in the hotel garage. Here are your keys."

Tanner took them. "I don't think I'll feel like going anywhere, but thanks."

"I presume you will want to visit your mother while you're here. Maybe you'll feel stronger by the end of the week."

"Yes, I'm anxious to see her again."

Joseph nodded. "You'll also be glad to know the last shipment of tanzanite has arrived and is secured in the company vault." Joseph closed his folder.

"That's good. I'll be glad when the courts release the stolen stones so we can assess the total value of the project. Joseph, do you know what this meeting is about?"

"Yes, but I'm not at liberty to say."

They rode in silence for a few minutes. Tanner flinched a couple of times, trying to adjust to being driven on the opposite side of the road. But that wasn't the only thing nagging at him.

"Joseph, is Angie okay?"

"Yes. She's been staying in her wing of the estate since she returned from Kenya. Her three friends arrived this morning. They've gone into Dallas."

"But, is she okay?" Tanner searched Joseph's face. Joseph would level with him.

Joseph met Tanner's eyes, appearing to consider for a moment before responding.

"She's been quiet since her return from Kenya. She seems heavy-hearted, and her eyes have lost their sparkle. Any idea how that happened?"

"She's been through a lot in the last couple of weeks. Give her time. She'll come around, and those friends of hers will help." He paused. It was a shame she wasn't feeling better.

"I want to see her while I'm in Dallas." Maybe she missed him.

"She will be at the meeting on Friday morning."

"Thanks."

Over a dinner of Japanese cuisine at one of those restaurants where the food is cooked in front of patrons, Angie opened her heart to her friends.

"I admit I was angry at Tanner for allowing our relationship to fizzle. He destroyed what we had. While on a stakeout, we discussed what had happened between us. Tanner explained his actions and apologized. As it turned out, we both made mistakes. But when he was shot, I knew I still loved him. His condition was critical, and I didn't want to lose him. I kept the pressure on his wound to stop the hemorrhaging."

"You saved his life! I'm not sure I would have been that calm," Elise said.

"You're a hero, Angie," Leslie said.

"The chaos helped as we got him to the hospital and prepped for surgery. I didn't have much time to think. Monitors were beeping. Nurses were starting an IV, taking his blood pressure, and temperature. Blood was on the bed and the floor ..." She took a drink of water, her hand shaking as she raised the glass.

Elise reached over and held Angie's hand sympathetically.

"I was praying for the Lord to spare his life as I wiped blood from his face. While rinsing out the cloth, he started moaning. I couldn't understand his slurred words at first. Then"—She paused and sighed—"He called out for Vickie over and over. I couldn't believe it. I'd loved him all my life, only to discover he

279

has feelings for someone else." A few tears slipped down Angie's face.

Leslie silently handed Angie a tissue.

Angie sniffed. "I cried then too. Maybe it's good he was unconscious so he couldn't see how foolish I was—"

Missy broke in. "He's the foolish one if he's chosen Vickie over you. Surely, she can't hold a candle to you."

Her friend's vehement loyalty and sudden hug made Angie's tears flow even faster.

"What did you do?" Missy prompted once Angie had calmed down.

"I did what any Ward would do: I mustered all my strength and put on a good front to cover up my warring emotions. I buried the pain and refocused on the situation. Over the next week, I saw him through the worst part of his recovery, said goodbye, and got on a plane. But—what do I do now?"

"Angie, you asked us what you should do. First, you break this engagement to Mason. Marrying the wrong man isn't the right thing to do. Then, give yourself time to time to heal."

"You've been through a lot, the news of your grandfather's illness, then the malaria. Not to mention the drama of the killer. I agree with Leslie. You need to walk softly, prayerfully for a while." Elise squeezed her hand.

"You need to guard your heart in this situation. The Lord will fight your battles. He's the one who can heal your broken heart and put the pieces back together. Let Him fix it." Missy sat back in her chair.

Angie was stunned. "Missy, that's the wisest thing I've ever heard you say. I needed to hear that today." Angie hugged the redhead. "Thanks."

Angie would do just that. God would fight the battle and fix the situation. She would wait on the Lord.

Missy winked. "I have my moments."

~

Mason paced his executive office at Ward Enterprises. Frustration concerning Angelica's silence angered him. "This 'ignoring her fiancé role' is getting old." He spoke to the walls. He dialed her cell and left another syrupy message when it went to voicemail.

He glanced at his watch, dialed an overseas number on his cell, and waited for the call to connect. On his third attempt, the call clicked through. He waited while it rang several times. No answer. He went to his desk, lifted the receiver, and pushed the intercom button. "Have I had any calls?" His brows furrowed. "Okay, thanks." He banged the receiver into the cradle, stood, and let out a deep breath with force. *Where is Wycliff? I should have heard from him by now. He'd better be in flight.*

Powering up his laptop, he stood as he scanned his e-mail. Technology moved more slowly than usual, adding to his angst. Not finding a message, he slammed the laptop shut. Pacing again, he rubbed the tense muscles in his neck. Distance put him at a disadvantage. With so much at stake and timing a critical element, he needed confirmation of the job's completion, and he needed it ASAP.

Chapter Sixteen

Mason stopped in front of the mirror in his office. He picked at some lint on his suit and glanced at his reflection. He put Angie's heart-shaped necklace into his pocket, grabbed his portfolio, and strode to the meeting.

He checked his watch, counting down the minutes until he was named the man who would lead Ward Enterprises into the future—*what else could this "high priority" meeting be about?* He perused the conference room, making sure it was prepared according to Ward's specifications. He'd asked Ward's secretary to join him.

"Judy, Ward wanted seven seats, with himself at the head, Joseph on the left, and me on the right. Next to me will be Angelica, and Maxwell Stoner, Ward's lawyer, will take that chair beside Joseph. Ward asked for two additional seats, but I didn't catch the names of those guests. Do you know who they are?"

"Let me check my notes." She thumbed through her steno pad and checked her cell. "That's unusual. Mr. Ward didn't give me that information. Sorry."

"Okay, thanks." Not wanting to draw attention to his lack of knowledge, Mason changed the subject. "Do you have the agendas ready?"

"They're printing as we speak. I had to add some last-minute but vital items." She closed her pad.

"You're very efficient, Judy. Thanks." With Angelica's recent return from Kenya, could the added items be news from Kenya? He smiled and moved toward the serving tables, surveying.

The caterer was putting the finishing touches on the elegant display of food and beverages. *Hors d'oeuvres* of mini croissants with assorted meats and cheeses were arranged on silver platters beside a colorful array of fruits strategically placed on white silk tablecloths. The crystal stemware was lined in perfect symmetry. A tall vase of red gladiolas formed a canopy over the exquisite display.

"Great presentation, Louis. Ward will be pleased."

The caterer smiled his thanks.

Returning to his office, Mason had a latte delivered to his desk and opened his laptop to check for a certain e-mail, which he did not find. Scowling, he spoke to an empty room. "When I said to keep me informed, I meant contact me regularly. Where are you, and where is my bag of tanzanite?"

Mason sipped on his latte, stewing. He strode to the window and stared at the skyline, framed in tumultuous clouds, rain slashing across the scene.

According to the meteorologist on Channel 13, a drizzly day would hopefully transform into sunshine by midday. Breakfast with her friends around a glass-topped table filled the dining area of her suite with a mixture of hilarious conversation and laughter.

When the chaos died down, Leslie said, "Angie, what is this meeting about? Why is it so important?"

Angie sipped her cappuccino and returned her cup to its saucer. "I'm assuming Grand-Papa is ready to reveal his plans for his company. I've never wanted to be in the lead at Ward Enterprises, but I'm anxious about starting this new chapter, whatever it entails."

"Will you see Mason today?" Elise leaned to the left to allow their waiter to remove her dishes.

"I'm sure he'll be there. He's probably miffed at me for not contacting him since I got home, but ending this engagement is first on my personal agenda. He's not the one." Angie stood. "You three have fun here today while I go to this meeting. I'll pick you up at five and give you all an update. We'll have dinner in Dallas."

"It's time to put your suit on." Missy showed her the face of her watch. "You can't be late for your grand entrance. You're good at those."

"Missy, you're not so bad yourself." Angie tugged on Missy's unruly curls.

"Well, if you call falling on my face in front of our graduating class a success, then I've perfected the skill."

Angie left her friends to their fun and donned her professional attire. With her briefcase in hand, she took a deep breath. The scripture ... *Trust in the Lord with all your heart and lean not to your own understanding* ... ran through her mind. It was perfect advice for this day, this time. But doing it was hard for a take-charge woman with means. She sighed, checked her reflection in the full-length mirror, and bid her friends goodbye.

Leslie whistled. "Wow, you look great. You're going to take their breath away, Miss Ward."

"Thanks. I want to look and do my part, but I'm trying to

trust the Lord with my future. You know I'm bad about trying to figure everything out, to fix things." Angie opened the front door.

Summer's sun broke through the clouds as Angie stepped out of the estate, slipped on her sunglasses, and strolled toward the waiting limo. "Hello, James. Is my grandfather going into Dallas with me this morning?"

"Yes, I am." His warm voice filled the air as he rounded the other side of the limo.

Angie pivoted and stepped into his embrace. "Good morning. How are you feeling?"

"Weak, and I can't seem to get enough air into my lungs. But I'm anxious to get this meeting underway." James opened Ward's door and waited while he gingerly slid into the sedan.

"Should we postpone this meeting?" Angie hurried to the other side and got in. A fist formed in her stomach.

"Nonsense, my dear. This day is too important, and I don't have time to spare. Joseph is bringing my portable oxygen tank. I'll be fine when I get to the office."

With how his jaw was set, she knew he would not be persuaded.

He sat back as Joseph arrived with the medicines and oxygen equipment. Without a word, Joseph hooked up the tank and handed Alexander the tube. Once oxygen was flowing, James drove them toward the Dallas skyline.

Joseph opened a Perrier and gave Ward some meds before turning to Angie. "Angelica, you look stunning and ready to enter Ward Enterprises as an executive."

"Thank you. I want to relieve Grand-Papa of some of his workload as quickly as possible." She glanced at her grandfather, his coloring a grayish hue. He was nodding off with his head resting on the cool leather of the headrest as they cruised the highways. "Joseph, I appreciate the way you watch out for him. He's comfortable with you."

"It's my honor. He's been a loyal friend for forty years." He reached over and gently pressed Ward's wrist while watching his watch. He noted Ward's pulse in a small notebook he retrieved from his suit pocket. "I want to keep him as comfortable as I can."

After several turns, a looming tower of black glass came into view: Ward Enterprises. It sparkled as a few rays of the morning sun broke through the clouds and glistened on the rivulets of rain clinging to the slick surface.

Stepping through the revolving doors, Angie thought of facing Mason—she couldn't put it off any longer. She crossed the marble floors ready to face a new challenge with the Lord's help. She held the elevator doors open for Joseph and her grandfather and punched the button for the top floor. When the doors opened, her grandfather stepped out first and turned to Angie.

"Welcome to Ward Enterprises, Angelica. An office has been prepared for you. I think you'll like it. It's two doors to the left." He patted her cheek in a grandfatherly manner. "I hope you'll be happy here. I have been."

She caressed his warm hand. "I'm happy here, at your side, Grand-Papa." She escorted him to his office door. "I'm asking the Lord to heal you."

"I asked Him too, but His answer was not yes. Let's enjoy the time we have and not focus on the inevitable."

"But you taught me to keep praying. It's not time to throw in the towel." She wrapped her arms around him and prayed she would have faith to accept whatever decision God made.

～

At nine-fifty a.m., Mason led Maxwell Stoner into the conference room. "You will find your name next to Joseph's on the far side of the table."

"Thanks." He removed some file folders thick with documents from his briefcase, stacking them for the meeting. The lawyer got a pastry and a cup of coffee. He stirred sugar and cream into his brew and complimented the caterer.

With Stoner occupied, Mason straightened the chairs around the table, easing toward the lawyer's files labeled *Alexander Ward Will & Trust, Ward Estate, Angelica Ward, Tanner Zarello,* and *Mason Malone.* There were two more files he couldn't see, but it would be too obvious for him to adjust them.

Hearing talking in the hall, Mason hurried to the door, anticipating Angelica's arrival. He fingered her present in his pocket—a yellow-gold heart pendant. With her by his side, things could only go up from here. His day had finally arrived. His dream was becoming a reality. Ward Enterprises would be his, just as soon as Ward made the announcement. Mason drew in a cleansing breath, forcing himself to appear relaxed yet professional, donning his executive demeanor. Out the window, the sun broke through the clouds, casting its glow across the room. *Lights, camera, action—it's show time.*

Alexander and Joseph entered and took their usual chairs. Judy followed, bringing a stack of folders for Ward, his pen, and a cup of Kenyan AA coffee. She selected some fruit from the buffet for her employer before returning to her office.

An unfamiliar man wearing a no-name suit and scuffed shoes appeared in the doorway. He went directly to the head of the table, where Ward stood, and they shook hands like two old friends as Ward smiled and welcomed him to the meeting. "Mason, direct my friend to one of the vacant seats, maybe the one beside Angelica's chair."

"Yes, sir. Please come this way." Mason showed the man to his chair and invited him to get some refreshments before the meeting began.

After pulling a file from his portfolio, the newcomer put it under his arm and went to pour himself some ice water. He strutted with confidence as if he owned the room.

Angie made a quiet entrance, heading directly to her grandfather's side. Ward's face lit up. "Welcome, Angelica."

"I love the office. It's perfect." She hugged Ward. "Thanks."

"I'm glad you're pleased, my dear. Joseph helped with the décor." Ward returned her embrace.

When she stepped away from her grandfather, Joseph moved closer and kissed Angie's cheek. "I hope your new office will serve you well."

"I'm certain it will, thank you. You're the best."

"It was my honor. I'm so proud of you—"

"I missed you, Angelica." Mason took her hand and kissed it. "I'm glad to see you at last. I asked you to call me the minute you returned." He feigned sadness. "I bought you a welcome home gift." He handed her the locket, allowing it to swing from his finger for all to see. "It's a heart, designed just for you."

"Thanks, Mason. It's a sweet gesture." Angie laid the locket on the table. "We need to talk."

He lowered his voice. "We could have shared many conversations if you'd called me."

"Sorry, Mason. I've had my days and nights mixed up. Jet lag does that to you, and the malaria left me weak. Did you know my friends are visiting?"

Great segue, Angelica.

"Your college friends?" Great, those simpering girls again. Though they might keep Angelica distracted and happy. If so, he could leverage her name for his benefit. He could work with that.

"Yes, my best friends—"

Alexander Ward cleared his throat. "Good morning, friends. Please take a moment and visit the buffet before we start our meeting."

Angie slipped from Mason to the display of delicacies and filled a small plate. Mason filled a crystal glass with water and downed it, but it didn't cool him. *Angelica has changed. Something's different.*

Beginning the meeting late was out of character for Ward. He demanded promptness at Ward Enterprises. Joseph seemed peaceful as he stirred his hot tea. Maybe Ward was waiting for the empty chair to be filled.

Angie sat in her assigned seat next to Mason. She retrieved a velvet box from her briefcase. "Mason, this isn't going to work. I'm not in love with you. Here's your ring. Our engagement is off." She slid the ring case toward Mason and left it beside the gold pendant necklace on the glossy conference table.

"Angelica, don't do this." He put his hand on top of hers. "I know we started our engagement on rocky ground, but we can fix it. Let's talk after this meeting."

"No. My answer is final." Angie turned away from Mason and introduced herself to the gentleman beside her, making small talk.

Touché. He proposed in front of an imposing crowd—she turned the tables and broke the engagement when he couldn't retaliate. *This is not over—not by a long shot.* Mason hated not being in control.

Judy entered with some medication. "Sir, this prescription was just delivered."

"Thank you, Judy. Give the prescription to Joseph."

After taking the tablets, Ward called the meeting to order. *Maybe that's why he was stalling.*

"Thank you for agreeing to meet with me. This is a day I have been planning for a long time. There are a few recent details that have altered certain timelines, but here at Ward Enterprises, we're always up for a challenge."

He seemed to be moving his mouth, but saying nothing. Mason couldn't understand where he was going with this.

"You each play a huge part in the future of this giant operation, and we have much to discuss."

Alexander paused as the conference room door swung open and the final attendee entered.

Tanner Zarello joined the meeting. Alive.

Mason stuck his finger behind his designer tie, loosening its chokehold as a sick feeling constricted his throat.

"Sorry, I'm late." Tanner made his way to the other side of the conference table.

"Glad you could make it." Joseph greeted him as he rounded the room.

Once seated, Tanner locked eyes with Angie. "Hi, Angie."

She sat statuesque, staring as if his arrival took her by surprise. "Hello, Tanner."

Well, isn't this a great turn of events? Angelica doesn't look at me that way. Mason's thoughts went into overdrive, making a new plan. Something went wrong somewhere, badly wrong. Mason wiped perspiration off his forehead and put his sweaty hand on top of Angelica's. "So good to see you, Zarello. We didn't know you were back."

"It's great to be home." Tanner brushed his gaze over Angie, then turned his focus on Ward, ending their verbal exchange.

Angie moved her hand into her lap.

Mason's gut churned.

～

Tanner's appearance set Angie's head spinning. He looked amazing, stronger. His black dress shirt taut across his toned torso matched his ebony hair and dark chocolate eyes. He sat straight and confident at the table—his presence filled the room.

Alexander Ward stood with effort. Angie could read the pain in his furrowed brow and squinting eyes.

"There are many reasons I called you here today. We will deal with them one at a time. As you must know by now, I have terminal cancer, and my days on this earth are numbered. I want everything in place before my health deteriorates further." He took a sip of water.

Absolute silence encased the room.

"Angelica, I've prayed about this since you were a little girl. Trust me. Trust the Lord. Everything will be fine."

Like flipping a switch, Ward's voice took on a commanding tone. His wizened features grew stern. All-knowing.

"But first, I must address an important issue. I've invited District Attorney Bill Roberts to join us today. To my dismay, some criminal activities have surrounded Ward Enterprises. We must rid our team of the Judas in our midst." He gestured toward the district attorney. "The floor is yours, Bill."

Roberts stood, walked to the head of the table, and shook hands with Ward. A Metro Police Sergeant stepped inside the conference room. The DA scanned the room, stopping his perusal to face Mason. Without explanation, the DA demanded, "Mason Ardwin Malone, please stand."

"You can't be serious!" Mason sat taller and grabbed the edge of the conference table with whitened knuckles. "What's this about? Ward, tell him who I am. I'm the one who helped you build this empire." Mason kept his seat and stared at his boss.

Alexander Ward didn't speak.

Bill Roberts stepped closer to Mason. "Mason Malone, I said, stand."

"Ward, why are you doing this? I'm valuable to you and this company. This is a big mistake—huge!"

～

Mason's visions of grandeur were crashing around his feet.

The DA ignored his protests and nodded to the metro officer. The metro officer stepped forward and read the charges.

Mason slammed his pen on the table and stood, directing his rage toward Ward. "Unbelievable! After all I have done for you and Ward Enterprises, this is how you treat me?"

The door of the conference room opened, and two additional police officers entered and grabbed Mason's wrists.

"I've done nothing wrong. I'm innocent. I've never even been to Kenya. You can't prove a thing. My hands are clean." He jerked away from the officers trying to put handcuffs on him, but the click of the cuffs confirmed his capture.

Angie's pulse raced as she witnessed in horror. *Danger lurks where least expected.*

"You're a snake in the grass." She stood as her outrage built.

"Angelica, do something!"

"How dare you?" She slapped him hard. He looked stunned. Her hand hurt, but it felt good—really good.

The police took Mason away as he shouted his innocence and resisted arrest with every step. The DA looked at Alexander Ward as he was leaving the conference room. "Thanks for your help with this case. The evidence you've provided, together with the Kenyan side of this case, will seal his fate. I'll update you later." With that, he was gone.

Tanner shook his head. "I should have known."

Shocked at Mason's arrest, Angie met Tanner's eyes across the room. She mouthed the word, "You were right."

"Let's take five before we continue with business. Get some coffee, friends." Alexander Ward put a file folder aside, sighed, and leaned back in his chair.

Tanner stood and approached. "Angie, can I get you some water?"

"With ice, please."

He moved to the buffet, confident in his stride. He was right—Mason had ulterior motives, and his divisive moves almost cost Tanner his life.

He pivoted and caught Angie staring. He clinked ice cubes against the glass as he delivered her water.

"I brought you some strawberries." He handed her some sugar packets along with the fruit.

"You remembered." Angie took the packets and sprinkled granules over the berries. "Thanks, Tanner." She put her hand on his. "I am sorry you got hurt as a part of Mason's plans."

"It's not your fault. The Lord protected us." He squeezed her hand and reached into his pocket, and brought out a ring box. "This is your graduation present. I'm so proud of you." He returned to his Kenyan chai but winked as he stirred his hot tea, blending the sugar and milk.

Angie opened the box, revealing a gorgeous six-carat tanzanite ring. "Thank you, Tanner. I love it." She slipped it on her finger.

Before he restarted the meeting, Angie moved to Mason's former chair and placed her hand on Grand-Papa's arm. "How did you know he was behind the attacks?"

He smiled. "A Kenyan prefix showed up on his cell a couple of times, and he strong-armed some of my friends to pay the company their loans ahead of schedule. It was obvious he was vying for my job—no matter the cost. He wanted to sit in my chair with you by his side. I saw you give his ring back. Smart girl." He patted her hand. "This is a great day, my dear. So, let me see your beautiful smile."

She slipped back into her chair and enjoyed her strawberries as the sunshine glistened off a beautiful tanzanite ring.

Chapter Seventeen

Angie turned her attention to her grandfather as he stood, commanding their attention.

"I feel responsible for the harm Mason has caused some of you personally and for the setbacks he created for this company. I saw promise in him, took him under my wing, and gave him opportunities. I am sorry I didn't notice his shortcomings sooner. Forgive me." He took a drink of water as everyone nodded sympathetically. "Let's get to the main item on the agenda today. My health issues have hurried the process, but I'm sure about the decisions we'll discuss now and peaceful about the future of Ward Enterprises." He took a seat, pulled his chair forward, and propped his elbows on the table.

"I want to begin with the question looming on your minds. Who's going to lead this company into the future?" He opened his portfolio and surveyed the room, stopping at Tanner.

"Tanner Zarello, I've been watching you for some years. You're a man of integrity with superior leadership skills and a mind for business—much like I was when I started Ward Enterprises. I've tested you, and you've met every challenge. You've proven your loyalty in trying situations. It's with great confidence that I offer the position of head of Ward Enterprises to you."

Angie read shock mixed with unbelief on Tanner's expression as he sat frozen. She was thrilled he was chosen and so proud of him.

"Sir, I'm speechless—I appreciate your kind words concerning my work ethic. But, I'm not presumptuous enough to pretend I could ever fill your shoes. You created a masterpiece as you built this company. Your blood, sweat, and tears are embedded into the fiber of every business relationship and among the staff you hand-picked."

Grand-Papa leaned back in his chair.

"I'm humbled you would consider me." Tanner paused, as if in thought.

"Does that mean you'll accept the position and take on this challenge?" Ward posed the question.

"Yes. I would be honored." Tanner went to Angie's grandfather and extended his hand. "Thank you, sir."

Grand-Papa grasped his hand and smiled. "Gentlemen and Angelica, I am proud to announce Tanner Zarello is now the President of Ward Enterprises."

Applause filled the conference room. Joseph and Maxwell Stoner congratulated him as he returned to his chair. Tanner locked eyes with Angie across the table.

"You'll do a great job, Tanner. You're a born leader." Angie smiled.

"Tanner." Grand-Papa drew his attention. "Joseph has reports of our holdings and pending business decisions for you to study. I plan to work for three more months. Could you be ready to take the helm at that time? I'm aware you'll need to return to Kenya to testify in court. The vice president has used his power to expedite this matter, bringing closure quickly. Once you return, you can shadow me. I will answer your questions, acquaint you with our staff, and introduce you to our board."

Tanner nodded.

Turning to Angie, Grand-Papa smiled. "Speaking of the Board, my dear Angelica, I welcome you to our executive pool. Your talents and education are the perfect addition to this company."

"Thank you, Grand-Papa." Angie glanced over at Tanner, who returned her gaze across the table.

"Angelica, Tanner, and Joseph, I also want to inform you that Maxwell has my will, life insurance, and burial details. He'll walk you through the process when the time comes. There's no need to dwell on those matters today." Grand-Papa looked at Angie.

Tears were pooling in her eyes.

"Angelica, you'll be well provided for. Trust me on this."

"I trust you, Grand-Papa. I just don't want you to leave me." She wiped her cheek.

"This was not in my plans. But I promise to stay as long as the Lord allows me."

Tanner felt her pain. *Everyone I love leaves.* He wanted to be her hero—to change that for her forever. Ward tapped his pen on the conference table, bringing Tanner's thoughts back into the meeting.

"Let's finish this agenda. There'll be some serious damage control necessary concerning Mason's activities over the last several months. To our advantage, his assistant kept good records and gave us a trail to follow. I'll attempt to remedy as much as I can, and then I'll itemize the loose ends for you, Tanner." His voice was strong, still the man in charge.

Ward continued. "We'll have Mason's belongings removed by this time next week. The auditors are combing through his files as we speak." Ward looked at his agenda and closed his portfolio. "We have one more item to discuss." He pulled an envelope from the pocket of his suit coat and passed it to Tanner.

"What is this?"

"A blank check. It's signed—fill in the amount. Think of it as a reward. You risked your life for this company and its employees, helping to bring Mason to justice and protecting Angelica. I want to thank you," Ward was adamant.

"I don't want your money, sir." Tanner pushed the envelope back toward Ward.

"I insist." He motioned for him to accept the envelope.

"That's not necessary." Tanner wouldn't pick up the check.

Ward stood, put his leather portfolio under his arm, and prepared to leave. He paused as if in thought. "You can have anything you want. So, speak up. What is it, Zarello?" He waited.

"Anything, sir? You mean that?" Tanner stood.

"Yes, name it. Now's your chance." Ward leaned on his cane Joseph provided, a smile tugged at the corner of his mouth.

"I want her!" He pointed to Angie without looking in her direction. "I want to marry your granddaughter, sir."

Angie was on her feet in a flash. Her chair rolled back and hit the conference room wall. "Wait! I'm not a bargaining chip. Don't make me part of your employment package. Tanner, you can't waltz in here and stake your claim. I heard what you said. You don't love me."

Ward smirked. Tanner groaned—Ward had expertly maneuvered him like the businessman he was.

"You have my permission, but now you have to get hers.

Just make it quick—I don't have much time, and I want to walk her down the aisle."

"Grand-Papa, you can't just assume I'll agree! I'm not a signing bonus or part of a deal." Angie forcefully stacked her papers and jerked open her briefcase. After stuffing them inside, she grabbed her purse and cell.

Ward's tone and features instantly shifted from master negotiator to grandfather. "Angelica, please don't leave yet. I know you entered one engagement to please me, and I won't force you into another. But, if you would still do one thing for me—stay and talk with Tanner. I don't think it will be like last time." Ward glanced at Maxwell and Joseph and leaned on his cane as the three men walked toward the door. "Let's order some lunch. Joseph, call that Italian restaurant you ordered from last week." They made small talk as they closed the doors.

Angie stood and perched her purse strap on her shoulder. Gazing at her grandfather as he struggled to walk, she waited.

Tanner hurried to her side. "Angie." He placed his hand on her arm. "Don't leave yet." Her body language conveyed an air of insult, confusion, and manipulation. Her clenched fists confirmed his assessment. She waited for the door to click.

"Tanner, you left me, you broke my heart, you called out for Vickie several times in the hospital, then you show up unannounced, and want to marry me—Give me a minute. I need to catch up here." She put her empty hand on her hip.

Tanner took her briefcase and slipped her purse off her shoulder, placing them on the table.

"You left to chase tanzanite—you left me behind. Why would you—"

He stepped closer, slid his right arm around her waist, and smiled.

~

The moment he touched her, she started losing her train of thought to stumble over her words. She hated herself for letting him have such power.

She took a deep breath to regain her momentum. "You may be my new boss, but you don't get to make decisions for—"

He silenced her diatribe with a kiss. Not just any kiss, but the kiss of a man in love. She was stiff and angry, but slowly relaxed in his embrace. The force of his lips on hers stole her argument—paralyzed her senses. When he leaned back to look at her, she stared into his ebony eyes.

"Tanner"—She stepped back a bit—"We need to talk, and I can't think with you so close."

He laughed. "It's because you're crazy about me. Admit it." He closed the gap between them again and ran his finger softly from her cheek to her lips.

"You called out for Vickie when you were in the hospital—I was taking care of you, but you asked for her, not me. Can you explain that?" She tried to think, to stand her ground. "And, what did you do, make a deal with my grandfather? Then, when you got an opportunity, you marched in here to claim your prize."

"Finished?" He waited.

"No, I can think of more things to say." *When you're not standing so close, distracting me.*

"Well, before you go on, let me say this: No, I didn't make a deal expecting you to fall into my arms. You're not a bargaining chip. I respect you and know how capable you are. I've watched you, studied you, and memorized the curves of your face. Every tanzanite stone reminded me of your eyes. I worked to prove myself worthy of you. Please listen to my heart." He kissed her again with tenderness. "I love you, Angie."

"Tanner, I grieved when you left. I cried because our relationship seemed to be unimportant to you. You hurt me. I was confused and alone. Then, when you were shot and crumpled at my feet, I knew I still had feelings for you. But now, what do I do? You called for Vickie several times." She held his gaze.

Tanner's brow wrinkled as he thought. "I don't know what happened while I was unconscious, but I'd just seen her being knocked out before I was shot. I had to be replaying the scene. I wish you'd asked me about this. Is that why you left?" He sat on the edge of the conference table.

"Yes, I had to." Tears pooled in her eyes. She held her hand up to keep him from interrupting. "Now you're here, Mr. Strong-and-oh-so-handsome, declaring your undying love."

"Angie, I don't have feelings for Vickie. My heart belonged to you. You have to believe me. I'm sorry for the pain I've caused you." He caressed her face.

Angie's resolve crumbled. A tear dampened her cheek.

"We've lost so much time. Please trust me, Ang—" He reached and caught the tear as it escaped her lashes. "I was a fool and prioritized proving myself to earn you instead of focusing on you and what you needed. Since then, I've dreamed of you for years, been tormented by my love for you. I cherish you, and cherish is more than love in my book." Tanner held her gaze.

Angie loved the essence that belonged to him alone. She fought a losing battle. Her heart trumped her excuses, her reasoning. He captivated her. Taking a chance to trust him again, she touched his lips and placed her hand on his cheek. She loved being in his embrace.

... lean not to your own understanding ...

"Tanner, I'll think about it." She slipped her hand to the back of his neck, pulled him close, and kissed him. It felt right —real. Angie reached for her things, masking her nervousness as she risked her heart again. "What's next, Mr. Zarello?"

"Let's continue this conversation over lunch, shall we? There's a great restaurant in the lobby of my hotel across the street." He opened the door and offered her his right arm. "Ready, Miss Ward?"

"Sure, Boss." She smiled.

Tanner pressed the elevator button. "I've been thinking. You're part of the 'executive pool' as your grandfather said, but we still have to decide on your exact position. You want to be my secretary?"

"No." The numbers lit up.

"A floor manager?"

"Nope." The doors opened. She pushed the 'down' button. "You have to do better than that."

"The cleaning lady?" He smirked at his suggestion.

"Nada, I don't clean."

"You did in Kenya. The resort is shining. I think you're perfect for the job." He allowed her to step out of the elevator and then followed.

"You could have a career as a stand-up comic. Want me to acquire you an agent?" She stepped out of the lobby where the midday Texas sun encased her.

Focusing on the traffic, Tanner crossed the street and entered Maggiano's Italian Restaurant. As the hostess seated them, his cell buzzed. He glanced at the screen. "Angie, I've got to take this. It's Dylan calling from Kenya."

"No problem. Tell him 'hello' for me."

Tanner nodded and put his cell to his ear as he went outside to the sidewalk for better reception. Dylan updated him on life at the inn and the upcoming court dates as Angie, observable through the window, perused her menu and spoke with a waiter, then twirled a strand of hair.

"Okay, I'll leave in five days. Do you know how long I need to be in Kenya?" Tanner guarded his sore shoulder from passing pedestrians.

"Two, maybe three weeks. How are things in Texas?" Dylan asked.

"Interesting, very interesting. I'll fill you in when I get there, but for now, my hunch was correct. Mason Malone has been charged as the man behind Wycliff's attacks." Tanner said, the knot in his shoulder finally releasing.

"Let's get these two convicted for their crimes so we can move on with life," Dylan said.

"Sounds like a plan. I'll fax my itinerary. See ya."

Tanner ended the call and returned to the table. "You look deep in thought." He took a seat and sipped his iced tea.

Before Angie could respond, the waiter returned to take their order. "The lady ordered salads for you both. What entrée would you like?" He held his pen over a tablet.

"I would like fettuccini Alfredo. Angie?"

"I'll have lasagna with extra meat sauce, please."

Tanner added Angie's menu to his and gave both to the waiter.

"What did Dylan have to say?" She sipped her Coke.

"Your street kids are getting fat, your bird is loud first thing in the morning, and the workers miss you." He smiled and sat back. "You miss Africa, don't you?"

"Yes, it gets in your heart."

The waiter returned with their salads and covered Tanner's with fresh ground pepper at his request.

"Tanner, how's your shoulder? Should you have come home so soon?"

"It was too soon, according to the doctor, but your grandfather needed me. I'm being careful."

Tanner prayed over their food when it arrived. "So, what were you thinking about? You were twirling your hair, a sure sign that brain of yours is working overtime." He took a bite of salad.

"This day. It's not been what I expected. I broke my engagement to Mason, and you surprised me with your arrival. Mason was arrested and dragged out in handcuffs. You're now the head of the company, and you say you want to marry me. Lots of excitement for one morning, don't you think?" She stabbed her salad.

"I guess it has been eventful. But it ended well, didn't it?" He winked at her when she met his eyes.

"The jury's still out on that one."

She wasn't going to make this easy. Silence ensued as they ate their salads.

Their entrees were placed on the linen tablecloth. The smell of oregano and Alfredo sauce rose from the plates. With their drinks refilled, they were alone again.

"Tanner, I need you to be patient with me. This is sudden, and we haven't dated recently. Now, I must create an amazing wedding in record time if I want Grand-Papa to walk me down the aisle."

Tanner dropped his fork. "Does that mean you're saying 'yes'?"

She reached for his hand. "Yes, Tanner, I will marry you."

He was on his feet in a second and kissing her. "You won't be sorry, I promise." He was smiling when he returned to his seat.

Tanner hardly tasted his fettuccini. His dining companion, his beautiful fiancée, filled his vision and overwhelmed his senses.

After declining dessert, Angie walked him to the elevator. His energy was spent, and she needed to get back to her friends.

"Let's make it four weeks from tomorrow." He put his right hand on her cheek, then slipped it behind her neck, pulled her close, and she melted in his arms, returning his kiss. When he pulled away, he lifted her chin so they were looking eye to eye. "Trust me, Angie. We'll work through each challenge as it presents itself. You're not alone. You will always have me."

Grand-Papa was leaving when Angie returned to the office. He handed her a set of keys. "I'm on my way to the garage. Want to see where your parking spot is?"

"Do I have a company car?" She took the keys.

"No, it's a gift from me. I hope you like it. Walk down with me, Angelica."

"Sure. You're tired, aren't you?" She punched the elevator button.

"Yes, but happy." He allowed her to enter first. "What do you think about the meeting?"

"Where do I start? It's a lot to process for one day ... I'm glad Mason's gone, I'm sorry you're sick, but Tanner is an excellent choice." The doors opened on the garage level.

"An excellent choice for the company or for you personally?"

Angie smiled. "Both."

"It's good to see your smile again. Now, your parking space is the first one on the right." He walked in that direction.

"Grand-Papa. That's a Rolls-Royce Phantom! Known for hand-built craftsmanship, incredible opulent interior, an embodiment of perfection, with—you added the optional dark exterior trim." She squealed. "I've always loved these cars. Thank you!" She hugged him.

"Enjoy the ride, you deserve it." He turned to his waiting limo.

"Grand-Papa"—Angie gathered her tumbling thoughts—"Did you know all along Tanner wanted to marry me?"

He stopped. "Tanner has been in love with you since you were sixteen. I know what true love looks like, my dear. He adores you. That's what I wanted for your future."

"I thought you wanted me to marry Mason!"

"I wanted you to make your own choice, so when you chose Mason, I stayed quiet. Unfortunately, my silence led you to think I wanted you to marry him. But I prayed the truth would surface. It always does. So, I pushed Tanner a bit."

"More like backed him into a corner. Did you have to make it sound like I was part of a business transaction?"

Grand-Papa opened his leather portfolio and pulled out the envelope he had offered to Tanner. "Look inside."

Angie pulled out the contents of the envelope Grand-Papa placed in her hand. "A blank piece of stationery!"

Grand-Papa winked and turned back to his limo.

Shaking her head in astonishment, she turned to her new car and pushed the key fob. Lights blinked, and the locks clicked. She pulled out of the garage in her Phantom with a new appreciation for her grandfather. *He's wise.*

Tanner was exhausted, but he needed to call his mom. He punched her number into his cell. On the fourth ring, her answering machine picked up. He listened to the recorded message and the beep. "Mom, I'm in Dallas. Ward asked me to lead Ward Enterprises—I said yes. I asked Angie to marry me

—she said yes. We need to talk. How about dinner? Call me." He smiled, knowing she'd call the second she listened to his message.

He tried to rest, but sleep wouldn't come. His mind was reeling. He texted Joseph, requesting that he take care of his flight details to depart on Wednesday evening.

Opening one of the files Ward had sent over, he scanned the details of several mines and their profit margins. After the fourth file, he understood the 'why' behind the tanzanite mine assignment. It taught him the terminology, the verbiage necessary to read the reports and recognize trouble spots. As an executive, he would know what questions to ask and what answers to expect. Ward used the experience to train him to take over Ward Enterprises. His learning curve had been drastically reduced by the Kenyan experiences, for which he was thankful.

He put the folders aside, picked up his cell, and punched a number.

"Joseph, do you have any friends at Tiffany's, Genesis Diamonds, or Shane Co.? I need a ring, a spectacular diamond." He grabbed the pad on the nightstand and poised his pen to write.

"What do you have in mind?"

"I want a one-of-a-kind heart-shaped diamond in a delicate setting with at least five carats. A ring perfect for a beautiful woman, a designer one-of-a-kind piece. Can you find that by tomorrow morning?"

Joseph laughed. "You aren't asking for much, are you?"

"Just for a miracle."

Saturday morning brought blue skies and sunshine with a promise of late evening showers by the meteorologist's prediction. Angie poured herself a cup of coffee after a night of updating her friends and wedding planning. Caffeine would help her face the day.

"Is there more coffee?" Leslie took a mug out of the cabinet.

"Yes, there's plenty," Angie ordered breakfast for them and took her brew to the sunroom, leaving the daily news droning on her kitchen TV. The doorbell chimed just as she got comfortable.

"I'll get it. Don't get up." Leslie hurried to answer before the bell rang again, waking Elise and Missy.

When Leslie stepped back into the sunroom, a bouquet of red roses blocked her face. "I can only guess who these are from." She handed the vase to Angie.

Angie balanced the vase and pulled the card from its envelope. "It says, *Lunch in the Penthouse Suite at noon. I love you, TZ.*" Tears blurred her vision.

"I think he means it." Leslie sat across from her and sipped her coffee.

Angie placed the flowers in the middle of the coffee table. "I know he does," she whispered as she stared at the blooms. "He loves me."

Chapter Eighteen

Tanner selected a television channel with continuous love songs and reduced the volume. Candles added a soft fragrance to the setting, and with their lunch waiting under silver domes, he released the wait staff so he and Angie could be alone in his hotel suite Joseph had reserved.

"This is a beautiful suite." Angie walked in and put her purse on the sofa.

Tanner hurried to her side. "But it still doesn't compare to you."

"You're flattering me," She murmured as she stepped into his embrace.

"It's not flattery if it's true." He kissed her softly, then pulled back a couple of inches. "Hi."

"Hello yourself." She didn't want to rush the moment. "You can do that again."

Tanner laughed and kissed her again, then took her hand and led her to the table. "Your lunch is ready." He removed the domes and took his chair across from her as salty steam permeated the air. "I hope French onion soup is still your favorite?"

"It is, and so is the shrimp cocktail, grilled chicken salad, and French silk pie." Angie beamed, her cheeks glowing. "First the roses this morning, and now this ... thank you."

"Anything for you." He poured their sweet tea and prayed over the meal.

"You and your entourage having a good time?"

"Yes, it's been great. We spent last night doing as much wedding planning as we could before they fly home today. They're thrilled for us." She dipped a shrimp and took a bite.

"I have to say I am too." Tanner buttered a roll for her and studied her as she grew quiet. "Is everything okay?"

"It's exciting, confusing, and overwhelming. One minute, I'm nervous about becoming your wife, and the next moment, I can't wait. Putting a wedding together quickly because my grandfather is sick panics me. I feel like we're missing part of our relationship by going from being friends to being married in a month. Sometimes I wonder if we can successfully transition into being a married couple with such little time spent together. But here with you, I'm relaxed. Safe. I know everything's going to be okay."

"It's going to be more than okay. We're going to be good together. Please focus on creating the wedding of your dreams and enjoying the process. Have fun, walk down that aisle, and we'll begin our new life, facing the future together as Tanner and Angelica Zarello. We can make up for lost time, taking things slow, and making it our goal to never stop dating. Trust me."

Tears formed on her lashes. She sighed as if trying to collect her emotions. "I do. But even those I trust have left me ... You know I fear being alone." She blotted her face with her napkin.

"Angie, losing your parents was tough, and your grandmother's death increased your fear. Let the Lord give you peace. He'll never leave you. You have His promises to stand on. The Lord has brought close friends into your life to fill some of the voids, and I'm here for you too." He reached across the table and squeezed her hand. "We'll walk this path together, you and me."

"I look forward to that." She took a deep breath. "Thank you."

"You're most welcome." He kissed her hand. "Why don't we eat?"

She dipped another shrimp into cocktail sauce. "Did you call your mom?" She took a bite.

"I did. She's very happy for us. She loves you. You know that, don't you?"

"Yes, and I love her. What did she think about you leading Ward Enterprises?" Angie dipped her last shrimp.

"Mom wasn't surprised. She said she knew your grandfather had plans for me a long time ago, but she kept it to herself and let it play out. She's happy I'll be stateside once the trial is over in Kenya. I'm having dinner with her tonight." Tanner gave Angie his last shrimp. "How about one more?"

"Thanks. Having you stateside sounds good to me too." Angie moved their empty dishes to a tray and tasted her chicken salad. "How do you feel about being president of Ward Enterprises?"

He smiled, "I've never been called a president before. The Lord has given me peace. Which means he will help me fill a big pair of shoes. I can't do it without divine intervention."

"I have no doubt you will be amazing. I will be praying about your transition as Grand-Papa leaves the job."

"I appreciate that."

Their conversation went from one topic to another. Angie

SHIRLEY GOULD

seemed to relax in his company, for which he was glad. She had a point—they hadn't had much opportunity to spend time together as a couple with forever in mind.

"How about some coffee with your pie?"

"Yes, please." Angie took their desserts to the sitting area.

"Good idea." As he brought their cups, the left one wobbled a bit.

"How's the shoulder?"

Tanner sensed her concern. He reached for her hand. "I'm making progress. But it's slow. Your grandfather's physician checked me over and seemed pleased with my condition. I hate to make that trip again, but I must finish this."

"When do you leave?"

"Tuesday evening. I'll be gone two to three weeks."

"But it's dangerous. Can't Dylan handle it for you?"

"Not this time. He needs my testimony to seal their fate." He kissed her hand. "Angie, it's not dangerous now. We got the bad guys, remember? I'll be safe. And you're going to be so busy, you won't have time to miss me."

She sighed but looked him in the eyes. "You're right. And I know you'll be back soon. I trust God's plan for my life, and He's brought all this together in a way only God could have accomplished. I trust you with my heart and my future."

"I'm glad to hear you say that. You're my world, and I'm coming back to you." Tanner reached into his pocket and pulled out an engagement ring with a five-carat diamond set in platinum. He went down on one knee and looked into her eyes. "Angelica Ward, will you marry me? I love you with every fiber of my being and want to spend forever with you."

She stared at his eyes, then his lips. "I'm so in love with you. Yes, I'll marry you."

He returned to the sofa, slid the ring on her finger, and kissed her soundly. "You won't be sorry. After a fairy tale

314

wedding and a romantic honeymoon, we'll have an amazing adventure as husband and wife."

She looked at the ring, then met his gaze. "The heart-shaped diamond is perfect. I love it."

He raised her hand to see the diamond sparkle in the sunlight. "A spectacular ring for an incredible woman." He kissed her. Then stayed close. "Ang—I truly saw your heart in Africa—your loyalty for the company, your love for those orphans, and your heart for me. A diamond-shaped heart is perfect for you."

"That's a sweet thing to say." Her cell buzzed with a message. She frowned. "Sorry, I need to get this. It could be about Grand-Papa." She looked at the screen. "Oh, it's Leslie, Elise, and Missy—I lost track of time, and they'll be here in a few minutes. I'm supposed to take them to the airport, but I could get a taxi for them if you want me to, so we don't cut our time short."

"No, they're good for you, and I need to rest. I'll call you tonight after my mom leaves. I have a lunch meeting with your Grand-Papa tomorrow. Could we have lunch on Tuesday? In four weeks, we can have uninterrupted time together." He stood and walked Angie to the door. "When I get back, will you meet me for dinner, just the two of us?"

"Absolutely. I'll look forward to it."

He took her face in his hands. "Thank you." He spoke softly —sincerely.

"For what?" She matched his whispered tone.

"For saying yes." He kissed her passionately, leaving her breathless.

He punched the elevator button. "I'll call you tonight, Ang—"

"Goodbye." She kissed him softly and stepped into the elevator. "Love you."

Her perfume lingered when the doors closed.

Angie chose three different styles of dresses in the same deep blue color for her bridesmaids. She gave the attendant the measurements for Missy, Elise, and Leslie, designating which style went with which person. Eyeing a horrible, old-fashioned dress, she snapped a picture of the ugly gown and sent it to her three friends with a text: "I've picked out your dresses for my wedding. We're going vintage. What do you girls think? I gave them your measurements." She smiled, anticipating their responses.

Leslie texted, "You have impeccable taste. I trust your judgment."

Elise answered second. "I'm so happy for you. I'll wear a toe sack if you ask me to."

Missy wrote, "If you chose it, I'll like it—or at least act like I do."

Angie laughed out loud.

After a morning of shopping, Angie went in search of her grandfather at their estate. The company limo was in the driveway, signaling his return from the office. On cat feet, she slipped into his study to see if he was strong enough for a visit.

Alexander smiled when he saw her in the doorway. "Good afternoon, my dear."

"I know you're busy. You got a minute?" She sat in front of his desk in a leather wingback chair.

"Sure, I always have time for you." He put his pen down and gave her his undivided attention.

"According to tradition, I need to have something old, something new, something borrowed, and something blue for the wedding. I have the new thing and the blue thing, but I was wondering if I could use some jewelry from Nana Joy and my mom for my old thing and my borrowed thing? It would make me feel like they're part of my special day."

Ward stood with the help of his cane and started around the desk. He extended his elbow in her direction. "Let's go see what we can find. I'm certain they would be honored."

She put her hand in the crook of his elbow and enjoyed the slow walk from his office to his bedroom. He pulled a framed portrait from the wall, allowing it to swing on its hinges. A couple of twists of the lock, and it opened, revealing a wealth of jewels.

"The two top shelves were your grandmother's, and the pieces in these drawers belonged to your mother. Do you have specific items in mind?"

"Is it okay if I look through their things?" She hesitated.

"Of course. All of it is yours, Angelica. Take your time. I'll rest on the chaise lounge, and you can show me your choices." He moved to get comfortable.

Angie caught a whiff of Nana Joy's perfume as she opened a velvet jewelry bag. Touching these special treasures brought her closer to the women of her rich heritage. After careful deliberation, she chose a delicate necklace featuring a single snow pearl on a white gold chain, with a diamond set at the top of the pearl. Noticing Grand-Papa's eyes getting teary, she showed him the necklace.

"Is something wrong?"

"No, it's a perfect choice. Nana Joy bought it for your mother to wear on her wedding day. Your mom was wearing it when she passed from this life." He touched the pearl dangling from her hand.

"Did Nana Joy have earrings that would match this necklace?"

"Yes. Look in the white velvet box on the top shelf. She had a substantial collection."

When Angie poured the pearls onto a velvet-covered tray, she found a pair of loops with woven strands of pearls. "These are perfect."

"Yes, I agree." He used his cane to stand as Angie replaced the precious pieces in their resting place. He locked the safe and swung the portrait back in place. They started their stroll to his office.

"Grand-Papa, was my mother like Nana Joy? I think of her that way."

"Yes, they were much alike, and you have characteristics of them both. You have your Nana Joy's heart and your mother's looks. But you also have my strong Ward constitution. Coupled with your faith in the Lord, you'll face all of life's challenges with grace."

"I wish you were going to be around for me to lean on. I'm going to miss you, Grand-Papa. You're taking part of my heart with you." Her eyes misted.

"Some of our journeys are longer than others. I'm torn between not wanting to leave you and longing to see my Joy and your mother again. We must trust the Lord's timing, no matter how hard it is."

They stopped at the door of his office. She hugged him, treasuring this moment.

The trial went on for weeks, in a courtroom melting in the stale air. The Kenyan justice system representatives wore robes and wigs. How, was beyond Tanner. Still, in the sweltering heat, it was a done deal when Tanner finally took the stand and gave his testimony against Wycliff and his accomplice.

Telling the story of how he almost died at their hands sealed their fate. Only logistics remained before they would be sentenced.

With a spring in his step, Tanner boarded a plane eight days before his wedding. He had arranged the rehearsal dinner via email with Rose, Angie's demanding wedding coordinator. At Tanner's request, Joseph assisted by reserving a white limo and acquiring their lodging for their first night as man and wife. It had to be perfect—beyond romantic.

He slept the first leg of his journey and enjoyed a meal at the London Airport. The hours couldn't pass fast enough. When his plane landed in New York, he texted Angie, even though it was the wee hours of the morning.

> I have missed you, my love. Have dinner with me, Angie? A car will be waiting for you at seven. I'm anxious to see your beautiful face and kiss you breathless. Love you.

He pocketed his cell and retrieved his bag from the overhead compartment. His cell buzzed, signaling a text.

> I'll be ready. Can't wait to see you. Love you too.

Tanner punched the off button and strode toward US Customs. He couldn't get home fast enough.

Angie's full-length mirror reflected her final decision to wear a zebra-print sundress and platform heels, with matching earrings. She'd changed clothes three times, wanting to look her best, but now she gazed in the mirror with satisfaction and a mixture of nerves and excitement.

James appeared at her door. "Good evening, Miss Angie. Are you ready?"

"Absolutely. I've been waiting for this night for a long time." She followed him to the limousine.

As the limo reached the restaurant, the bellman opened her door. "Angelica Ward?"

"Yes, I'm Miss Ward." She accepted his extended hand. When she stepped inside, her stomach tightened. She rubbed her sweaty palms on her dress. The place was empty except for an alluring man standing at a table for two by a glowing electric fireplace. Soft music set the mood as roses scented the air. Candlelight flickered as Tanner met her in the middle of the restaurant, where she walked into his embrace. "Tanner."

He placed a soft kiss on her lips. "I missed you." He deepened his second kiss.

She cradled his face in her hands. "Welcome back." She ran her thumb over his lips. "It's so good to be with you again."

"I've longed to see you, Ang—Please have dinner with me." With his hand on the small of her back, he led her to their table and pulled out her chair.

"Where is everybody? This place is usually packed." Angie looked around for other diners.

"I rented the restaurant so we could have a private dinner, just you and me."

"Isn't that a little extreme?" She took a sip of her iced water.

"I wanted you all to myself and couldn't take a chance on someone spoiling our evening. I've taken the liberty of ordering for you. I hope that's okay," he said.

"Sure, you know what I like." She studied his face. "You look stronger. You're feeling better."

"Yes, I can use my left arm without pain in my shoulder."

The waiter delivered their salads. Tanner took her hand

and prayed over the food and their time together. He didn't let go of her.

"Thanks for tonight. I've missed you." She squeezed his hand. "Also, I've been needing to ask you something."

"Shoot." He bit into a crusty loaf.

"Can we live at the estate when we return from our trip? I don't have a lot of time with Grand-Papa, and I'd like to be close. What do you think?"

"Absolutely. I knew you'd want to. Can we stay in your wing? We can make other arrangements later."

"That's what I was thinking. Thank you. Time is so precious."

"And growing more precious every time I'm with you." He leaned back for his entrée to be placed in front of him. Salty steam from the *au jus* rose from the heated plate of prime rib. "This looks like a great cut of meat."

"It's very tender." She cut hers.

"I've been thinking about your new position at Ward Enterprises. I think I know the perfect job for you."

"The perfect job? This I've got to hear." She put her fork down and waited.

"Well, when the new guy takes over, namely me, I want you to be the director of the benevolence department, the compassionate part of the operation that donates the money we make—like to those street kids, for example."

Angie sat back in her chair. "I love that idea. I even have the plans already drawn up. You're a genius." She leaned over and hugged him. "It's the perfect job for me."

"I'm glad you're pleased, and I can't wait to see your plans. I want to make you happy." He placed his hand over hers.

"You make me happy, Tanner."

Their conversation moved from details of the trial to

wedding plans, to her new car, in between bites of divine cuisine. When they finished, the waiter removed their plates.

"I have a question for you. Have you heard of the Seychelles?"

"Yes, they're beautiful islands in the Indian Ocean with huts built out over the water. Why?"

"I'm going there with my wife." He smiled and studied her reaction.

"Really? And when do you leave?"

"Sunday afternoon."

Angie leaned over and pulled him toward her. She kissed him soundly. "That's amazing."

"There's more. We have to make a stop in Kenya for a couple of weeks to finish the trial. You want to see those kids again?"

"Yes, I do." She moved away from him so their dessert could be placed on the table.

While sharing a piece of cheesecake with berry topping, they discussed their schedules for the upcoming week. An appointment with the minister, getting a marriage license, and dinner with Grand-Papa would fill the next day. Fittings for his tux and her wedding gown would be done separately. The schedule of friends flying in would take them different directions for a bachelor party, a lingerie shower, hairdresser appointments, and tuxedo fittings.

Tanner reached over and took her hand. "I know we haven't had much time together lately, so let's do our best to see each other when we can this week and talk often. Still, I want you to enjoy this week without pressure from me. After Saturday, we'll begin life together as husband and wife forever." He leaned over and kissed her.

She smiled. "You're on."

Chapter Nineteen

Angie gave her wedding coordinator the drawing. They were meeting in her suite at the Ward Estate.

"It's going to be the wedding of weddings. I'm glad to serve you, Miss Ward." She gave Angie an update on all the details of her special day, then closed her portfolio.

Since Angie was returning to Kenya, an ingenious plan percolated within her. She made a couple of calls to put it in motion.

"Yes, I need this completed by Friday morning. Please deliver the documents to the estate before noon, addressed to my attention. Talk only to me. This is a surprise." As she closed her cell, she smiled at her scheme.

The sound of bells dangling on the front door greeted Angie, Missy, Leslie, and Elise as they entered Bridal World. Their flip-flops slapped the marble floors as air-conditioning relieved them of the Texas heat.

"Welcome to Bridal World, where fairy tales come true. My name is Alexa. How can I help you ladies? The bubbly blonde stood ready to assist potential customers.

"Deanna is expecting us." Angie looked toward the mirrored area by the dressing rooms and smiled.

"Angie, everything's ready. Come this way." Deanna hurried to greet the bride. Melodious love songs filled the air as Deanna led them to tufted loveseats and served white grape juice in champagne flutes. "Ladies, make yourself comfortable while Angie gets into her gown."

Angie hurried to the dressing room. She stepped into the gown and, with a whoosh of fabric, swept over to stand on the pedestal to show her friends. Deanna straightened the train. The gown's sequined straps sparkled under the chandeliers. The fitted bodice accented her slim waist before it flared into rows of ruffles.

Elise had tears in her eyes. "What a gorgeous gown, Angie. It's stunning. You look like a model in a bridal magazine."

"It's a perfect choice." Leslie locked eyes with her in the mirror. "How do you feel?"

"This hasn't happened the way I'd dreamed it would—but this is the dress, and he's the right groom."

Leslie squeezed Angie's hands. "I agree. You've found your soul mate, and he adores you."

"Wow! I told you you'd be the most beautiful bride ever. I was right again." Missy's applause and giggles brought smiles to the ladies.

Deanna put Angie's veil on her black hair. Leslie took photos.

Angie pivoted to pose and noticed Missy staring at a gown on a mannequin. "Missy, you like that one?" Toile, flowers, and white lace surrounded the redhead like mischief walking in the clouds.

"This is the one I want. I like the tight waist and floral design that starts on the shoulder and extends to the floor, like a sea of petals. Don't you love it?"

"You're right, it's the perfect dress for you, even if it's not lime green. Now, all you need is the groom."

"Well, it never hurts to plan. You never know when the right guy will come along. A girl must be prepared." Missy wrote down the name and style number of the wedding gown and gave the information to Deanna.

"Thanks, Miss Anderson. I'll keep this on file with your measurements." She turned to Angie. "Your planned presentation is ready, Miss Ward." She helped Angie out of her wedding gown and bagged it for her.

"Okay, you three. I want to see each of you on the pedestal in your bridesmaid dresses. Deanna will tell you which dressing room is yours. Come out at the same time."

Angie got comfortable on the viewing settee and waited. She could hear Missy's squeals. All three ladies burst into the showroom, talking at the same time, delighting Angie.

"I love this dress. It's exactly what I would have chosen." Elise was looking at the back of the dress in the three-way mirror. Its plunging back was highlighted with straps of crystals crossing perfectly before wrapping around her waist in the front. "Your text made us think we were wearing that awful dress. I'm so relieved."

"I'm glad you tricked us." Leslie's eyes were wet. "This is a beautiful deep blue dress. I've never had a gown of this quality."

"Leslie, I thought this flowing tanzanite-colored gown with crystal straps would be gorgeous on you, and I was right."

Missy was standing on the platform, twisting and turning in front of the mirror in her empire-waisted gown in deep blue with multiple crystal straps crossing her shoulders. "Angie, I was worried. But I look so good, so you're forgiven."

"The styles fit your personalities. I hope you like tanzanite blue. Here are your dress bags. After you change, we'll go shoe shopping. You can't wear these dresses without amazing stilettoes."

Missy hugged Angie as she headed to the dressing room. "I wonder where they sell glass slippers?"

~

Tanner put a gift for Angie in his carry-on and slipped his journal into the front zipper pocket as his cell rang. "Hello, beautiful. What's up?"

"We are on our way to the estate. Are you at your apartment? I'd like you to meet my friends."

"I'm here. Come on by. I'd love to see you and meet them."

"We'll be there in about ten minutes."

"Sounds great." He pushed the off button and put away their plane tickets.

When he opened the door, Angie smiled at her fiancé. "You sure it's okay for us to drop in?"

Tanner stepped closer, placed his hand on the side of her neck, and kissed her gently. "You can come see me anytime." He put his arm around her shoulders. "Now, where are your partners in crime?"

Angie motioned for her friends to come closer. "Tanner, I'd like you to meet my best friends, Elise, Leslie, and Missy."

Tanner extended his hand to them in turn. "I'm glad to finally meet you all."

"We've heard a lot about you," Leslie spoke with kindness and sincerity.

"You're almost as good-looking as Angie said you were." Missy teased.

Tanner laughed. "I've heard some stories about you, Miss Anderson. I'm happy to finally make your acquaintance."

"Right back at ya," Missy said over her shoulder as she pivoted, surveying his apartment.

Elise stepped forward. "I'm happy for your good fortune. You better not break her heart."

Leslie added, "Again."

Tanner held up his hand. "I promise."

Missy butted in. "That's good because we watch cop shows, and we know how to hide a body."

Tanner laughed at their wit and spunk.

Angie stood, mouth agape, at the turn of the conversation. "Ladies, I think it's time to go. How about you wait for me in the car?" They bid Tanner farewell.

"I'm sorry, Tanner." Angie's face heated.

"They love you, and I don't blame them for being skeptical. But I think they're great. You've got a serious confidant in Leslie, a servant's heart in Elise, and a jack-in-the-box in Missy to keep you laughing."

"I'm glad. They're dear to me, and I know you'll win them over."

"I'll do my best. By the way, Dylan's original flight was canceled. He arrives on Friday afternoon."

"I'm glad he'll still make it in time."

"Yes, he won't let me down. Now kiss me and go enjoy your three musketeers. Next week, you're mine." He wrapped her in his arms, pressing her against the length of him, and kissed her.

Her cell phone vibrated in her hand. She ignored it at first, not wanting to interrupt their kiss. When she finally pulled it close, she stiffened in Tanner's arms.

"What's wrong?"

"Grand-Papa has collapsed. I must get to the hospital immediately. Oh, I can't lose him now," Angie cried.

"Send the limo with your friends to the estate, and text

them to pray. We'll call and update them once we know something. Let's go to the hospital together." Tanner reached for his keys and locked his door behind them.

"Why would Grand-Papa be in the cardiac unit when he has cancer?" Angie looked at Tanner as they exited the hospital elevator and hurried to join Joseph, who introduced them to Dr. Weston.

"Miss Ward, this morning your grandfather experienced a mild heart attack caused by a small blood clot traveling to his heart. We have him on blood thinners and want to keep him for observation until Friday, but he's adamant he has to be somewhere on Saturday afternoon." He smiled at Angie and Tanner.

"Has the infection of the lining of his heart returned?" Angie reached for Tanner's hand.

Doc Ellis stepped forward. "No, this incident has to do with a new cancer medication that affected his blood and ultimately his heart. We've adjusted the dosage, and he will be feeling better soon."

Joseph cleared his throat. "So, is he stable at this time?"

"Relatively stable. It takes time for medication to take effect, but we're keeping a close watch over him for the next twenty-four hours." Doc Ellis spoke with authority.

"Thank God," Tanner breathed.

"Yes. Can we see him?" Angie glanced from one doctor to the other.

Dr. Weston nodded. "Just keep your visit short so you don't tire him."

"Thank you, doctors. I appreciate your personal care for

him." Angie shook hands with the men. "We'll be here until you feel certain he's going to be okay."

"Your Grand-Papa's a fighter. He won't be leaving this world until he has completed everything on his bucket list." Doc Ellis winked at Angie.

Angie smiled through teary eyes as she, Tanner, and Joseph slipped into Grand-Papa's ICU room. She took his hand in hers.

"Are you feeling better?"

"Yes," he whispered. "Just weak."

"Tanner, I'm glad you're here with my girl. You, too, Joseph." Ward struggled to speak.

"She's not alone. I'm staying by her side. You relax and allow the medicine to work. The Lord isn't going to take you before your time." Tanner spoke with comforting authority.

Ward looked at Angie. "We made a good choice." He smiled and allowed sleep to come.

Tanner waved at Dylan when he rushed into the sanctuary for the wedding rehearsal on Friday, after the rehearsal had started.

Rose handled the addition like a pro. "Dylan, we're glad you could make it. You can take your place between Tanner and Drew. Face toward the back of the sanctuary until the bride arrives, then turn facing the bridesmaids." They went through the lineup one last time to get Dylan situated and proceeded to the rehearsal dinner.

Tanner had a true Texas-style meal catered in a country western-themed room. Thick T-bone steaks grilled to each individual's liking graced tables covered in leather tablecloths. Cowboy boots served as vases for bouquets of Texas bluebonnets, and country love songs played softly throughout the evening.

"What a great idea. I love the Texas theme." Angie stood next to Tanner.

He put his arm around her. "I'm glad. I didn't want to have anything similar to tomorrow's event."

"You're pretty smart for such a good-looking guy. There won't be cowboy boots used in tomorrow's decorations." She smiled and hooked her arm through his elbow so they could welcome their guests.

After an evening of great food, amazing music, and gift presentations to the wedding party, Tanner stole a few moments with his fiancée. "How are you?"

"I'm concerned about Grand-Papa. Joseph said he is improving, and I have to trust him. Other than that, I'm good. It was a wonderful dinner. You did great."

He smiled. "With that Sergeant you hired as your wedding planner, this evening would have been perfect without me. But, you've done most of the work."

"I gave it my best shot. Are you packed?"

"Yes, are you?"

"I finished this afternoon." She looked down, then met his eyes. "I'm nervous."

"Don't be. Angie, it's you and me, like it's always been. Just trust me. I know this has happened fast, but our love isn't new. Just focus your eyes on mine, and you'll be fine." He kissed her hand. "The Lord is with us."

Rose turned the music down slowly without anyone noticing. But all eyes were on the dance floor when she turned the lights on the happy couple.

Tanner put Angie's hand on his shoulder and looked into her eyes. "Dance with me?"

"But there's no music—"

At that moment, a guitar began strumming softly. The sound grew louder as George Strait entered the room. Tanner slipped his arms around his fiancé and took the lead.

George's thick, country drawl rasped about promises and hearts, lifetimes and dreams, and Tanner prayed it would all come true.

"I will love you forever and a day."

"You mean that, don't you, Tanner?"

"Cross my heart." He kissed her forehead and spun her around the dance floor, enjoying the feel of her in his arms.

A tear made its way down Angie's cheek as the song ended. He held her close.

She whispered. "Thank you for the song, Tanner."

"It was a gift. I haven't had many opportunities to share my heart, but that's about to change. This is the last night I have to let you go. Tomorrow, you'll see me at the end of the aisle, and I'll be the guy with the biggest smile." He kissed her again. "Goodnight."

"Goodnight." Tearing herself away, she turned to look at him again before stepping out of sight. He was still staring.

Sunshine and blue skies greeted Angie on her wedding day.

"Belgium waffles, crispy bacon, and strawberry syrup await the bride!" Missy called Angie to the breakfast table.

"Good morning, bride." Leslie greeted her.

"Morning." Angie yawned. "How about some coffee?"

"Coming right up." Elise served her favorite brew.

Leslie put her hand on Angie's. "You ready to get married?"

"Yes, more than ready."

After a soak in her luxurious tub, an hour with her hair and make-up artists, and last-minute packing, Angie closed her make-up case and sighed.

"It's almost time." Leslie stuck her head through the door.

Angie smiled. "I know. I'm going to marry Tanner today."

"Congratulations, my friend."

"I took a peek at the décor. The sanctuary is magnificent. The ice blue and silver accents added the perfect pop of color to the crystal vases with the white gladiolas. Great job, Angie." Leslie hugged the bride.

"Do you like the flowered archways?"

"They give a fairy tale feeling to the sanctuary. It's perfect, Angie."

"Can you help me with my veil?"

"Sure." Leslie picked up the headpiece.

"It seems surreal being the bride standing in front of the mirror." Angie put her head back for Leslie to secure the combs with pins in her glossy black hair.

"I have something for your three." She gave them each an envelope with their name on it. "After my honeymoon, I want you to meet me for ten days of vacation—in Africa!"

"In Africa?" Missy squealed. "You're joking, right?"

Leslie was speechless.

Elise hugged Angie. "This is too much. Africa, I can't believe it!"

Leslie struggled to speak. "This is extremely expensive. I can't—"

"It's not a multiple-choice question. You must, because it wouldn't be the same if we weren't all together. I won't take 'no' for an answer. You've got to experience Kenya with me. So, pack your suitcases and your cameras. Safari is simply amazing, and the children need to know we care and God loves them."

They hugged her and expressed their appreciation with

giggles and tears. Angie opened a black box. "You three want to see Tanner's ring?"

"Absolutely." Elise moved close, crowding between Leslie and Missy.

"I wanted a rugged-looking ring with a tiny sparkle of diamonds." Angie opened the ring box. "It's a white gold nugget ring with three diamonds mounted in the middle. They represent today, tomorrow, and forever."

"It's perfect for him—classy but tough." She gave the ring to Leslie. "Leslie, you're in charge of this ring until I put it on his finger."

"You could always add a smaller diamond to the setting with the arrival of every baby you have—just a thought," Missy said.

"I love that idea." Angie smiled.

After a soft knock, Grand-Papa stuck his head in the door. "You ready, my dear?"

"Yes, Grand-Papa. I'm over here. Come on in."

With the help of his cane, he got out of his wheelchair and stepped around a three-way mirror, and his breath caught when he saw Angie. "You are a vision, Angelica, absolutely gorgeous. There are only two other brides who have rivaled your beauty, your mother and your grandmother."

"Thank you. I wish they were here, but I'm so glad you made it. How are you?"

"Much better. Do not concern yourself about me today."

The photographer captured the moment when Grand-Papa kissed the bride and put a penny in her shoe, following a Ward tradition.

"The Lord is smiling on this day. He and I have discussed your future, and today, you're stepping into your happily ever after. I'll wait for you in the foyer." Ward kissed her cheek and slipped out of the dressing room.

As the two o'clock hour approached, excitement surged through the atmosphere. The pre-wedding music began. It was time.

～

Tanner checked his watch. Waiting in the wings of the church hall, he paced the room.

"You getting nervous?" Dylan slipped into the coat of his tuxedo.

"Impatient, not nervous. The time can't pass fast enough for me." He reached for his jacket, stuck his hand in his pocket, and took out his keys. "You might need these."

Dylan slipped the keys into his pocket.

"Does all of this wedding hubbub bring back bad memories for you?"

Dylan paused. "It does. I know how you're feeling right now. The love is strong, the bride is amazing, and you're ready to start your future together. I get it, man, but I have peace and closure. God's choice for me hasn't come along yet. Today is about you and Angie."

"I'm glad to hear you say that. Thanks for standing with me."

"My pleasure." Dylan checked his watch. "You're up."

The door opened, and Rose paused to boss the ring bearer into submission before entering and eying Tanner. "You ready?"

"Yes, ma'am, more than ready."

She opened the door and held it. "Then, let's move." She looked at her clipboard and made sure the men entered in order. "It's show time, boys."

Chapter Twenty

When the clock struck two, Rose sent Missy down the aisle. Elise followed, and then Leslie winked at Angie and turned to walk down the aisles. The junior groomsmen and bridesmaids strolled together to take their places.

"Oh, no." The wedding coordinator sighed.

"What's wrong?" Angie frowned.

"The ring bearer decided he would rather drop petals. He grabbed some out of the flower girl's basket and threw them in the air." She shook her head. "Now, one flower girl is waving to all the people as she passes by." She closed the double doors and sighed again.

Angie smiled, but then her stomach tightened as she moved into place and put her hand through Grand-Papa's outstretched arm. He put his hand on hers and looked into her eyes.

"Angelica, are you ready to marry Tanner?"

"Yes, I'm ready."

On cue, Rose opened the doors of the sanctuary. The "Bridal Chorus" rang out as the guests stood in honor of the bride. Amid glowing candlelight, she began her journey under gorgeous archways with the sun shining through the stained-glass windows, making the setting ethereal with a touch of magic.

All eyes focused on her, but hers were locked on Tanner's as she flowed down the aisle. He was a vision in a tux. Angie tucked this moment away in her heart to remember always. She smiled when he winked at her as she and Grand-Papa reached the end of the aisle.

Their pastor welcomed the guests to witness the joining of two lives, which would be forever one. He spoke about the seriousness of marriage as designed by God Himself before asking who was giving this woman to be married to this man.

Grand-Papa cleared his throat. "I do."

Angie turned and wiped a tear off his cheek. "Love you, Grand-Papa."

"And I love you." He placed her hand into Tanner's and went to his seat.

The moment Angie's hand touched Tanner's, a special peace, as if the Lord's blessing was resting on this ceremony, this union, filled her. As he threaded his fingers through hers, the strength of his grip signaled security and love.

Surrounded by flickering candles and huge bouquets of flowers, with all the people they loved in attendance, they exchanged vows to love and cherish each other forever. At the appropriate time, she put the ring on his finger.

"I love it." Then, he put her band on her finger and kissed her hand.

When the minister pronounced them man and wife, Tanner kissed her softly. They turned to their guests. Angie put her hand through Tanner's elbow. After being introduced as Mr. and Mrs. Tanner Zarello, cheers erupted, and the music started—their cue to leave. As they entered the foyer, Tanner embraced his bride and held her tightly. She clung to him in response.

He pulled back so he could see her face. "I love you, Mrs. Zarello."

She smiled. "I like the sound of that."

"Then, I will tell you every day."

"I'll hold you to that."

"Holding me sounds good. You want to skip out now?" There was a twinkle in his eye she hadn't seen before.

"Let's have some cake first." She kissed him with promise in her embrace.

"I'll eat fast." He whispered into her ear.

She laughed.

The reception passed in a dream-like blur for Angie. A soft breeze played with the billowy white tent. Ice sculptures glistened under crystal chandeliers.

Dylan stepped to the microphone. "As the best man, I would like to personally congratulate Mr. and Mrs. Zarello and wish them enough love to last a lifetime, enough trials to keep them clinging to one another, and enough children to fill the Ward estate." The crowd laughed. "Please raise your glasses as we toast two wonderful people as they start their lives together."

Leslie stepped forward. "Today we've witnessed the joining of two beautiful lives. I pray for the Lord's richest blessings upon their future. Watching your story play out has made me believe in fairy tale endings. You're an inspiration to us all. Love you both."

After releasing a pair of doves representing launching their lives together, Angie and Tanner hurried to the staircase to throw the bouquet and garter.

"You ready, girls?"

A crowd of single women pressed forward. Leslie had her camera poised, ready to catch the action. As Angie turned, the bouquet hit Leslie's lens and landed in her hands. Leslie looked at Angie and sheepishly lifted the bouquet. The ladies applauded.

Tanner tossed the garter to a throng of eligible gentlemen in the crowd. Drew jumped high, snatched it, and grinned.

Angie stopped Rose. "Please announce the arrival of the limo.

"You ready to go?" Tanner asked.

"Absolutely." She smiled.

"Mrs. Zarello, your chariot awaits."

Raising the hem of her gown, she followed him through the doting crowd. Wedding guests lined the walkway, holding paper cones filled with white rose petals. On cue, the song, "God Gave Me You," filled the air. Angie and Tanner hurried to the white limo that sported a 'Just Married' sign. White petals floated through the air, resembling snow as they showered the newlyweds. Magical.

At the limo, Angie kissed Grand-Papa while Tanner hugged his mom before he helped Angie into the luxury limo. When the door was closed, Angie breathed a sigh of relief.

As they drove away, Tanner began picking rose petals out of Angie's hair. "That looked like a blizzard." He placed a handful of petals on the seat in front of them. "Amazing wedding, especially the moment you appeared. I was captivated. You're the most beautiful bride I've ever seen."

"Thank you." She leaned in his direction as the limo took a corner. "I have a confession to make—I've wanted to marry you since I was a little girl."

"Really? You should have proposed."

"When I was eight. I don't think so!" They laughed.

"I've got a gift for you. Unzip my carry-on bag. Look for the blue ribbon."

She opened his bag, reached for the gift, opened the ring box, and found a platinum band with tiny diamonds embedded around Swahili words. "Tanner, this ring is beautiful. What does it say?"

He stuck his head in the door. "*Nina penda wewe sana,* meaning—I love you very much. The words you said to me before you left Kenya. Wear this ring when it's not safe to wear your heart diamonds. It's my effort to keep a wedding band on your finger at all times. Would you pull my journal out of the carry-on? I'd like you to read it."

"Okay." Reaching into his bag, she pulled out the thick book. She immediately realized it was the journal he'd kept since he was fifteen.

She opened it slowly, reverently. As she read, her breath caught in her throat. All the entries were about her. He wrote that she was the only one he could ever love, and he would wait for her forever if he had to.

Her heart was racing. She thumbed through the journal, finding photos of herself stuck between the pages. Turning to the back of the book, she read an entry dated two weeks ago.

Lord, I'm passionately in love with Angie. Mine is the only reflection I want to see in her tanzanite blue eyes. Please help her see my love is true—it's eternal.

Angie couldn't read anymore. She held the book to her chest like a precious gift. Tears spilled onto her cheeks. She had his heart, his whole heart. Her unwarranted nerves vanished.

"Angie, baby, why are you crying?" He tightened his embrace.

She leaned back to see his face. "I feel your love in your

journal. The Lord has given me the desire of my heart—He gave me you!" She kissed him, pressing herself against him. "Tanner, you're mine, and I'll never let you go."

"Yes, I am, Mrs. Zarello." Tanner gave her a toe-curling kiss —sealing his promise they'd be together forever—she'd never be alone again. Never.

THE END

About the Author

Shirley Gould is an inspirational speaker, an African missionary, and an author. She's the founder of Kenya's Kids Home for Street Children, an orphanage in Kenya. Her passion for missions drives her to share her stories and adventures to inspire others toward fulfilling the Great Commission.

She has written non-fiction for thirty years and is writing Christian Fiction novels. Her debut novel, *The Sahar of Zanzibar,* was released in May 2021. On July 25, 2023, *Escape From Timbuktu* was released. The sequel, *Sunset Over Swaziland,* was released on March 23, 2024. On November 19, 2024, *The Kissing Ball* was released. Her novels are sold on Amazon.com.

She lives in the Nashville, Tennessee area, enjoying her seven amazing grandchildren, Madi, Jake, Finley, Charlotte, Judah, Blakely, and Lyda.

Also by Shirley Gould

The Paradise Inn Series

The Kissing Ball—Book One

Wealth and beauty have Angelica Ward dodging paparazzi at every turn. When a photographer's drone knocks her unconscious, she falls into Emerald Lake. Tanner Zarello, the maid's son she's had a crush on for years, dives in and saves her.

After giving CPR, with Angie cradled in his arms, Tanner's feelings for her shift from the friend zone to thoughts of capturing her heart. He will have to prove himself worthy of the heiress to have a ghost of a chance.

When Angie takes on the job of orchestrating events and décor for the Christmas season at the Ward Estate, Tanner volunteers to assist, which thrills her. She has plans this Christmas and is relying on the kissing ball to see her dreams come true. Working with Tanner, she feels protected as she deals with the persistent photographer's antics.

When the paparazzi infiltrate Angie's space, showing stalker tendencies, Tanner apprehends and restrains him until the police arrive. He is arrested and charged.

The danger escalates at the season's last event, and Angie's life is threatened. Will Tanner get there in time, this time? Questions about their social standings, his job assignment, and her feelings for him won't matter-if the paparazzi-turned-stalker succeeds ...

The African Skies Series

The Sahar of Zanzibar—Book One

In a scary case of mistaken identity, Olivia Stone is threatened by Aga Kahn, a powerful Indian ruler, because she could pass as the twin of the missionary's deceased wife. Kahn calls her the Sahar of Zanzibar who has returned from the grave to torment him and demands that she leave the island or face his wrath. She'd come to exotic Zanzibar in search of adventure, but she experiences much more.

A handsome widower, Missionary Eli Deckland, steps between Olivia and the angry Indian, rescuing her. There's an instant connection between Olivia and Eli that escalates when he comes to her rescue

Hearing about her life-threatening situation, Austin Bendale, a decorated soldier turned security services specialist, purchases a plane ticket and comes to the rescue. But things aren't as they seem. Hidden agendas are inciting riots, humanitarian funds are dwindling, and orphans are disappearing.

When you put one determined woman and a never-say-die hero in this life-and-death situation—using her gifts and his brawn—can they ignore the sparks between them, escape the chaos, solve the mystery, apprehend the guilty, and get across the border in time?

Because the sun is setting over Swaziland ...

Get your copy here:

https://scrivenings.link/sunsetoverswaziland

Stay up-to-date on your favorite books and authors with our free e-newsletters.

ScriveningsPress.com

again and again. Amid the chaos, Eli tries to prove Kahn murdered his late wife. After several attempts on Olivia's life, she's kidnapped. Eli joins the police to find her before it's too late.

As every moment passes, Olivia's life is in more danger... Will she be saved in time? If she is rescued, would it work between her and Eli? With an ocean keeping them apart, will their feelings fade? The answer is in the African skies ...

Get your copy here:

https://scrivenings.link/thesaharofzanzibar

Escape from Timbuktu—Book Two

Elliana Bendale can't believe her first assignment as a photojournalist is in ... well, Timbuktu.

Yes, it sounds remote, but it's an enchanting ancient city in West Africa, and if she does this right, this project could open the door to a world of exotic assignments. And even better—her translator is a ruggedly handsome Frenchman. What could be more exciting?

Beau de La Croix is not who he says he is. But posing as an interpreter enables him to gather intel about the terrorists threatening Timbuktu. No one needs to know he's a double agent—especially not Ellie.

Unfortunately, the number one enemy in the world has figured it out, and suddenly Ellie's photojournalist adventure includes dodging bullets, traveling down a crocodile-infested river, and literally running for her life.

What has Beau gotten her into? And if they survive, can she say goodbye to her hunky hero? Or is his life as a double agent too much excitement for a feisty Texas girl?

When Beau's worst fears come true, what will he do to save the feisty reporter he can't seem to shake?

Get your copy here:

https://scrivenings.link/escapefromtimbuktu

Sunset over Swaziland—Book Three

Grant writer Jocelyn Millender travels to Swaziland to get humanitarian aid for the devastated, disease-infested country. When war threatens, all travel is suspended. She's trapped, scared, and in danger.

www.ingramcontent.com/pod-product-compliance
Lightning Source LLC
Chambersburg PA
CBHW071751110726
47908CB00006B/1761